A Bride's Price

Arnold Mundua
Papua New Guinea

Paperback ISBN: 978-0-6459322-5-6

First Published in 2024 by

**First Nations Writers Festival International Limited
T/as First Nations Publishers**

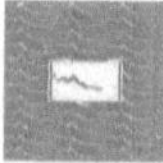

A Registered Charity (ABN 79 655 932 979)

2/53 Junction St, Nowra NSW 2540, Australia
Phone: +61 491 851 353
Email: firstnationswritersfestival@gmail.com
Web: www.firstnationswritersfestival.org
FB: www.facebook.com/firstnationswritersfestival.com

Cover Design: Busybird Publishing
Cover Photo: Natasha Arnold, [In the cover photo]
Typeset: Busybird Publishing
Line Edited: Anna Borzi AM 2024

Printed and bound in Australia by IngramSpark

Author's Note

Writing fiction is like finding and filling in the missing piece in a jig-saw puzzle to produce a complete picture. The writer has to piece together the various strands of the story to make it captivating and keep the reader engrossed. When I developed my interest in writing I decided to write on a subject familiar to many readers, that will keep them engrossed, entertained and above all compelling. Keeping this in mind, I chose love, romance and the adverse effects of unrequited love as the theme for this book. This is what you are about to read, my experience compounded with the vision I had formed. Together it is embroidered to form this fascinating story,

The story is set in the highlands of Papua New Guinea in the 1970s and 80s when Jiwaka was still part of Western Highlands province and when email and mobile phones were non-existent in the country. It is written from a forester's perspective, one who is most commonly stationed in the 'forest', away from the many common privileges and excitement of modernisation.

The story is not intended to offend any person, gender or institution but to bring into focus the importance of decision making in conjugal life. And more significantly, how a decision can affect people. This forms the subject of this story.

The story is about love, romance, polygamy and murder. It is based on PNG's cultural ways of thinking, living and doing things, especially in the highlands where polygamy is rife and part of the traditional culture. It is written to entertain, but also to make people, especially our PNG girls to be aware of the possible consequences of not making proper decisions about love and marriage.

In light of this fact, the whole novel has been construed as educational in nature.

This book is entirely the work of fiction. I have no better place to set my story elsewhere then my little Bokan village in the Upper Simbu Valley, under the foot of PNG's highest peak, Mt Wilhelm in the Gembogl district of Simbu province. While all locales, tribal names and clan groups do exist as described, all characters and events are creations of my imagination.

Any similarities of events, names and/or resemblance of persons living or dead is a coincidence.

Dedicated To

Yakop Yaka Baglau, Getru Mangre, Ageta Tom, Yosep Pigle-nagile, Anasas Munabo, Arnold Dor Yaka and Arnold Umba Ambane, who have all been my strength during my walk in life.

1

A Bolt from the Blue

The sun had finally gone into hiding behind the mountains in the West. Along with it went the comforts of the day. Outside our home, the temperature was gradually dropping. In the next hour, it was expected to be chilly and freezing in the entire valley. I was gathering firewood to make a fire in our house for a cup of hot coffee to battle against the imminent cold, when Kolkia Andambo, our neighbor and clansman, informed me that Cathy Gior died at the Mt Hagen General Hospital. Cathy was the daughter of James Gior and Angela Kumo, one of the most beautiful and envied girls from the Siako clan, whom I knew some years ago. I was, therefore, taken aback by the news when Kolkia announced the story.

"Are you sure, you are not kidding, Andambo?" I asked, when he finished.

"I am not kidding, Joe", Kolkia said, "Cathy is dead"

"This cannot be true…who told you that? I mean, how did you know? Where did you get all the information from?" I gabbled, trying to find composure, as the questions rolled out.

"It is a big news, Joe. Everyone is talking about it right now at Mondiagl-kaugla", Kolkia said, "The Siakos are discussing to contribute money too. They are planning to hire a motor vehicle to take them to Mt Hagen to attend the funeral tomorrow" He continued, almost confidently without any trace of uncertainty in his voice.

I remained startled and could not believe every word that was coming out of Kolkia's lips. I knew Cathy was having marriage problems with her wealthy millionaire husband for some time. Her face would be bloated and full of scars and bruises whenever she came home. I vividly recalled the last time I saw her outside the Lae Showground; the complexion of her beautiful face totally distorted by swellings and bruises from a fresh beating.

"Good grief! What happened to you?" I had asked.

"That old bastard did it again," Cathy had said, referring to her husband, Peter Kupal.

"But why? Why did he have to do such a terrible thing to you?"

Cathy never responded. Her husband stepped up and both disappeared into the show ground with their entourage. Yes, there were miscarriages in her marriage, but an early death for her age was unbelievable, difficult to accept and beyond reasoning. Why did she die? How did it happen? What was the cause of her death? I suddenly felt a lump in my throat, and a pang of sorrow sinking deep inside me. I tried to find out more from Kolkia but dissimulated when I noticed the presence of my wife, Anna some few steps away.

Kolkia Andambo said very little about the cause of Cathy Gior's death, as he too was unsure of the nature of the death, but briefly hinted from what he gathered that it resulted from a brawl with one of her husband's other wives. "But that could not be confirmed as yet", Kolkia explained, "We will get all the facts, and perhaps all the details from Cathy's uncle Philip, when he returns from Mt Hagen. He was said to be the first to take the news and left on the next PMV to Kundiawa to find out if it was all true that Cathy died. Maybe, he'll return tomorrow and the news will be confirmed when he returns.

"I see---so Cathy Gior must have really died", I said, as I stared thoughtfully into the open space before me.

"That's right! That's what I gathered at Mondiagl-kaugla", Kolkia said, "The Siakos are waiting for Phillip too. They wanted to be really sure before hiring a truck for their travel to Mt Hagen to view the death".

There was weird silence in the house after Kolkia left. My wife Anna, who is also a Siako girl from Cathy's village, said nothing about the news she'd just heard. She did not even mention it, nor did she want to discuss anything about her clan sister's death. She appeared not shaken and affected by the news too. Strange, but it was common sense and I need not ask or touch on the topic. I remained calm instead and tried to forget what I had heard, but awkwardly, found it almost difficult to contain myself.

Cathy retrospectively was no ordinary person. She was once my childhood inamorata and a former girlfriend. Everyone in my Bokan village and the neighboring villages knew of our relationship, and the subsequent break up. My wife Anna was no stranger to the relationship too. As a kindred and clan 'sister' to Cathy, she was one way or another, closely associated with Cathy Gior and myself prior to our marriage. She even involved herself in stealthy errands between us before the dissociation and really there was nothing I could hide from her, or anyone when word reached me that afternoon that Cathy was dead. A pang of sorrow engulfed me deep inside, but I could not openly express my commiseration, as I respectfully did not want to upset Anna.

As my incredulous mind pondered in grief, memories of the wonderful times I had and shared with Cathy Gior, came vividly flashing back into my mind. I remembered the first time we met. She was only ten, a mere fourth grader in Dengalgu Primary School at Toromambuno, and myself thirteen, then a grade seven pupil at Rosary High School in Kondiu. I reminisced with nostalgia, the glorious moments we shared together in the long years that followed, and the anticlimactic ending to our ill-fated relationship. Though our relationship failed fruition, the experience was great, exhilarating and fun-filled. It sure was a long time ago, but seemed only yesterday.

2

The Dramatis Personae

Wake up, Joe---wake up!" my mother said, briskly shaking my legs. "Hmmm! What's the matter? You are disturbing my sleep", I complained, and annoyingly pulled the blanket over my head, not wanting to be disturbed again.

But mother did not go away. "It's Thomas---your school mate", she said, with tones of excitement in her voice, "He is here to see you. Can't you sit up, and greet your friend?"

"Oh, Thomas…is he still here?", I asked, still drowsy but already awake in a flash at the mention of Thomas.

"Yes! He is standing right beside me now, waiting to see you. Come on! Why don't you get up, and meet him?"

"Ooooh, my gosh! What's he doing here at this time of the day? It's too early and freezing to walk outside", I said, as I struggled to get out of the blanket.

"What? You call this morning, when the sun is almost over your head?" Thomas promptly took over the conversation from my mother. "Why don't you sit up and check the day before it gets noon?" Thomas said.

I drowsily removed the blanket to my waist, turned around and sat up on the bed, my eyes still half closed. Sitting on the earth floor near the fireplace, waiting in anticipation for me to rise up was Thomas Goir, my friend and classmate at Rosary High School. Sure enough, he was early in my house. His feet were wet all over from the morning dew he'd collected from the wet grass along the way, as he walked to Bokan. His fingers were evidently numb from the freezing temperature outside, and I could see him spreading them above the glowing embers at the fireplace to put life back into them.

"Aaaah! Good morning, Tom. It's too early to step outside, you must be up with the birds", I called out from the bed, as my mouth opened up to let out the first yawn of the day, with my arms stretching out to relax the pressed muscles from the long night's sleep.

"Yes, Good morning, Joe! The birds were up first, then me", he said with a glowing smile. "And you? What's keeping you that long in bed?" Thomas jokingly asked in his usual seriocomic tone.

"Did I sleep that long? I said, as I cleaned my eyes.

"Off course, you did. Why don't you check the day outside?"

Rubbing my eyes clean, I peered out of the door at the blazing daylight outside.

"Oh---No! It must be going up to 8 or 9.00 o'clock, I think", I suddenly exclaimed, after assessing the morning light outside. Thomas shrugged. "I don't know…but, you thought I lied, didn't you?". "Not exactly! But surely, I must have taken the longest sleep in my life. And maybe, if you had not come along, I could have woken up in the afternoon".

"Well, thank me, then". Thomas twitted.

"You deserve nothing better, Tom", I retorted back at his facetious demand, "Really, you ought to be punished for disturbing me in my sleep"

Thomas chuckled and I laughed too. The day was a tranquil Tuesday morning of April. Thomas and I were best of friends at school. Although a Siako from the neighboring Ende-naige-ingugl village, we considered each other 'brothers', and a member of each one's own family. Ironically, many observers mistook us for two identical twin brothers when they saw us together. And it all retrospectively began seven years ago on a chilling February morning when we enrolled ourselves at Denglagu Primary School at Toromambuno. Our mums brought us there on that fateful morning and little did we knew, nor our teacher, a Catholic Nun Sr. Erreny, that there was more to come, when she paired us together behind a double-desk in the Standard 1 classroom. From the simple giving and sharing of common interests and material items in the classroom, our friendship grew and developed into an unbreakable bond, that, consequently, in the later years, was to involve our parents back home for a life-long rapport with frequent exchanges of gifts, that included the choicest food items and packages.

Thomas clearly was no stranger to my house. His visit that morning betokens that of a friend, out to check on his best pal after losing contact for some time. It was almost four days ago since we last saw each other. We had traveled home together from Kondiu for the first term holidays and he had gone straight home to his parents at Ende-naige-ingugl and I had come straight to my Bokan home. Nothing was heard from each other since then, and probably too eager to find out what I was doing all this time he came over to Bokan that morning.

"Where's mother?" I asked, as I removed the blanket away from my legs.

"I don't know", Thomas said, shaking his head. "She went outside while you were getting up".

"And Paul?".

"Him too…he wasn't around when I came in".

"Did mother indicate where she was going?"

"No…but she should be outside somewhere".

"Doesn't matter, Tom; she's probably out feeding the pigs. Can you check the fireplace? She should leave something there for me to take for breakfast"

"Yes, I can see two pieces of cooked *kaukaus* here", Thomas said, holding the baked *kaukau* tubers up in his hands.

"I feel like eating something, can you pass them to me, please?", I said, and then, asked Thomas, "How about you? You hungry?" Thomas did not wait. "I walked here with an empty tummy, Joe. Off course, I'm hungry too", he said. "Then, you take one, I'll have the other".

"Thank you! I'll help you out with this one", Thomas said, as he cuffed away the ashes from his *kaukau* after handing me the other.

The *kaukaus* were of the *Tainde-ambu* variety and while we were breakfasting on them, Thomas briefly told me about his last three days with his parents.

"My father is putting up a new house", he said, "Our old one is about to go down and he is replacing it"

"Your father envies big houses, the new one must be a big one too".

"It certainly is, Joe. And I was very busy over the last three days. I helped him to cut the bamboo for the walls for the last three days. But it involves a lot of work, you know. We had to cut the bamboo up at Dunugl, and carry it all the way down to Ende-naige-ingugl over our shoulders. We worked like mules from 6.00am till late. My shoulders are aching deep, and today I decided to shirk for a break, and took off while father was not watching".

I now established why Thomas was so early in my house, and let out a foolish smile when he finished.

"So, you decided to escape and hide away here with me today?", I said.

"No! Not exactly here," Thomas quickly replied, "I am going up to Toromambuno. I only called in here to check you out first before moving on to the school".

"Oh, is that so?"

"Yes"

"What are you going to do up at the school, anyway?"

"To my brother's house"

I paused and eyed Thomas curiously, obviously stunned at the mention of a brother teaching at Toromambuno Primary School.

"You never had a brother in the school last year, and all the other preceding years too when we were there. And now you have one teaching there?" I said, with a puzzling countenance.

"Yes, my elder brother, James. He's teaching there now", Thomas said.

"James? You never told me you had a brother of that name. Have I met him?"

Thomas thought for a while.

"I can't recall the last time we met him together. But he spent all his years in schools in the Southern Highlands, and rarely came home. It was only this year that he got transferred to Simbu. He's now teaching at Toromambuno. And that's why I am going up there to pay a visit".

"That is a surprise to me. You are lucky, Tom, to have a brother ahead of you, unlike me. Is James married, or single?"

"Married, off course. His wife is from the Wandike Auge-nigl-ende clan. Do you remember Philip, our Standard 3 class teacher from Wai-mambuno?"

"Yeah, Phillip Koane…his wife is Salume Korai. Their house is just across the river."

"That's correct. Teacher Phillip's sister is my brother's spouse".

"Then, she must be Kumo---Angela Kumo, because teacher Phillip has only one sister who goes by that name".

"Yep! It's her---Kumo", Thomas affirmed, "She is James' wife"

"Okay, just give me a minute, I think I remember seeing your brother once too. Is he the tall slim fellow with thick beard?"

"He shaves too, but sometimes he is very bushy around the chin area".

"It has to be him because I saw him together with Kumo over at teacher Phillip's place one time. They were probably here on holiday or something"

"Then, it must be him; so, you've seen him already", Thomas said.

"That was him alright. But how come, I did not know James was your brother all these years, Tom?"

Thomas again gave some thought to my query, and then said, "Well, maybe, he doesn't know of you…or, perhaps I never told you about him"

"It has to be that, or something else…what are you going to do up at his house, anyway?"

"I am not going anywhere. Like I said, I planned to shirk from work today, so that's where I'll be till late"

"I see".

There was a moment of silence as we concentrated on the *kaukaus*.

"And you?", Thomas finally asked after we finished the *kaukaus*. "What are your plans for today?"

"I don't know---in fact, I was still sleeping when you came around. And I still have not fully recovered yet. So, maybe, I'll go back to bed again, and complete my sleep".

"Bed? Oh, come on, Joe! You're not an old man to go back in there again", Thomas jested with a frowning look. "Listen, why don't you come along with me to the school and pass the time there with me", Tom said.

It was not at all a bad idea, and I tried to recall if there was anything that I was suppose to do during the day. But nothing lined up.

"Well, I don't see a problem there" I said, "It's just that I don't have a fixed plan for today, and the bed is the next option. I can join you to the school if you like. When do we leave?"

There was already delight in Thomas' eyes. "When you are ready", he tersely replied, already pleased with my assent to accompany him.

"Then, give me some time. I'll look around for mother and let her know where we'll be going first. She gets annoyed sometimes when we disappear without letting her know of our whereabouts".

"Let's go out and find her together then".

Mother was nowhere to be found outside the house. We hurried to the pig's house where she was expected to be at this time of the morning, and she was there with Paul, my only younger brother of eleven. Both were feeding the pigs. She had just finished and the empty *bilum* was now over her head like a netted veil when we arrived.

"What are you two boys up to now?" she called out, as we emerged in her sight.

"Looking for you"

"Oh, why…is there a problem, or something?"

"No…we are going up to the school".

"School? Toromambuno?"

"Yes…so, we've come to tell you before we leave".

"And did you take your *kaukaus* I left behind for you?"

"Yes, we did. There were two pieces. So, we shared them between us". Mother gave us an askance look and smiled. "Then, I don't see any reason why you have to come all the way here to tell me all about it", mother twitted. We chuckled and turned back the way we came to hit the road, refusing my little brother Paul who was begging to join us.

The sun was already up and the Mondia-nigle defile was gradually warming up as we left. Naturally, my Bokan village, being nestled at the foothills of the high-rise Kindi Range in the east, the Bismarck Range to the north and the Gogor rise to the south was always the last to take in the early morning's sunshine. And ironically, it was always the first to give it away in the afternoons with the facing Yandina Range in the west blockading the afternoon rays. But now, it was all lit up. The pristine Tar and Mondia rivers that meandered through the curvature of the defile from the Kombil-ke and Mogoma catchments along the Bismark Range glittered lustrously in the bright sunlight as they purled gently over the shining brown algae coated stones and boulders. Both the rivers met a few meters to the northwest from my house front, naturally demarcating the confines of my little Bokan home to the west. A few meters downstream from the confluence was the suspension footbridge of *Casuarina* saplings to allow access to the main walking track on the other side of the river without drenching the toes in the icy cold river.

The main walking track across the river stretched north-south. To the north, the track linked the villages of Gadin-mambuno, Dini-pene and Mondia-nigle. Further upstream was Kot-dame where the forest line from the Bismark Range meets the ever-expanding subsistence gardening activities undertaken by my Miuk-Kwiopa clansmen. The track continued to the Mondia Pass after ascending the Ken-kugl ridge-way; first reaching Oiye-boglkwa, then stepping onto the vehicular track at Mogoma, across the Mondia Pass and over into the depressions of Bundi, the land of the Gendes (or *Geregls*, as we pronounce them), our traditional neighbors on the other side of the Bismark Range. Descending further to the lowlands below was the Ramu Valley.

It was on this very track that Fr Alfons Schaffer, Fr Antonius Crannsen and Br Anton Baas, the three German pioneer Catholic SVD missionaries, under the guidance and escsort of the ever popular Kawagle of Mingende, walked almost fifty years ago in November 1933 into the densely populated highlands from Madang after trekking the mountainous terrain of the Ramu and Bundi; whereupon first contact with white 'ghosts' was made by our so-called stone-age ancestors with the missionaries.

Surrounded by tall *Pandanus* stands, close to the river edge opposite Bokan, is the village of Kama-mambuno, where some twenty years later, will be the concourse for the defile dwellers, appropriately calling themselves the *'Mondia Karamaps'* to enjoy a game of cards or darts to pass time in the evenings before heading home. South bound, a few hundred meters downstream, is Wai-mambuno village, formerly a place for sojourn by the colonial patrol officers and once the central ceremonial ground for the famous pig killing festival of the neighbouring Wandike Auge-nigl-ende clan.

The Yandina Range ultimately drops to a scarpment at the entrance into Wai-mambuno and traversing the drop to the other side is Mondiagl-kaugla, the Siako territory. The Simbu River, originating from the lakes, Piunde and Aunde, and catchments around the base of the towering Mt Wilhelm in the north, gushs past heading south to meet the mighty Whagi, then Purari and eventually feed the Gulf of Papua.

A log bridge connects the eastern bank to the precincts of the famous Mondiagl-kaugla market on the western flank. A few steps across the market is the Gembogl-Kundiawa road that links the entire Maugl-wak tribe to the outside world. The road ultimately serves as the western perimeter of the popular Mondiagl-kaugla market. Across the market on the far side of the road begins the ascent of the western face of the Upper Simbu Valley, with Degl-bagl just above the road, Gunda-bugl and Daka-mambuno sandwiched in-between, and Puglan-gigl further up on the upper reaches of the Banda-mambuno Range.

Many people were already at Mondiagl-kaugla when we arrived, buyers and sellers alike in multitudes.

"Look! The people…nearly everyone is here"

"I told you, Joe, you woke up late. People were already here when I crossed over to Bokan this morning. And today is Tuesday – market day! I hope you haven't forgotten that too."

"Bugger me, I forgot today is Tuesday", I said, as my eyes scanned the market for anything interesting. At the far end corner behind some big stones were nurses from the Gembogl Health Centre, running an immunisation clinic for the babies and children. A blue government Toyota Land Cruiser was parked close by and many mothers were seen crowding around that area with their children and babies. The wailing from the inoculated ones was loud and clear, and could be heard from where we were as we ambled past.

"Don't let my father see us", Thomas warned, as his eyes consciously searched the market.

"I can't see him anywhere. I don't think he is here yet. Where was he when you left him?"

"On the roof of his new house. He was up early with the birds".

"Then, don't you worry; I think he is still up there on the roof".

We briefly stopped for a minute, or two, to chat with friends, but did not prolong our sojourn, as Thomas still does not want us to be seen by his father. We stepped out onto the main road and continued up towards the mission station. Behind us was Ende-naige-ingugl – Thomas's village, enshrouded beneath the giant *Casuarinas* except for a few houses on the bench in the foreground that were partly obscured by the crown canopy of the Gum trees growing alongside the road.

By the time we reached the Poko-dame bend, Mondiagl-kaugla and Ende-naige-ingugl were both gone. They were out of sight. Up ahead before us was Nigl-guma village and the road junction to Keglsuglo. Behind the houses, partly obscured by the thatched rooftops, was the sawmill operated by the Mt Wilhelm Local Government Council, sandwiched between the Mission Station and the village. The roofing iron sheets of the sawmill shed could be partly seen glittering above the thatched rooftops. Above the treetops, towering down in alpine blue, was Mt Wilhelm, the country's highest peak of 4508m projecting graciously high up into the cloudless blue sky.

In the brilliant morning sunlight, the mosaic patterns of the tundra grassland above the tree line at Bugla-wai-nogua and the barren rocky faces with the serrated frosty capped summits reminded us of the grandeur of the Swiss alps, the Himalayas and the Andes we had seen in color magazines, and calendars pin-ups.

A lot of people were standing at the road junction to the Mission Station and Keglsuglo, but we paid little attention to them and sidled past. Up ahead was Toromambuno Catholic Mission Station, geographically sandwiched between the Tombogl and Sugla-mambuno Ranges that stretched north-south at equal lengths from the base of the towering Mt Wilhelm to Nigl-guma. Between them meanders the pristine and crystal clear, but icy, Kualke River.

A few steps forward from where we stood was the entrance gate into the glebe and under the aging *Casuarinas* we could see the Mission's cow paddock and the station's buildings, most notably the sister's convent which was in the forefront. A few meters back, slightly to the right in the background was the monster church. The steeple and the silver finial rood atop the spire could be seen through the transparent *Casuarina* canopies.

But we did not continue up to the school as we had predetermined. When we finally reached the entrance into the station, our attention was somehow gravitated towards the buzz of sawmilling activities taking place just outside the station perimeter. We had seen the sawmill in operation many times before, but, maybe, we had missed the activities for a while too long while away in Kondiu and curiously stopped to watch the sawmillers as they went about performing their routine duties, milling the round logs taken out from the forests around the base of Mt Whilhem and the Bismarck Range. The technical application of knowledge and running of electrically powered saw milling equipment in the production of lumber was eye-catching, causing wonder and admiration, and we observed everything both with curiosity and envy for a very long time.

It was some good hours later that we finally decided to continue to the school, but that observation was later to have major influence in my career choice after completion of High School. Forestry was where my career path would lead me.

We entered the mission gate and stepped onto the nicely laid stone pavement that stretched for over a kilometer into the mission station. It was constructed in the 1960s. Our parents, under the supervision of the early missionaries and their laymen had expertly laid the stone path, consisting of close to half-a-million stones collected from the nearby Kualke River long before we were born. Our eyes reviewed the familiar sights of the station grounds with nostalgia after some weeks away in Kondiu. "Nothing has changed", we mused as we advanced.

Many fading memories of the recent past deluged our minds. We reminisced on the afternoons during Agriculture class when we would be directed by our Class Teacher to go out into the cow paddocks with wheel burrows and collect cow dung to fertilise our school gardens with classmates. We laughed and continued up to the Sister's convent, past the titanic Catholic church, where we would often pause for a prayer, or genuflect in worship, as was always encouraged by our teachers.

Next to the church was the mission canteen, where the price for a thick chunck of fresh beef was very cheap. We talked about it and walked past and stood by the canal, then Br. Lambert's garage and finally on the bench overlooking the sluice and mini dam below where the water source to the mission's power turbines started. It was picturesque from where we were, given the panorama and beauty of the natural settings. The seemingly simple engineering skill, applied in the design and construction of the dyke, the sluice and the barrage dam across the Kualke, diverting the water source from the main Kualke River to the hydropower turbines, was amazingly interesting. For our juvenile and underdeveloped minds this was a wonder. It certainly was, and is still an engineering masterpiece of the German Lay worker, a Herman Sieland, who constructed the power station in the 1960s.

Br Lambert also had a piggery down there by the river side and a huge boar was seen wondering around in the pen.

Behind us, across the mission gardens to the west were the three classrooms with the black creosote coated walls, we had occupied as primary school pupils for the last six years, ending last year. It was there that we were tamed, groomed and nurtured academically for our future betterment and prosperity in the modern world. Up ahead was the school playground and across the field on the edge of the playground were the teachers' houses.

We walked past the byre, and crossed the playing field. James Gior's house was to our right in the second duplex.

3

Infatuation

There was no one in the house when we arrived. The main door was closed but there was noise of someone in the kitchen, which was a separate building at the back of the duplex.

"I can hear someone in the kitchen", Thomas said.

"Me too"

"Let's go and find out", Thomas said, and led the way. I followed closely behind. When we finally checked, we found a small girl desperately trying to roast some freshly dug sweet potatoes on a smoldering fire.

Unfortunately, our presence was somewhat unexpected and we surprised the poor little girl with a terrible shock when we stood at the door.

"Thomas!" she abruptly said, almost taken to her feet

"Yes, it's me … me and my friend"

"You both scared me", the girl said, shaking her head and smiled after regaining her composure.

"Oh, we're so sorry, then", Thomas apologized, "We didn't actually mean to scare you; we heard some noise in here, so came over to check".

"It was me, Tom. I was struggling to break this firewood", she said pointing to a crooked piece of firewood that was lying next to the fireplace.

Thomas, who happened to know the girl very well, later introduced her to me as his niece, Cathy Gior, the eldest daughter of his brother James Gior's three children. He then introduced me to his niece too.

"This is Joe…Joseph Tamgo", he told his niece. "He is my classmate and we are best of buddies at school".

Cathy put out a genial smile and extended her right hand. I took hold of her hand and we warmly shook hands as we greeted each other.

"Everyone is out", Cathy said, as she pulled her hand away from me, "I don't know where they went, so I can't tell you exactly where they are now"

Thomas frowned, as if he was on an errand, but said nothing thereafter, and instead, looked around for a place to sit. I joined him and we both took our places near the fireplace, opposite his niece.

Cathy explained to us that she was hungry and was trying to improvise some quickies for her famished tummy. Just next to her, beside the fireplace, was a dishful of attractive looking uncooked sweet potatoes that appeared to have come out from a new plot of *kaukau* garden, presumably a first harvest from the plot.

"You boys can join me if you like", she said. And with almost empty tummies, it was an offer we could not refuse. "That is kind of you", we chorused, "We had only one *kaukau* each before we came up here and we are hungry too"

"Yeah, this is an opportunity we both can't miss", Thomas added.

Cathy smiled and we all laughed as we settled down around the fire, which was now burning well with our assistance.

We kept the moments alive while waiting for the sweet potatoes to be cooked. There were plenty of chatter, jokes and laughter. Cathy was full of wit. She was friendly, affable and open in everything we talked about. She was loquacious too and did most of the talking. Like all other young Primary School kids, she asked us many questions about Kondiu and about the everyday life in a high school. What kind of things did you learn? Are they hard? Do you have any European teachers there? What kind of food did you eat in the mess? We answered all her puerile questions with delight, and at one stage, jocularly remarked, "You'll find out everything for yourself when you get there after completion of your sixth Grade". Cathy giggled and laughed disapprovingly at our remark, but coincidentally, our prophetic prediction was to be fulfilled two years later.

The sweet potatoes were finally cooked and after a self-serve meal, we continued discursively with our chatter. It was now already past mid-day but the afternoon was never boring. Maybe, the stories were exciting, thrilling and jocular, which, consequently, caused laughter the whole of the afternoon and kept the mood high, but for me personally, it was more than that. It was Cathy herself. It was something extraordinarily amazing about her that attracted my attention, and henceforth kept my mood very high during the entire afternoon.

Despite her very young tender age she was already charming enough to attract a boy's attention. She was pretty, and quite unbelievably, it was undeniable too to admit that all the necessary feminine ingredients of a beautiful girl were already there for a boy to be infatuated. I noticed that at first sight, and upon arrival, admired her from the beginning. The longer we stayed, the dottier I became about her, and it was not long before I felt a growing affection for her; an affection never before experienced for any other girl in my life. It was a totally new feeling, something unique and novel to my occassional aggressive, selfish and hostile attitude towards girls in the past. Maybe I was precocious. But certainly, there was something that cannot be denied here. I had fallen in love, I think. And yes…for the very first time!

Our convivial moment came to an end when Thomas finally announced that we should head back home. I agreed with Thomas verbally, as the sun was starting to go down behind the mountains in the west of Puglan-gigl, but ironically, deep down in my heart, there was a compelling vehemence of reluctance. I wanted the conversation to continue for as long as possible.

"How about Cathy?", I said, looking at Cathy first, then Tom, and then wittingly emphasised, "Nobody is here yet and she's going to be all alone after we leave". I looked straight into Thomas's eyes, this time in the hope of buttoning us back for a few more moments. But it was Cathy who spoke first. "Oh, don't you worry about that?", she said, "I can stay here by myself. It is getting late and everyone should be well on their way to the school by now."

I said nothing more. The voice came from the 'special' one, that I was concerned about and had longed to remain close with. Nothing more came out of my lips, as I recoiled in disgust. "Yeah, she can stay here by herself", Thomas said. "She was alone when we came around and found her. She should be alright", Thomas further added, cementing his earlier decision that we should leave. I felt hurt inside but reluctantly stood up.

"Oh, ok", I said, "If that is fine with Cathy, I think we should leave". Off course, every word uttered was not really coming from my heart. And together, we bade Cathy goodbye and stepped out of the kitchen. Cathy returned our afternoon greetings and stood at the door watching us, as we crossed the playground and disappeared from her sight.

Thomas and I parted when we reached Mondiagl-kaugla. He proceeded down the road to Ende-naige-ingugl, and I crossed over at Mondiagl-kaugla and walked to Bokan. But my journey home that afternoon was peculiar. My mind was deeply obsessed and besotted with Cathy's beauty, that I plodded home at a snail's pace, with the usual ten minutes walking distance extending to well over an hour by the time I got home. The smiles, laughs, jokes and everything she did that afternoon I relished in my mind with increasing enthusiasm and desire. I ignored all the 'waylays' and 'accosts'. It seemed a bit crazy at that juvenile age; myself at only thirteen to indulge in such dream and fantasy over a ten-year old girl but, maybe, that was how life was meant to be as you grow older. Without any doubt, it was the beginning of another chapter in my life.

I could not settle down comfortably in the following days. The constant indulgence of daydreaming became so intense that the preternatural yearning for Cathy Gior gained momentum. And quite alarmingly, it was so overwhelming that I couldn't wait any longer to see her again. Deep inside there was a constant itch to go out and look for Cathy, and impulsively I took a stroll across to Mondiagl-kaugla two days later in the hope of finding her, or Thomas, if possible. Coincidentally, my timing was perfect. I met Cathy Gior with some of her friends at the Mondiagl-kaugla market. They were on an afternoon stroll too; talking, laughing and enjoying the afternoon sun as they approached the market from Nigl-guma. Out of sheer desperation I quickly raised my hands to lure her attention, and when I secured it I beckoned her across to where I was sitting. She waved back after picking me out, and leaving her friends behind, she quickly crossed over towards my direction with an alluring smile, even though I had only known her from the day before.

"Good afternoon", I said, returning her smile in full radiance. She returned my greetings and was even prettier this time.

"You are alone, where is your friend Thomas?" she asked, as she settled down on a boulder next to me.

"I don't know. I haven't seen him since our last meeting at the school", I said, "Maybe, he is at Ende-naige-ingugl, helping his father out on their new house"

"You two are always together. That's what I heard"

"Yes, but I'm alone this time…so, you must have done a bit of research on us, did you?"

"No, it was grandma, Thomas's mum who told me all about you two when I mentioned to her yesterday about our meet on Tuesday", Cathy said, smiling. "We are out on an afternoon stroll", she quickly added.

"Same for me too. I just arrived a while ago", I told Cathy, hiding my true purpose.

We exchanged some jokes in reminiscence of our first banter at the school. Cathy was, as usual, affable and friendly during the badinage. Already, she was garrulous and I could feel the convivial atmosphere returning. Hence, it did not take long for my internal desires to kindle for her again. And, with the absence of Thomas, I felt totally absorbed and the atmosphere rather more sensationally romantic than ever. Deep inside, I was already burning and shaking with excitement to verbalise everything in my mind. I wanted to tell her how deeply I felt for her and what had happened to me over the last two days. Foremost was my eagerness to ask her if we could possibly enter into a boyfriend/girlfriend relationship, a very bold and precocious move against our delicate age. But that did not matter so much to me for the moment, as I was already at the brink of spitting out everything, or otherwise, anything about my infatuation to the very one sitting just next to me.

But then, just when I thought nothing was going to stop me from spitting out my internal desires and feelings, I somehow, on impulse and by sheer control, managed to inhibit my undertone, fearing that she was, maybe, too young to think about boys at this time and boo me. Furthermore, I had not known Cathy long enough to proceed with my impromptu plan. This was only our second meeting and I felt it would be a total disgrace if she declined. Most likely, I'd be walking home with my 'tail between my legs' and ruefully agreed that it was not the psychological moment yet.

I briskly mooted on a subject to keep our conversation alive.

"Do you like getting letters?' I asked.

"No".

"Oh! Why is that?

"Well, I never received one in my life, so I am not in a better position to make a judgement on that".

"Oh, really?", I said, looking straight across into Cathy's eyes.

"I guess so…I mean, it sounds a bit fusty here", Cathy said, "But as a matter of fact, our teacher just recently taught us how to write letters and mail them out. We have been taught how and what to write on the envelopes and so on. But I've not written one out yet, nor do I receive any. Let me put it this way! Simply, there is no one to write to".

"Alright, I see what you mean," I said thoughtfully, and then asked, "What if I write you a letter when I get back to Kondiu next week?"

"That will be fantastic", Cathy said, almost jumping up to her toes, and was excited as ever. "I've never received a single letter in my life before and, it will be a first and great experience if you write me one", she added.

Cathy's response was so alluringly enticing that I could not hold back my excitement to start on a letter immediately. In truth, I dearly needed to somehow establish a permanent dialogue as a bridge to Cathy and, quite miraculously, we have just achieved that.

"I promise I'll write you a letter when Thomas and I return to Kondiu next week", I said, gleefully, "I'll even inform Thomas to write one too, so you can expect a letter, or maybe two, if Tom writes too, around the second week after we leave here"

"Fantastic, I'll reply to all your letters if you both write", Cathy said delightfully, "This is a promise".

We had not conferred long enough. And I was briefly explaining how the mission mails operate between Toromambuno and Kondiu when her friends called her to walk back to Toromambuno. I tried to drag out our conversation for a few minutes more to keep her back from her friends, but she promptly stood up, tapped me lightly over my shoulders in farewell, and left to team up with her friends. I sat watching her go with envy and admiration, as they walked back to the school. She never looked back. And, as it turned out later on, that afternoon was to be the last time I saw Cathy Gior before returning back to school.

I wasted no time in writing a letter for Cathy when I arrived at Kondiu. I reminded her that Thomas and I had returned safely to Kondiu and that our meeting at her place that Tuesday afternoon during the holidays had been a pleasant and memorable one. I also indicated in my concluding paragraph that I enjoyed her company too, and ultimately post-scripted the letter with the line, *'Hope to hear from you soon'*, hoping that she might empathise my interest in her, even though nothing romantic was penned. I was very cautious not to write anything distressing, annoying or confusing. And, with her address carefully written out on the cover envelope, I dropped the letter into the red mailbox in front of the school office for dispatch, hoping all along that it reached her safely.

Thomas, on the other hand, was apathetic. He showed little interest in writing a letter to Cathy, even though I mentioned to him about the letter I wrote to her. Maybe, he was not interested in writing letters---which may be fine with him---but our fraternal relationship took a different turn from my standpoint. He was now my inamorata's paternal cousin and from hereon I stealthily held him as my stepping-stone to Cathy Gior. My perfunctory attitudes towards him veered. This time, I regarded him an important person in my life and obsequiously was docile towards him, trying all I could to be complacent and submissive in everything and anything I did for him. But I did not reveal anything to him yet. I mentioned Cathy once in a while during our rambles and meetings to let him moot up a conversation, obviously to open the doors for me to unbosom everything I had in my mind. But, for some reason, he would say very little, or otherwise nothing at all about his niece and instead broached something else, leaving me in a depressed mood. I wished more often if he would only empathise with my true feelings about Cathy and what was really going on deep down inside me, but this apparently was to take some time, it seemed.

As the weeks and months went past, the school activities in Kondiu occupied most of our time with less time to think about anything else. But Cathy Gior always had a place in my mind. I remembered her almost everyday and frequently wondered if she was alright and had received my letter until one Saturday. It was during the movie night at the Bishop Cohill Auditorium, during the intermission, that I heard my name called out in the front by the School's Headmaster, along with the other students, during the mail call. My heart jumped almost immediately at the mention of my name.

"It's from Cathy", I confidently guessed in my mind, as I walked up to collect it. And, true to my thoughts, it was her letter. Her crabbed handwriting was conspicuous on the cover envelope. Almost at once, a seraphic feeling swept through my entire system. It was a feeling never experienced before and was the most exciting moment in my life. In truth, it was my first time ever to receive a letter from a girl. And although, it was not a love letter, or anything close, the fact that it came from a secretly admired one was more than enough to send me into the dream world.

"Thank you very much for your very nice letter", Cathy acknowledged in her opening paragraph. She also acknowledged my company and that of Thomas over the holidays as her most enjoyable moment. "I enjoyed your company and hope to see you both again soon", she wrote. Many other little stories of home and her latest experiences in the classroom featured in the next paragraphs of her single-page letter. Finally, at the bottom of the page, she penned off her letter with the line, *Hope to hear from you soon*', the very words that I had post scripted in my letter to her.

The sentence was, off course, banal. But for me, personally, it was more than that. With all the dreams and fantasies about her still causing a stir and firmly rooted inside me, the line was something vicariously sensational and prematurely got me aflamed with burning passion and desire for Cathy. I re-read the line over and over again ruminatively with indulgence. And more still, I could not wait to put pen on the paper to write for her eyes. The following morning, I started on a very lengthy letter, acknowledging receipt of her letter. Many other stories about Kondiu followed. I made sure lot of good things about her was penned for her eyes. Again, I was plain and discreetly careful not to sound too romantic, but implicitly I was allegorical, wittingly hoping that she sensed my true mind in every sentence I wrote for her eyes.

I did not waste time in getting the letter away. She wrote back fast, replying to my letter as she had promised to do so. Soon there was a continuous flow of letters between us, eventually resulting in a binding brother/sister relationship established through the mail. Cathy would end her letters with, *'From your sister, Cathy Goir'* and I would reciprocate with *'From your brother, Joseph Tamgo'*. It sure made me feel good and, I was proud, although it was not exactly what I was hoping for. But this was only the beginning of many things…the beginning of many things yet to come!

4

The Nostalgic Moments

Cathy got prettier and prettier every time I saw her with the change of time, days, weeks and months. Her beauty ravished me. But I remained vigilant and was always careful not to think insensibly or act irrational, as she had already taken me for a 'brother'. Certainly, I would be insane to act otherwise. And if I do, then most likely, she would lose all the trust and confidence in me and, maybe, abandon me forever, I thought. Deep down, I did not want this to happen and, instead, bestowed her with all the fraternal affections she needed, hoping all along that one day she will make my day.

But quite disappointingly, our locations became a concern to me when I paused to think about it. Kondiu and Toromambuno were located well over 100 kilometers away from each other, separated by huge rivers and mountain ranges, and I felt like we were stuck at each of the North and South poles. Thus, I treasured the school holidays most, as these were the only moments I was able to see Cathy in person, and enjoy her companionship. During the few breaks I went home, I tried all I could to spend as much time with Cathy as possible to enjoy her presence. She was gregarious and quite pleasingly became fond of me too. We would spend long hours together at the markets, or after the church service on Sundays, chatting and enjoying the comfort of our closeness. Christmas holidays alone were always the most enjoyable moments for us both, as the school holidays extended for many weeks before the commencement of the new school year. This prolonged our stay in the village for extended periods, and on many occasions I would invite her to the many social activities, dances and video night shows in the neighboring villages. At other times, I would invite her to village games played on Sunday after church service. She would accede obligingly without reluctance and obediently accompanied me to whichever destination I suggested. And I was thrilled promenading her to these venues.

We behaved in this way for over two years. Then came the most exciting moment in our platonic 'brother/sister' relationship. Cathy was selected to enroll at Kondiu as a Grade 7 student the following year, towards the end of November. She passed all her Grade 6 examinations and was among the twelve other Grade 6 pupils selected from Denglagu Primary School to attend Rosary High School. In Kondiu, her name appeared on the school notice board together with the names of all other new Grade 7 intakes selected from other Catholic Agency Primary Schools in the province. Thomas and I were both surprised and pleased with her efforts in making it to high school.

"We'll be together in Kondiu next year", I ranted, as I congratulated her when we went home for the Christmas Holidays. "Your name appeared on the school notice".

She smiled approvingly.

"Yes, I know", Cathy said, looking bright and radiant. She was already informed by her school headmaster and was well aware of her selection to high school. She was in an all time high; looking forward to the day when she would set her foot in Kondiu when I congratulated her. And when classes began at the start of the new school year, she enrolled herself as a Grade 7 at Rosary High School, while Thomas and I proceeded to Grade 10 in the same year.

Under the supreme care, guidance and administration of the Catholic De La Salle Brothers and the Sisters of Mercy Nuns, Kondiu was a place of great learning. Located in a beautiful quiet fertile valley, in an idyllic setting along the eastern banks of the turbid Whagi River, Kondiu has always remained a household name as the land of the *'Kaia-nigl-mam'* amongst the Maugl-waks, specifically for the giant tubers of the sweet potato variety that went under that name (*kaia-nigl-mam*) the land relentlessly produced. Since its inception, the school was the only secondary education institution for the Maugl-wak students who attended Denglagu Primary School. History has it in the annals that in the early years, the Maugl-wak students traveled on foot to Kondiu for education at a time when motorised road systems were non-existent in the province. Many pioneer old students still remember the tedious two-day walk; trekking the mountainous terrain of the Upper Simbu valley, trailing the strenuous Ki-Kombuglo and Guie-waie Gaps, crossing the turbulent waters of the Wara Simbu and Singa-nigle, and then trudging through the countless stretch of tribal lands before finally reaching the school. With the motorised road system in place, this tiring journey was reduced to a half day by Four Wheel drive from Toromambuno to Kondiu.

Kondiu also has a notable place in the province's education history for being one of the earliest learning institutions. Established by the SVD missionaries of the Catholic Church as a *Tok Pisin* school in the 1960s for boys undergoing Catechism training after relocating its original school at Kumbu near Mingende, Kondiu gradually expanded and taught Primary School a syllabus. Over the years, as the number of Catholic Primary Schools mushroomed, Kondiu again introduced and worked out a high school syllabus to impart secondary education to the ever-increasing number of students in the Catholic Agency Primary Schools, thereby gradually pacing out the *Tok Pisin* and primary school syllabi. As Kondiu progressed and expanded with the change of time, the Catholic SVD missionaries, who had, by then, decided to concentrate on pastoral commitments, handed over the realms of the school to the Catholic Christians brothers of the De La Salle Order. It was under the new regime that co-education was introduced, setting a milestone with the first lot of girls, retrospectively graduating four years earlier. Cathy's intake was amongst the eight lots of girls enrolled at Kondiu after co-education was introduced.

Although many things may have changed to which Cathy Gior was not accustomed to back home, she was able to acclimatise quite well in her new environment. Though we could not be so sure of her situation in the girls' area, we were optimistically sure that she settled in well under the watchful eyes of the Sisters of Mercy nuns in their confinement on the hilltop. There were a couple of other senior grade Maugl-wak girls too, to keep Cathy company and we knew for sure that she would be fine.

During the brief moments we met, Cathy would speak of her sister Anasas and little brother Apa back home and how she missed them both. But we encouraged her not to think too much of them.

"You'll soon forget them as the weeks go by", we'd keep telling her, reminding her of the busy weeks of schooling that lay ahead.

We were not wrong. After a month into the year, she found no time to think about her family back home, or ever made a mention of her siblings again.

Cathy and I still maintained our brother/sister relationship in Kondiu, but I was very careful of the school administration that comprised of Christian brothers and nuns who were tough and pedantic on the school rules and regulations. Boy/girl relationship was totally banned. Stiff penalties were imposed on any suspicious relationship of that kind, found among the students at the school, and I was careful not to raise any eye-brow or cause any speculation among the students and staff. But, in spite of the rules, we enjoyed our close brother/sister relationship. Sometimes, I took her out on some *Walk-about* Sundays to Mingende, then Kunabau and back to Kondiu. Thomas, at times, accompanied us during these Sunday walks but ignored us on many occasions. Maybe, he was beginning to realise how deep our brother/sister relationship was developing in front of him, but that could not be confirmed as yet, and too, that did not matter so much to us either. And we ignored him instead most of the time.

As the end of the year was drawing close, the schoolwork load got heavier. The Grade 10 students, including Thomas and myself, were preparing for the final National Examination that was due in October. The exam would be a test of brilliance amongst the Grade 10 students nationwide, and equally a test of proficiency and competency in the teaching profession amongst the respective Grade 10 teachers across the country. And our teachers worked hard and round the clock to see that we did not go down, or let them down in the forthcoming exams. There was frequent revision of past examination papers in class and during night study hours. Like all other Grade 10 students, Thomas and I swotted tirelessly everyday. And despite all the odds, and to my delight, I scored fair marks after the exams. A succession of 'Credits' followed by several 'Upper Passes'. I was glad to have scored no 'Pass' or "Fail', and hence was selected to enroll at the PNG Forestry College in Bulolo at the start of the new academic year. Forestry College was my first choice in the school leaver's application form, filled out to the National Selection Unit, and I was content when I got the offer. Thomas, on the other hand was brilliant in the exams and scored a succession of 'Distinctions' in nearly all the subjects after the exams. Pleasingly, he was among the top twenty Grade 10 students produced in the country for that year. He was accepted for continuation to Grades 11 and 12 at the Passam National High School.

The ecstasy of the graduation day arrived in mid-November. It was the moment everyone was looking forward to. At this moment, Kondiu would release her batch of Grade 10 'products' to venture out into the whole wide world in search of academic fame, fortune and prosperity. After celebrating the final Church Mass in the Kondiu chapel, Thomas and I finally graduated with the 82 other Grade 10 students in the Bishop Cohill Auditorium. Our Grade 10 certificates were presented to us, one by one in front of the packed auditorium by the Chairman of the School Board of Governors in large yellow A4 envelopes, when our names were called out. It was a sensational moment but sad when it was all over, as it soon became evident that it was time to separate from the many good friends and classmates of four years, many of whom would not be seen again for a very long time. And, for some---never again! Sadly, as anticipated, when the graduation was over, students from nearby areas around Kup, Gor, Papnigl, Mindima, Wandi, Mingende and those who had parents attending the graduation with a motor vehicle left soon after the occasion. Others, including Thomas and myself from distant locations in Simbu stayed back in Kondiu to be dropped off in Kundiawa early the following day on the school truck.

The departure on the following morning was a hectic moment filled with extreme excitement. After four years of 'imprisonment' in Kondiu, it was a relief to leave this place of total isolation and I had little time to think about Cathy Gior or anybody else after the graduation. My selection for enrolment at the PNG Forestry College in Bulolo remained the primary cause of all the excitement, as there were many things that were soon going to be the 'first' in my life. Accompanied by the notification letter was a Students' Travel Concession Card. With the card was a National scholarship (Natscol) airline ticket number. And I was to pick up an airline ticket at the Talair company office in Kundiawa. Triumphantly, I was looking forward to the first aeroplane flight in early February, dreaming almost every moment, how it will be like looking down from the air while cruising in the small metallic 'dot' in the sky. The journey to Bulolo likewise will be the first ever trip for me to venture out of Simbu. And I was excited, as ever, at the prospect of seeing the many new places---especially Lae, the city I had always heard about. The sight of the seascape, the coconut trees, the canoes, the ships and the many other things of the coast that I had always heard about, or seen in pictures, would be great experiences among the many others. And I was looking forward to all such and everything else with great indulgence.

When the school year commenced in early February, I got myself in readiness for my first ever trip out of Simbu province to Bulolo, located in the hinterlands of the coastal province of Morobe. On the evening before my departure, my lovely parents prepared a little farewell dinner of boiled chicken and vegetables for Thomas and myself prior to our separation. Before serving time, my younger brother Paul, who was helping our mother in the fireplace, went on an errand to Ende-naige-ingugl and fetched Thomas. Both arrived just in time, when my parents were jointly preparing the food for us in a dish. When the meal was set, "You two boys have been very good friends for a very long time", my mother said, looking straight in our eyes with smiles of sadness. "You both have played together, eaten together, slept together, schooled together and are now going in different directions. We have prayed relentlessly to our God for your safety and success at all times, and I think He blessed you both handsomely. You will be going to places where we have never seen and heard of---Joseph to Bulolo-Wau and Thomas to Sepik. We will continue to pray for His continued support, blessing and protection. And because you will be separating, we have decided to host this meal for you to enjoy before you go out on your own. You can share this meal as our compliment towards your success and for future enrichment in your endeavors. Enjoy it, then go out there to where ever you have been called to go and settle down in your new environment with peace and sound mind".

Following that, she said Grace, and after the "Amen", pushed the dish of food to our front. There were sweet potatoes, English potatoes, peas, beans of assorted kinds and many other local vegetables; delicacies that were usually rare during ordinary meals. The food was plentiful for two persons and we invited my brother Paul to join us. He accepted our invitation and soon we sat around the main dish enjoying the chicken, along with the other foods and vegetables.

It was a heavy and delicious meal. The vegetables, in particular, were all local, home grown, nice and scrumptious with the chicken. We enjoyed it with much delight but, in oblivion and to my dismay, this meal was to mark our last taste of homegrown highlands vegetables. In the next month, we both were to miss these favorite greens for a very, very long time. In our new locations we were bound to taste vegetables that we were unfamiliar with since birth and would be, either struggling or forced to adapt to their taste. For me alone, the famous *kru sako* of the Watut Valley was to be the supplement for the next three years. The complimentary meal also was to betoken other things too. After a very close and steady fraternal friendship of giving, sharing and eating together, this dinner was going to be the last meal for us to sit together, share and enjoy. In the next month and after, we were to be miles away from each other, thus gradually and sadly moving away from each other and gradually losing contact as we venture out and concentrate on our adult endeavors.

I woke up early the following morning. My mother was also up but almost earlier than myself. I was going to leave for a far away destination- -Lae, and therefore woke up early to prepare my breakfast of baked *kaukaus* in the ashes, the last such meal. Since she knew that I'd be away for a full year, she wept silently as she prepared the sweet potatoes for me in the open fire. I pitied her as I went about packing my bags with the assistance of my father, who was now awake too, but doing everything in silience. After a very cold bath in the chilling Mondia, I got into some new clothes my parents had bought me. And just before the sun was up, I left Bokan for Mondiagl-kaugla to catch the early PMV to Kundiawa. My parents accompanied me with a little group of neighbors to see me go, my baggage changing hands amongst them, as we walked to Mondiagl-kaugla.

It was still early when we arrived at Mondiagl-kaugla. The market was empty of any moving creature and, the road was clear too. Over the thatched rooftops of the Siako homes, clear white plumes of smoke from the early fires of dawn curled up lazily into the sky, an indication that the inhabitants were already up. Down the road, beneath the giant aging *Casuarinas* at Ende-naige-ingugl, the distinct white smokes could be seen wafting away lazily from the rooftops in the breezeless morning. Briefly, I thought I saw Thomas and Cathy waving at me on the bench in the foreground, but it was all just my imagination. No one was yet outside in the chilling morning. And it will be truly sad that I'll be missing them both, my two very best friends, I mused, as I starred in the direction of Ende-naige-ingugl.

Then, just as my eyes were about to move away from Ende-naige-ingugl, two figures appeared on the bench, above the road. The figures were steady for a while, as if in discussion or checking out something in our direction, and then briskly walked down to the road. In haste, they scurried up the road towards us. Surprisingly, the two moving figures I'd seen earlier must have been that of Thomas and Cathy Gior. Both were smiling gorgeously as they neared us.

"We are here to see you go, Joe", Cathy quickly said and smiled, when they reached us. "That is kind of you two", I said, and smiled back with emotions. "It's nice to see you both again for the last time too. In fact, I was just thinking of you both", I said. "We just can't let you go without a farewell handshake, either." Thomas added, and both expressed their sentiments with consolations, while I briefly outlined my day's travel plan.

"Take care, make sure that you don't get into trouble along the way", Cathy advised, when I finished.

"I am confident I'll reach Bulolo safely", I assured them. "The college bus will be there at the airport for pick-up, too. So, I'm sure I'll arrive safely"

"That sounds perfect. Make sure that you jump in the correct bus too". Thomas further advised.

"There should be a sign, or at least something there on the bus for me to see and embark. That's what it says in the letter. So, I don't think I'll have problems there"

"Good. Take care!"

We had not waited long when the first PMV of the day roared to a stop in front of us. We ended all our conversation. I hastily threw my baggage onto the back of the PMV amidst handshakes and hugs. Before I embarked, I quickly scribbled the Forestry College address onto a piece of paper and away from the many eyes, I placed it Cathy's hands.

"The new address, you can use it to keep in touch", I whispered to Cathy as I got on the truck.

Cathy quickly took the paper from my hand but hardly looked into my eyes or at the piece of paper in her hands. Her face blushed and she was ruddy all over. I hugged my mother, then my father and then the few other neighbors who were there to see me go. I hugged my long-time friend Thomas Gior too. My mother was already in tears, when I settled down on the PMV. It was a very emotional moment for her, and of course, myself too. For it was she, that I always loved and remembered wherever I went. And not forgetting my father too. When the truck finally pulled out, Cathy did not wait. She buried her face in a towel that she took along and sobbed too. Thomas waved amidst his sad smiles.

"So long and safe trip, buddy", he voiced.

"Same to you when you travel next week", I called back and returned his waving.

I was also sad to leave my little brother Paul. He said nothing but I knew he was affected too, as I could still see him and the others waving at me for as long as the PMV was still in their sights. I felt my throat drying up fast. I could also feel my eyes welling up with tears as the truck increased its speed. And when the truck negotiated the first bend, "Goodbye! See you all later", was all that came into my mind, as we meandered down the Upper Simbu valley to start my long trip to Bulolo---my thoughts, already traveling well ahead of myself to the unforeseen destinations I'd be covering during the day.

We reached Kundiawa just before 9.00am. The flight to Lae was going to be a connection from Goroka, according to the ticketing officer at the Talair counter. I had my booking done a week earlier and, was automatically included in the passenger manifest when I checked in.

"10.20am is the departure time", said the ticketing officer, as he handed me back the ticket and a boarding pass.

Feeling high and elated, I walked out of the counter in high spirit to wait for the carrier to come in from Mt Hagen. At around 9.45am we heard the sound of an approaching aircraft from the west. Looking across to the Digine Mountains along the Kubor Range we spotted an aircraft that was navigating its way at a very low altitude, just above the Whagi River towards Kundiawa. With the runway facing the high-rise Dom mountains to the south the aircraft was traversing the contours of the rise in the background until it swayed north, just above Kel for the landing. The plane, a Banderrante, finally flew in and landed at 10.00am. The baggage cart was pushed forward. The pilot was out on the tarmac, walking around his plane. He was checking his aircraft from the outside. I was more focused on my bag as it was pushed towards the aircraft, and after the baggage loading, a boarding call was announced. I excitedly joined the queue with my heart panting at the departure gate for my first ever aeroplane flight to Lae.

We were directed to our seats, as we entered the aircraft under the watchful eyes of a cute flight attendant, presumably of Sepik origin, who was standing at the doorway. With her help, I managed to get the seat belt fastened. Several others were also assisted by the flight attendant and soon the exit was sealed off. The pilot also entered the aircraft and headed towards the cockpit; then took his seat beside the co-pilot. We were ready for departure and I knew any moment the propellers would be turning. After some buzzing and humming sounds, the propeller to the port began to turn. My seat was close to the window on the right to the front. There was, most likely, a very good view of the scenery below while in cruise. I felt almost relaxed, comfortable and excited too, but, as the propellers turned, my heart panicked at the violent vibration. The spectre of the propeller coming off the wing and then leaving me in halves scared me to the nerve as the blades turned to the maximum. I remained speechless with my eyes to the front as the pilot went through the pre-flight instruments.

We eventually moved forward, slowly and gently across the tarmac to the runway. Houses, trees and the other features outside slowly moved back and went into hiding from my window as we slowly moved forward. The pilot finally positioned the aircraft at the upper end of the strip for the take-off. After a brief pause, the pilot stepped on the brakes (or that's what I thought), revived the engines, and finally let go of the braking mechanism into take-off mode. We taxied down the runway at possibly 200 miles per hour. As I looked out of the window, I saw the trees, buildings and everything outside racing past and disappearing behind me.

One last glimpse of the provincial capital was the Simbu Lodge, Simbu's premier Hotel where the future king of England, the Prince of Wales, and heir to the British throne, HRH Prince Charles had rested himself before moving on to Mt Hagen during his highlands tour in 1975. It raced past and quickly disappeared from the window. As soon as the Hotel went out of sight, I suddenly remembered the huge steep drop at the end of the airstrip but, before I knew what was actually happening, we were already in the air.

Below, I could see the trees, cars, houses and people gradually reducing in shape and size as we lifted higher. There were occasional moments of fear down my spine when we encountered turbulence as it was lifting, but I remained composed when I noticed the other passengers sitting relaxed in their seats. But my composure was only temporary from the outside, as deep inside, I felt terrified as the plane was lifting and hardly bothered to look out of the window until the plane completed its ascend and eventually leveled itself.

We finally swayed east and cruised at a minimum altitude, just above the Okuk Highway towards Goroka. It was a beautiful day. The early morning fog had, by then, cleared out completely and the scenery below was picturesque from above. The breathtaking panoramic views of the rugged mountainous terrain, with razor back ridge tops, stunned me with curiosity and excitement as I peered out. Equally fascinating were the crowded villages linked by tangled strings of road network through some of the most adventurous and daring parts of Simbu. The mosaic patterns of subsistence gardening on the difficult and very steep slopes were yet another amazing discovery, and for the very first time in my life I saw how my densely populated province of Simbu, its content and geography looked like from the air. And how amazing it was. Sure enough, I felt privileged to have seen some of the greatest and breathtaking geographical features on earth right in my home province.

We flew past Kamtai station, the district administrative center for the Sinasina-Yogomugl populace and Muaina High School. A few moments later, Mt Elimbari and Chuave High School came into view from my window. Just below me was Chuave Government Station. We flew past them and, quite interestingly, all the features and objects---the cars, houses, trees, and even people---looked like toys from above and, quite easily, any toy fanatic kid could have mistaken the scenery below for animated toys.

After a brief moment, over a stretch of rugged moss forest, we flew over the grasslands of the Ungai valley and, finally, above the verdant Lapegu Pine forest plantations along the slopes of the Ungai Mountains. It was with amazement and wonder to look down at the distinctive and huge spread of man-made forest on the arid grassland slopes of the Ungai Range. Unfortunately, little did I know, while peering down at the pines, that I was literally on my way to study the science and silviculture of forest plantations of the kind below me. Far from my knowledge, we were to make a field visit to Lapegu to see these pines, as part of our field excursion, several months later. In the distance ahead of us was the township of Goroka. The runway was clearly visible in the town center. The pilot maneuvered his aircraft south, following the Ungai Range and, later, directed the course towards north for a perfect landing.

Goroka was the base of the Talair airline company and over ten aircraft were parked on the tarmac, some in the hangar, undergoing service and maintenance. The Banderrantte was to continue to Port Moresby after refueling and I was off-loaded in Goroka with a couple of other Lae-bound passengers to make a connection in another plane. We were given almost an hour to wait and it was an opportune moment for me to venture out for a quick sightseeing. With nothing else to care about at the terminal, I soon found myself jostling in and out of the Gouna Centre, then along the pavement down the main street to the Steamships supermarket. After a quick look around, I went past the Papua New Guinea Banking Corporation, and found myself in front of the Collin &

Leahy supermarket. There were a lot of people sitting or standing around there, but none that I knew of. Following the backstreet, I loitered across to the front of the Bird of Paradise hotel. I could see the Gouna Centre from where I was, and hurried back to the airport terminal.

It was almost one hour, ten minutes when the next plane---another Banderrantte---was readied for departure at 12.30. A boarding call was announced and I hastily made my way across the tarmac to the waiting aircraft along with the other Lae-bound passengers. As a matter of fact, I was desperate to reach Lae before sunset, as I do not want to miss the college bus that was expected to wait there at the Airport. I felt restless for the entire period I waited and boarding the aircraft was a total relief. The pilot was already in the cockpit and had one of the propellers away from the entry door running. Again, a flight attendant welcomed us on board and soon the plane was in the air.

It was a perfect afternoon and, again, the scenery below was beautiful and picturesque for a tourist's camera. I was, again, fascinated by the huge extent of landmass that spreads out along the route the plane took, but, unlike my green Simbu, it was all arid grassland below. I could see the Okuk Highway snaking through the undulating grassland terrain below with cars and trucks of all make, moving back and forth like busy ants. But quite surprisingly, I was stunned at the very scarce distribution of houses and villages along the route, largely contrasting that of my densely populated Simbu. The entire lifeforce seemed to concentrate along the riverbanks and roadsides, leaving hectares and hectares of uncultivated grasslands barren. How fortunate are the people of Eastern Highlands, I thought, as I stared at the huge landmass below. The Eastern Highlanders were truly blessed with very good flat lands, unlike Simbu, I mused. Familiar names of places, like Henganofi, Kainantu and Yonki, appeared in my mind, but I could not mark them out from my window. And it was when I traveled by road some months later that I was to recall some of the landmarks I had seen from the air.

Just before Henganofi, I noticed a formation of rock on an elevated grassland plain, conspicuously eye-catching, conical and uniquely reaching high with a perfect smooth-off at the top, thus resembling the bust of a person carved out from solid rock. Interestingly, as a *Phantom* comic fanatic, I thought at first sight, the landmark to be that of the famous 'Phantom head' peak, created by Lee Falk in his renowned *Phantom* comic series, located somewhere in the jungles of Bengal. I smiled inanely, as I stared at the peak, but it soon disappeared from my window.

We finally went into some clouds just above Kainantu and the plane yawed frighteningly at the turbulence. I remained still, griping the seat to my fore, for the entire moment the plane was bouncing up and down. Outside, it was all white and, briefly, a menacing thought of a possible mid-air collision with another aircraft appeared in my mind but the thought quickly disappeared when patches of grassland appeared below through several pockets in the clouds.

By the time we were out of the clouds and into the open, we were above, what I'd later learn as the famous Arona Valley, the site of a future dam which was to supply electricity to the entire Highlands provinces, Lae and Madang. In a matter of minutes, we were above Kassam Pass and, later, over the Markham Valley, all flat from above.

Finally, just before 2:00pm, we circled above the Huon Gulf for the landing. And for the first time, as the plane turned to set course for the runway, I caught a glimpse of the seascape, its expanse, and remained too startled to utter a word or sound as the plane went in for the landing.

The Banderrantte finally touched down and taxied up the runway. It decelerated speed, then pulled away from the main runway and soon came to a stop outside the terminal. I was glad that we made it to Lae safely. There was excitement in my mind too. After the long, connected flights, I couldn't wait any longer in the plane to get outside and so was everyone else too, I presumed. But alas! As we waited for the ground crew open up the exits, for the very first time, I began to experience the odds of Lae city inside the aircraft---the blazing tropical heat and sultry climatic conditions of the coast. Unbelievably, I was already soaked up and drenched in my own sweat---something never experienced before---as I remained in my seat for the exits to open. I could feel the nylon shirt on my body completely saturated with sweat and firmly stuck to my body. I felt completely uncomfortable and, almost instantly, remembered my highlands climate and its permanent cool temperatures.

I also recalled the cool pristine Tar and Mondia Rivers in front of my house and immediately felt the anguish to go back to Simbu. But it was a hopeless thought, as I cannot turn back. I was now many miles away from Simbu in a foreign land, that I'd never been before. All I was expected to do now was to travel out to the car park and locate the bus with the Forestry College sign, find a seat in there and travel to where ever the driver goes. Failure to locate the bus could mean a dead end for me, and I remained restless as we waited for the ground crew to attend to our carrier.

The exit finally opened and I stepped out onto the tarmac, a relieved man after the intensive sweltering. But alas! It was even worse outside. With the deflecting heat coming up from the bitumen coated surface on the tarmac and coupled with the sultry climactic condition of Lae, I imagined myself being dip-fried right there. That was not all. Coupling the scorching heat with the sights and sounds of Lae city, I found the sudden change of environment, just too much for me to take in all at the same time, especially a rural highland bumpkin like myself. In no time the growing elation and excitement of the journey plummeted to the lowest, as I walked into the arrival lounge.

The baggage cart was later pushed into the lounge. As I collected my baggage from the cargo trolley, a yellow Toyota Land Cruiser with a 'Z' number plate pulled into the car park. It had 'Forest Service' sticker on both sides of the door, and a tall middle-aged person – presumably of Markham origin, was at the wheel. At the back was some luggage and youths who appeared more like students, sitting with their eyes towards the incoming flight that had just landed, as if to check on someone arriving. I quickly walked across to the driver, but before I spoke the driver asked first. "Are you a student for the Forestry College?'

"Yes, I am", I answered back, looking on.

"Good, this is the pick-up vehicle for Forestry College students. `You can put you bag on the truck and jump on", said the driver, as his eyes scanned the terminal again.

Feeling relieved and safe at last that I have got into the right hands in that strange place, I gladly threw my bag in the back and boarded the yellow Z-plated Toyota land cruiser. I had expected a bus but did not make a mention of it to the driver or the others there because all faces were new to me. I soon learnt later that the other boys on the pick-up vehicle were all students too, some of them were to be my classmates in the following week.

Soon after confirming the last flights into Lae for that day at the Air Niugini and Talair terminals, we departed Lae for Bulolo, arriving late in the night, a tiring journey that took us almost three hours to reach.

5

The Ripples

The PNG Forestry College was located on the outskirts of the Bulolo Township surrounded by hectares of *Araucaria* pine forest plantations. Filled with history and historical relics of the past gold dredging era of the 1920s, 30s, 40s, 50s and the 1960s, Bulolo, unlike Lae, was cool and balmy. The climate was more like the highlands than the coast, though torrid, at times, during the day. But, on the whole, I felt more comfortable and relaxed than the very first moment I stepped out of the plane in Lae. There were a couple of Simbu students in the college too. They came forward and introduced themselves to me, and I felt at home almost instantly in that far away location. With them around, I quickly acclimatized myself to the new environment and soon made many new friends, on my own, with other students.

Everyday new and continuing students kept coming in from different parts of Papua New Guinea. Several were overseas students from the neighboring Pacific Island countries such as Samoa, Vanuatu, Solomon Islands and even Marshall Islands. At the end of the second week, when normal classes began, the full class was twenty-eight in total, enrolled in the first-year program. Amongst the twenty-eight was myself and, as it turned out later, it was the final total. Courses offered were all forestry orientated. Field practicals and outdoor classes were frequent as they were formulated into nearly all the forestry course programs offered with the semester and mid-semester breaks allocated for field trips and excursions. The field trips and excursions were compulsory for all students to participate, and hence, there were no holidays for individual students as we had experienced in high schools. Personally, I found the overall course programs interesting and exciting. And coupled with the K13.00 fortnightly Natschol pocket allowance and the frequent fortnightly visits to the Pine Lodge hotel bar---located less then a kilometer away from the college down on the upper reaches of the Bulolo township---for a stubby, I soon forgot all my old friends.

I, nevertheless, remembered Cathy Gior once in a while, but perhaps, did not have the time to write her letters. Obviously, I expected her to write to me first, using the college address I had supplied her before I left. At times, I wondered why she did not bother to write to me and decided I should write to her again, instead. But then I demurred when some discouraging thoughts crept into my mind. She was now 14 and I was 17. At 14, Cathy was just old enough to construe logically what was happening around her. Back home, we belonged to two different clan groups, the Siako and Denglagu clans, where inter-marriage of the young was allowed between the two clans. The clan distinction was there and Cathy knew it too. And I surmised her to have intentionally decided to refrain from writing letters to me purposely put a stop to our brother/sister relationship when she realized the dangers and where our relationship might lead us in the near future.

The perception could be right, or not right but logically it was undeniably possible. I felt nervous when I thought deeply over it but then with the never-ending fire of love still burning inside, I decided to give it a try by writing something. I started the letter with an apology for not writing her any letter for sometime, then wrote about the college and how I was getting along. I was brief. I reminded her of the college address again and finally, in the bottom line, I post-scripted: *"Hope to hear from you soon"*. And to further surprise her, I enclosed a K5.00 bill from my Natschol allowance.

I had not waited long when one afternoon, after class, about three weeks later, I received Cathy's reply to my letter. She was pleased, just as I was, to have received my letter after so many months. She thanked me and briefed me about her schoolwork, her first term holidays at home and queried about my new environment at length. I enjoyed the letter. Every line kept me on my toes and had me breathing heavily with anticipation as to what the next line will hold for me. But, most of all, her pithy endearment, '*I missed you a lot*', in her concluding paragraph, had some sensational effects and had me staring at the letter with hallucinations for a very long time.

It was pretty ordinary on the paper, but I found it gnomic. Already, the fire of desire was starting to burn inside me again, as I cogitated over her selected words. Was this any indication of Cathy's interest in me, and the beginning of what I have been waiting for? Or was it just a sisterly gesture of expressing her true feeling during my absence? Whatever it was, I had yearned for such an endearment or anything closer that would indicate a requital of my covert affection. And the excitement intensified and was so overwhelming that I could not contain myself. I gazed ruminatively at the letter for a long time with indulgence, and read over and over her selected words later in the night before dozing off. Early in the morning, in a pent-up mood, I replied to Cathy's letter. I commended her for her nicely-written letter. "You are smart girl", I wrote, and without taking any chance, indicated that I missed her a lot too. I was careful not to rush and mention something that was abusive or romantic to confuse her, as I was not really too sure of the true state of her mind. Finally satisfied, I got the letter away through the post.

Cathy Gior's letter was placed on the study table just next to my bed where I could easily pick it up and glance through it anytime I felt like. It was truly a special letter and I didn't want to lose it, or let is disappear from my sight. About a week later, on a Saturday morning, Yakopus Kaiglo, a PNG Forest Products employee, who worked in one of the forest mills across the College, came into my room on a weekend visit.

Yakopus was a young man in his mid-twenties, who hailed from the Siako clan as did Cathy and Thomas Gior. His father, Ignas Dagir, a forest plantation supervisor, moved with his family to Bulolo in the early 1960s. Yakopus was raised and grew up in Bulolo and lived all his life there. I first met him at the Bulolo market during the orientation week in February. I was introduced to him by another tribesman, Tony Kagl. Tony was also working with PNG Forest Products as a technician at the Bulolo plymill factory. After the introduction and gradually getting to know me better in the subsequent weeks, Yakopus made frequent visits to the College, especially on the weekends, to meet and chat with me before returning to the Forestry Compound where he lived with his family. That Saturday morning, as he sat on my bed, he saw Cathy's letter on the edge of the study-table next to my bed, and while I was out to fetch him lunch from the college mess, he must have picked it up and read it. He was still holding onto the letter when I returned.

"Whose letter is this, Joe?", he asked, as his eyes busily went through the lines.

"Which one?"

"This", he said, waving the letter.

"Oh that…it's from my girlfriend", I proudly boasted when I noticed Cathy's letter in his hands. "Have you read it?" I asked, but he never answered. Instead, he pried further about the author.

"Your girlfriend?", he asked.

"Yes, my girlfriend." I came back gleefully, all perked up, and soon started painting a marvelous picture of Cathy with my words.

Yakapus smiled as he took in every word that I put out about Cathy, but strangely he hardly spoke a word. Too arrogant to suspect anything dubious, I proudly went on and on about my relationship with Cathy--- how it all started, how I won her, how we fared along etc., etc.---all pure lies, off course! I felt like a hero, but it was not these sweet lies that kept Yakopus silent. Unbeknown to me, or otherwise far from my knowledge, Yakopus must have noticed something familiar in the letter but for some reason, he did not reveal nor say anything, as I babbled away. He was, as I found out later, trying to collect and fit in the missing bits and pieces together in order to establish the author of the letter, before opening up. He listened attentively with smiles as I talked away and, then suddenly in a flashing smile, as if now too confident about the author of the letter, exclaimed.

"Congratulations! I am pleased to learn that you have befriended my cousin".

"What? What do you mean 'my cousin'? Is Cathy Gior related to you?", I asked, almost taken to my feet, the smiles and the romantic mood suddenly gone from my body.

"Yes, Cathy and I shared one great, great grandfather. She's from the collateral branch of the family. I only saw her once when she was an infant. She must have been a big girl now", Yakopus confidentially said and explained as he stared at the letter in his hands. I dug deeper to ensure, Yokopus was not referring to the daughter of James and Angela Kumo. But I realized too soon that I was defeated very badly. "Cathy's father taught in Mendi for many years", he said, "But now I hear that he is teaching in Simbu. His wife Angela Kumo was a tough woman, a real hard nut to crack"

I squirmed inside and cowered with fear, as I sat motionless in shock, not daring to speak a word again. It sooner dawned before me that, inanely, I had just made out a false claim on Cathy Gior in front of someone more closely related to her, a blood relative, not an ordinary listener. My body prickled as I realised my mistake. Almost at once, fear swarmed up my spine and penetrated through my jittered body. I remained speechless all the while Yakopus took his lunch. I tried to concoct an excuse in my mind to apologise for my lies, but I had said too much and, nothing convincing settled in my fear-crippled mind.

Briefly, Yakopus had not been to Simbu his whole life and I felt slightly relaxed when I assumed that he was not likely to be up there for a while yet to impart the lies to Cathy, or anyone back home. In retrospect, I never saw him up there and he surely will never be up there for a very long time, I thought. But unfortunately, I was wrong and misjudged in my assessment. The following week, Yakopus' rec-leave was due and strangely he had planned to go to Simbu for the very first time and spend his entire leave there after being away in Bulolo for many years. Why he made that decision, I would never know, but the revelation scared me further, almost to the point of causing a heart attack, even though Yakopus never mentioned anything to me about his plans in Simbu. But as being closely related to the Giors, I discerned that he was likely to hide nothing, and spill out everything I had said of Cathy, and possibly tell Cathy's parents too, if he goes home. And I feared my lies with extreme concern. What a mess I had caused with my loud mouth, I regretfully thought, as I sat looking hopeless opposite him.

Yakopus finally decided to leave after he finished his lunch. He may have sensed the sudden change of my mood, or perhaps had not yet, but did not say anything, even though he was composed. He switched to something else, as if nothing went wrong. If he had sensed it, then he kept it to himself.

"I'll call in here again on Monday", he said, as he stepped out of the door, "...and if you wish to send anything home, have it ready for me to pick it up when I come this way"

"That is, if I have something ready", I told him, as if everything was fine with me and as usual walked him out to the main road before sending him away.

Still in total despair over my lies, I had nothing for him when he came around on Monday. "Just pass word to my parents that I'm fine". I told him.

"I certainly will", he assured, and amidst laughter, joy and excitement over his coming trip, bade me good luck and left for Simbu to take his much-deserved three-week rec-leave.

The mid-semester break of two weeks in mid-September was about a week away and my class was gearing up for a field trip to Aseki in the Menyamya district. I had waited almost four weeks after I wrote my last letter to Cathy Gior but so far had not received any response. Maybe, there was a mishap somewhere, I thought, but my lies to Yakopus still lingered in my anxious mind and I eclectically assumed two things, which might have happened. Cathy had either decided to end our relationship by not writing to me, perhaps after sensing the tone of my last letter, not to her liking, or the most prickling of all; that Yakopus had embarrassed her with the lies I had made about her when he arrived home. It was logically possible at both fronts and the thoughts reverberated in my mind whereever I went. But the latter worried me most as I knew that Yakopus would not hold back anything if he ever met Cathy.

And, as expected, I was not wrong after all. In early October, after returning to Bulolo from the two-weeks Botany trip to Aseki and Menyamya I received a rather mischievous letter from Cathy that had been waiting there for me when I was away in Menyamya. The letter was a bit unusual in its appearance: the cover envelope had no sender's address, something Cathy never left out in her past letters and it was thin as if the envelope contained nothing inside. "Perhaps, she forgot to put the letter into the envelope before sealing", I thought, as I tore open the envelope.

But alas! I was wrong. The most shocking part of the letter was yet inside. On a carelessly torn out page of a school kid's exercise book, with nothing more, was a single sentence scrawled across the middle link of the page in bold block letters was the inscription *"DON'T WRITE ME ANYMORE LETTERS OR TALK TO ME".* Yes, it was all scrawled and rubricated in bold red ink, and signed, 'Cathy' at the bottom of the page. There was no date or anything else to make a further reference. In total shock, as if being told off directly to the face, I felt a lump in my throat, as my eyes went over the words again and again. My mind went blank, as if the only entry into a dark room was shut off. That was not all. Inside me, I felt like a bucket of cold water poured over a burning fire. I felt totally hopeless as I pensively stared up at the inscription, then up at the ceiling, trying to think out what might have possibly gone wrong. But I couldn't come to a clear understanding. I was confused too, and for the moment everything was just too much for my confused mind to take in or comprehend. Something had gone terribly wrong somewhere, I muttered. And what could that 'something' be? I kept asking myself hopelessly, but my thinking went too short to establish or rest on an answer. I was indeed a hopeless man. What now lay ahead was a painful assignment to solve the mystery.

The month of October went past like the wind. Yakopus Kaiglo returned from leave during the first week of November. As usual, he called into my room one weekend. He for sure must have enjoyed his leave and was excited as ever when he dropped on my study chair. He did not waste time and regaled me with all the happenings back home; about his trip, his holidays, his other engagements and finally his meeting with Cathy when she went home for her school holidays in September.

"She's such a beauty, Joe", he said, "I was particularly surprised at her speedy growth", he ranted about his niece. I said nothing, even though I took in everything he said. And I could not judge whether Yakopus realised my recent change of behavior when the subject of Cathy Gior came up but he blabbed on trying to impress me more; perhaps shook me up and put me into the mood on the subject. But I remained phlegmatically stolid, showing very little interest in his blabs. I had received a very tormenting one-sentence letter from Cathy only days earlier and already a façade of lies was discernible on his face as he talked away. Inside me there was also a strong revulsion to believe his specious embroideries too.

"How long did she stay at home before returning to school?" I asked, rather bluntly.

"Oh, just one week. It was a term holiday" Yakopus said. And that was all I seemed to want to know of Cathy.

I did not ask any further question, nor did I respond to his holiday tales. I might be angry with him, literally holding him solely responsible for the cause of Cathy's sarcastic letter, but there was something else too. I could sense that he was certainly hiding something from me that he wanted me to find out for myself. I could read it in his eyes, and could also pick them up in between the lines as he was talking. He was seemingly lying to me from the way he talked and behaved about Cathy Gior. And almost instantly, there was a psychological urge to trust him no more and I did not believe anything he was throwing out. I felt restless, the more I got carried away with the thought. But, apparently, there was no concrete proof to question him over the letter. Yakopus eventually left after that meet but I spent sleepless nights at the college in the coming days, just thinking over it. In the end, I bravely reached a conclusion that it was all pure suspicion after all and with the second semester exams due in two weeks, I decided to concentrate on my studies rather than to take my mind away from it.

During the next two weeks, I concentrated mainly on my studies. I banned Yakopus Kaiglo from visiting me at the college, as I didn't want to see him again. The exams were finally over and I cleared all my exams with 'good passes'. About a handful of my classmates were discontinued because their results were below the set pass mark. I was eligible to return the following year to proceed to second year with the remaining others. I was generally pleased with myself, as it was a remarkable achievement, particularly when I realised many Grade 12 intakes drop out after the exams.

The College finally issued Natschol airline tickets to students on the last day of the close-up week. My ticket had the booking for me to travel from Lae to Kundiawa and return via the same route in early

February, the following year. It was going to be my first trip home after being absent for a full year and the excitement was very high. I was glad at the prospect of seeing my family again, especially my parents and younger brother Paul. I really missed them so much and it would certainly be a great reunion for us all. I would also meet my old friends, Thomas who'd be there from Passam and many others too and I planned a great holiday.

But then Cathy bothered my mind with consternation when I paused to think about her. She would be there at home for the Christmas holidays too and I feared my lies again. I was not quite sure what to do. A series of hypothetical questions kept pounding in my mind. "Should I confront her, explain, apologise and supplicate for a pardon, or should I just avoid her?" I kept asking myself over and over. Other disturbing questions stormed my mind too. "Has she told anyone about my infatuations? Is she going to jump at me and boo me when I cross her path?" She appeared a Goliath before me and the more I thought about it, the more embarrassing it became for me and I soon felt uncomfortable, a bit scared and rather reluctant to go home.

But home is always where the heart is and, in the end, when I finally arrived at Bokan I kept myself on guard at all times to keep myself away from Cathy's eyes, and did all I could to avoid her when I sensed her presence nearby. I was literally scared to come face to face with her. But Cathy Gior was no fool, either. She kept her distance too. She was no longer the affable and most inviting girl with that beautiful smiling face I had known in the past. This time, she was somebody completely different, a stone-hard face girl with a mask of pouting lips whenever she crossed my path.

However, the uncomfortable moments did not last long. Seriously, I had expected the worst from Cathy after knowing very well that I was actually at fault with all my lies to Yakopus Kaiglo in the first instance. I had expected a confrontation of some kind with Cathy over these lies. But for some reason, there was nothing of that. And with nothing hostile or deprecatory evident nor forthcoming, as the days went by, I gradually felt more relaxed again. There was sense of peace and soon the fear inside me was gone. "So, Cathy is not going to do anything about it. It's going to fizzle out soon". I gladly thought.

But the serene state of my mind was ephemeral. Some two weeks later the constant avoidance between us raised yet another concern and anxiety, and soon began niggling me. It made me reconsider the stand-off between myself and Cathy and our distorted relationship. I reflected on whether we should continue to avoid each like this, and eventually move away from each other. But that thought did not really sink in well in my inner thoughts. Cathy Gior was undeniably beautiful and the daunting spectre of losing her altogether perturbed my composure. Seriously, there was the portending risk of losing her to someone else, if we continue to avoid each other. And I felt hurt and uncomfortable when I realised the risk involved, particularly the risk I was taking.

"I can't let this happen", I mused, almost jealously.

Without a second thought, I immediately decided that we should come together again, talk this confusion out and, maybe, sort it out once and for all. Hopefully, there was a little misunderstanding somewhere that needed a little bit of explanation, and perhaps some clarification too to get over with the problem. Moreover, I had a feeling that Cathy would want it that way too.

But unfortunately, when I approached her, this was not at all possible. Cathy was still inflexible in her approach towards me, trying all she could to avoid me and my overtures for a possible reunion. Her shabby attitudes created more embarrassing situations when I tried to accost her. She ignored me in just about every attempt I made. I felt abashed, wretched and dejected on all occasions but I did not give up. I persevered relentlessly despite the oddity of her attitude. But sadly, every attempt was futile.

Then, after ceaselessly brooding over the matter, a viable thought settled in my head when I realised that I could not succeed alone.

"I need a middle man…someone who could approach Cathy, should explain everything and do all the talking for me", I thought.

I quickly remembered my friend and toe hold, Thomas Goir, who was home from Passam for the holidays. We had met a couple of times over the last two weeks and I immediately went out to find him one morning at his Ende-naige-ingugl home. And as expected, he was there in his house when I arrived. We chatted for a little while and I quickly told him about Cathy, her sarcastic letter and the latest twist of fate.

"You see, I really don't know why, but something about me is really bothering her", I said.

"Why? Why did she have to do this?"

"I really don't know, Tom. And that's why I'm here?"

"What! You want me to find out for you? Is that the reason why you are here?" Thomas exploded with a guffaw.

"Exactly, that's precisely why I am here." I frankly told him.

"I want you to approach Cathy and find out what is really upsetting her".

Thomas looked at me in the eyes.

"Oh, come on Joe, you know each other very well. You don't really need me for petty jobs like this".

"I tried, Tom", I said, almost sorrowfully. "And she keeps avoiding me"

"Avoiding you? Alright, let's go and find her together then. Maybe, that should make things easier for you both to talk it out".

"No, Thomas", I quickly cut in.

"Why?"

"Cathy is not the same person this time. I got a feeling she'll throw everything she's got at me if we go together. I'd like you to do this alone", I explained to Thomas.

Thomas smiled.

"Why are you so worried about that, she's only a woman and nothing more…"

"Wrong, Tom. She's more than that. Believe me!"

Thomas laughed and then scratched his head for a while, as if looking for a better solution. "Alright, I'll come to Bokan, if I have anything interesting for your ears. Otherwise, meet me at Mondiagl-kaugla", he said. That sounded more gorgeous.

"I sure will…I can't wait any longer to find out from you", I said.

Thomas showed up a day later to report his findings to me at my Bokan home.

"Cathy's furious", Thomas said with a grin, as though it was something funny.

"What is it that is upsetting her?" I asked.

"She mentioned somebody…but I can't remember now. He came up from Bulolo and hawked to everyone here that she was your girlfriend; so, she got upset over it".

"Just as I suspected", I interrupted furiously.

Thomas expressed surprise on his face, shrugged his shoulders but said nothing, and remained silent, as if to hear my side of the story.

"Did she mention anything else?" I asked.

"About what?"

"Well, anything about me?"

I was expecting Cathy to rubbish me in front of his cousin. But surprisingly, it was the opposite.

"No, she said nothing of you. I didn't even hear her mentioning your name and I was wondering why you were dead scared to face her."

"Then, why did she continue to avoid me now?" I asked with astonishment.

"I don't know, it's between you and her. You two can sort that one out at your own time", Thomas jested.

I looked at Thomas and let out a smile of approval at his proposition. It was worth doing the way he suggested, if circumstances permited, but this was unfortunate. On the other hand, deep inside me I felt the hatred for Yakopus Kaiglo gradually building up. My suspicion about Yakopus was right. It now proved positive that it was him that sabotaged our beautiful brother/sister relationship. I was angry, as I mulled over it, but soon after felt hurt and realised that it was my own fault. I opened my filthy mouth first. It was my mistake, and there was no reason to blame him or anyone else for that matter, but to accept the repercussion regretfully. Maybe, I should tell Thomas the whole truth, I thought, and if possible, verbalise my feelings for his niece to him and the turmoil I was going through and get this love thing sorted out once and for all. And, maybe, he could step in and help me out. But, again, on second thoughts, I reckoned this was far too extreme. This was, perhaps, yet another crazy idea to get me into yet another trouble again.

"Just forget this crap, Tom", I said, pretentiously trying to cover up the whole episode. "They are all pure lies from a lunatic".

Thomas shrugged his shoulders.

"What can I say? I know nothing about this".

"Of course, you don't. Maybe, Cathy will have a change of heart one day." I said, sounding sorry.

I lied. I had certainly disavowed any knowledge of all the allegations mooted by Cathy. But, in reality, I had prematurely encroached too far in my infatuations and consequently paid the price by losing my inamorata in a blunder, which left me in a *fait accompli* state that holds no one else at fault but myself.

My forestry studies in Bulolo finally ended on the first week of December. I successfully completed my three-year diploma program and was awarded a Diploma in Forestry in a huge graduation ceremony held at the College Library.

Unlike the Kondiu High School graduation, the Forestry College graduation was filled with surprises, specifically because apart from high profile dignatories, the ceremony was also attended by Timber Industry personel who were there to recruit fresh college graduates. Amongst the graduation surprises for me was a job offer. A week prior to my graduation, I was offered a job as a Resource Forester with PNG Forest Product Pty Ltd in Bulolo, the plywood company operating just across the other side of the College. It was something unique, as I had never applied for the position, and unbelieveably I was automatically made an employee of the company even before I graduated. And at the graduation lunch after I was advised by a company representative to commence work after the New Year and was furnished with an airline ticket to travel from Lae to Kundiawa and return the same route, even though I was eligible for a Natschol ticket home. The arrangement excited me, and, as I boarded the plane in Lae to fly home, I dreamt at length about the new job I'll be taking up after the New Year, and what I will be telling my parents about my job offer when I reach home.

When I arrived home, I had another big surprise in stored for me too. Unlike other holidays, this time, my homecoming welcome was made extraordinary by my parents by providing a pig to feast on with my friends to celebrate my graduation. It was their graduation present for me, they said. Speechless, I accepted their present with gratitude. Indeed, it was a huge show of appreciation for my academic achievement and the following morning, a *mumu* was arranged. Organized by Paul and his friends with my father at the helm, I left all the responsibilities to be taken care of by them. I had other commitments to attend to first before joining them later.

As I always did every time, whenever I was at home from the coast, I left for Nigl-guma early in the morning to seek anti-malaria antidotes at the aid post. I had normally taken the advance dose to suppress any malaria symptom that was likely to develop from the change of climate---i.e. from the humid tropical heat at the coast to the cool high altitude highlands, when I was back home. As a *mumu* was underway, I sneaked out and reached Nigl-guma in record time. Up ahead was the Mission Station, the familiar silvery finial cross of the Catholic Church clearly visible through the Casuarina canopies.

As I neared the turn-in gate into the aid post, far up ahead near the sister's convent at Toromambuno, I saw a tall young lass walking down the stone pavement. She was traveling alone from the Catholic mission station. I couldn't recognise who she was but I noticed a rather conspicuous style of walking that I was familiar with, an ambulatory style typifying that of someone I knew. "Is that Cathy?' I mused, as I was about to turn into the aid post. The young woman eventually got closer and when I looked up to check again I saw a grin on her face. The grin stopped me in my tracks and when I paused to check...Alas! It sure was Cathy Goir. She physically had changed tremendously over the last two years and certainly was beyond recognition. She had slightly doubled in size since the last time I saw her. And my rather myopic eyes had trouble recognising her. But she must have seen me in the distance, doubled her pace and was walking straight towards me, smiling as she approached.

Already panic-stricken, I let out an ambiguous smile across my face. But before I knew what was actually happening, and without even saying hello she threw her arms around me. "It's been a long time", she said, as she wrapped her arms around me with a strong hug, almost choking me dead. Still clinging on to me she apologised dearly to me for everything she had said and done to me over the past two years.

This was a totally unexpected encounter, least or never expected and I was astounded, surprised and pleased, all at the same time, as I grabbed Cathy in my arms. I hugged her tight as if I had found a long-lost family member for the first time after many years, all the while trying to figure out if she was really Cathy Gior. But who else was out there who would come forward, wrap me up and apologise? It has to be Cathy. And yes, it sure was Cathy. I could feel her. I could hear her. Her familiar voice sinking in as music into my ears.

Forcing my head slightly back, I took a quick look into her eyes. My eyes could not qualify for a second glance as they rested on her face. She had grown into a beautiful girl over the last two years and there was not a mark of contrast to dispute her beauty. She was sixteen and the feminine features of sixteen were all there. I tried to recall whether I was in a trance but I was not. Right in between my arms was Cathy Goir, my inamorata and dream girl, something least expected when I set out that morning.

"Yes, it's been a long time", I finally responded almost absent-mindedly, as I held her, unsure when to let her go free from my arms. I couldn't voice anything further. I was already lost for words. In truth, my lips were confused to find the appropriate words to voice or put together for her ears.

"When did you come?" Cathy asked excitedly.

"Yesterday".

"Yesterday?" she exclaimed ebulliently with expressions of surprise on her angelic face, as I slowly let her free.

"Yes, I arrived yesterday afternoon'" I shyly answered with a smile.

"I didn't know that"

"You don't have to", I joked, putting more smiles on her face, as she rolled her eyes.

Cathy was in the village since late November. She had graduated from Kondiu High School but had not received any job offers yet. She was returning from the Mission station after checking the incoming mails. She briefly explained her situation with anxiety and later inquired about my presence there.

"I am going to the aid post", I said, and briefly explained why I was going there.

"Let's go together then. I want to get this sore dressed too", Cathy said, pointing to a sore on her right foot that had obviously healed and didn't really require any treatment at all.

"Alright, let's go then". I shyly mumbled, as she took the lead.

The aid post was crowded with patients and we loitered across at a snail's pace to let the queue shorten its length. It was the first time to come together and talk after being out in the cold for over two years. And I felt rather strange and retrospectively guilty at times, of the past. I talked very little during our conversations and was even more discreet each time I said something, letting Cathy do most of the talking. Cathy told me all about her frustrations again in not receiving any job offers.

"You know it really annoys me. Many of my classmates have already got their offers, and I really don't know why I did not receive mine", she said, looking across to my face anxiously. "It looks like, I won't be getting any offer".

After a brief pause, Cathy then asked me how I was doing in Bulolo.

"I have just graduated", I proudly told her. "I'll be working with PNG Forest Products Pty Ltd next year and I am going to start straight after the New Year".

"True?

"Yes"

"Oh, congratulations then…that's good news! Maybe, I'll accompany you to Bulolo when you go", she exclaimed, and looked at me askance.

The gnomic remark raised my eyebrows, as if my ears had heard something outlandish, and I stopped in the middle of our walk and gazed at Cathy in surprise and disbelief.

"What do you mean?" I suddenly asked looking straight into her eyes with a frown.

"Well, you will at least need someone to do the dishes, and off course, the dirty clothes too, wouldn't you?"

A complacent smile spread across her dimpled face.

"Cathy, you don't really mean that, do you?"

"Off course, I mean that…I'm serious", she replied back, looking away as she moved on again, taking the lead.

I followed closely behind like a puppy, trying to comprehend her unexpected, but pithy statement.

"I am not getting any job offer and besides I don't want to stay around here in the village either", Cathy came back again.

"What did you put down in your School Leaver's Application Form?" I asked trying to put her back into our earlier discussion.

"Well, my first choice was Balob Teachers College, and second was Lae Secretarial College".

"And you have not received any thing from either institutions yet?".

"No…nothing"

"I see".

Nothing more came out of our lips for a moment. I thought about asking for her final grades to determine where she was likely to receive a job offer, but then held back when I thought I might embarrass her if she had performed poorly at school and more so in her final exams. Instead, I encouraged her to remain calm.

"Don't you worry, this is only the beginning of December", I said, "We have not come to the end of the month yet. You will still get your offer and I am pretty sure it's on its way right now", I added encouragingly.

There was a smile of relief on her face at my encouraging assurance. And she indicated some seconds later that she was practically joking about traveling with me to Bulolo. I let out a smile as I took in her words and the change of her mind.

Perhaps she was joking, but on a serious note, I realised to some degree that it was no jape. It was certainly more than that, as during our brief moment, Cathy's persona and attitude changed dramatically. I could tell spot-on that she was not the same Cathy Gior she was two years ago. And there was no secret about it, either. Cathy had reached puberty and acquainted herself to all the changes of womanhood and her persona clearly denoted that she was now ready to accept courtship with boys. I perceived that this could be one of the reasons why she came forward after all these cold years to apologize and reconcile with me again. Off course, there may be other reasons too, but whatever it was that prompted her to come forward and apologise, light was again shed into my heart. Cathy Gior was back into my life again.

6

Rays of Hope

My holiday was short. I purposely decided to curtail it because I wanted to go back to Bulolo as soon as possible and take up my new job quickly. The superme dream of being on the payroll and collect my pay packets every fortnight excited me most, more than anything else, that I did not want to waste any time. A few days after the New Year, I bade farewell to my family and friends and left for Bulolo.

My parents were proud to see me go and, like all other times, accompanied me to Mondiagl-kaugla. But unlike in the past, I left Bokan this time as a young elite, not a student anymore. And as we waited for the PMV they laid down some ground rules for me to take note of during this next phase of my life. They cautioned me to be thrifty at all times and look after myself. "Be good and don't take beer. Beer is no good," they said. "Don't accommodate unnecessary visitors to the house, always ask the Almighty for His protection". I listened attentively with occasional nods as they added more and more rules, guidelines and advises when the first PMV roared to a stop beside us.

A little crowd, comprising of my relatives, friends and parents, bade me farewell with hugs and handshakes at Mondiagl-kaugl, as I got on the PMV to begin my journey to Kundiawa. My eyes, though surreptitious, quickly scanned Mondiagl-kaugla for Cathy Gior. I had told Cathy the previous afternoon about my departure in the morning but could not find her anywhere in the group. Maybe, it was too early for her to get up and come on the road to see me go. It was the same further down the road when the car moved past Ende-naige-ingugl. She was not there either.

I boarded the afternoon 1.00pm flight for my trip to Lae on a Talair Banderanatte in Kundiawa, touching down in Lae airport just before 3.00pm after a brief stop over in Goroka for refuel. Unfortunately, I couldn't continue to Bulolo on the same day, as the Bulolo leg of the journey was to be a connection the following day. I spent the night outside Lae with a relative at the Nine-mile settlement.

I was up early, the next day, and checked in at Lae airport at around 7.00 am when the terminal doors opened. Departure time was 9.00am and two hours later I boarded the flight bound for Bulolo. It was a beautiful day, and the clear blue sky was free of clouds. From high above, some 2000 meters above the sea level, the Twin Otter cruised peacefully without any turbulence along the historically world famous and once the busiest air route, to Bulolo. The discovery of gold in Bulolo and Wau had made this air route the busiest in the entire world in the 1930s. It was recorded that between 1931 and 1938 over 40,000 tons of cargo and more than 7,000 passengers were airlifted from Lae to Bulolo using the German built G31 Junkers. In the same period the whole of Australia airlifted only 4700 tons of cargo, and so were other major air routes around the world, thus making Bulolo the busiest air routes in the world at that time. There were also many other global aviation records set and broken during that period too, and as the Talair Twin Otter cruised peacefully along the same old route, I remained glued to the breathtaking features passing below me through my window, trying to picture how these brave men, women and aviators of the past managed to achieve such feats. Some even losing their lives, like pilots Les Trist at Wampit Gap (May 1931) and Frank Dayton (December 1032) at Wau Aerodrome. In their memory two streets in Lae have been named after them.

The beautiful landscape and the picturesque scenery below were indeed marvelous scenes from the air. I had traveled along the Bulolo-Lae Road many times before but never had I seen such a beautiful country from the air. The panoramic view of the Zenag plains, the Mumeng landscapes and the Baiyun hydro power station with the water canals, were some of the spectacular scenes from the air, many of which reminded me of the arid grasslong terrain of the Americas in western movies. Equally fascinating from the air was the verdant spread of man-made forest plantation in the Bulolo-Watut valley, as we neared Bulolo. The many hectares and hectares of magnificent contrasting army green color of pine forest canopy spread among the arid *Imperata* grasslands was strikingly a spectacular scene, and denoted the extent of the plantations into the far corners of the valley from above.

The plane eventually dropped altitude when we approached Bulolo and made a perfect landing at the runway a few minutes later. The exits opened, and I once again stepped on the soils of Bulolo, the historical gold mining township, this time not as a student but a young college graduate to pursue my career in the world of forestry.

There was still ample time left before lunch hour struck and I immediately set out for the Resource office. The office was a separate building next to the Ply Mill and John Smith, my would-be boss, welcomed me into the office when I showed up. He was pleased to see me back so soon.

"I thought, you won't be back until February", he said with a pleasant smile as we exchanged handshakes.

"Yeah, well…I decided to start early", I said, smiling.

A Kiwi by nationality and forester by profession, Smith knew me personally. He had assisted me enormously in the previous year with my final year project titled, *Economical Aspects of Contracting in the Forest Industry*, when I was a student at the college. My research project had required substantial amount of information and data from the company and I frequented Mr. Smith's office more often for interviews and information regarding the economical aspect of contracting in the company. He showed keen interest in my project and had assisted me to the fullest with all the information and data I had required from the company. He was present when I made my oral presentation at the College. I must have pleased him and, using his discretion as a Divisional Manager, Smith made it possible for the company management to offer me a job in the Resource Division, which he headed. And I was pleased to work with and under him.

After introducing me to the other employees and would-be workmates, Mr. Smith directed me to call in at the personnel office and formalise my employment contract with the company before commencing duty. It was the first official duty of the day, as I found out later when the timesheet was collected. The Division's vehicle was made available and he had one of the employees behind the wheel to drive me to the personnel office.

"Make sure, you come back here when you finish", Smith called out as we pulled out.

It took about thirty minutes to get the formalities done at the personnel office. To my surprise the Personal Manager was a Simbu man from the Kamanuku tribe. His name was Martin Kuglame. He seemed prepared, or pehaps was expecting me even before I entered, and after the formal introductions, he placed all the necessary papers before me to go through and pen down my signature in the appropriate spaces. I went through the papers, signing where ever I was required to sign. It was my first experience going through the protocols of formal employment, and I felt nervous. But when I was done, I felt relieved, satisfied and above all excited. I was designated as a Resource Forester and my job description required that I was to lead teams out on forest resource surveys in the timber concession areas acquired by the company. The job description also indicated that I would be required to spend weeks, and even months, in the bush while on survey assignments. As a young and energetic fresh college graduate, I was pleased and felt even more excited. The job was certainly going to be full of adventures and I looked forward to meeting all the challenges with anticipation and enthusiasm, as I walked out of the Personal Office.

When I returned to the Resource Department office, Mr. Smith directed Abraham out of the car and took over the wheel. "Finished?", he asked, as he settled behind the controls. I said, "Yes".

"Ok, Let's go and leave your bags", Smith said, smiling. After I put my bag on the truck, Mr Smith roared down the Huxley Street to the single quarters, located further down in the town area, next to the Bulolo theatre. There, he handed me the keys to Room No.3 of Donga.No.5, an old, but well-maintained building close to the Bulolo Bakery. "This will be your new home, until we find some better place for you later on", Mr. Smith said, as he handed me the keys. I removed my baggage from the pickup, and walked up the steps. Mr. Smith watched from inside the car and as I opened the door of Room No. 3, "You can rest now, and start tomorrow", he called out from the pickup. And bagging my assent, he drove out and headed back to the office.

The room was small, but cozy and just pleasant enough to call it my new home. There was a spring mattress on the bed, a wardrobe in the corner, a chair and a couple of other furniture items set in the room for tenancy. I unpacked my bag and temporarily arranged my room. Moments later, as I lay back on the bed to rest after the tiring journey, and off course, a sleepless night at the mosquito infested Nine Mile settlement outside Lae, I let my mind drift back down memory lane. I recalled all the difficult times I had slogged through in the past thirteen years. I also recalled the difficult scholastic years in community and high schools, the endless assignments and sleepless nights of swotting at the College and let out a complacent smile of satisfaction. So, after all these difficult years of schooling---6 years in Toromambuno Primary School, 4 years in Kondiu High School and 3 years in Bulolo Forestry College---I have finally landed on a paid job, I thought gratefully---the ultimate prize and reward for all these difficult times and efforts I had put up with. Surely, it was the beginning of another chapter and challenge in my life.

I was out on my second forest survey when my nineteenth birthday fell due in July. The survey was conducted at Bundun, near Gurako, along the Lae-Bulolo Road in the Wampit area. The field camp was set up about half-a-kilometer from the main road, close to the Bundun Lutheran mission. It was a convenient location, more central between the city of Lae and the township of Bulolo. As team leader of the survey party, I expended some money for some SPs [beer] to be carted into the camp for the celebration. I had two prime reasons to arrange for the SPs: firstly, to drink on my birthday and, secondly, to splice the mainbrace, i.e. to let the crewmembers enjoy some beer after three weeks of continuous hard work in the bush. The arrangement was a surprise and, in a way, first of its kind, arranged by a team leader. I received many words of praise from my five-crew members who were hell-bent and thirsty alcoholics.

"None of your predecessors had ever done that before", they would say, as they complimented me with smiles and hugs of appreciation.

From a nearby retail outlet, the boys, with the assistance from local helpers, carted six SP cartons into the camp. After taking a decent meal of boiled chicken with coconut milk and vegetables, we commenced our drinking as early as 5.00pm in the afternoon.

There was plenty of beer for everyone and each person drank at his own pace. It was a 'help-yourself-mate' kind of drinking and we moved on smoothly. But the boys started talking above the normal tones when the first carton was emptied. I knew, they were gradually getting drunk because I felt giddy too. We chattered, joked and laughed as is always common in any carousal. Many stories from the boys were smutty jokes of their unusual experience with girls. They would moot on a story about their past flirting and affair with a girl, then highlight the funny part of their experiences and we would all laugh over it.

It was a hilarious moment for everyone, including myself. The stories were, of course, dirty and obscene in some cases but most were romantic tales that elevated our composure and moods. I contributed nothing. But suddenly, the stories turned psychedelic and a certain face intercepted into my mind that could not easily go off during the carousal.

Some of the stories from the boys reminded me of Cathy and I remembered her in the middle of my quaffs with hallucination for the first time, after nearly six months in Bulolo. My mind vividly recalled the last time I saw her back home. I remembered the situation she was in before I left for Bulolo. My mind started musing on the many dubious questions that were gradually becoming a niggling in my mind. "Has she received an offer yet? If she has received one, then where could she be now—Balob Teachers College or Lae Secretarial College? Or, is she back home then? I thoughtfully recalled the morning she threw her arms around me at Nigl-guma Aid Post and her proposition to travel with me to Bulolo. Maybe, she joked but I could still vividly recall her exact words. "I must write a letter to Cathy", I thought at last, "I'll write home first and find out exactly where she is, then look up her address in the phone book and write directly to her", I pondered.

Apparently, my plan to write to Cathy Gior, when I got back to Bulolo after completion of the survey, was short lived. In early August, when I returned to Bulolo after the forest assessment survey, I received a letter from the Resource Manager of Vanimo Forest Products Pty Ltd, offering a position of Forest Surveyor with the Bunning Brothers, a logging company, operating in the Vanimo timber concession area in the Sandaun province. The offer was made in direct response to an application for employment I had made to the company, prior to my departure for the Bundun survey. An attractive remuneration package was offered with the position that suited my liking and I immediately accepted the offer without any question through the telephone.

Mr. Burger, who was later to be my divisional boss, received my call, acknowledged my acceptance and assured me of an airline ticket coming my way for my travel to Vanimo. Excited and glad that I would be leaving for a new destination, a place where I had never been before, I tendered my resignation to my boss two days later, after collecting my airline ticket from the Talair agent in Bulolo.

The resignation was accepted with much regret. "Well, we cannot hold you back against your decision. I wish you well up there", Mr. Smith said, as he handed me my employment reference.

On the following day, I packed my bags for my trip to Vanimo. I was booked to fly out from Lae and travel via Goroka, Mt Hagen and Wewak. Interestingly, it was to be the longest airplane trip for me too. I was looking forward to it with excitement. But, as I was packing my bags, something else came to my mind, something good and pleasing that I could not refuse. I decided to take my flight from Mt Hagen instead, so that I could travel up the Okuk Highway by bus and sojourn at home to check out Cathy Gior before traveling on to Vanimo. It was a pleasant thought, as it was to be a perfect opportunity to see Cathy again and brief her about my transfer while conveying the same news to my parents.

With my mind set, I left Bulolo and continued up the Okuk Highway in a bus to Simbu. Unfortunately, when I arrived home, I learnt that Cathy had left. She was no longer in the village. I discovered soon after, through my brother, Paul, that she was accepted at Balob Teachers College in Lae and was now a fulltime student there since February.

"She rarely comes home. In fact, she came around here in June for the holidays but went back again: Paul said. "That was a big miss", I thought, as I wondered why she could not contact me in Bulolo from Lae.

I could have visited her in Lae from Bulolo too, had I known her placing earlier. As it turned out, it was late now to turn back. I shook my head in disbelief. But at least, I would know where she was and that was more than enough for me to know about Cathy.

I continued my trip to Mt Hagen, the following day, after briefing my family of the transfer and boarded the Talair flight to Wewak. After a brief stopover, I continued in another plane to Vanimo. I had telephoned the Resource Manager from the pay phone some hours earlier from Mt Hagen and he was there at the airport when I arrived. He came forward and introduced himself as Peter Burger and led me to his car. Unlike Mr. Smith, Peter was an Aussie forester and I learnt that he was a man of very few words, but his orientation was good. It reflected that he was sure to be a good boss. After driving me around and introducing me to various company personnel he finally drove me to a duplex apartment at Wesdeco compound, where I was given the keys to one of the unoccupied flats. I unloaded and moved into the flat with my baggage. As it would turn out, this duplex was to be my home for the next three and half years.

My first task, after settling in at Vanimo, was to write a letter to Cathy Gior. That was what I had planned to do when I traveled in the plane but then demurred when something mischievous came to my mind and smothered my plan to write. It was almost a year since I last talked to Cathy. She apologised and even hugged me, but I was unsure whether she would write back to me this time. The Bulolo incident too, on the other hand, was also not properly resolved when I left, and I thought deeply as to whether I should write. I thought over and over again.

Then bravely, soon after brushing aside all odds, I finally gathered a pen and paper. It's better to write and find out, than to sit back and anxiously think about it, I thought, as I began the letter. I congratulated Cathy on her acceptance to Balob Teachers College in my opening paragraph. It was a belated congratulatory message but there was no other better time to extend that than the moment I wrote the letter. I tried to think of some other stories to add in the later paragraphs but, strangely, nothing came into my mind. It seemed that there was no real purpose for writing the letter. Frankly, I was bothered by the bitter memories of the past incident, which still had lingered in my mind. And after moments of fruitless thinking, I ended the letter with a short postscript, advising her of my new location and the subsequent change of my address. "You can write to me at the address supplied, if you wish", I wrote at the end of my letter at the bottom page. I then quickly looked up the Balob Teachers College address in the telephone directory and mailed out the letter the following day.

Alas! It was not long before I received Cathy's reply to my letter. I had returned from the field one afternoon. The cover envelope was without a sender's address and, at first, I assumed the letter to have come from Paul back home. But when I opened it, my heart beat doubled and my breathing got heavier and heavier with anticipation when my eyes caught sight of the Balob Teachers College address on the front page of the two-page letter. Without wasting any time, I quickly ran my eyes through the contents. Cathy thanked me for the letter I wrote and apologised for not getting in touch with me in Bulolo from Lae. "You were always out in the bush every time I rang", she wrote. She was also surprised to learn of my transfer to Vanimo and wished she would come to Vanimo one day and see the border province for herself. She then briefly wrote about her studies and how she was getting along in the College.

I enjoyed the letter as usual, but again, the lines like '...*missed you*' and '...*hope to see you soon*' in her concluding paragraph could not make me take my eyes away from them easily. The lines aroused my mood and inflamed my passion for her more and more again. Also interesting this time, was the fact too that I noticed a slight change in the type of letters that she usually wrote for me. I thought I found some of her lines to be allegorical and obliquely adumbrating her lust for me too with hints of love and romance, something never seen before in her past letters.

Without elaborating further, 'Bang!' went the noise, as I hit the nearest object with excitement, when I finished reading the letter. Cathy was in some ways developing an interest in me too, I thought. I read through the letter again, and thought deeply for sometime, but decided not to jump to a conclusion as yet. I understood, she was seventeen and, perhaps, it was the perfect moment for me to open up and let my infatuation be known to her, I thought. But again, I decided against it at that point of time. I resolved that it was improper through the mail, in retrospect of the Bulolo experience, and decided upon the forthcoming Christmas holidays to be the appropriate time to approach Cathy verbally, when I go home for the festive season.

I replied to the letter without any delay with the Christmas holidays just around the corner. Unlike the first letter, this time I had many things to write for her eyes. I realised that I did not run short of words to start a new sentence. In truth, the new hope Cathy's letter brought had caused many things to flood into my head. With the address carefully written on the cover envelope, I sent the letter away but, unfortunately, my two-page letter did not reach Cathy Gior. And sadly, I was to learn that a year later.

Perplexed and anxious, my first impression after not getting any response from Cathy, was the Christmas rush-hour around the corner. She may not have the time to reply, and wanted to write when she got home and then forgot, I thought, or otherwise she had already left before the letter reached the college and she never collected it. For the latter, she was sure to pick it up when she returned to the College after the New Year, and maybe, would send her reply early in the following year.

Unfortunately, I never went home on the anticipated Christmas period. I remained back in Vanimo instead, due to work commitments. And when classes resumed the following year, I expected a letter from Cathy Gior, a reply to my last letter. But apparently, nothing came from her. My frustrations grew as the weeks rolled by. By the end of February, I presumed Cathy to have decided not to reply to my letter. Spitefully, there was reluctance to write anymore letters to Cathy too, apprehending that the Bulolo saga might be repeated again, even though the itch to write a letter to her remained a burning desire in my mind. Sadly, I withdrew in deep thought one more time, hoping that nothing was serious after all.

7

Pangs of Love

I went home for the first time in December for my annual leave after arriving in Vanimo the previous year. It was almost two years since I last saw my family and was glad to be with them again. My brother Paul, now in his fifth grade at Denglagu Community School, had already grown up. Father and mother, though reaching senescence and hoarier than the last time I saw them, were racy and sprightly active in their rustic semblance than ever. I was proud to see them both. Mother, like all mothers, wept as I entered the house. Above all, it was a joyful moment for us all to be with each other again.

Though safely home, I was always, as usual, conscious of the change of climate and weather and the adverse effects it could have on me, clinically. And, on the second day after my arrival, I was passing through Wai-mambuno, on my way to Nigl-guma, when teacher Phillip Koane, who was digging a pit in front of his house, called out his morning greetings.

"Yes, good morning, Phillip", I responded.

"When did you come?" he asked, with a surprised look after taking in my morning greetings.

"The day before yesterday," I replied.

"Good to see you. It's Christmas time and we are expecting many home comings and many new faces at this time of the year".

"Yeah, it's always the same everywhere", I voiced back in return.

After a few banters, Phillip asked, "Where are you heading now? It's a bit too early"

"I'm going to Nigl-guma…to the aid post".

"What for—to see someone there?"

"No, I am going there for some anti-malaria dose from the APO. I don't want to contract malaria," I told him.

"Brilliant! That is absolutely good thinking. You must always do that whenever you come back from the coast. The change from living in hot climate, and then to cold climate can sometimes make way for malaria".

"I always do that whenever I come home", I replied.

"That's good, Joe, I really hate malaria" he said.

Shortly after, he mooted on his latest experience with malaria fever. "I was near death", he said, "Every joint was aching and I was very weak. I thought I was going but somehow recovered". I listened as he ranted on but my curious eyes could not move away from what he was doing on the ground in front of him. "What are you doing there? The earth is too cold to dip your fingers in there right now", I asked, cutting his tale.

"I am digging a *mumu* pit", Phillip said.

"Oh, I see. What for? Early Christmas party?

"No…tryin' to catch up on something, Joe. I'm putting on a belated birthday party and I am thinking putting a porker into this pit along with the food. But the pit is small so I am trying to widen it up abit".

Phillip switched from malaria and briefly told me about a belated birthday party he was hosting for his daughter, Suaire, who was turning five, on the following day. He spoke of the food, the guests and how he was going to host a party. Then, quite unexpectedly, as a neighbour in the same commune, or perhaps, being one of his former pupils, he invited me to attend his party as a guest too.

"There'll be plenty of food and drinks", he said, "If you have nothing to do tomorrow you can come along and enjoy the evening".

"Thank you for the invitation. That is very kind of you, I will surely come around", I said, accepting his invitation, and eventually left for Nigl-guma.

The following day, I attended the party with a carton of **SP** for Phillip and a little dress, as a birthday present for his daughter. I bought the dress, upon accepting Phiilip's invitation, at the Mission Canteen after visiting the aid post. As I entered Phillip's place at Wai-mambuno with my gifts, his wife Salume exploded with an *aglange* of appreciation. I felt nervous, for Salume's *aglange* drew a lot of attention, but it was the conventional way of greeting, welcoming and formally appreciating a gift in public. I humbly accepted Salume's gesture. Her hubby teacher

Phillip came next and thanked me for my contribution and took away the carton of **SP** from me. This was followed by several more hugs and handshakes of 'welcome' and 'thank you' from the other host members, who were assisting Phillip and Salume to host the party.

I noticed after settling down that it sure was going to be a huge party. There was plenty of food, including pork that had been cooked in the *mumu* pit dug by Phillip the previous day. At one corner of his house was a pile of **SP** cartons neatly stacked to the roof, about fifteen in all. "These are all for tonight", he whispered into my ear, as we walked past the stack, eventually adding my contribution to the stack, making it sixteen.

"I think that's plenty", I mumbled to Phillip, amazed at his preparation.

But Phillip had his reasons.

"Well, don't you forget; it's happening right here in the village, so you must always cater for uninvited guests too"

I shook my head disapprovingly.

"It is an expensive execise to host such parties in the village", I said.

"It is, Joe…never try to host such events that involve free meals and drinks in the village. It could lead to hatred, jealousy and can sometimes be fatal too, if a *kumo–kwimbo* is not too happy".

Phillip knew what he was talking about.

"I think I agree with you, Phillip", I said.

It was an overcast day and, at around 4.00pm, in the afternoon, most of Philip's guests had arrived, many in pairs, other individually and some in family groups. A handful were teachers, his teaching colleagues from the school. And off course, there were also uninvited guests too, as Phillip had predicted, and I presumed this latter group comprised mostly his own clansmen and women and relatives, who just sneaked in to be part of the celebration.

There was a sudden flurry of rain outside and the big house was gradually packed to its capacity with just about everyone inside, all sheltering themselves from the flurry outside. Amazingly, the huge house, constructed of mostly local bush materials---*kunai* roof and *pitpit* wall, took in everyone comfortably. And looking around there was still space to take in some more. I sat myself in the far end corner of the house on a high raised bed with my back to the wall.

There was noise of people everywhere and, a little while later, my attention was drawn to the exchange of greetings at the doorway, whereupon those sitting near to the doorway were greeting and welcoming some new arrivals outside. Two couples entered the house, but with the entrance light in the background causing a silhouette, it was impossible to identify who they were from where I sat until they settled down a few meters away. It was James Goir and his wife, Angela Kumo, Phillip Koane's brother in-law and sister.

There was someone still outside and, again those sitting close to the doorway were calling out, inviting the one outside to come in. "There's plenty of space inside, come in", they all urged, while excusing those in the house to make way, and create a path for the one outside to walk through. Some few seconds, later, a young girl in her teens, reluctantly entered the house. She was tall, perfectly light skinned and slightly fat, but not too fat, the right kind for a beauty contest, excused herself as she stepped into the doorway. My eyes peeled wide open as she made her way in but I could not really establish who she was, as she too was silhouetted against the doorway light behind her. But for some reason my eyes did not move away from the girl. "Who could that be? Look at the thighs", I said to myself, as I sat admiring every bit of her as she navigated her way through the space that had been opened up, and greeting everyone along her path with handshakes and hugs as she walked past them.

Suddenly, as if my ears had heard something strange, I turned virtually frozen when a certain name filled the house, as everyone started applauding and greeting the girl. "*Ambai* Cathy!", they would all exclaim, as they reached out to greet the girl. "Look at you, you are already a big girl now", some said. "Cathy? Is that Cathy Gior?" The questions went off like an alarm inside me. My eyes remained glued to the girl wherever she went. Then as she turned to greet someone seating in my direction, I noticed the girl. Although she changed slightly in the recent times, I could still figure her out. And no doubt too! With the parents already in the house, the pretty girl was none other than the couple's beloved daughter Cathy Gior, making her way in to join them in the house. She had come along with them, but perhaps was reluctant to enter when she saw the house filled with people, something typical of most college girls.

I could feel my heart throbbing and pounded like a six-pound hammer against my chest. I wanted her to come over and take a place on the bed too. Has she noticed me? I thought, almost restlessly. But Cathy was still going in the other direction. Damn! She's she's not not coming this way; I complained inside me. Desperately, I tried to attract her attention and before Cathy would find a place to sit, and I quickly *psssst'* across. She must have heard me through the noise and when she turned, I waved her across to where I was sitting. She let out a smile after a swift glance and quickly excused herself across to where I was sitting. My thoughts ran wild as she was crossing over, again excusing the crowded pack in between. Inside me, I was here, there and everywhere, all at the same time, with my heart pounding as I tried to figure out whether all this was real. And it was real for sure. Cathy Gior, my dream girl, was making her way towards me. I quickly opened up a space and she dropped right beside me.

"Whew! Am I not glad to see you, Cathy?" I exclaimed, as she settled down. We greeted each other with a big hug. It was a bone-crushing hug and for the first time I could feel the marvelous curves of her beautiful body as it pressed against mine. It worked thrilling magic in my body and I could not contain myself. She had doubled in size too, and I found my arms a bit too short to give her a good wrap up.

"You're terrific…just terrific!", I said, "Look at your enormous size. What have you been dieting on lately?" I comically added. Cathy giggled with a smile and teasingly hit me on my lap with her clenched fist.

I soon discovered that Cathy had just graduated from Balob Teachers College, a fortnight ago, after successfully completing her two-year teacher training there. She applied for a teaching post in Simbu but had not yet received a posting notice from the education authorities in Kundiawa. "The posting list has not gone up on the notice board yet", she briefly explained.

"That list won't be up until mid-January", I jovially remarked, as though I was a teacher myself. But I was right too.

"Exactly! That's what everyone is telling me", she said, amidst her smiles.

I then quickly asked her about my last letter that was never replied and why she did not bother to write back. "Which letter?", Cathy asked, and to my disappointment, she retorted back, blaming me for not writing back to her again. "What? Are you saying that you did not receive my letter?" I asked, staring disbelievingly into her eyes.

"Nothing", she responded, shaking her head.

"Oh, I'm sorry then", I apologised with astonishment. "I replied to your letter. I addressed the letter correctly too. Are you sure you didn't get my letter?" I double-checked.

"I received nothing and I told you that already", she replied with an askance look, and further added, "How many times will I tell you that I did not receive a thing from you?"

She was serious this time, and I could already sense some tone of disappointment in her voice. A silence followed, as I tried to think up what might have possibly happened to the letter when Cathy spoke again.

"I thought, maybe, you were busy writing out to other girls", she said, almost teasingly with a titter. As if I had heard something strange, my two ears stood tall when they caught Cathy's banter.

"What do you mean?" I asked, looking straight into her eyes with my eyebrows arched to the forehead.

"Oh, nothing really… just joking", she said with a laugh, and playfully slapped me on my lap before looking away.

Like many modern birthday celebrations, Phillip Koane hosted his daughter's birthday party after careful planning and, though not sumptuous, there was just enough food and drinks for everyone. There were soft drinks for women, children and non-drinkers, **SP** for those who were fond of beer and food for everyone. The number of **SP** cartons increased every time a new guest arrived with his or her donation. Someone would present a carton or two of the favorite ale to Phillip as a friendly gesture of his contribution towards Suaire's birthday party, a customary Melanesian way of denoting support, brotherhood or true friendship.

Unfortunately, it was the birthday cake that was missing for little Suaire to make a wish and blow out the candles on the occasion of her fifth birthday. Perhaps there were no cake shops around with the nearest shop located 35 kilometers away in Kundiawa, to place an order. But generally, the cake did not really matter so much in a rural setting like Wai-mambuno where birthday celebration was not a common practice, or even part of our culture. It was copied from the white man and most village folks present would otherwise wonder why a little slice of cake was going around, when there was plenty to eat, drink and feast on.

The rain outside finally subsided and Phillip mobilized the host members and organized for the party to begin. The main part of the celebration did not take long, as it was more or less informal without the cake. But the theme of the gathering served its purpose. First, little Suaire was led into the house. She was radiantly garbed and led to a section of the house, carpeted with linen. Everyone cheered her with their 'Happy Birthday' greetings and handed out their presents. A dish of food, containing a whole cooked chicken, was placed before her to be enjoyed with her little friends. Snack foods, includes lollies were also distributed amongst her little friends. It was truly an enjoyable moment for the little ones, with some of them having a taste of these sweets for the first time. When that was completed, it was all over for little Suaire and her gang and the rave-up for the adults began.

The food was served first and in a more typical 'Simbu fashion', according to family units in dishes. Distant relatives and guests were served on disposal 'plates' of steamed fig and banana leaves. Phillip's wife, Salume served me food on a plate. She did the same for Cathy too. We were perhaps regarded as special guests amongst these group of village folks, maybe because of our exposure to the outside world. There was pork, *kaukau* and some vegetables on our plates. Drinks were served a few minutes later when the leftover foods and dishes were cleared away. Those who preferred beer were served with **SP**s, while others had soft drinks. I preferred beer and took my first bottle of **SP** soon after I finished the pork and returned the plate.

I was served my second bottle some ten minutes later. I could be fast in my consumption rate, but I guess I was thirsty, and perhaps over excited with Cathy at my side. Cathy chose to have a soft drink and was served a can of coke. It all went smoothly and we both enjoyed the fun, just like everyone else. But after my third beer I felt slightly dizzy in my head and tipsier than moments earlier. I could feel the effects of the ale taking its toll as I was pouring more and more into my mouth and down my throat. Cathy was still holding onto her first can when I finished all my three beers. I offered my fourth bottle of **SP** to her, all for fun, off course! I wanted to see how she'd react; whether she would accept or refuse, but she smiled innocently and refused my offer.

"I'm doing fine with this", she said, hoisting the can of Coca-cola higher up for my eyes.

"So, you don't take beer, do you?"

"No! Beer stinks and tastes rubbish", she said, and looked away with a chuckle.

"I see, so that's why you don't like beer?".

"Correct", she said, and looked into my eyes again with smiles.

"Then, grab yourself another soft drink." I said.

"I will, but later". Cathy said, with the smiles never failing to leave her beautiful face.

Some two hours had passed and many, who took beer, could be heard communicating well above their normal volume. Our poor papas, who were taking beer after many moons for the first time, were already drunk after their first bottle. Favorite primeval *giglanges* of their bygone years quavered euphoniously out of the lips. One would start up a tune and the rest would join in chorus. Together, they would end it sweetly in baritones primeval to the modern generation. Elsewhere, the singings picked up in little groups, and in less than an hour, the entire house was rocking to the tunes of the *giglanges*. Under the effulgence of the Coleman lamps, I could see heads of all shapes and sizes moving to the rhythm of the folk songs. I could see my father, who had arrived later at the invitation of Phillip, sipping his drink and singing away cheerfully with his friends. All their beers were at half full. Interestingly, most were sipping their third or fourth bottle, but were already drunk, unlike the many young bloods quaffing their countless beers in the dark corners. I enjoyed watching the papas most, with envy.

It was gradually getting late in the night outside. By now nearly all mothers, children and non-drinkers had gone to their homes. Those who remained behind were mostly thirsty drinkers of the favorite ale. Three heads away from us was Cathy's mother Kumo, closely keeping watch over her husband James, while he boozed away happily with his other teacher colleagues, who were equally enjoying the great night. Cathy, who had been sitting with me during the entire celebration, remained my belle and made my night a pleasant one. Her soft occasional touches thrilled my nerves deeper everytime when we were in contact. At times my groggy and drunken eye would gaze amorously at her beautiful face for long wonder moments, which at times, became very difficult to avert them. Cathy might have sensed my somewhat provocative gazes but remained by my side unaffected. On intuition, she was equally enjoying my company too. She would occasionally put a teasing smile and playfully hit me to distract my attention whenever she sensed the leers from my drunken eyes taking too long.

"Do you like beer?' she would ask with an askance look.

"I guess, I do", I would respond, staring provocatively into her eyes.

"Better quit", was all she would say, hit me, then rolled her eye with smiles and looked away.

I was now half-drunk and with all the singing well above the noise of anything else in the house, Cathy and I had to shout at each other in order to converse. In many instances, we had to bring our heads very close together for one to talk, and the other to listen. This went on for some time, and I guessed it raised some eye-brows too. But we were not bothered one bit. Then, at one stage, quite unintentionally, one of my hands pressed down hard on one of Cathy's fat thighs, close to the groin area for support, as I was leaning across to catch something she was telling me. I didn't notice my ineptitude until after Cathy struggled to contain my massive weight resting down hard on her groin. Unaware, this part of the female body was certainly an 'out of bounds' zone and I felt guilty and abashed the moment I realised my hand there. I quickly winched back my hand in guilt, trying awkwardly to apologise. I looked into Cathy's eyes, anticipating a disappointed face. But surprisingly she timidly smiled instead. She spoke no word on my inanity and continued as though nothing had happened, with her eyes quickly scanning the house as if to check if someone had been watching us, or had seen everything. Fortunately, no one had seen what happened. They were all carried away with their drinking.

I was almost drunk and Cathy's turn out towards my inanity was captivating. I had touched an area rarely touched by many hands and it enormously inflamed my carnal desires to such an extent that an aphrodisiac feeling swiftly inundated my composure. Deep inside, I was imbued with love and desire and most of all, courage was already building up in me. After all these years, I resolutely decided that this was the psychological moment I had been waiting for a very long time, the perfect moment to verbalize everything I had always dreamt and fantasized about her. And to my advantage, I was taking beer, I thought. It is common knowledge that a drunkard could do anything mischievous and escape with in unaffected. "So, what am I waiting for?" the question popped in my mind. I didn't waste any time. Inching closer, "Cathy?", I said, nudging her with my elbow. "Yes?" She leaned forward, and, "What is it?" she asked. I took a deep breath, and then I said, "I don't know whether you'll like it but there is something I had always wanted to tell you and, had been keeping it all to myself for a very long time". Cathy lifted her head and looked into my eyes. "What is it?" she asked, and eagerly moved herself closer.

"It is personal and confidential too", I said, "just between you and me, you know"

"Oh, I see"

"And if you promise to be a good girl, I'll tell you everything now".

"Trust me", Cathy said, wanting to know everything almost at once. She appeared desperate, and even excited too. "Maybe, I'll like it too", she added, almost provocatively with a titter, as if she had already known what I was going to tell her.

This turnout boosted my confidence further and I was already fired up and set to spit out everything. Though drunk, I was overexcited too. I moved closer again. I took a quick deep breath again to ease any frustration that might cause a hiccup on my confidence and play havoc on my progress that moment. "It's like this", I said.

"I am listening"

Then, just as I opened my lips to let out the next sentence for Cathy's ears, out from nowhere, something in silhouette darted past us like a missle and smashed in the fireplace that was about a meter and half away from us, causing an explosion that caused confusion and chaos everywhere, taking everyone up onto their feet. It was an unopened **SP** bottle containing full beer. The singing stopped at once. In a matter of seconds, a fight broke out at the far side of the house where the bottle had darted out, causing a stampede. We could not confirm from our end, who could have been involved, but it was certainly a big fight that sent everyone running amok. Thick billows of dust from the earth floor clouded the scene.

Cathy and I stood up in total confusion as the brawl got out of hand. Elsewhere, there was mad rush for the only door, and before I knew what had happened, Cathy left me and went for the door too. In a matter of second she disappeared into the darkness. I tried to follow her but could hardly run. I was too paralytic to move a step forward. Phillip quickly intervened with the help of his boys and soon subdued the commotion some ten minutes later. I soon learnt that the two Kaugla brothers, Mathias and Kua, had put up the fight while trying to settle a flabby feud between them while they were under the influence of alcohol. It was Mathias, the younger brother, a common ruffian, that swung the bottle, which annoyed his elder brother who, in turn retaliated.

The Kaugla brothers disturbed what was supposedly a great night, and everyone, including Phillip, was upset at the loathsome disturbance. I quickly looked around for Cathy Gior when everything settled and returned to normalcy but she was nowhere to be seen, nor were her parents. It was obvious the family had gone home along with the many others when the fight erupted. I recalled the sensational moments just before the disturbance and shook my head disapprovingly in dismay. Regretfully, it was truly a lifetime opportunity that went begging. I had just missed my golden chance to impart my life-long dreams and desires to the girl that I had secretly loved, admired and longed for. I hoped the Kaugla brothers realised what they have done to me, I thought. They simply have ruined what was supposedly a great and historical night in my life.

I sat on the edge of the bed with my head between my cupped hands, thinking deeply about the mishap, which had caused this entire disturbance. Should I follow Cathy to Ende-naige-ingul? I kept thinking over and over, but held back my inclination, as it was already going up towards the early hours of dawn. When I looked around the house almost half of the people present before the fight were no longer there. They had gone home, just about every one of them. There was no more singing. All our older men, including my father, had left. I blamed the two Kaugla brothers for disturbing, what most invited guests, including myself and many others, thought as the best party ever hosted by anyone in the little Wai-mambuno community.

The drinking continued again amongst a handful who had remained behind. The Kaugla brothers joined the carousal too, quaffing away their beers intemperately, as if nothing disgusting had happened between them, only seconds earlier. I was infuriated and was even furious at the sight of their presence but held back my temper, as I was only a guest of Phillip and did not want to start another commotion again.

"Anything left?", I called out to the one giving out the **SP**s. He was none other than Koima, Phillip's brother-in-law and little Suaire's maternal uncle.

After checking the carton, he passed on a bottle to me. Fortunately, it was the last bottle from the carton. "You're lucky, this one is the last bottle", said Koima, as he handed over the beer. He alerted the others that I was served the last bottle. "Gentlemen, there's nothing more in stock", he announced to everyone, and threw away the empty carton.

Soon, there was talk amongst the drinkers for a possible contribution of cash to cart in some more beers to keep the night going. Many put forward their money, including teacher Phillip. But I was not with the group. My mind was elsewhere. I was thinking deeply about Cathy Gior, the failed attempt and what I was going to do in the morning. I also planned to go out and look for her and tell her everything that I had just wanted to tell her only moments earlier. The more I thought about it, the drowsier I became and, before long, I plumped onto the bed behind me and got lost in a deep sleep.

8

Obsession Unburdened

I was raised from the bed by the noise of some children romping about outside the house. I sat on the edge of the bed, scruffy and disheveled, trying to think out and recollect the night's rave-up but the hangovers of the heavy drinking suppressed all my quick senses of thinking. When I looked around after rubbing my eyes clean, I saw bodies, about a handful, lying everywhere in the house that reeked with a malodorous scent of beer. There was heavy breathing, snoring and snuffling all around and I could not clearly recall everything. But slowly images of the night's party appeared in my mind. I remembered the food, the beer, the singing, then the fight and suddenly Cathy Gior. I remembered I was trying to tell her something when the fight erupted and disturbed us, and the party too. Then I recalled my plan to approach her at her Ende-naige-ingugl home, first thing in the morning and finish off what I was trying to tell her during the night.

Without a second thought, I got onto my feet from the bed, stepped out of the house and rushed down to the nearby pristine Mondia that was flowing, some thirty meters from the house front. I stood by the water edge and after a quick splash of the freezing water onto my face from my cupped hands, I hurried across to Mondiagl-kaugla, wiping my face dry, as I scurried along. A little crowd of four people gathered around a roadside betel nut vendor, enjoying the morning sun as they chewed his nuts. With little regard, I slowly walked past, after exchanging the morning greetings, and proceeded down the road towards Ende-naige-ingugl, planning everything I was going to do and say as I walked. It took me less than five minutes to reach Ende-naige-ingugl. I was elated too. But, as I stumbled to the entrance gate, I scrupled and momentarily paused. Something touched my nerves and I consciously panicked to continue further into the village. I realised that I was not drunk anymore.

And with that I could feel the courage to proceed into Ende-naige-ingugl deserting me. It disappeared.

Seriously, Ende-naige-ingugl was a Siako village, inside Siako territory, and I would apparently be a 'foreigner' or 'stranger' on that turf. Hence, I found no genuine reason to walk right into the village at this very early hour of the day. It was likely I would raise speculation in the minds of the many who'd see me there. "What's that Denglagu young man doing here at this time of the morning?", many would ask. By custom that was embarrassing and I stood thinking hard on what to do, but nothing worthy entered into my mind.

Should I turn back? I kept asking myself, but I was already at the gate, and had no desire to turn back. I was still thinking when I suddenly remembered my old friend Thomas Goir, who, I was told, had arrived from Port Moresby, the previous evening. Cathy had told me all about him and of his arrival in the night at party. I had not seen Thomas for more than two years and a smile glowed across my face when something assuring settled into my head. He'll be my person of interest, I thought. If anyone should ask about my presence there, it was to see Thomas Gior, and no one else. It was a perfect plan for my visit to Ende-naige-ingugl at this early hour and I let out smile of satisfaction, when the hurdle was removed from my head.

Without wasting any more time, I jumped over the entrance fence and walked into the village. It was all quiet inside. It was also my first time, after more than five years, to enter Ende-naige-ingugl village again, and found the housing arrangements quite different from what I was used to, or had seen some years ago. Many new houses went up in place of some former ones, while a couple derelict homes I had known in the past, remained standing in a state of dilapidation in their respective locations. Some dogs barked, as I walked past their owner's homes, but none dared to come near me. I quickly asked the first person in sight. It was Martin Kindua, a Siako I personally knew.

"Is Thomas Goir in?", I asked.

Martin was surprised to see me too.

"He arrived from Port Moresby two days ago. He should be there. That's his house, over there", he said, pointing to a group of houses on the far end of the village.

"So, Tom's parents are still living in the same house", I said, "I was here when his father was constructing that house five years ago"

"Yes, that's the same house. Thomas should be in there"

"And that new house?"

"That belongs to James Gior and family. You can walk past, there are no dogs there", Martin said.

"Oh, alright. Thanks", I said.

The Goirs had their family homes built next to each other on the far westernmost corner of the village. There were two houses, the foremost belonging to James Goir and family, while the next behind belonged to Thomas's parents that I was familiar with. I headed in the direction of Thomas' house. Fortunately, Thomas and Cathy were both together outside their homes when I arrived. They were basking in the early morning sunlight that was shooting its brilliant rays from across the serrated Numbu–Bauglwake mountain range in the east. Cathy had been regaling Thomas about the night's incident at Wai-mambuno. Both had their backs to the sun in the direction of my entry and I surprised them when I showed up from behind.

"Welcome to Ende-naige-ingugl!", Cathy voiced, sounding in a perked-up mood, as if she was excited at my presence. She quickly rose from her location and greeted me with a handshake.

My old friend Thomas wrapped me up with a big hug, and I hugged him in return too.

"What brings you here at this time of the morning?" he asked with grin, as Cathy looked on with smiles.

'To see you, of course…how do you expect your long-lost brother to ignore you when he knows you are here", I responded back smiling, as though I was there specifically to see him.

"Cathy was just telling me all about you, and the party last night at Wai-mambuno", he said.

"Yes, Teacher Phillip hosted little Suaire's birthday party and we were all there together last night", I told Thomas.

"That's what she was telling me now, and everything that had happened there".

"A lot of things happened last night. She should have plenty to tell you", I said.

Then, before I could say anything else, Cathy quickly inquired about the fight and how we got on in the night.

"There was no more beer. So, we dismissed all and I went straight to bed. In fact, I searched for you after the fight but couldn't find you. So, I assumed you to have walked home".

"I helped mum and we walked my drunken dad home. But listen, I'm so sorry, I had to do this without letting you know. Truly, I was scared to the nerve...the explosion, the fight and the stampede. I was dead scared, you know. So, I had to make for the door and escape into the night", she confessed.

"It's alright, I know, it was not your fault and that's understood", I said, as if nothing had mattered that night after she left.

Then, quite unexpectedly, Cathy asked, "What were you going to tell me last night just before the fight?" As if iced in a deep freezer, I turned frozen, as I took in the question.

I never expected Cathy would ask me that question quite so soon. She stunned me off-guard and I turned to stone and could not answer her immediately. I had literally gone in there to finish off last night's talk but, now with all the courage gone, I found it almost difficult, and even brain dead, unable to deliver the talk, even after Cathy asked. I felt sweat all over me and even guilty too, but pretended as if nothing was abnormal.

"About what?" I asked, putting on a dubious face in dissimulation, as if to have forgotten everything I did and said last night.

"Can't you remember?", Cathy asked, "You were trying to tell me something last night when that bottle flew past us and caused the explosion near the fireplace, which got everyone onto their feet. The fight then broke out seconds later, followed by the stampede", she said, recounting everything accurately with the mnemonic view to assist me remember the events of last night.

Again, pretending to think deeply, as if trying to remember a thing, I shook my head negatively.

"No, no...I can't remember at all", I said. "I think I was too drunk to remember a thing now", I added, shaking my head. Cathy paused for a moment.

"Oh, well, just forget it, then. Maybe, you'll recall everything again some other time", she said, submitting to my game.

Thomas stood listening with very little concern all the while we conversed. He appeared lost on the subject we were on but did not bother to ask. Some moments later, Cathy joked about some of the funny scenes she witnessed in the night at the party. We laughed about it. Thomas also shared some of his similar experiences in Port Moresby. We asked questions about the city, and he answered them to our pleasure. We talked and enjoyed the morning sun for about thirty minutes when a piquant piece of thought sailed into my mind. I never planned it and wasn't too sure whether it would work out, but I excused Cathy if I could talk to Thomas alone.

"What about me?" Cathy asked, staring at me in disbelief.

"A-a-ahem, I think, it's a bit secret; men's talk, you know. So, we'll talk first and maybe let you know later", I said with a quick smile, as my drowsy eyes looked directly into hers.

Astounded and also curious at my rather strange leer, Cathy called out, "Don't tell me, it's about girls". She joked with a guffaw, as if she had already known what I was going to tell Thomas. "Maybe…but just stay put. It won't be long", I said, as I grab hold of Thomas' left arm.

I quickly walked Thomas to the other side of the house and stood him against the wall. He appeared confused at my latest twist of behavior. "What are you doing?", he asked. But I put my pointer finger to my lips, "Shhhh…", I said and beckoned him to remain calm. Checking both ends of the house to ensure Cathy was not following, I began. "This is a long story, but I'll make it short", I said. "Oh, is that so? I thought you took me aside to plan a bank robbery?", Thomas joked, smiling. I smiled too but did not waste any time. "Listen", I said, and began by first, explaining why I was there at Ende-naige-ingugl, and then secondly, why I wanted to speak to him alone. Again, Thomas laughed, but this time did not voice anything.

Taking a deep breath, "Tom, I really don't know what went into me right now but I am about to unveil a top secret to you. Whether you like it or not, we've been brothers all along, so please keep it to yourself", I said. "Spit it out", Thomas said with a burst of laughter, as if he already knew what I was going to unveil. And as he listened, I opened up, beginning with my decade long secret.

"You know very well that I am always fond of Cathy, and I know you are well aware of that too", I said.

"What do you mean? I don't know a thing about that", Thomas interrupted again with yet another burst of laughter.

"Well, last night at the party, I was going to tell Cathy something---something about how deeply I was fond of her. I was also going to ask her if we could possibly enter into a permanent boyfriend/girlfriend relationship. But unfortunately, the fight dispersed us, ending a really sensational night. And I never even told Cathy anything of what I had planned to tell her. I am here this morning purposely to tell Cathy what I had intended to tell her last night. But I just can't do it now".

"Why? What do you mean?"

"I don't think I have the courage anymore to do that right now. You see, last night, I was drunk and it was all right for me, but now I am sober and all the courage is gone. I don't think I'll stand up and talk".

Thomas smiled. There was evidence of understanding in his eyes and that pleased me, though I felt slightly embarrassed after what I had emptied before him.

"I thought, both of you already established a steady relationship years ago", Thomas finally said.

"Oh, most people think it this way when they see us together more often, and I think, even you too, but really we haven't yet..."

"Okay, so what exactly do you want me to do right now?" He cut me short.

"I want you to just tell Cathy that I love her and ask her if we could enter into a permanent boyfriend/girlfriend relationship".

"Is that all?"

"Yes, that's all", I said and cuffed him with a playful tap on his shoulder, feeling even more embarrassed this time.

Thomas again burst out laughing, this time with a loud guffaw.

"You are taking about a very small thing, a doddle that does not really need my assistance at all", he remarked, amidst his laughter. "I mean, she is only a woman just like the many others out there and besides, you know Cathy better that I do. You can do that all by yourself. That's not as hard as what you may be thinking, or it?" I wasn't too dumbfounded to answer him immediately, with my thoughts running amok. Then, "Come! Let me take you to her", he said with a sudden pull on my arm.

"B-b-b-but Thomas...not today. I told you, I am already sober", I voiced and reluctantly pulled back, "You know, Tom, I am too shy to approach her now", I said.

"You are a chicken, a real chicken...", Thomas muttered with his childish smile, as he released my arm. Then after a few seconds, "Alright. I'll talk to her then", he said, "Don't you worry, I'll be on your side, and I don't think she will decline either. You can come after me if you want". And with that said, Thomas walked away to find his niece.

"I'll remain here...but I am counting on you", I blurted out behind him, as he disappeared around the corner of the house to find Cathy.

The next few minutes were the most terrible moments in my life. My heart pounded harder and harder against my chest every time I looked in the direction where Thomas had disappeared. I did not sit properly. As the seconds ticked past I pondered on the unheard discussion, taking place on the other side of the house. What is Cathy telling Thomas now? Will she agree to everything that Thomas would be telling her? What if she says, no?

I was still thinking when Thomas appeared again from where he had disappeared.

"Come on, over here", he howled at me, with a radiant smile glowing across his face.

He had his right thumb up too---certainly indicating good news. Upon noticing this I instantly assumed he had succeeded in his mission. My heart prematurely jumped with joy and a sigh of relief escaped from inside me. I felt like walking out of an examination room that very moment, totally relieved after anxiously studying hard, day and night without any respite. I was over the moon and even before Thomas revealed anything to me I was on the verge of jumping up and shouting to the whole wide world that I was Cathy Gior's boyfriend. But I remained composed and tight-lipped as Thomas reached me.

"It's okay with her…she's all yours now", Thomas finally announced, smiling, as he approached me, seemingly taking everything very lightly like he always does. I stood motionless, taking in everything he spilled out, and tried to figure out whether this was all real or just another dream. And then, suddenly, "So, what are you waiting for now?", Thomas growled. "Get out there and talk it out with your 'wife'", he urged, with a congratulatory push.

I smiled guiltily, and felt even more nervous as I reached out and hugged Thomas in appreciation. But as a long time friend he was calm, as though nothing dramatic had happened. And with him around and subsequently involved, I was already out of control. I was excited as ever and couldn't stand still inside. I wanted to know everything. Shaking restlessly with enthusiasm, excitement and desperation I confronted Thomas with many puerile questions.

"How did you do it? …I mean, what did you tell her? And what was her reaction?" I asked, wanting to know everything from the start.

"Oh, come on Joe, don't be childish. You sent me on a mission to tell Cathy that you loved her, and that was exactly what I did. What else did you expect me to tell her?"

"Sorry, sorry Thomas, but it's just that I can not stand still inside. I am over excited and already over the moon. Can't you see me shaking? Anyway, what did Cathy say?", I mumbled.

"I told you, it's alright with her. She agreed to be your girlfriend, she's yours now", Tom said. Then, "Come! Follow me!", Thomas roared at me, leading the way towards Cathy Gior. Hesitantly, I followed closely behind him like a tethered puppy.

"Bro, you've just done something great for me", I whispered to him from behind as we walked. Thomas looked back. "These are small things…what are brothers for?", he exclaimed with smiles, winking his left eye at me, as he proceeded.

Cathy was sitting with a radiant face when we showed up and she spoke first. "Is that what you were trying to tell me last night?" she asked gleefully, smiling. I guiltily nodded, even though I wasn't quite sure what subject she was referring to from last night.

"I think it is", I said, feeling a bit more nervous, but Cathy laughed instead.

"You have many wonderful moments to tell me all this. Why did you have to leave it till last night?"

"Well, maybe, I was too stubborn to speak out", I shyly mumbled between my trembling lips. And then, in order to avoid further embarrassment, I bravely reached out to take her hand while she was talking. Cathy smiled and took hold of my hand.

It was slightly a shaky moment but history was in the making. Cathy Gior and I conversed for the first time as a boyfriend and girlfriend after calling ourselves brother and sister for over a decade. Thomas stood in silence, watching us with a smile of approval a few yards away, as we talked and exchanged our smiles. I believed he was enjoying the scene too and I found no better way to express my gratitude to him. It was ten years ago that he had introduced me to his seven-year-old niece on that fine Tuesday afternoon at Toromambuno Community School. Today, he had just bound us for a much-desired relationship that I had dearly longed for since that afternoon. He was truly a great friend and I owed him a depth of gratitude for everything he did.

We sat for a while but very little came out of our lips. Maybe, we were yet to adjust ourselves to the latest twist of fate. Cathy was now my girlfriend and, likewise, I was her boyfriend. Perhaps, we needed time to re-start our relationship all over again, and off course, with a different approach. But for Thomas Gior, nothing affected him. He remained calm right through but for some reason nothing more came out of our lips. Maybe, we ran out of stories at last, but the silence touched my nerve. Guilt was slowly creeping in, as the miracles of the remaining alcohol melted away in my body and I excused Cathy and Thomas for a dizzy head from the night's hangovers.

"I desperately need a bed rest", I said, then quickly asked, "Can you both meet me later in the afternoon at Mondiagl-kaugla?" My excuse seemed a surprise and Cathy quickly looked at Thomas.

"Where are you going to take your nap?" Thomas asked.

"At home…Bokan!".

"Alright, we'll catch up with you later in the afternoon", both chorused, looking on. "And perhaps you might want to clean yourself up too, you look terrible", Cathy added, smiling. I smiled back but did not voice anything.

I rose from where I sat and walked out of Ende-naige-ingugl, passing through the row of houses and aimed for the main exit. Not a soul was around and the place looked deserted after everyone had disappeared in the morning into the gardens. In less than a minute, I was already standing in the middle of the road. I checked the road. There was no one when I looked up and down the graveled track. Leaping high into the air, I exultantly punched the air in jubilation, as I pranced delightfully up to Mondiagl-kaugla. The day was truly the proudest moment of my life. Recalling my triumph, I had finally succeeded. After a full decade of secret admiration, I had finally got my dream girl in the manner I had wanted---to become soul mates, a feat to be recorded in the annals of my memory for the rest of my life

I had lied about going home to take a bed rest. It was really the nervousness in the first hours of my triumph at Ende-naige-ingugl that prompted me to leave early. So, instead of going home, I waited the whole day at Mondiagl-kaugla market, waiting in anticipation for Cathy to arrive from Ende-naige-ingugl. My desire to be with her was burning rapidly after the success of my trip in the morning. She arrived at the market around mid-day. She was alone. I could see that she had showered and got herself into some fresh clothes. She was certainly looking beautiful and majestic in her fresh clothes too. I could not work out whether she saw me, but I quickly whistled and waved her across to where I was, as she walked up the road.

"Where's Thomas?" I asked, when she finally stood in front of me. Cathy shrugged her shoulders.

"I don't know. He disappeared right after you left. I went back into the house to take a nap, and don't know where he went", Cathy said, as she looked around for a place to sit.

"How about you? Did you take your sleep?" she asked, after settling herself on a rock next to me.

"No, I was here the whole day after I walked out of Ende-naige-ingugl"

"Why? You still look tired. You should have gone and taken some rest. I took mine right after you left and am feeling better now".

"Well, good for you" I said laughing, "but me, I guess I waited for you here all day" Cathy let out a chuckle and we laughed.

The market was gradually packing but we sat ourselves away from the other people and soon were in communion with each other. Unlike our past conversations, the tone of our language gradually changed in style and habit from those of the past. We were no longer a 'brother' and 'sister'. This time, we were two beginners trying to discover love and romance. Many hidden agendas that were never discussed before and had long remained covered poured out of our lips. I brought forward everything; I had held back all these cold years. I made sure that I left nothing out, as this was the moment I had eagerly waited for. Ironically, she had similar things to tell me, which surprised me more than ever; ambitions and desires that she had kept secret to herself. I realised then that she has had the same passion and fondness for me over the years too. And quite surprisingly, she had been waiting for this moment too.

Our conversations took us back to many incidents of the past. We reviewed with nostalgia all the years that we plodded through together and laughed over them. When I asked about the one sentence nerve-racking letter, she wrote five years ago that froze our brother/sister relationship for almost two years, she responded, "The letter was written out of frustration and embarrassment caused by Yakopus Kaiglo", and then apologised, although it was a long time ago.

"I never meant to write that letter, and it was never written from my heart", she said. "In fact, I regretted it later on but it was too late, the letter has been posted. I felt quite guilty to approach you ever since then".

"I see…Well, had I known that earlier, it would have been better, but it's all over now", I said calmly, and then added, "It's not the end of the world yet, let's forget the past and start anew".

Cathy smiled.

"That's right, let's forget and start fresh again. It really caused some terrible moments, I know, but I don't think we lost anything yet", Cathy lamented and teased me on my arms, rolling her eyes provocatively at me.

"No! Not at all", I said, and we both laughed.

Cathy Gior and I met more frequently than before and we enjoyed every minute of our unions. Every moment together was sweet like honey. Retrospectively, it was a dream come true at last for both of us. But unfortunately, our glorious moment was to be short-lived. Time finally caught up with us. My recreation leave was up and it was time for me to say goodbye and return to Vanimo. I didn't want to leave Cathy, and Cathy also felt the same. She didn't want me to go away from her. Maybe, we had discovered love at last, and hence did not want to depart from each other. But regretfully, she has to stay and I must go. It was our career obligations that we had to honor and prioritise.

Cathy was yet to be notified of a school posting to teach but that wouldn't happen until mid-January and I was to leave without knowing her definite placing. On the evening before my departure, that would be the following day, we talked for the last time at Mondiagl-kaugla.

"I don't want to see you go away", she said with a pale face, "I don't' want you to leave me behind. Let's go to Vanimo together". I looked away with an empty mind, and then back at her. I could see she was really upset.

"No, we can't do that, Cathy", I said patting her arms, "You will have to teach. I will write letters. I promise, I'll write to you as soon as I touch down in Vanimo. I'll use the mission address for the start and you can inform me of the change of your address later on in your letter".

We spent a very long time together before retiring to our homes later in the evening. I left the following morning with truly a broken heart for Mt Hagen to catch my flight to Vanimo via Wewak.

I kept to my word when I arrived in Vanimo. As soon as I settled into my duplex apartment, I immediately started on a very lengthy letter for Cathy. I wrote anything that came from my heart that was worth mentioning, and anything that would please. I reminded her of how beautiful she was. And then, for the first time I wrote: *I love you*. I felt rather strange at first to pen the line, as I was always conscious and careful in my past letters not to put out such effusion openly. I paused momentarily to figure out if I was doing the right thing. Yes, I was! Our relationship had taken a different turn now. Cathy was now my girlfriend and not a sister anymore. And there was no reason in the world why I should not have written, *I love you*, in my letters to Cathy from then on. The time of panicking, frustration and embarrassment was over and she certainly expects plenty of *I love you*, in my letters from this time on. Smiling gorgeously at my anaylsis, I folded the letter into the envelope.

It was within a week that I received a letter from Cathy. It was a complete surprise and I was amazed at the prompt reply. "That's fast", I murmured, as I opened the letter, but no. The letter was not the reply to mine. It was post-dated to the day I left Bokan. She had written the letter on the day I left, maybe in the afternoon, and got it posted away the following day. Cathy wrote of her loneliness and the miseries that my departure had caused her.

"I missed you", she wrote, and further added, *"And I can't wait any longer to see you again"*. I stared at the lines. Words of love and endearments effusively formed the full text of her two-page letter. She wrote everything that was down deep in her heart, which she had not verbally expressed during our meet. She had them all on the paper. I re-read the letter again and again, as if feeling her presence right before me. I knew she certainly had waited for this moment for a very long time, just like myself.

I was wondering whether to replay to Cathy's first letter when a second one arrived a week later. This time, it was in reply to my letter. She disclosed in her second letter that she had been given a teaching posting to Hobe Community School in the Karamui district. She also indicated the change of address and advised me to direct all future letters to that address. Her letter was short, but contained sensational words of love, just like her first letter. I replied to both the letters in my single communication with all the best wishes, and off course, sweet words that I could think of and finished off in my closing paragraph that I missed her too. I addressed the letter to her new address.

She wrote back without delay. I did the same. Our letter writing once again picked up pace and became a non-stop priority. Every time, we would go a step deeper in our exchange of words and emotional feelings. All possible and potential romantic terms, jargons, catch phrases and locutions that crossed our heads would form the main body of the letter. Cathy would write up to six and seven pages of full-length letters and I would do the same, in return, trying to overtake her by an extra page. Hieroglyphic illustrations of a heart with an arrow piercing through the center would take their place in any available space in our letters, indicating broken heart at the most. Favorite lyrics of love songs by popular artists and recordings groups from within and abroad would be plagiarised and paraphrased in our letters to contemplate our emotional feelings for each other. I was moved by the lyrics of the song *Lonely is the Night* by the pop group, Air Supply after Cathy skillfully paraphrased the lyrics in one of her letters to me. She would also dedicate a song or two using the local NBC Radio Station *Karai Blong Mambu* through its Listener's Choice programs, but I never had the chance to pick up the songs because of the poor reception in Vanimo.

9

The Moments of Agony and Ecstasy

Nothing was more exciting in life than the moments when Cathy and I would receive a letter from each other. We then had to put away everything and spend good long hours reading the letters, dreaming and fantasising over and over, before shelving it away for later reading. Despite the many letters we wrote to each other, our anticipation for still more letters from each other became an everyday desire and dream. I kept Cathy's letters in a folder. And as more and more letters came in, the folder got thicker and thicker. By the end of the fifth month, I had to use a paper binder to keep every page of her letters in place. They were all sensational love letters, letters that anyone would want to keep and run his eyes through everyday. Interestingly, our folders eventually became good romantic reading materials. At times, when I found my day boring or stale, I would reach out for the folder and go through some of the letters to enlighten my day again. I hoped Cathy did the same too.

One fine Thursday afternoon, in early November, I received a letter from Cathy in the office mail tray. As it was always usual for me, my heart jumped with joy when I recognised her usual handwriting on the cover envelope. Picking up the letter, I quickly walked out of the office and sat myself in a secluded spot, away from all disturbances to read the letter. I accustomed myself to Cathy's promptness in her letters, but unlike her many other previous letters, this particular one was a bit unusual and rather extraordinary. It was thick, as if it contained something solid, but soft and tender when pressed. There was certainly something inside. And when I tore open the cover envelope, the letter emitted a sweet scent, something nice that smelt more like a perfume in my nostrils. Suspecting perfume at first, I spread open the letter only to find in the centerfold of the first page, loose petals of a beautiful red rose. They were nicely prepared and pressed, as if from the hands of a field botanist, with the crimson color, the scent and everything else still fresh and intact.

"This is for you with love", Cathy wrote in her letter about the rose.

I had seen flowers being exchanged to symbolise love and romance between couples, lovers and friends, and so was amazed by Cathy's yet another extraordinary way of expressing her love to me.

"I could have been presented with a bouquet of red roses if I had been around close by", I thought to myself, recapturing some of the scenes in Hollywood movies, as I admired the loose petals in the letter.

But, on the contrary, I soon learned some hours later that there was something more to it than just another gesture of love. It soon occurred to me that after I finished reading the letter, unlike Cathy's other past letters, I found this particular one almost difficult to put it away. There was an unusual urge and desire to keep reading the letter over and over again, which I did many times later in the house and later in the night until sleep deprived me any more rights to continue reading. And quite strangely, in the long night, my thoughts and desires for Cathy Gior escalated, and eventually soared to an height, never experienced before. Her phantasmal image continued to appear like apparition and remained glued like a poster in my mind. I had received many similar love letters from Cathy before, but never had I been hypnotised by any one of them, and this particular one was seemingly strange. I could not sleep and stayed up all night. Then, without any objection I immediately suspected love poisoning. I suspected Cathy to have enchanted the letter with incantation, or used a love potion of some kind in the recent letter, hopefully to net me permanently for herself, I thought.

I walked to the refrigerator in the middle of the night and took a glass of cold water, but that did not help very much. I tried to induce sleep but it never came. The insomnia effect of the suspected love poisoning was unbearably overwhelming. Worse still, my preternatural desire for Cathy soared and increased to such a peak that, strangely, I decided right in the middle of the night to fly to Hobe Community School, and see Cathy. It was an extraporaneous decision and I couldn't clearly recall what exactly forced me into making such a decision, but my mind was already fixed. Attempts made to reconsider the decision failed on all occasions. My next plan was to concoct an excuse for my boss to take a break, an excuse that will convince my boss to allow me to take leave. And it did not take long to think one up. I planned to take compassionate leave on the pretext of visiting my sick mother in Kundiawa General Hospital.

In the ensuing hours towards dawn, I commenced on a single page letter, purporting to have been sent from home, outlining that my mother was sick and in critical condition in Kundiawa General Hospital. I emphasised that she was due for a major surgery and the doctor's prognosis after the operation was not too good. I concocted other stories of home to make the letter sound genuine and authentic to the boss and carefully folded it into Cathy's cover envelope, which had my name, address and the recent post-marked stamp.

I was up early in the morning. It was Friday. Peter Burger, my boss would be there in the office with all the other divisional managers for an early morning audience with the General Manager. I planned to confront him before that morning brief so that my concern can be raised at the briefing. Without taking any breakfast I rushed to the office. But Peter Burger arrived late, some twenty minutes later in his utility pick-up. Navigating his way through the small crowded car park he pulled into his parking space. I confronted him as he stepped out of his car. I had not rested well last night, and Peter Burger immediately noticed my weary eyes almost going to sleep in the sockets of my haggard face and eyed me with curiosity.

"Are you alright?" he asked.

"No, boss", I quickly replied, simulating compassion and anxiety on my face.

"I can see that", Peter said, "Something wrong?"

I quickly slipped my hands into my side pocket and produced my fabricated letter. Without speaking a word, my boss beckoned me to follow him into the office.

"Now what is it", he asked, as he settled himself into his chair.

"This letter, boss", I said, holding the letter up in front of him, "It's from home. I received it yesterday afternoon".

"What is it all about?"

He listened, while I explained the contents and the situation I had created back home, his eyes occasionally glancing at the letter in my hand.

"Well, that's serious, what do you intend to do now?" he finally asked, when I finished.

"I'm thinking of taking a week off to Kundiawa and visit my sick mum in the hospital, if that can be allowed by the company," I said, looking sad and depressed.

Peter sat in silence for a few minutes, glanced at the letter in my hand, and without daring to take it, or even read it, let out his view.

"Listen Joe", he said, "I don't think the company will furnish you with an airline ticket for such travel on leave without pay. It's against the company's policy, you'll have to meet your own airfares".

"I am prepared to do that", I said with a bit of emotion. There was silence for a moment. Then, as if something vital came to his mind, Peter spoke to me again with an inquisitive gaze.

"When is your Annual Leave due?", he asked.

"Mid- December---about four weeks from now", I replied.

"Well then, since you have a more serious case at hand, why don't you apply for your three-week annual leave, and qualify for an airline ticket".

"That's a great idea…thank you, boss", I replied back enthusiastically. "I'll do exactly that", I said.

Peter assured me that he would talk about my leave and travel with the general manager during the morning audience and come back to me.

"Don't go away", he advised, and disappeared into the General Manager's office.

I was waiting at the front office counter when Peter showed up again some thirty minutes later, and motioned me to follow him into our office.

"When do you want to leave?" he asked.

I knew the GM must have given his consent.

"As soon as possible. Tomorrow is the best time I can think of, if we can get everything arranged today", I said, with a little bit of demand.

"Tomorrow? Saturday?"

"Yes, boss", I said, unmoved with my decision.

"Ok, make sure you get a leave form filled out, signed and copies made available to the personnel officer and the accounts section respectively now. I'll get both sections to speed up things for you.

"Thanks boss", I called back, and disappeared happily to the personnel office to collect the necessary leave forms. My plan had worked out perfectly as expected and I was already over the moon as I pranced towards the Personal Section.

It was a pay week Friday and I collected all my dues, including my leave entitlements at 4.00pm in the afternoon. My airline ticket, leave pay and fortnight earnings for the pay period ending that week, were all paid in full. The airline ticket had a confirmed booking for the next day's Px flight to Mt Hagen via Wewak. With joy in my heart, I walked out of the office. I knew very well that my trip was going to be a very special one, filled with adventures and exciting moments that couldn't go by without being captured, and so quickly purchased a Fuji brand 135mm camera in the Garamut Enterprise supermarket. I loaded it with a 36-slide roll of film. I also purchased some extra rolls for spare. Without wasting anymore time, I hurried home early and packed my bag for the next day's trip to Wewak, Mt Hagen, Kundiawa and finally Hobe.

I made my bag as light as possible. I packed two shorts and two shirts for my use and two 'T' shirts with the border design I had bought for Cathy as memento at Sandaun Printing, the local screen print shop in Vanimo. Satisfied and with everything set and ready for departure, I took a stroll down to Narimo pub for a few beers with friends and workmates, and to pass time in order to speed up the night. And as usual, every pay week Friday, the pub was packed. I found almost everyone in the beer garden, all my friends and workmates. Within minutes, our table was heaped with beers of all varieties; white SP cans, brown SP bottles, wines and individual favorites that took us into the late hours.

The Px flight to Mt Hagen was to depart Vanimo at 11.30pm after a quick return international flight into Jayapura, just across the border in the Indonesian province of Irian Jaya. With my head still dizzy after the night's heavy drinking, I checked in at 10.00am when the F28 Foker aircraft was lifting off for Jayapura. It returned fast and by 11:45am we were up in the air again, cruising between Wewak and

Vanimo. At about 1.00pm, the plane finally touched down at Kagamuga airport after a brief stopover in Wewak. I picked up my bag at the arrival lounge, and got onto an airport bus to town, where I transferred to a waiting 15-seater Toyota Ace that was making an afternoon return run to Kundiawa.

There were some vacant seats still available in the bus. The operator preferred to have all his seats fully occupied and made several rounds in the township, making occasional stops at the usual bus stops, hoping for passengers to board. And after non-stop patterings of his intended route, "Simbu…Simbu…Simbu…Kundjip…Minj…Whagi Bris" by the side crewmember, passengers gradually filled up the remaining seats. Soon, we were all set to pull out. Some ten minute later, after refueling at Kalakai Service Station, we zoomed out of Mt Hagen, heading down the Waghi valley along the Okuk highway, heading east for Kundiawa.

The Toyota Ace was fast and made a direct break neck run to Kundiawa, making only three stops along the highway to offload and take in new passengers at Minj, Ga-nigle and Kor-nigle. It finally arrived in Kundiawa at 2.10pm. It was Saturday afternoon and there was not much activity in the town. Most shops had closed by 12.00 noon for the weekend, and the town was almost deserted. I quickly crossed the street over to the police station. I decided to take the shortcut rather than going around the main street, and hurried along the back alley to the front of Sika Store, crossed over to the PNGBC bank and finally the airport. There were some people crowding around inside the airport fence, and one of the steel containers in the airport had its doors wide opened. I quickly walked into the group of people crowding there. I wanted to check if there was any aircraft making a run to Negabo. Otherwise, I planned to spend the night in Kundiawa.

There was an MAF Cessna at the tarmac, but no sign of the pilot. "The plane just flew in from Karamui and won't be making any more trips there", some by-standers informed, "…but the Simbu Aviation is doing a last run to Negabo and the plane is still in Bomai", another said.

That was great news! I thanked them, and quickly hurried across to the ticketing officer at the Simbu Aviation counter, who was operating in the steel cargo container that had had its doors wide opened. The ticketing officer happened to be Toby, a tribesman from the Wandike clan. I had known him personally, and after a moment handshake, I quickly enquired about the Negabo flight.

"There is only one flight going to Negabo, the last flight for today. You're going down there, are you?" he asked, as if he knew about my plan.

"Yes, I am going there," I quickly replied.

Toby shook his head seriocomically and asked, "Its late, are you visiting someone down there, or just taking a joy trip?"

"I am visiting Cathy…Cathy Goir!", I frankly told him.

"Cathy Gior? The daughter of James Goir and Angela Kumo?"

"That right, she's teaching down there".

"She was up here about a month ago, and went back with a couple of other young Siako kids. They haven't come back up yet, so they should all be down there", said Toby.

"That's good. I am going down there to see them", I said, and asked, "Will there be enough space available in the flight, that's going?"

"Sure, there'll be plenty of space. There are only three passengers going on this flight, plus some medical supplies for Negabo Health Center. I can put you on, if you like", Toby said, and looked up to me.

"Put me first on the passenger manifest", I demanded, without wasting a second.

"That will be K35.00", he said.

I quickly slipped my hands into my pocket, produced some bills and counted out to him the K35.00 fare.

"The plane should be coming in any minute. It has already left Bomai", said Toby, as he issued me a receipt for the fare.

It was not long after we finished that we heard the fading drone of the single engine Cessna coming up from the South. Toby and I rushed out of the container. Just beneath the South Simbu mountain ranges, around the base of Mt Wikauma following the Whagi River a moving dot rolled forward, enlarged and eventually dropped altitude above Kel for landing. "That's it, the plane is coming", Toby said, and disappeared into the container. The Cessna finally touched down and taxied up the runway and came to a stop in front of us, next to the MAF Cessna. The Australian pilot got out from the cockpit and after helping the passengers out, directed the ground crew to ready the plane for its next and final run. It was Toby who took over from there to prepare the plane while the pilot was going through the passenger and cargo manifest. Later the pilot went around the aircraft, checking his machine from the outside, including the fuel content.

It did not take long. Some twenty minutes later, boarding call was announced and we boarded the aircraft. I was directed by the loadmaster, Toby, to sit next to the pilot, obviously to balance the light aircraft at the front that was fully loaded with boxes containing medical supplies for the Negabo Health Center in the back compartments of the aircraft. "You can be the co-pilot on this run", Toby joked, as he directed me to the front seat next to the pilot. The three other passengers took the back seats just behind us. The pilot helped us with the seat belts, and five minutes later, we were up in the air.

We trekked the mighty Waghi River south from the air. The pilot, who had been flying this route many times before, maneuvered his single engine Cessna at a very low altitude down the South Simbu gorge. It was my first experience to fly in one such aircraft, and I sat restlessly next to the pilot---who appeared cool and relaxed just across me---hoping every minute that we got to Negabo, safe and soon, as he meandered through the gorge following the river south. We passed the Gunage Range with its eye-catching vermilion and octane soils on the left. I saw the Segima Health Center with its tin-sheet roofs, where I had once traveled there with a friend in his Four-Wheel Drive. It was picturesque, given the natural beauty of the geography and the subsistence activities on the mountainous terrains, surrounding the Health Center.

On the opposite face of the gorge, to the right, was Omkolai with Gumine station in the background, and on the bench above the Maril River was Dirima Catholic Mission just before the station. We passed Kilau, then Nomane and, minutes later, we were above the rain forest plains of Karamui. I could see the richly blessed conifers of *Hoop* and *Klinkii* pine stands spreading out on the plains, in the gullies, and along the ridge tops below me. I had learnt of these Araucaria stands, some years back, at the Forestry College and was amazed at its dominance and extent. There were only three areas in PNG where this tree species was found growing naturally; Bulolo-Wau in Morobe province, Jimi Valley in the Western Highlands province and Karamui plateau in Simbu province. And here I was looking down at the Karamui stands as they spread out below me in the plains of the Papua basin. Ancient as they were, it was truly a magmificent sight, seeing them sticking out in their conical form from above the canopies of broad-leafed forest, as if attempting to reach the skies. And with the white elongated strands of lichens that hung loosely covering the branches and blowing gently to the direct of the breeze, it gave a wonderful impression of a thousand decorated Christmas trees standing on the plains to greet Fr Christmas and his reindeers. As a career forester it was an opportune moment to fly across this forest area, and I enjoyed the scene with great admiration. A few minutes later, we circled above Negabo station.

The Negabo airstrip was constructed next to the Sub-Health center, and I could see people gathering up at the far northern end of the strip to 'welcome' the incoming aircraft that was going to land soon. The pilot approached from the south to make the landing and, as the plane was going in, I spied from above to my right, some houses in a clearing just outside Negabo station with tin sheet roofs. In the same direction, further down depressed in a valley among the Oak forest, I saw another lot of houses; about two with tin sheet roofs, and a couple of others with sago thatched roof tops. A murky dry weather road seemed to string the two places to Negabo station. I was to learn soon after touch down that the first lot of houses I espied was Tua Community School, and the next further down was Hobe Community School, the school where Cathy Gior was teaching. And it was where my final journey was going to end.

The landing was a bit rough on the newly-constructed runway, but the pilot, who had landed his craft there many times before, taxied his plane to a stop at the usual northern end of the strip. He stopped the propeller and went out to open the exits from the outside. We made our way out but I attracted a lot of attention, as I disembarked. I was a new face amongst the passengers disembarking in that rural location, and many eyes followed me wherever I went. Briefly, I imagined Cathy Gior rushing across to greet me from amongst the onlookers, but nothing like that happened. The other three passengers were whisked away by their friends and waiting family members. I soon learnt that they were all resident government officers---two of them Health Workers at the Negabo Health Center and the other an Agriculture officer attached to the IFAD-funded South Simbu Rural Development Project, based at Negabo. I let my eyes wander among the rural crowd to see if I could catch sight of any familiar face I had known before, but the search was futile. There were not many passengers for the return trip, and with a lone passenger beside him, the pilot lifted off again for Kundiawa.

It was 4.04pm on my watch, and the sun was almost sinking in the west. In the next thirty minutes or so, it would all be an evening without the sun. Darkness would close in next and, on perception, I was expected to act quickly, before it was dark to find my way to Hobe. With my handbag in hand, I quickly walked across the field. I decided that the best person I should ask about Hobe, was one of the passengers, we had traveled together on the flight. I could not locate the other two, but the third passenger was still there, gathering his bags and the medical supplies together with his wife and children and other helpers. Tapping him lightly over the shoulder, I excused him. He turned, and upon noticing me, got to his feet.

"Hi, my name is Joe", I said.

"Mine is Tine, we traveled together, did we?", said the officer, with an amicable smile. He was friendly, and had a typical Sinasina intonation with his diction. I was to learn later that he was one of the CHWs at the Negabo Health Center.

"Yes, we travelled together. But I am new here, and a bit lost".

"Oh, okay, what can I do for you?", Tine asked.

"I am trying to go to Hobe", I said, "But I am not sure which direction, or road to take. Can you show me where Hobe Community School is, please?" I inquired, as a matter of urgency.

"Are you a teacher?" Tine asked, a bit curious.

"No, I'm not a teacher, but I am visiting a friend who is teaching there. But this is my first time around here", I said.

"Oh, I am sorry, then. Hobe is far down that way", Tine said, pointing out to the east; to the direction of the buildings I had seen from the air. My eyes keenly followed his hand.

"Is that the road to follow?" I asked, pointing out to a portion of a pitch-black earth surface road, that disappeared into a dense Oak forest, overlooking Negabo.

"That's it. It's quite a distance from here. You'll have to walk a couple of hours, two at the most, to get there".

Tine briefly explained and pinpointed the popular landmarks and common features along the route, as I listened. "Just across there and beyond is Tua Community School", he said, "Hobe Community School is the next, further down in the depression. That road across there ends at Hobe Community School. It will take you sometime to reach Hobe from Tua", Tine said.

Then, glancing at his watch, Tine offered to accommodate me with his family at their home, as it was getting late. "You can travel down early tomorrow morning", he said. But I thanked him for his kindness, and obstinately refused. I had seen both Tua and Hobe from the air, and was confident to make the trip safely to Hobe before dark.

"I'll be fine. I think I'll make it to the school in time before night fall, alright", I assured Tine. "Thank you very much for your help. I truly appreciate your kindness", I said.

"Well, good luck then, and safe trip" Tine replied, smiling. Without wasting anymore time, I bade farewell to Tine and his family, and set out on the last leg of my journey.

Negabo station was built on the high grounds on the southern slopes of Mt Karamui, an extinct prehistoric volcanic peak. Hobe was depressed in a location on the south-eastern base of the same peak. I had to descend eastward to reach my destination. By good luck, the declivity, to my advantage, made my journey at that crucial time of the day much easier. In less than twenty minutes, I was already approaching Tua Community School. A signboard, welcoming visitors to the school, was clear and visible at the entrance gate of the school. I walked past the school and continued at a non-stop pace along the dark earth road. New faces along this road were rare, and I saw some teachers coming out of their houses to check out who I was. But I did not bother to stop or confer with them. 'Good afternoon' was all I managed to throw at any of the closest one I passed, and continued at a steady pace.

On my clock, it was ticking towards 5.00pm and, on perception, I was racing against time to get to my unknown destination when there was still light. I had seen it all from the air. The last journey would upredictably be the difficult part of my entire trip with the hike to come. I steadily doubled my pace to about forty steps per minute through the thickly dense Oak Forest, crossing countless cool pristine rivers and creeks, and over the many log bridges, until I arrived, at what looked like, a flood plain along a flat topography. Moments later, I came across some old abandoned garden sites. There were signs of people frequenting the places around there, and bush tracks leading off from the main road into the surrounding forests areas. Hopefully, I was more or less getting closer to some villages, I thought. And I was not wrong. A few minutes later, I came across the first lot of houses, a village. Domesticated animals roamed freely under the high post houses that were made of thatched sago palm leaves. A bawl from a baby was heard in the nearest house, and there were voices heard in the next house. I asked the first person in sight and realised that I was only couple of hundred meters away from Hobe Community School.

Feeling relieved at last, I continued down the road, this time at a lagging pace and eventually climbed over a fence, that took me into the front yard of, first, the Masi South Simbu Rural Development Project's Agriculture Extension Center, and next, the Hobe Catholic Church. The latter was a huge building constructed of bush materials. Tine briefly mentioned them both up at Negabo airstrip, and they were in their respective places, as he had described them. Hobe at last, I thought. The school should be nearby somewhere around here, I thought. Feeling relieved, I paused to look around for a while to locate the school but, with the darkness now slowly closing in, I couldn't see clearly from where I was. But never had I known, that only a few steps behind the church building, was the Community School. And only a few seconds walk, from where I was standing, was Cathy Gior's house.

There were gardens around the church and the adjacent areas surrounding the church. The road I had followed narrowed and finally petered out in front of the church. After the brief respite, I followed a track that went around the church to the back, and good golly, there right in front of me in the dusk, through the banana field, were the two buildings with the tin sheet roofs I had seen from the plane. There was no mistake. I was now looking at the only two double classroom buildings in Hobe Community School. A glimmer of joy swept through my exhausted body. My journey had finally come to an end, as in a few moments, I should be comfortably sheltered with Cathy in one of the houses just across the garden, I thought.

Gee, I should have noticed that along time ago, I thought, feeling more relaxed, as I tried to recount the amazing odyssey, which had taken me into this unknown territory; in the low land jungles of Papua, and close to the border of the Gulf and Simbu provinces. I tried to think up whether this was all real, but it sure was. I was not dreaming, nor was it a hallucination. I was standing within the precincts of Hobe Community School, where all my voluminous letters ended up, and from where all of Cathy Gior's sensational letters had emanated. Cathy was surely expecting a reply to her latest letter, but ironically, this time it will be the author who will be knocking at the door—unbelievable! I smiled inanely at the thought. Perhaps, there was a better reason why one had to risk taking such a long, tough and costly trip to an unknown territory but, in truth, it was the power of love. I now learnt that love had its own games to play on its victims. Certainly, if there was something in the whole wide world so precious in life to risk one's own life, even if it means to cross a turbulent waterway, climbing a high mountain or braving through a stormy night, it had to be love.

I was now standing in the middle of a crossroad to the school, the church and some houses next to the church. Further up to my front was a track that I later learnt to link Haia, another remote station in Karamui, to Negabo. I was going to take the track leading to the school when suddenly a young man in his 30s' stepped out of a large sago thatched roof house, and conveyed his evening greetings. He was to be Luke, the catechist of the nearby Hobe Catholic Church and was later to become a very important person during my stay. He must have seen me, a total stranger, from inside his house.

"Are you looking for someone?" he asked, as he reached out for a handshake.

"Yes, I am", I said, as I greeted him, "I am looking for a lady teacher who is teaching here".

"Is she Miss Gior?" he asked?

With only one single lady teacher at the school, Luke did not make any mistake.

"Yes, Miss Gior", I said, almost exictedly.

"That's her house over there", he said, pointing to a sago-thatched roof house that was only a few steps away in front of us. "Come, follow me, I'll take you there", Luke said, and led the way towards the house.

With my heart pounding, I followed closely behind, trying to picture what will happen in the next minute when we stand at the door. He led me through the banana field, and some 60 seconds later we stood in front of the sago-thatched house, that was erected high above the ground on wooden stilts. There was light in the house and muffled noise of young people, laughing boisterously inside, but the door was closed, obviously to keep out the deadly mosquitoes that were buzzing around in great numbers. A record player was doling out a popular PNG tune, well above the noise of the mirth.

Posing himself on the ground in front of the door, Luke called into the house. I stood back and listened but no response came. After a second attempt, the sound volume of the cassette player was lowered, and the door suddenly opened. A gangling youth, in his early teens, stood at the door and, after a moment of gazing, jumped to the ground and rushed across to greet me. It was Siune Sakrias, son of a Siako relative of Cathy. I recognised him immediately. Soon after, everyone in the house raced for the door to check out, when Siune raised the alarm of my arrival. "It's Joe-Joseph Tamgo", he kept bawling. Toby was right in Kundiawa. There was Poka, son of Cathy's aunt and Anasas, Cathy's own younger sister. Cathy had brought them all to Hobe to keep her company in this lonely remote school. There was instant joy in the eyes of everyone, when they saw me.

Cathy Gior showed up last and could not believe her eyes at all, when she stood at the doorway. She was preparing her next day's lessons when the announcement of my arrival interrupted her from her work. But this was of little concern, as it turned out later. My presence must have meant more to her that evening, because she packed up and put away everything and never bothered to touch them again. We threw ourselves at each other, as if we had not met for ages, when I walked up to the house, and remained in that fixture for a long while, before letting each other free. She later told me, while we were alone in her room, that she almost fainted at first sight, when she saw me with Luke outside the house.

After greeting me, Cathy invited Luke into the house for a cup of hot Milo, which was still hot near the fireplace. Luke gratefully accepted and left soon after he finished his cup, thanking everyone. I was served rice and bully beef for dinner. It was a well-deserved meal, as all my energies had been exhausted and lost during the tiresome journey. How these imported food items ended up down there in that remote school puzzled me too, as I gobbled them but did not bother to question where they got them, as my presence in the house was still unbelievable. Cathy still could not accept the fact that I was there amongst them.

"It that really you, Joe?" she'd keep asking me with leers. I would occasionally force a laugh, as I ate. And once or twice, amidst my mouthfuls, "I guess, I am", I would say, with chuckles that would put smiles on the faces of everyone.

And, "I really can't believe your presence here at all", Cathy would say, adding, "Maybe, I'll believe tomorrow when I find that you are still here".

"Oh, come on, Cathy! That's even worse than our biblical Thomas. It's me, I'm right here now. I don't think you need a concrete proof to believe my presence", I said, "Don't be surprised if you find me snoring in bed with you tonight", I joked, putting laughter and smiles on the faces of the youngsters.

When the noise of the laughter finally petered out, I recounted the story of my odyssey. Everyone was amazed at my tale and a lot of puerile questions followed next, that kept the whole evening alive till late. Later in the night, when Cathy and I were alone in her room, "It was the call of love", I twitted. "This is the longest and the most adventurous trip of all time that I ever took in my life in a single day. Interesting indeed, and if anything tragic had happened to me along the way, it would have certainly been in the name of love". Cathy giggled, leered at me provocatively for a while and fell into my arms for a night of never-ending smooching, couplings, rousing and more smooching, couplings and rousing, that I was to remember for many years later.

10

Fun, Romance and Embarrassment

My stay in Hobe was full of fun and romance. I enjoyed every minute of it. During the day, I'd stay at home with the three exuberant Siako striplings while Cathy went to take her class. She would come back whenever she found time to check on us, chat for a while, and then return back to her class again. After 3.00pm when classes ended for the day, it was all our time. Cathy and I would leave everyone in the house and spend most of the afternoons alone in her classroom, or go for rambles around the school gardens, checking her agricultural plots. We would engage ourselves in many long hours of emotional discussions that were splendidly full of dreams and romance. She told me everything, she had to tell me, and I did the same in return.

"About the rose", I asked one evening, as we took a stroll around the school garden, that she'd enclosed with the letter, she sent to me. "This was no ordinary flower, was it?"

"Did you get the flower?", she quickly asked, looking into my eyes with a grin.

"Off course, I did".

"Did you like it?"

"Beautiful! It was still fresh, the aroma and everything".

Cathy smiled.

"I picked it up at a friend's house up in Negabo", she quickly said.

"It sure was beautiful. I placed it in my diary and it's still with me", I said. Then, "Can I ask you something?" I said.

"Yes, what is it?"

"Was there anything else in the letter apart from the rose?" I asked.

Cathy paused with a frown, thought for a while and then, "No, I don't think I enclosed anything else other than a rose. What else did you find in the letter?"

"Oh, nothing really, it's just that I find that particular letter containing the rose a bit unique from all your other letters".

"How? I mean, what happened?", she asked, curious and almost knowingly.

'Well, first, it emitted a beautiful scent when I opened it. Secondly, I could not sleep, or put the letter away after I finished reading. Thirdly, my desire for you soared and glowed like a burning fire. And fourth, I had to board the next available flight out of Vanimo just to see you. Anyway, to make a long story short, I thought I was love poisoned through that letter".

"What do you mean by 'love poisoned'?", Cathy asked curiously, and from what I thought I saw, Cathy was slightly shaking, when she answered me.

"Well, I suspected the rose to have been enchanted with a love potion, or some incantatory that really played its charms on me, good and proper".

Cathy did not speak for a while. She appeared startled and remained mute, as if being trapped somewhere. Her eyes fell and the smile faded away on her face, as qualms of guilt began to surface. I instinctively realised that I could be getting closer to revealing something, with the peaceful atmosphere dramatically changing in the last few seconds. There was scruple and frustration in Cathy's eyes too, as if she was struggling to admit something. But that was introspectively not necessary. I certainly did not mean to cause any frustration or harm, as it was only out of sheer curiosity that I had asked about the rose, and quickly laughed it out in order to dismiss the sense of anxiety in her, and possibly neutralise the anxious situation I had placed her in.

"Look, I am sorry, I didn't mean to hurt you, or cause any frustration", I quickly confessed. "You see, I was a bit confused after receiving it, and off course, reading that letter containing the rose, because I couldn't go to sleep or put away the letter. I thought I was love poisoned. Really, it's only an assumption that I'm trying to prove right from you while I am here. So, please don't get me all wrong".

"It's all right, I understand", Cathy muttered, after some moments of deep thought.

"That's good, thank you for your understanding. In fact, I loved all your letters. There is nothing wrong with all of them. They truly kept my moments in Vanimo alive without you there. And they still are, even today, Cathy" I said.

Cathy smiled. It was a gorgeous smile and a provocative one too, and as I remained dazzled at the sight of the perfectly lined teeth between her soft lips, "If you don't mind, Joe, I might just as well explain what happened", Cathy said.

"No, not at all! Go, right ahead, just spit them out. Anything you say is music to my ears"

Cathy exploded with a burst of laughter at my hyperbolic remark, and then after a few moments let out the truth.

"To be honest, I know nothing about magic and love potions", Cathy said, "A nurse friend in Negabo mentioned the power of a proven love potion she had in her possession, and how to go about using it, in a general discussion. I became interested, and when I asked, if we could try it out in one of my letters to you, she agreed. She needed a flower, and we picked the rose behind her house. She did everything that was required to be done, and gave me the rose with the instructions to put it in the envelope together with the letter and send it away. I only supplied your name, and complied to the instructions she gave me".

"So, the rose was the culprit behind everything, correct?", I said, laughing.

"I never really believed that it will work, but it must have worked", Cathy cut in.

I let out a smile.

"You can't believe this", I said, "Whatever your friend did to that rose, the magic, or whatever it was, did work two hundred percent with all its power and might, and had a tremendous effect on me".

"Oh, no…please.", Cathy mumbled, placing her hands over her lips.

"Yes! It really worked on me, Cathy, good and proper. Believe me. Otherwise, you may never see me here", I admitted.

"Then, I am so sorry, Joe", Cathy apologised, trying all she could to secure my forgiveness. "Should I get back to the nurse friend and advise her to destroy, or reverse the power or…or withdraw whatever she did to that rose?" she asked later.

"Off course not. And that's not even necessary, either", I quickly cut in. "Don't even worry about it, Cathy. Whatever your friend did to that rose did not do any harm, or cause any inconvenience. As a matter of fact, it does not hurt to be with you right now. Don't you think so? I'm in heaven really, believe me. It's the letter that I was curious about. But I don't think, you really need love potions or incantations, or get someone to orchestrate such things to bring me closer to you because I am already nailed to you. You should know that I was already nailed to you along time ago when we were kids, trying to roast *kaukaus* together at your place". Cathy chuckled with provocative glances, and I knew she was recalling the scenes at Toromambuno on that fateful Tuesday many years ago.

"That was many years ago", she said.

"That's right. And all you have to do now is to simply write, or pick up the phone whenever you need or want me. I'll certainly be there, when and wherever you will want me to be."

"I don't think, I'll ever do that again in the future", Cathhy said with a look.

"Well, I don't think, it's necessary either", I cut in.

"Believe me, there won't be anything of such in the future"

I had decided to stay with Cathy for at least two weeks in Hobe, and spend the remaining week with my parents at Bokan before returning to Vanimo. But, quite unexpectedly, this itinerary was cut short by a mysteriously frightening incident in the first week. It all started when Cathy swooned and became comatose on the night of the fourth day. The incident happened without any symptom of a common illness or fever, as we were wrapping up for the night, after a pleasant day of swimming and mountain climbing at a nearby mountain, overlooking the school. It all happened so suddenly while Cathy was laying on the bed to dose off. And I wouldn't have found out, had she not let out strange moans of agony in her sleep. I tried to wake her up by shaking her frame, but she remained unmoved and continued to let out terrible moans, with her body gradually stiffening. I never came across any incident of that kind before in my life, and panicked almost immediately in the room when I learnt of her situation. I quickly alerted Poka, Sakrias and Anasas to come into the room, but they were equally held spellbound, and were just as scared as I was. Panic-stricken, we called in the headmaster of the school, and the other three teachers into the room. "What happened?" they all asked, as they entered, but we were short for explanations. "She just passed out mysteriously", was all we told them.

I tried to explain what actually happened in the room but the incident was something paranormal and beyond a non-medical specialist's intelligence, and very little came out of my lips. There was talk of possible causes, but all were superficial, based on assumptions. I was practically lost and remained a worried man all along, as the talks wore on. The absence of a medical person nearby, with the locale of the nearest medical facility, some five kilometers away in Negabo, and the non-availability of a mechanised transport system narrowed all my hopes for immediate medical attention, and these were of greatest concern to me, as we sat watch over Cathy Gior.

Suddenly, amidst our discussions there were abrupt movements coming from Cathy. She would struggle to speak something, but after some efforts, nothing came out of her lips. And if she did mumble something, it was just some odd sounds and nothing more. Anasas, being the only female amongst us, occasionally moved up to her elder sister to comfort her and begged her sister to talk, but Cathy would fall back into a coma again, seconds later.

The latest development brought something into the mind of a young teacher, and soon he disclosed the likely cause of the catalepsy.

"I think she is being visited by an incubus", the teacher said, almost confidently, "I think, I saw you all during the day at the top of the mountain across the school. According to the local belief here, certain spots on that mountain are forbidden to young girls, and I think she trespassed one of the boundaries".

"I think you are not wrong", the headmaster immediately cut in, nodding his head, "Cathy's abrupt body movements, and the indecipherable sounds meant that she is actually trying to communicate with somebody, some mysterious person".

In a remote jungle area, where myths and superstition are accepted and believed widely, the teacher sounded correct in everything he said.

Being apparently lost and confused, we were ready to believe anything with the cause of the illness still dubious in our minds and there was no way we could ignore or dispute the teacher's diagnosis. Immediately, Luke was called in to verify the teacher's assumption. The local catechist, who had always remained solicitous about the spiritual welfare of the Hobe community, urgently demanded to know the whereabouts of Cathy during the day after viewing her condition.

"We swam at the creek near the school ground, and then climbed that mountain across the creek by going around the precipice to the summit. After taking some photo shots of the school, we travelled back down the way we went up", I briefly explained.

"Did you reach the top?"

"We did. That's where we stood to take some photos".

"Then, you have trespassed into the forbidden ground", the catechist quickly interjected, saying, "That area is out of bounds; a forbidden ground to all females, especially young girls. Cathy is certainly possessed and crippled by the spirit, who dwells there".

We were stunned at the revelation and hardly raised a voice to speak. Luke was a local. He knew everything and anything about the area, and we believed him with all our hearts everything he said. We knew, Cathy was fine and healthy prior to the sudden catalepsy, and there was nothing dubious in Luke's revelation to convince us that he was wrong. I was already scared, as he was going through the superstitious details about the area. Upon concluding his talk, he wasted no time, either. He went straight to the remedy and confidently, led a prayer of exorcism to drive out the incubus from Cathy, the spirit that possessed her. He had Holy water with him too in a bottle, and started sprinkling them in the room, in all the other rooms and then went outside, and did the same around the house. Satisfied, Luke entered the house again.

For a time being, Cathy's abrupt movements stopped, but she did not regain her consciousness and, instead, dozed off into a peaceful sleep, unlike moments earlier. It was also getting late in the night, and the headmaster left with his teachers, promising to return and check her progress in the morning. After spending a little while with us, Luke also left. He assured us that everything should be all right for Cathy.

The assurance from the catechist brought some sense of relief to me, as I was the most affected one about Cathy's situation. I had reasons, far more tormenting than the incident itself. Poka, Sakrias and Anasas also withdrew to their beds for sleep.

I remained alone with Cathy on the bed, but sleep did not come to me, given the situation I was faced with. I momentarily felt relieved, as I watched Cathy dozing off peacefully after the exorcism. I still counted on what Luke did, but I was still not yet satisfied of her recovery, and anxiously stayed awake with my eyes open, wondering during the entire night, why I had to come all the way there and get tangled into this situation, till dawn of the next day.

Despite the long hours, we stayed during the night, and everyone woke up early. Cathy still had not yet recovered, and I arranged with the headmaster, when he came around in the morning, to send a student up to Negabo, with a note to seek assistance from the SSRDP Agriculture Officer there, who had a four-wheel-bushman-bike to travel to Hobe, and transport Cathy up to the Negabo Health Center for medical attention. This was arranged. And shortly before 7.00am, a student runner was on his way with the note to Negabo.

Cathy's condition was stable in the house, but we were still kept in suspense for most of the time during the day. Her teaching counterparts made constant visits to check on her progress, and so did Luke, who continuously exorcised the room with prayer and other primeval rites he deemed vital and necessary. Then, to our pleasure, at around 10.30am, Cathy moved for the first time. She spoke for some time and dropped back to sleep again. This brought us a sense of relief and lulled our anxiety. Everyone began to speak of Luke and his powerful exorcism practice. In reality, it was also for the first time that I had ever witnessed such a situation, where exorcism was performed and presumably worked. And I believed and trusted Luke too. Exorcism truly appeared the prophylactic treatment required for Cathy's situation, after all, I thought. But despite the positive sign of recovery, I still preferred a professional medical treatment and prognosis.

It was nearly seven hours later, that we finally heard a fading sound of an engine in the upper reaches of the Negabo plateau. The sound grew louder and louder, as it got closer. And with no other machine or engine running in this part of the world, we knew our 'ambulance' had finally arrived. Within a short while, the four-wheeled, Yamaha engine, bushman bike pulled into the front yard of the school ground. It was Joseph, the DPI officer, we had traveled together in the plane to Negabo, four days earlier. "So, that's where you ended up", he said, smiling at me, when he came over to us. "You just made my day", I said, as we greeted him heartily and, after briefing him of the situation, helped Cathy onto the bike. Luke and the teachers, along with the Siako striplings wished us well when we were ready to go. And amidst waving and well wishes from the Hobe folks, we set out. Cathy was frail and too debilitated to remain steady, and I wedged in along side her for support but, later walked to ease the burden from the combined weight uphill.

After a slow and somewhat tedious journey up the murky Hobe-Negabo road, we finally arrived at the Health Center. A little crowd of curious folks watched us, as we pulled into the front of the outpatient wing. Fortunately, Cathy must have regained full consciousness during the long trip, and managed to walk all by herself to the Health Center; this time, unaided and without even looking for support, or help from anyone. And quite surprisingly too, she also talked as if nothing frightening had happened to her in the last twenty-four hours, and started chatting with some of her nurse friends in the Health Center. I was a bit astounded at the latest state of her condition, and the sudden change of her attitude, but still did not fully recover from the nightmares I had had in the night. I looked on, as she went about greeting and hugging her friends, talking and laughing, as if nothing terrible had happened but I was reluctant to ask or even query her about the state of her condition. All I was pleased with that moment, was the ground on which we now stood, where proper test and medication was now readily available to treat her.

A nurse, who knew Cathy Gior personally, and later introduced to me as Betty, attended to Cathy's case. Could she be the one who 'poisoned' the rose? I would never know. We explained everything that had happened to Cathy, making sure that every information was clear and correct to the last detail. The young nurse, who appeared to be vigorously active in her duties, carried out all the pre-diagnostic tests required on Cathy to identify the common cause of the illness. She attended to it like an emergency case, but to our dismay and also surprise, she found nothing.

"There is nothing wrong with you", the nurse concluded after the examination, and gradually packed away the medical apparatus she had used on Cathy. I stood dumbfounded. Moments later, to my astonishment, Cathy also admitted the same.

"I feel nothing abnormal too", she said, adding, "I feel perfectly fine".

I was surprised at the latest exchange of words and watched in wonderment, as the nurse and her patient gabbed away. It must be an absolute joke last night, I thought, as I stolidly watched as the two women talked and laughed away. But it was too much for me to keep watching and I could not hold on any longer.

"You gave us a terrible nightmare last night. Are you definitely sure you are fine?" I suddenly interrupted, annoyed and irate.

For the first time, I felt anger, deep down inside me but I sulked. Cathy noticed the queer look, and the morose expression on my face, and quickly diverted her attention towards me. She had already sensed the pent-up anger inside me.

"It's strange", she calmly admitted, "I really can't understand, but I feel nothing wrong in me now. I feel absolutely normal, just like yesterday and the day before".

"That's unbelievable; I mean, I can't believe this", I said in a mollified tone, looking puzzled.

"Me too. I can't believe this, either. You know, I was a goner last night".

"So, what could be the possible cause here, then?", I asked.

"Maybe, the catechist was right", Cathy said, "It could be the work of an incubus. We must have certainly trespassed into a forbidden ground upon that mountain top".

"That's right! It could be that," the nurse affirmed, joining us in our conversation. She was preparing a syringe with porcelain for Cathy. "I have been living and working in here for three years now", Betty said, "And this place is full of superstitious myths and beliefs. Certain sites and spots around here are no-go zones for women, especially young girls, and I think Luke did the right thing. Exorcism is the only prophylactic treatment for this sort of cases around here. Modern medicines won't help and the locals here know it better".

"I am considering a transfer out of here", Cathy said, as Betty planted the needle into her right buttock.

It was a windy and chilling afternoon. It was overcast and after the examination and treatment Betty invited us to her house for coffee. She asked us to stay the night with her, as it was getting too late to travel back to Hobe, but Cathy refused.

"I already missed a day's lesson. We must go back", she insisted.

"Then, take my umbrella with you, because the clouds are thick and grey outside. It might rain on the way".

We thanked Betty for her hospitality and set out for Hobe around 4.00pm in the afternoon. The good nurse was not wrong in her prediction. A few meters out of Negabo station, just before reaching the precincts of Tua Community School, we encountered the heavy downpour. Fortunately, we took Betty's umbrella along with us, so graciously cuddled under it. It was a big umbrella, perfect to shelter two teen bodies and we were comfortably safe from the downpour.

But alas, despite the wet and damp weather condition, our cuddling, in no time, developed an inevitable lovey-dovey sensation along that lonely jungle road, that we soon got lost in a world of romantic emotions filled with effusions, smooches and peckings, forgetfully ignoring. the downpour hitting us and the nightmares of the yester-night that had haunted us, making the Negabo-Hobe walk in that teeming rainy afternoon the most pleasant and enjoyable journey in our lives. If there was any moment that richly paid off for the most daring and very long distance trip that I undertook from Vamino to Hobe, I guessed it had to be this Negabo-Hobe walk with Cathy through the lonely rainforest track of singing birds and curious eyes of the wild, as it was here that I believed Cathy and I exposed, demonstrated and experienced all facets of true love and romance in all its entirety.

"I hope you won't give me any more nightmares again tonight", I teasingly reminded Cathy with a smile, when we reached the precints of Hobe.

"Not tonight, Joe" Cathy said, "It's going to be different tonight.

You'll see, I promise", Cathy responded with a leer, as she climbed over the fence at the entrance.

Everyone was anxious about Cathy's condition and there was joy when word reached the school grounds that we were coming back. A child from the village up the road had raced before us to the school and informed everyone. Luke and the teachers and the three worried Siako striplings were all there to meet us when we arrived. They were pleased to see us and crowded around us, as Cathy recounted her ghastly ordeal.

"I'll never go over to that mountain again", she told everyone, "I think Luke is right in what he said".

"I agree with you", the headmaster said in support, and imparted what he learnt of the evil place from the other locals. Luke also cautioned Cathy, and talked more about the evil mountain.

"For as long as I will be here, that place is out of bounds for me now, even the river", Cathy promised Luke.

"The river's alright, but stay away from the mountain. Better not go there again", Luke advised.

Normalcy returned in the house, but Cathy Gior's sudden illness and recovery so shivered my nerves deep down that I no longer felt comfortable to remain at Hobe. I decided to leave the following day. The after effect of what would have likely happened, if Cathy hadn't recovered, drew fear and haunted my memory. I knew, on perception, even before Cathy recovered that I was already in trouble. I knew that I would be solely held responsible for Cathy's ordeal if news of the tragedy leaked to Ende-naige-ingugl. 'She was fine until I showed up and took her up to the forbidden mountain', everyone would be saying. And worst of all, Cathy's parents and relatives would explode in rage with me for almost killing her by taking her up to a restricted place, forbidden to women. Later, in the night, I let Cathy know of my intention to leave in the morning. She looked puzzled, "You must be kidding", she said, and begged me anxiously to stay back for a while, maybe, for another two, or three more days but I politely refused. I was adamant on my decision. "I am sorry, but I'll have to go", I insisted, "My boss is expecting me back soon, and I'll just make a quick trip home from here, before I return to Vanimo", I said.

I had lied, and was swarmed with guilt for lying to Cathy too, but frankly, I didn't want to use her illness and recovery as an excuse, because I did not wish to make her feel responsible for my early return. Cathy was indeed sad, and did not speak a word for some moments, but finally agreed with some reluctance. Then, as a surprise departure gift, I put up a suggestion, if she would like to spend her Christmas holidays with me in Vanimo, knowing very well that I won't be coming home for the Christmas season. "All travel expenses will be covered from my end", I said. As if I had struck a nail on the head, Cathy jumped up to her toes with joy, and threw her arms around my neck with excitement, almost choking me to death. "That would be wonderful", she said, "I'd very much like to see Vanimo and won't miss the opportunity. How will I get up there?", she asked.

"Well, I am thinking of sending you an airline ticket for your travel to Vanimo. How about that?"

"Oh, wonderful, thank you very much".

"I'll arrange that at the Air Niugini office in Vanimo, and you can pick up the ticket at the Air Niugini Reservations Office in Kundiawa when you go up for the break after the close-up here. When do you close-up for Christmas?

"That's great", Cathy said, and quickly ran her eyes through the Education Calendar that was pinned on the wall in her room. With the help of her pointer finger, Cathy came up with the specific dates of when and what will happen towards the end of the school year.

"We will close-up here on December 2nd", Cathy said, "…which is a Friday, and by Monday 5th I should be in Kundiawa".

"Good…can you give me a call when you get there?"

"I will certainly call…how can I forget you? I'll call from the SSRDP office in Kundiawa. I know several people in there who have access to telephone lines".

"Great! You do that because I will have your ticket number ready when you call. We will then arrange, and set a date for your travel, so that I should wait at the airport to pick you up".

"I'll do everything, as you say", Cathy said happily.

"Good, make sure, you don't forget a thing".

"I don't think I will".

"Excellent" I said.

It was a fine Thursday morning. The Simbu Aviation Cessna makes about two flights a day into Negabo, sometimes more or less, depending on the number of cargoes and passengers consigned and en-route to the area. The first flight normally goes in at around 10.00am, and the second comes in usually after mid-day in the afternoon. In spite of the long-distance walk from Hobe to Negabo, there was still a possibility of catching a flight out of Negabo before lunch. But otherwise, I could still jump on the afternoon flight, if I couldn't make it to Negabo before the first flight lands, and I started packing my scanty belongings together.

Eager to accompany me on the return trip was Anasas Gior. She had stayed long enough, I believed, with Cathy in Hobe and, maybe bored to remain there any longer, insisted to travel home with me when she learnt of my departure. Cathy consented to let Anasas go, and quickly arranged with the headmaster for a 'Travel Pass' for her travel. The Pass was a piece of paper issued by the Provincial Division of Education, designed with the Simbu Provincial Government logo affixed at the top, spaces and columns for passenger details in between, and spaces for signature, name and designation of the authorising officer in the bottom left corner. Anasas' details were carefully entered in the appropriate spaces and was signed by the headmaster. All Ananas had to do was to produce the Pass to the pilot, and board the plane without paying any fare. I was amazed at the way the Travel Pass worked but, later, learnt that this was one of the privileges put in place by Simbu Provincial Government for its public servants serving in the remote parts of South Simbu. The pilot accepts the pass, and collects his dues from the Provincial Treasury after producing the pass at the Finance Office in Kundiawa. How amazing and I truly marveled at the way the Simbu Provincial Government was looking after its public servants in the remote Karamui. So, Cathy was not totally lost in that corner after all, I thought.

Anasas and I bade farewell to everyone---Sakrias, Poka and Cathy---with strong hugs, and immediately after breakfast, set out for the long walk to Negabo. It was a sad and heart-breaking moment, as we walked down the steps of the house. I feared for a change of mind any second that could make me reverse my decision, and extend my stay. But this did not happen. I was perhaps brave. We crossed the banana field, and headed in the direction of the Catholic Church. When I looked back, not one person moved from their initial position. I could see them all there, waving at us from the verandah, under the sago thatched roof building. Anasas waved and I waved too. "Bye, we'll see you all later", I called back. Almost instantly, I could see Cathy breaking down and disappear into the house, not wanting to see how we left. It was the last glimpse of my dream girl. I slowly turned. A lot of thoughts ran through my mind but I pushed them aside, and with a painful heart began the long walk to Negabo.

It was a fine day, and we arrived well in time before any flight landed. An incoming flight was expected soon, and there was already a small crowd at the usual northern end of the airstrip when we arrived. We joined them, and had not rested a while when the Simbu Aviation Cessna, making its first flight of the day into Negabo, circled above us to make the landing. A few minute later, the plane taxied to a stop where we waited. The pilot and a single passenger got out of the aircraft. Some minutes later, after off-loading some boxes, the pilot made a call out for passengers traveling to Kundiawa. As it was common in all remote airstrips, it was a 'pay-as-you-enter' ticketing and boarding method, and Ananas boarded first after producing the Pass to the pilot. I watched carefully how the pilot would react to the pass, but after going through the details inscribed therein, he quickly slipped it into his chest pocket. I followed next after paying my fare with cash of K35.00. Two other male passengers followed next and five minutes later we were up in the air again.

Our first stop was Karamui airstrip. But we could not continue to Kundiawa, as en-routed. After touch down, the flight was re-scheduled to make a quick Karamui-Bomai-Karamui run. The pilot advised us to wait around and we disembarked to wait for the plane to make the Bomai flight, before we would continue the Kundiawa flight again. With five new passengers taking their seats in the aircraft, the Cessna coughed out smoke, had its propeller running, and in the next minute, it was up in the air again, heading west towards Bomai. It was an opportune moment to take a sight-seeing walk around the Karamui District Headquarters, and Anasas and I quickly took the opportunity. But Bomai was less than twenty-minutes flight away, and we did not cover the area thoroughly, when the plane touched down again with its load of Bomai passengers. Everyone disembarked and we boarded again, this time with two new passengers in Karamui. The Cessna lifted off again, all seats fully occupied, and twenty-five minutes later, we touched down at Kundiawa airstrip. As I stepped out onto the tarmac, I recalled back to my adventures in Karamui and let out a complacent smile. "Back to civilisation at last", I gladly thought. Will I ever go back there again? No, never again, I thought. Maybe, I will, if Cathy Gior wants me down there again, but not on my own.

I quickly walked Anasas to the Gembogl PMV stop, next to the Piunde Gas Station, and sent her away in a waiting Toyota land cruiser, that was traveling to Mt Wilhelm High School. I stayed back. I wanted to visit some friends in town, and of course, visit the bank too and draw some funds for my family and friends at home. I was out for two years, and it would be foolish of me to show up without any presents or gifts. "I'll spend a night here, and come up tomorrow", I told Anasas, as I put her on the pick-up. She waved back and bid me good luck, as the land cruiser pulled out, to begin its forty-kilometer journey up the Upper Simbu valley.

My quest for Cathy Gior did not go without opposition. The following afternoon, when I went home, I received the first ever, and the most unpleasant reception from Cathy's overbearing mother, Angela Kumo. As anticipated, Kumo was not at all happy about my trip to Hobe, after she learnt everything from Anasas the previous evening. When I arrived at Mondiagl-kaugla in the afternoon, I was snubbed and publicly humiliated with embarrassing invectives for almost causing Cathy's death in Hobe.

I wasn't too sure, how long Kumo had waited for me, but as I got off the PMV, my attention was drawn to a raucous snarl at the far end of the market place. A woman stood up from amongst the many, and howled something down towards the direction, where I had gotten off. Unfortunately, my poor eye sight could not clearly establish her identity, or what she was after, or what she was up to. However, she was certainly fired up, and I could establish that from the distance. With her voice still above anything else, she walked towards my direction, snarling her resentments, as she walked. I had no idea, who she was or what she was snarling about, as I never expected any presentiments of any kind. I was away in Sepik for two years and had no enemies at home. But, then some seconds later, when the woman finally got closer to a distance within my visibility range, my heart trembled and almost ceased pumping when I noticed the woman to be Angela Kumo, Cathy Gior's mother. Almost at once, I felt prickles all over my body, as premonitory shivers of fear shattered through my nerve system. It was clearly evident, Anasas Gior had told her everything to the last detail, and I was in for the worst, heading towards a pot of boiling oil.

Standing at a vantage point, some few meters out, Kumo inveighed me for almost causing death to Cathy. With a fierce countenance, and hostile glare, she belabored me with invectives, which I had never experienced before, never expected from anyone in my life before, and most of all, something least expected from a prospective mother-in-law. There was cordial dislike and animosity in her tone, clearly denoting her dislike of me. And then, she publicly denounced my association with Cathy.

"I never had you in mind, you are wasting your time", she yelled at the top of her voice "There are many other girls out there that you can set your eyes on, but not Cathy", she roared.

She remonstratively asked me why I had to travel all the way to Hobe and almost put Cathy into a coffin. "What were you looking for in Hobe? Have you got a relative living down there", she asked, above the noise of everything else, "What would you do if she had died down there? Do you think, you can ever replace someone like her for me?"

It was just too much, but the questions kept coming. I said nothing, and didn't bother to say anything, with my head hanging loose down my front. Any attempt to voice something in protest to get out of the diatribe, would certainly mean adding fuel to the fire. Hence, I hopelessly remained mute and still during the entire moment Kumo had her field day.

Kumo barked on and on without a break. It was a fine afternoon and she captivated the attention of nearly everyone in the market with her raucous invectives. A huge crowd closed in and circled us; Kumo at the one end, me on the other taking all the invectives and all around us were the many thousand eyes moving between Kumo and myself. Naturally, I perspired a lot, letting out litres of sweat during ordinary moments, and that afternoon, not one sweat gland held back its contents. All over me I could feel twice the amount pouring out over my body. And with the afternoon sun emitting its final rays down on us from above Puglan-gigl, I was wet all over.

Frustrated and blushed crimson with embarrassment, I decided to walked over to a boulder at the roadside, where there was ample shade to cool off, but this seemingly added more fuel in Kumo.

"Why are you trying to run away?", she howled after me, "We are not yet finished, you just can't walk away like this".

Still, I said nothing, and continued to move forward, ignoring her accusations. Angered, she let out everything again---another fresh volley of invectives.

Angela Kumo may have found the entire moment a perfect opportunity to scare the devil out of me, and keep me away from her daughter forever. She must have planned this encounter last night, after learning from Anasas that I'd arrive in the afternoon, and executed it perfectly well in front of the public. She threw everything she got at me, and tried to get me into responding to all her accusations, but I listened in silence, not daring to open my lips. She tried again several times more but still nothing came out from my lips. Maybe, satisfied, and perhaps considering me defeated and totally eliminated, she finally left, cautioning me never to be seen together with Cathy again.

I momentarily felt relieved after the 'volcano' disappeared. But not altogether. Inside me, I found it almost difficult to recover from the humiliation, and public disgrace she had caused with the diatribe. It was truly a regretful predicament, and some onlookers, who witnessed everything, came forward and sat beside me with words of comfort to console me. Others solaced me with words of encouragement. "It common everywhere", they'd say, "… she attacked you publicly, because she's going to prize you with her daughter".

Some had other thoughts, "It is a common disposition of mothers everywhere", they'd say, "You are a young man. So, don't mope down and worry too much about it", and pat me on the back.

Many were indignant over the harangue, and condemned Kumo's impolite attitude. They considered it was a quibble that was practically none of her business. "It's something between the young, and there's no real need for Kumo to come out in public over it", they'd protested.

Most mothers, who were there that very afternoon, selling their garden produce, pleaded their sympathy to me, and cursed Angela Kumo's ill-mannered attitude. "Who does she think she was talking to? She must have reserved her daughter for a white man. We'll wait and see, who she is going to marry her daughter to", they said.

I took in all their pleas, along with those of the other sympathisers with pain, guilt and regret.

"It's alright, let's forget about it", I said, putting out a pretentious smile, trying all I could to remain as philosophic as possible.

Amongst the onlookers, who also witnessed my ordeal, was a young lass, a former Mt Whilhelm High School Grade 10 student, who had failed to secure a place at a tertiary institution in the country. She had retired back to the village, and stayed at home with her parents. Her name was Anna Thortia. She came from the same Siako clan as Cathy Gior. Her father Goie Bagle, a prominent and outspoken village leader, was the Councillor of the Siako clan. Anna saw everything that had happened to me on that fateful afternoon and was deeply annoyed at the way Cathy's mother inveighed me. My ordeal struck her hard on her sympathetic heart, deep down, that she was to remember that terrible predicament of mine for a very long time.

When the crowd finally dispersed, I could not remain any longer. I was still tormented and in a moment of turmoil. When everything seemed quiet, and all attention was drawn away from me, I sheepishly sidled across the market, trying as best as I could to avoid the many eyes, and crossed over the Mondiagl-kaugla Bridge. Once on the other side, away from the many eyes, I doubled my pace and scurried home to find my two smiling parents, always there to hug me ardently into their wide-open arms. Both were glad to see me. Mother, as always, broke down after not seeing me for two years. It was a happy family reunion after a long absence. But I divulged nothing of the Hobe trip, nor my recent predicament to them. Somehow, I felt reluctant to tell them. It was a day later, when my parents heard of Kumo's outburst at Mondiagl-kaugla through some neighbors, that they queried me. Both were angry at first but, later, encouraged me to forget about it. Like the many onlookers and sympathisers at Mondiagl-kaugla, "It's a common habit with many mothers", my mother advised with solace, "She'll talk good to you in the end. This is a common attitude with many mothers…especially, when it comes to dealing with the affairs of their first-born daughters".

"That's right, this is typical with many mothers", added my father.

I accepted everything my parents said, and discarded Kumo's undue attitude. But I tried all I could to avoid her during my stay. I had already felt the burn---the 'heat of the burning lava', and learnt what kind of a woman she was, and did not want to cop yet another one. I was not so certain about James Gior. I was sure he has heard about the Hobe incident, and of course, Kumo's behavior towards me too, but he was different. An introvert, he was humble and perhaps understanding too, although he spoke nothing about the undue actions of his wife. However, I sensed guilt in his eyes, whenever I crossed paths with him during my brief stay. Maybe, he condemned his wife too, like the many other sympathisers, but was rather too scared to speak out in front of his bossy and overbearing wife.

I spent the remaining two weeks with my parents at home, not daring to venture out of Bokan. After being away from home for nearly two years, I found the pleasant taste of home-grown carrots, broccoli, cabbage, cauliflower, green peas and many other locally produced vegetables, appealing and appetising after dieting on *aibika* and *tulip* shoots and buds in the Sepik. In the remaining days of my stay, I made the most of it and spent my entire holiday feasting on them.

11

A Misunderstanding Crops Up

My 'emergency' recreation leave was finally over. On the second week of November, I traveled back to Vanimo and resumed my normal duties. Much to my surprise, when I showed up in the morning at the office on the first day of my arrival, I found a letter waiting for me in the mail tray. It was from Cathy Gior. She had written the letter on the day after I left Hobe, and the letter arrived early and was lying in the tray, waiting for me all this time I was in Bokan. The letter contained all the sweet talk of any first-time young lover. Cathy described in elaborate details, how sweet the memories of my visit to Hobe lingered in her head. She wrote about the first time experience she encountered with me, our romantic rambles, our pep talks and promised never to forget them. Other endearments followed in her later paragraphs with carefully selected words, that could easily send me packing again for round trip to Hobe. She finally penned off by asking me to write back soon.

As requested in her mail, I replied the letter and thanked Cathy for her hospitality during my stay with her in Hobe. I wrote about the rest of my stay in Bokan, and in a brief paragraph, made mention of her mother's aggressive attitude towards me when I arrived at Mondiagl-kaugla from Hobe. "She roasted me good and proper", I wrote. But in the next sentence, I emphasised that she shouldn't worry too much on this. "I do not take it seriously, nor do I mind at all. So, don't let it bother you too much about it", I wrote.

In my main story, I reminded Cathy again to give me a call, as soon as she is in Kundiawa, after the school close-up. With the Christmas holiday break-up for schools, only two weeks away, I instructed Cathy to do exactly what I had told her to do in Hobe. I mailed Cathy's letter away through the post, the following day.

A week later, I checked in at the Air Niugini sales office in Vanimo, and paid for Cathy's airline ticket at a cost of nearly K200.00 to fly from Mt Hagen to Vanimo, via Wewak. A slim saleslady served me and it was arranged for Cathy to pick up the ticket in Kundiawa. "Christmas flights are always fully booked. Make sure she books a flight early", said the saleslady. "I'll advise", I said. Satisfied, I walked home with the ticket number to be relayed to Cathy, when she would call me on December 5.

The excitement to have Cathy in Vanimo soared, as the days seemingly slowed, but steadily went past. In my apartment, I pasted a count-down calendar for the months of November and December on an eye-catching section of the wall in the living room. I had it there up for a mnemonic purpose, to remind me of what to do in the ensuing days, leading up to Cathy's arrival, ticking off the days as they passed. On the 1st December, I started preparations for Cathy's visit, as I expected her to be in Vanimo anytime during the week. I executed a major clean-up at my house, both inside and outside. I then bought some new curtains for the windows to replace the old ones, and a new table cloth for the lone dining table, which had long been without one, since the day I moved in. These were bought at a reasonable price at Hlongta Trading, next to the Garamut Super Market. I also bought some kitchen wares that were long due in the house. All empty SP beer bottles, stacked in the house, were thoroughly cleaned out and dumped at Wara KongKong Rubbish Dump. For the front and backyard lawns outside, a lawn-mower was hired to level out the ankle-high overgrown grass. Surprisingly, after everything was neatly arranged and set, I ended up with a new-look residential unit, that was far better than the original, and many other homes I had entered in the whole of Vanimo. And I was personally moved by the changes I had made to this company apartment.

In the office, I excused myself with the boss from field duties and spent most of the time in the office, just in case Cathy turned up from Hobe, and rang me up after an early close-up. I also notified Peter Burger why I wanted to remain in the office that week. And being always a good and understanding boss he did not object. No calls came through during the first four days of December. But I well knew the actual close-up would take place on December 2, which was a Friday. The next two days will be a weekend, and on December 5, Monday, I definitely expected Cathy Gior to call from the SSRDP office in Kundiawa, as this was the d-day we had planned to talk on the telephone, and make further arrangements for her travel to Vanimo.

Come Monday morning, December 5th, I entered the office in a pent-up mood and settled into my chair in high spirits. It would no doubt be an extraordinary moment and first time ever to converse with Cathy over the telephone, and I was shaking with excitement, as I started the day. I spent the time, doing odd things from 8.00am in the morning, till 6.00pm afternoon in the office, ignoring the lunch-break, as I waited. Imagination ran wild too, but apparently, no call came through. My heart jumped every time, when the phone rang up at the switch in the front, but sank when the line was transferred to someone else in the office. At the end of the day, when no call came, I was briefly lost, but assumed Cathy to have not arrived in Kundiawa yet. "She must be still in Hobe", I thought to myself, "…or else she would have already given me a call today".

I spent the next day, 6th of December, in the office again, desperately waiting for Cathy's call, but still no call came. Doubts began to cloud my mind, when I saw the sun heading over towards the Osima and Bewani mountains. When the office closed after five, I retreated to my apartment with mixed feelings, brushing aside all negative thoughts popping up in my mind. After the seventh day, Mr Burger wouldn't allow me to spend any more time in the office, as there was already a backlog of jobs, piling up in the field. "We need the Krisa road-line to be flagged and surveyed", he said. So, I left all my messages with the switch operator. I also left the Air Niugini Ticket Number with the operator, with instructions to convey the same to Cathy whenever she called, and take whatever message she intended for me.

With high expectation, I arrived every afternoon from work in the field and checked, but sadly it was all still the same. The switch operator would, either shake her head negatively, or just plainly spoke out from her corner, "Nothing, Joe", and sends me home with a troubled mind.

By the end of the week, I couldn't withstand it at all, and began to wonder what could have possibly happened to Cathy. We had pre-arranged everything; the dates and what she was supposed to do, thereon. I even reminded her again in my last letter to her two weeks ago to stick to the original plan. But this is not happening, something must have gone terribly wrong, I thought, as I mused over the situation.

But the misfortune did not deter my determination from having Cathy in Vanimo yet. I still had faith, and was confident, that she would call up anytime, in the next couple of days. But the second week of December silently passed without any signal from Cathy, no calls, no letters, whatsoever. Sadly, I realised that Christmas and New Year eves were just around the corner. It was quite obvious that Cathy was not coming. I immediately suspected her talkative mother, who was the only threat to our relationship, to have intervened, and stopped Cathy from communicating with me, or even make the trip to Vanimo, in her bid to disband our relationship.

Then, in the following week, just before Christmas eve, I received a letter from Cathy. My heart jumped, as I quickly tore open the envelope. The letter was post-dated, November 29. I quickly ran my eyes through the content, and noticed that is was Cathy's reply to my last letter. She had written it while she was still in Hobe, and she advised on what she would do when she was in Kundiawa, and urged me to be around, near the phone, to take my call on of December 5. She enclosed some of the photos we took in Hobe. They were all beautiful shots. She appeared in some of the photos and was photogenic in nearly all of them that she appeared in. I saw the devil's mountain in some of the photos, and recalled the superstitions and myths surrounding that mountain, and the terrible nightmare I had had. "Devil's Peak", I said. The letter didn't say much. It appeared it was Cathy's last letter of the year before the close-up of school year, as she was quite brief in almost everything she wrote in the one-page letter.

On Christmas day, all my hopes and expectations of Cathy's travel to Vanimo diminished forever. I knew it was the peak period of the year, and the chances of coming, or getting on the plane was slim, as I knew all flights will be fully booked. "Something terrible must have happened", I muttered, day and night when I paused to think about it.

After the New Year, I gave up all hopes of seeing Cathy in Vanimo. I got on the phone and rang the Air Niugini reception desk in Kundiawa. I enquired on the ticket, to find out if someone had picked it up. The lady in the phone asked for the ticket number, and when provided it, I heard fingers tapping on the computer buttons over the phone.

"You there?", the lady asked, some seconds later.

"Yes, ma'm?"

"The passenger hasn't picked up the ticket yet", said the voice.

"Has someone enquired for it?"

"I wouldn't know about that"

"It's alright. Thank you, I'm only checking", I said, and hung up the phone, not knowing what to do after thereafter. I was literally confused and lost.

I remained in suspense, and was still wondering, when I received a letter from Paul, my younger brother, in the third week of January. It was dated December, 15th. Paul wrote to me frequently but only when there was something important for me to know back home. This time, Paul wrote to me in great detail the most disappointing news, I had never wanted to know, or to be told. "Cathy has taken up with someone else", Paul wrote, "He is a Inaugl from Sitnigle, His name is John Mitna, and he works as a Coca-Cola salesman, based in Mt Hagen. They've come together in early December, and are spending Christmas together at Ende-naige-ingugl with the Giors. Cathy's currently having a good time, taking driving lessons in the salesman's utility at the abandoned Keglsuglo airstrip. She's enjoying every minute of everything with the salesman, and by the look of things, she's got carried away completely".

In his concluding paragraph, Paul advised me to simply keep my distance, and put Cathy Gior out of my mind. "She's not like what she used to be before. I think, she's gone off the track a bit. I suggest you to quit your relationship with her", Paul, wrote.

"No...no...no! This cannot be true", I protested, as I vaguely stared at the letter in front of me. I never anticipated that Cathy would do such a thing to me, by simply going off with another guy, as if I was already dead, and found Paul's letter very difficult to believe. I started reading the letter again, and then again, and finally a fourth time, to make sure

I was reading everything correctly. But it was all stated there, on the paper right in front of me, all clear and lucid in all its entirety. I suddenly felt my knees weakened, my mind went blank---an instant blackout, as if I had walked into a dark tunnel. I felt, I was already on the verge of collapsing to the ground. There was the clear blue sky when I looked up, and the good earth when I looked down. All around me, I could see the trees swaying to the direction of the wind, and the birds chirping happily, and flying around freely from tree to tree, enjoying their normal day. On the roads, the cars roared past, leaving billows of dust and people moving around in the streets minding their business. It was just another normal day, as usual. But I was a sick person, a badly injured one. I could not recover from the mental disorder Paul's letter had caused. I felt a lump in my throat, lost and empty like a zombie, as I walked to the Steamships Kai bar. With a malaise, I ordered a soft drink, but found it tasteless, and solid as it sank down into my throat. I bought a pie, but couldn't eat it either. My appetite for food plummeted.

I went home early, and spent a restless evening trying to brood on the possible cause of the reported infidelity. Many hypothetical questions pounded in my head. Why did Cathy have to do this? Have I done something wrong? Or, have I written something in my last letter, which could upset her? But there were no answers to all the questions. Maybe, someone intentionally hoaxed the letter instead of Paul to vitiate, or sabotage our relationship; a swindle perhaps, I thought. But the calligraphy was all the same when the letter was juxtaposed with Paul's other previous letters.

Then, after a long while, something gradually settled into my mind. I remembered my father's adage, and words of wisdom when he used to advise me: *"Never go to bed with your girlfriend, or you'll regret the day she discovers the realities of life, and goes out to explore the depths of it"*. At first, I took it as an old man's chitchat, trying to caution me against fornication, and the rapidly increasing teenage sex that was now becoming very popular amongst the modern kids. But soon, I realised the true side of his wisdom. I remembered my trip to Hobe, and the never-ending nights of lust and coupling under the flickering lights of the lantern lamp in Cathy's room. I recalled every word that came out of my father's lip. "The old man is not wrong", I regretfully mused. When I deflowered Cathy Gior, I had not only debauched her virginity, but also introduced her to the myths of love and sex, the realities of life after love. And she has gone out to explore the depths of both.

The next few days were my saddest moments of my life. My interest in work declined. I was frequently absent from work, sometimes malingering for two consecutive days. My anger distended with expletives, and my mind brimmed with menacing thoughts. I could not sleep well in the nights. Why did Cathy do this? I kept asking myself, day and night, as I tried to put things into perspective. But with no instant communication available, it was practically hopeless. And after getting nowhere in the end, I introspectively blamed myself and, above all, my forestry career for losing Cathy. "It would have been better, if I had taken up a different career", I told myself, "There are not many forestry activities in Simbu; why did I take up forestry and come this far, and lose Cathy?", I painfully thought.

Then, as if struck by lightning, a thought of hope, something contradictory to my earlier curses, suddenly flashed in my mind. "Why not pursue my forestry studies further for a degree?", I thought, "I'm still young. Perhaps, I'll rise to eminence one day, which might pay off richly in the future, and retributively open Cathy's eyes".

Without dwelling further on it, I found myself next to the telephone, dialing the number for the Faculty of Forestry at the University of Technology in Lae. I called the Head of the Forestry Department, Professor Andrews. The professor was engaged by the operator, and after a brief personal introduction, I inquired if there was any space available for non-school-leaver intakes.

"Oh, plenty…there's plenty of space available this year", Professor Andrews said, over the telephone.

"Thank you, Professor", I said, and then quickly disclosed my plans to him, "I'd like to enroll this year too, but did not formally apply. And I am calling to find out if that would be possible", I said.

"No, this is not possible, all applications closed in June last year", the professor said, "But we can give special consideration to your interest, because not many non-school leavers applied last year. We received only two applications, and there are still spaces for two or three more non-school leavers available this year. But you'll have to pass an entry mathematics test first before we can consider your enrollment".

"Oh, thank you so much, Professor. I can take the entry test. How do I get the Math's papers?"

"We can send them through express mail service. All you have to do is, just go through it, complete the answer sheet and send it back to the Mathematics Department here at the University".

"I'll do that, as soon as I get the papers", I said.

"But you'll have to be quick, because student registration starts next week".

"I'll do my best, professor, but again it will depend on how soon the papers arrive"

"I'll make sure you get the papers this week", Professor Andrews said.

"Oh, Great. Thank you, Professor, I'll look forward to that", I said, and we hung up.

I initially planned to sponsor myself in the first semester after I made the decision to enroll, and let the National Scholarships Office take over the sponsorship in second semester, as this was the norm for non-school leavers. But luck came my way, when I rang the Natschol office in Port Moresby for possible assistance, or if there was any scholarship package available.

"Hello, you still there?", said the deep male voice from the Scholarships office, who'd taken my call earlier, after being transferred from the switch.

"Yes", I said.

"Lucky fellow, you're fortunate to have called", said the voice, "There is only one scholarship available, and I am pleased to inform you that you have just secured it. Congratulations!", he said.

"Oh, thank you very much", I said, "I can't believe this"

"You have to, son! You just called in the nick of time to bag that opportunity. Now, give me your details, and also a current fax number, where you can pick up your notification letter".

In no time, I relayed all my details required by the Scholarships officer, including my employer's facsimile number.

"Okay, fine…make sure you produce a copy of the fax I am going to send now to our officer in the campus, when you go in for registration", said my new friend.

"I certainly will", I told him happily. And after exchanging well wishes, we hung up.

An hour later, I received the notification letter of my sponsorship from the National Scholarships office. I was over the moon.

The sponsorship was an absolute godsend, and I was delighted about my success so far. Looking back on my life, I have had many success stories behind me, but the latest two achievements made over the telephone---my acceptance to Unitech, and securing a National Scholarship---within a single week, were something incredible and certainly unbelievable. Personally, I dubbed them, as miracles from the creator. The successes came at a time, when I was mentally troubled, and in my most miserable moment. They truly brought new hope into me, and immediately, Cathy's misdemeanors against me were gone from my mind, as I waited for the mathematics papers to reach me. They arrived two days later, via TNT under my employer's address.

I took the papers home, and carefully went through the notes, instructions and questions in the work sheet. But alas, I was a hopeless student in Mathematics at High School, and going through what was in front of me, I realised there was no way I was going to score a tick to any of the questions before me. Another thought immediately entered my mind again. I quickly secured the help of our company surveyor, who was a great mathematician to fill out the answer sheets for me, instead. He consented although it was indeed cheating, but with a National Scholarship already secured, my surveyor friend realised it would be unwise to fail the entry test. And as, he took the lead in answering the questions, I took the back seat and towed along without a slightest clue on some of the questions. It was a twenty-question exam, and from the way my surveyor friend was attacking them, they seemed too easy for him. And in less than an hour, all twenty questions were answered in a four-page answer sheet.

I faxed the four pages away, and later mailed the original answer sheets through the post on the same day. I also called Professor Andrews about the answer sheets. A few days later, the University notified me of my success in passing the entry test, again through the fax, and also my eligibility to enroll at the campus in the coming week. I punched the air in jubilation, as I went out to look for my surveyor friend to break the news.

Student registration at the University of Technology in Lae would commence on February 4th, and end on February 10th. Classes would commence, thereafter and a fee of K30.00 was charged for all late registrations. Without wasting anymore time, I quickly tendered my resignation to the company, clearly outlining the reasons for my resignation. Due to the limited time I had, I also demanded my employer that my going finish entitlements be processed without delay, as I was already in the middle of the registration week. I had served the company with loyalty and distinction for over three years, and my requests were honoured with sentiments of sadness and regret. My boss, Peter Burger wished me success in my studies. "We are going to miss you, but you still young and have a long way to go. I wish you all the best in your studies", he said. The general manager, Mr Kevin Rust personally called me into his office, and bade me farewell with a bank cheque for K1675.00, and a Talair airline ticket to fly out from Vanimo to Mt Hagen. I had preferred a Px Ticket, but the company decided on Talair instead. I did not mind. I was flown into Vanimo on a Talair aircraft four years ago, and would be leaving on a Talair again. A perfectly worded letter of employment reference, bearing Mr Rust's signature, also accompanied my going-finish entitlements in a sealed envelope. I thanked Mr Kevin Rust in return for everything, and after a brief chat, shook hands in farewell and stepped out of his office. The other Admin staff were waiting outside in the general administration office car park area, after learning of my departure, and after emotional handshakes of farewell, I left the office for the last time. Sadly, it was my last and final exit from that office, that had assisted me greatly to cut down all the costs of the telephone calls and the facsimile machine I had used lately. With deep regret and emotions of sadness, I headed straight for my apartment to prepare for my departure, the following morning.

My departure was a short notice, and rather a surprise to all my friends and colleagues in Vanimo. Practically, there was not time for a farewell gathering. I must leave, as soon as possible in time for the registration, I thought, and packed my bags in the night under the lights. I would be boarding the early Wewak flight, that would take me to Wewak, with stops in Laitre, Lumi, Nuku, and Aitape. That was the normal flight route for the Vanimo based Talair aircraft. Then I would change flight to Mt Hagen for the second leg, in another Talair aircraft, with the Vanimo based aircraft making its return flight back to Sandaun province.

I was up very early in the morning, when one of my supervisor friends tooted his horn to drive me to the airport. I switched on the electric jug for the last time for tea, after my last breakfast of fried rechauffes, consisting of rice and bully beef, I packed my bags, jettisoning items, that I thought, would be of no use to me. My longtime neighbour, Raphael, who had shared the duplex apartment with me, helped with some of my baggage and soon got everything onto the waiting land cruiser. He was sad when he learnt of my departure a week ago, and was very emotional to see me go and we wrapped each other with strong hugs. "PNG is a small place", he said, "I hope to see you again someday, all the best and safe trip", he added. I also farewelled his family, and gave away most of the unwanted items, I had considered to be of little use, including the new window curtains, the table cloth and the kitchen wares I had bought lately to please Cathy Gior. With a final check in every room, I locked the door of the apartment, which had been my home for nearly four years for the very last time. I then gave the keys to the supervisor to return them to the personnel office, later in the day.

We drove straight to the airport. Some of my best friends were already there. They had gathered there to farewell and see me go. They helped me to the check-in counter where I got my luggage weighed, a suitcase and a mountain bag. I kept the weight-less waist bag with me. Six other passengers also checked in. When boarding call was announced at 7.30 am, tears streamed down my cheeks in rivulets, as I walked to the waiting Britten Norman Islander. I had just farewelled some of my best friends, whom I had called brothers, and was going to leave a place,

I had called home for almost four years. I was not too sure, whether I would ever return, or ever meet these friends and place again. Only time would tell, I thought, as I settled on my seat. And as the plane crossed the tarmac to reach the runway, I saw the many hands waving from the side and averted my wet eyes, not wanting to see them again. "Goodbye, fellas! Goodbye, Vanimo!", was all that crossed my mind, as the Norman Islander raced down the runway, and final lifted off.

I spent the next hour sleeping in the plane. As anticipated, after stops in Litre, Lumi, Nuku and Aitape, we finally touched down in Wewak at 10.45 am. I continued my journey to Mt Hagen after a change of aircraft---a Banderrante, arriving at lunch time in Kagamuga airport. The weather was fine in Mt Hagen. It appeared there was no rain for quite sometime, as the mid-day sun was burning hot and not a cloud was seen over the mountain tops and ranges surrounding the Whagi valley. After a quick bus ride to Kundiawa, I finally reached home before sunset, surprising everyone. Both my parents were home and took to their feet when I stood at the door way.

"What brings you back here again?", my father queried, a little while later, after greeting me, "I thought, you just completed your leave a month ago"

"I'm going back to school again", I said.

"Oh, school? "But, I thought you already completed your schooling in Bulolo".

"Yeah, well…that was the first stage, papa. This time, I am going in for the next stage of schooling, a level much higher than the first one", I said, as he listened attentively, trying all I could to find better words to make the explanation easier, and more understandable on the different levels of education in the world. "I'll be schooling in Lae, this time---in the big school, called university---not Bulolo, and will be leaving tomorrow".

There was disagreement in my father's eyes, as he listened. And, on perception, I could see that he did not really took in my explanation well. He was a typical rural illiterate father, who practically knows nothing about the modern education types, and I knew needed a proper layman's lecture on the subject.

"And the school fees?" he suddenly voiced, with an anxious countenance. I knew the question was forthcoming.

"Don't worry…don't even think about it, because there won't be any school fees", I quickly responded, with a smile. "The government will take care of all that, just like it did in Bulolo",

"Then, that's good! How long will it take you to complete that school?", he muttered, as I lugged my baggage into the house.

"Three years", I answered reluctantly.

"What? Did you say three years?"

"That right…three years".

"Oh, my gosh! That's a long time", my father came back sharply, shaking his head in disbelief, "I don't think, we will be around to benefit from your schooling; me and your mother, will be long gone, by then".

"What do you mean?" I knowingly asked, with reluctance, trying to act as if I was curious.

"Can't you see, my son?", my father said, with traces of concern in his voice, "We will, sooner or later, turn into bones and, most likely, be archaeological relics by the time you finish that school." my father said, with traces of concern in his voice.

"Oh, come on papa, don't be so morbid about death", I joked, and burst out laughing, trying to mitigate my father's anxiety. He recoiled in deep thought, but asked no more questions. I knew he wasn't really too serious about it too, because he was always a driving force to have all the children in our village in the classrooms. "Education is number one!", he'd be heard, saying in public places, and telling other families. And, as anticipated, a soft smile spread across his face, as he shook his head, perhaps indicating disapproval at my decision. But I overlooked him.

"Alright…do what you think is best for you, son. But remember, me and your mama will not be around much longer", father conceded.

A little while later, mother joined us. She had returned after attending to the pigs. Paul arrived in the night when word of my arrival reached him at Maina Vocational School that afternoon. He had moved to board at the school a week earlier, and was pleased to learn of my arrival. It was going to be his final year at the school and we were all pleased about his progress.

"Did you get my letter", he inquired, when we were alone.

"I did"

"That's good, I wrote everything down for you to know what happened here, over the Christmas holidays".

"I read everything", I said.

Paul told me everything again about Cathy Gior, and her new boy; this time, in full detail and at great length, everything that he had not mentioned in his letter, as I listened.

"Both had left about a week ago, when the school year commenced", Paul said, "John is believed to have gone to Mt Hagen, while Cathy returned back to Hobe to take up posting there again".

"Have you any idea how Cathy met this guy?" I asked.

"Not one bit. We were surprised when we saw them together here".

Paul suspected Cathy Gior's relative Siako brothers, who were usually regulars at the back of John Mitna's company utility, to have arranged Cathy for the salesman. "But that cannot be ascertained, nor can it be confirmed", Paul said.

"Interesting! So, where have they been living all this time, when they were together here? I thought you stated Ende-naige-ingugl in the letter"

"Exactly! Cathy's place. They rarely go to John's place at Sitnigle, because John's got his other wife there".

"Oh really?"

"Yes, that's what I heard"

"That's interesting, how did Kumo react to that? Did she explode, like she did to me last November?"

"I don't think so, because she was housing them".

"So, Kumo was housing them", I repeated.

"Well, the pickup is always seen parked at Ende-naige-ingugl, so where else could John Mitna be residing?"

"No wonder, I had waited anxiously all that time for Cathy's call", I said, annoyed at the thought, "I think, it's the color of money, or perhaps the red company Four-wheel Drive, with the Coca-cola ribbon that attracted both mother and daughter".

"It could be that. But I don't think you are wrong", conceded Paul, "The best thing you can do now is forget Cathy, and find someone new".

"I already dropped her before I got on the plane", I said.

"That's good", Paul said, "You know, it's sometimes uncomfortable to walk past the two lovebirds, as an immediate family member of Joseph Tamgo".

"I know", I said, and knew he was right.

I spent a restive night with my parents after Paul walked back to Toromambuno. Very early in the morning, before the cock crowed, and without arousing anyone's attention, I stood by the roadside at Mondiagl-kaugla and caught an early PMV to Kundiawa. Before proceeding to Lae, I walked to the Air Niugini office, and inquired about the ticket I had intended for Cathy Gior. It was still there, unclaimed. I needed money and would certainly need plenty in school, now that I won't be on a formal payroll again. After collecting the cash refund, I jumped on a Toyota coaster 25-seater bus, and continued my trip to Lae. A young teen-aged Western Highlander was behind the wheels, and made it to Lae in seven hours, arriving there at 5.00pm in the afternoon. I was two days early before the close of student registration. I joined the queue on the following day, and before the day ended, I was a full-time Natschol student at the PNG University of Technology.

12

Rapprochement

It was almost five years ago, since I last sat in a classroom. At first, I found, at times, difficult to adapt myself to student life again. I deemed the classes, lectures, tutorials, assignments and the many other school activities boring and a total waste of precious time. I recalled with nostalgia, my former job as a Logging Foreman, and the social activities in Vanimo that I participated in, as better and more enjoyable than schooling, and wanted to withdraw from studies after the second week. But, as the weeks rolled by, I met new faces and made many new friends. My new classmates realised my problem too, and were friendly, generous and cooperative, when I approached them for assistance. They kept me in company and gradually, with all the continued support and words of encouragement from my new found friends, I finally managed to settle into the classroom. And in total contrast to the above, with relentless flow of assignments piling up every week, and studies for tests becoming almost a fortnightly headache, I was kept bolted down to my study table and busy almost every day and night, allowing me no time to pause for anything else. Then, quite amazingly, without realising it, we were already in the middle of the year, and due for the mid-semester exams. And of course, after the exams was the three-week mid-semester break. "Days are flying like a rocket", I thought, as preparations were underway for the exams.

The mid-semester exams were finally over, and I was glad to take a break after the four months of studies and sleepless nights. Immediately, after the exams, I went straight home to Bokan. I had plenty to tell my parents when I got home. During our afternoons, I regaled them of my experiences in the country's highest learning institution, about my new friends and of the many other interesting things I encountered in Unitech and Lae, over the four-month period. In other afternoons, our next-door neighbours would pay postprandial visits to our house, to chat and enjoy the evening with us before withdrawing to their homes. And again, they would sit around and listen to some of my tales. Soon I became a good storyteller in the house, regaling everyone with my past experiences in Bulolo, Vanimo and the many other places I had visited, which they never had a chance to see; names of places they only heard about.

One evening, as I was sitting in the house with my parents and some visiting relatives, Konda, the son of our next-door neighbour, who was playing marbles outside with the other children, came running to the door, panting, as if on an errand, and howled into the house. "Joe, there's a little boy waiting out here to see you".

"Who is he?" I asked.

"Tongia".

"Where is he from? And what does he want?" I pried, but there was no response. Konda was already back in the playing arena, continuing his marble game with his peers. I momentarily paused to capture the little boy in my head, but Tongia was an unfamiliar name to me, and an unpopular child in Bokan too. "He must be a new kid", a relative said. "Sounds like it", I said, and gently excused the relatives, and went outside.

Across the playground, I saw an unfamiliar little boy of about six, watching enviously at the other kids like him playing marbles on the ground. Noticing my presence, he immediately scurried across to where I was standing.

"You wanted to see me, eh?", I called out, as he neared.

"Yes, it's Cathy, she wanted to see you", the boy gabbled nervously, scratching his head.

"Cathy, who?"

"Cathy Gior", Tongia replied.

"The teacher lady?" I asked, knowingly and surprised.

"Yes! She sent me to get you; she's waiting for you over at Wai-mambuno, at teacher Phillip's house".

"Why did she want to see me?"

"I don't know…she is waiting for you. You can go out there and find out", Tongia responded, almost curtly.

I had forgotten Cathy for quite a long while, and the mention of her name and the conversation with Tongia, had me starring absent-mindedly into the open space for some time.

"Did she really send you?" I inanely asked again, to make sure that he was not kidding, after coming back to my senses.

"Why would I be here? I told you, she's waiting for you at Wai-mambuno, and sent me to get you. Or, do I have to repeat that again", Tongia came back at me, somewhat harder this time, like a full-grown adult.

I was amazed at the way Tongia responded, and stood agape, literally stunned to let out any further question. Realising that nothing more was coming from me, little Tongia hurriedly left the way he came in. I remained undecided, as to what I was to do. Many hypothetical questions inundated my mind; why did she want to see me? Should I walk over, and see her? But on the contrary, the many questions that flooded my head were only temporary registration of protest against her infidelity. Deep inside me, my heart started to pound faster and my blood pulse doubled with excitement. Hence, my overburdened mind could not debate, or argue any further. The whole moment was like an extinguished fire lighting up again, and suddenly, I realized there was not time to waste.

"Tongia", I called out after him, just as he was about to disappear into a bend. Catching my call, the kid stopped in his tracks, and looked back.

"Tell Cathy, I'll be there in about twenty minutes".

Tongia tacitly nodded head, and without wasting any more time disappeared into the bend. It was the last time I saw this clever kid.

I hurried back into the house, and almost uneasily got into my shoes.

"You seem to be in a hurry", my mother queried.

"Yeah, some friends wanted to see me out on the road. Tongia just delivered the message", I said.

Then excusing the relatives one more time. I stepped outside and trotted over to Kama-mambuno. Avoiding friends and neighbours, who were there, as usual to enjoy the afternoon conferences, I scurried down the track to Wai-mambuno, all along trying to put everything into perspective. I had always wanted to find out about her deceptions, and this was the opportunity. Perhaps, she would explain everything, I thought. And then, she would tell why she wanted to see me too.

Phillip Koane's residence was a big house. The door was open, but there was no sign of life inside the house. It was the same house where we had celebrated his daughter, Suaire's fifth birthday a few years back, but this time, the inside was renovated and partitioned into rooms for habitation with *pitpit* blind. Philip's wife, Salume who proved to be a gifted housecrafter and talented landscaper, attractively beautified the residence with decorations inside, and the grounds outside with colorful ornamental and flowering plants. Briefly, as my mind drifted back to the birthday party, and what had followed thereafter on that night, I heard someone laughing behind the house, a female voice. Perceiving Cathy Gior there with a companion, I slowly walked around the house, admiring the nice surroundings, as I headed towards the curtilage, my heart beating vigorously in anticipation over what surprises were in stored for me on the other side. Reaching the finally corner, I found Cathy Gior chatting with Salume, Phillip's wife on a nice secluded backyard lawn, surrounded by flowers and colorful ornamental shrubs away from the public eyes. Both women were sitting together, gabbing away and enjoying the last afternoon sun, that was looking down at them from Yandina Range, towering just above Wai-mambuno. Philip was absent.

My arrival was almost unexpected, and I stunned both the women with surprise when I showed up.

"You scared the hell out of us, Joe", Salume exclaimed, as I emerged into full view. I momentarily stopped in my tracks.

"Oh no, no…I shouldn't be scaring you, you sent for me and should be expecting me anytime, any minute", I joked, with a grin, "And, I guess, I am not trespassing either".

"No, not at all. I think someone here was expecting you and, I think, we forgot that", Salume responded, laughed and, looking across to Cathy, rose to her feet. She then extended her right hand for a hearty handshake of greetings. "I can't see teacher Phillip anywhere", I said.

"He's out there somewhere, but someone here waited to see you all afternoon", Salume said, with a grin.

"Oh, is that so", I replied, but no one answered. Instead, the two women smiled, almost guiltily at me.

Salume did not last long. After a few moments of pleasantries, she left us all alone to mind our own business, and left, as if it was already pre-planned.

After Salume was gone, what followed next was a nightmare. As soon as she disappeared, the noise of the laughs, smiles and greetings suddenly disappeared. Strangely, an eerie silence followed. A few steps in from of me, on the perfectly trimmed lawn was Cathy Gior. She sat cringed with her head down in a servile fixture, occasionally putting on casual smiles, as her eyes found mine. I was apparently lost too, and not knowing where to start, "Hello, Cathy", I merely said, as I settled down about a step away from her, obviously feeling void after the long separation. Cathy maintained her smile, but did not respond. Why? I don't know, but slowly I began to notice something. My presence must have been the most difficult moment in her life. And already, I could read on her face, that she was having some kind of problem facing me. There were signs of guilt all over her face, and she appeared almost undecided where to begin.

"So, you sent Tongia to fetch me, did you?", I asked, trying to ease her troubled mind, and start her with a conversation.

"Yes, I did", she shyly replied, with suppressed smiles.

"Yeah, that's what Tongia said, so what is it, then?", I voiced, almost curtly, as if I was still tormented by her infidelity.

Cathy did not answer immediately. She had definitely wanted to see me for a purpose, but I realised she could not let it out easily. "There is no need to feel shy about anything. I mean, I was pleased to learn that you sent for me. I know, you have something for me", I said, trying to relax her troubled situation.

"I just called you over to apologise, that's all", she muttered through her trembling lips, breaking the long difficult moment of silence in herself.

I raised my head, but her response mnemonically drew the curtains away from the bitter memories of her infidelity, and inside me I felt pangs of anger and jealousy, slowly flaring up.

"Apologise? About what? What do you really want to apologise about?" I asked, almost daringly.

Cathy did not answer. I was, perhaps quizzical, placing her in an awkward situation to continue, and she stopped altogether. She very well knew that I was implicitly trying to reprove her deception, in requital for the upset she had caused to me, and remained still again. Then after a long silence, she meekly admitted, "About not giving you a call last December".

"Oh, the call! Okay! What about it? I think its past and gone...with me, it's all history now. Really, I don't want to talk about it now, or even in the future. But you must have something to talk about", I said.

A weird silence followed again. The perception that she was in for something much bitter than what she expected, became apparent to her in the brief moment. My responses were flippant and ambiguous, incurring more guilt and shame. And she found it difficult to speak, causing silence after silence.

"I heard, you were busy trying to learn driving over the holidays", I psyched myself, breaking the silence, "I mean, this could be one of the reasons, why you forgot to ring me".

Cathy's head dropped, this time, even lower. I must have somehow hit the nail, somewhere on the head, and she remained like a statue for the entire moment. There was atmosphere of guilt, frustration and even embarrassment all around her. Taking the upper hand, I took the opportunity to requite her deception with mockery and interrogation. "By the way, who was that glamorous Salesman instructor, showing you all the driving skills? I heard he is a great teacher for taking driving lessons. Have you obtained your Driver's License yet?", I asked, mocking her. Cathy could not take in anymore of my interrogative mockeries, and remained idle, hopelessly defeated in self-reproach. A shower of guilt and embarrassment saturated her thoroughly, and the complexion of her face blushed, as if to burst into tears any minute. Correctly, I was expressing something she did to me, that was incontrovertibly culpable, and I had no regrets. I enjoyed it.

But, apparently, her fixture and semblance in the long while slowly raised pangs of sorrow, whenever I eyed her. And with a sense of pity, crossing my heart after several glances, I decided to stop my interrogative mockeries at once. I was introspectively mean and harsh, I thought. I am a professional, a university student, but was behaving like an unprofessional, I thought. I was truly and indeed mean and harsh. She invited me and I did not even get her side of the story, and jumped the gun. Why do I have to talk like that, when she offered to discuss everything with me, I mused. Realising my mistake, I penitently recoiled, and slowly put on some smiles to instill back normalcy in my approach. But the silence did not end. Then, after some good minutes, "It was not my idea to get involved with him", she finally muttered, when I ceased to speak anymore. Tears rolled down her cheeks and wet her guilty face as the words tumbled out. But the lines detonated yet another lot of anger inside me. "Him! Who? What was his name, anyway?" I asked, again curtly at the mention of the unidentified person.

I was already boiling inside, obviously, hurt and angry, and of course, topping it off with tons of jealously. In no second, the pity and compassion demonstrated a minute ago were all gone in a flash. My sudden change of behaviour shocked Cathy too, and she paused amidst her tears, and eyed me through her tears, as if checking whether to respond. Then, in the most-guiltiest manner, "John! That Coca-Cola Salesman", she timidly murmured. And with liters of tears streaming down her cheeks, she recounted, ignoring my anger, the long story of her relationship with John Mitna.

"It was these Siako boys", she began, mentioning some names that hooked her to the salesman. Pervaded with curiosity, I remained attentively still, as she rambled on. "It all started, when the boys urged me to jump with them on the Salesman's utility, a Coca-Cola company landcruiser, that was traveling up to Gembogl. I refused, telling them that I had a long-distance telephone call to make. But they insisted, and even offered to take me to a phone, where the Salesman would arrange for me to ring at no cost, for as long as I wanted. Placing my trust with the boys, who were all my brothers, I jumped on the pickup. But we never got to the phone, the boys had promised. The salesman was busy with his clients, going in and out of shops. And in one instance, he went into the bank and spent close to two hours, and by the time he settled down to drive us home, it was already closing time after 4.00pm. And so, I never made any call, but…"

"Alright, that's enough", I interrupted.

Cathy's account resurrected many disturbing memories, that had melted away long ago, and I could no longer take in everything she'd be telling me. Hence, I stopped her in the middle of her story.

"I don't want to know rest of your fairy tale", I said, "I think, I already know what happened next. Can you switch, please…can you talk about something else? Like, why you called me here, I suppose you said you called me to apologise. Is that correct?"

Cathy gently nodded.

"Okay, shall we get on with it. But first, let me remind you of something too. I heard wonderful stories about you and your new guy. I also heard Kumo accepting the new guy into her house too. Most of all, it was you, who broke ranks with me, and not me. So, you must be sure, I mean, you must be really certain about what you are trying to do now. Because I am gradually recovering, or perhaps recovered from a nightmare, a terrible ordeal over the last couple of months, that you forced on me".

Cathy remained quiet for some time. She heard me talking in the tone of a mature person, and dare not to look at me in the eyes. I was telling her the truth, the absolute truth and she knew it all. Then almost suddenly, while still sobbing, and with what I supposed as tears of repentance in her eyes, she opened up. "If I am not sure of what I am doing, I don't think I'll send for you", she said. She hit the nail right on the head, shutting me off completely with her selected words. And, as if that moment was the only opportunity she had left in the world, Cathy let out her mind, not daring to give me a chance to talk. She spilled out everything she had planned for the evening, and anything that she needed to tell me.

"I tried to write to you and apologise on the very first day I arrived in Hobe", she confessed, "but found the pen 'too heavy' to lift, and off course, write for your eyes. Wherever I went, I was haunted by my own guilt. I would start up a paragraph on a paper, but then squash it, and threw it into the fire, because I could not continue the page further. The sense of guilt was overwhelming, every time I touched the pen for you. I felt restless every time I think about it. What have I done? Why did I do it? were questions that I lived with every day and night. I kept asking myself, 'What shall I do? Should I own up and face you?' And, if I do, 'Will you be able to accept me back?' These were some of the tormenting questions that bogged my mind every day and night. I also felt scared too, and ashamed to own up, but then there was always hope that you will forgive, if I own up and apologise. First, I tried to get in touch with you in Vanimo, but discovered that you were no longer there. I asked around for your whereabouts, but nobody dared to tell me, because the odium I had incurred was overbearing and nobody wanted to talk to me about you. It was during the recent Easter break, that I learnt of your enrolment at Unitech, Anasas reported your recent arrival, so I came over here with Tongia, and sent him over to get you. This is my side of the story", Cathy said, looking up to me, "I know you won't like it", she added, "but I am so sorry about everything, and what I put you through. Believe me, I am truly sorry".

Cathy's confession was rather sad and touching. I couldn't be so sure, if she had prevaricated her story, but she certainly left me speechless and had me staring at the earth in front of me. She has had a brave heart to come forward, admit and apologise. And I began to pity her story too. But I did not give in to her story right away.

"You got yourself to blame for all these", I calmly told her, "You can rest the blame on the Siako boys, whom you called, brothers for linking you up with John Mitna, or whoever he is. But really, you ought to blame yourself after all. You're old enough to make sensible decisions for yourself, whether to give, or get, refuse or take anything offered to you. You are old enough to think better. You cannot remain credulously naïve, and malleable all the time to outside influences. Sometimes, you'll have to stand firm, and make firm decisions for yourself".

I was homily and didactic in my later talk, but soon perceived that I was talking too much. I was putting too much into Cathy's head. I should stop, I thought, and immediately paused to allow Cathy regather herself, and think over and weight out the words, I had put forward to her. I knew, they were too much for her to take in all at the same time, especially taking into account the current state of her mind. But she needed them, and I was glad I put them out.

As Cathy pondered on my analysis of her tale and 'advices' I reflected on her apology. 'Should I accept her apology?' I asked myself, and occasionally eyed Cathy through the corner of my eyes. She was drying her tears with the back of her hands, and wiping her nose dry from the incessant wettings there. Her face was pale and still wet in some spots. I noted she would burst into tears again, if she ever made any attempt to open her lips again. I sympathetically did not want that to happen. I pitied her appearance, the way she submitted herself that afternoon, and eventually decided to end all our talks from there. Already Cathy had admitted herself guilty, and there was no point in requiting her deceptions, or interrogating her further for the reproofs.

"Let me tell you my side of the story", I began softly, to share my side of the experience. "You certainly caused an unbearable grief, when I learnt of your adventures with the sales guy. You never realised that, but it was truly a terrible experience. In fact, I had always trusted you, and never expected this would happen. And when it did, believe me, the whole sky fell on top of me"

Cathy remained speechless all the while she took in my story. She did not even dare to either see me or open her lips.

"But let's leave it as that", I said, "I don't want to talk more about it. It's all history now, but for one thing, I promised never to see, or get involved with you again in the future. But again, as it turns out today, I am somewhat surprised …well, rather please too, I'd say, that you have decided to come forward to apologise. I never thought, you'd do that. Honestly speaking, I thought you had left me permanently. And, one thing for sure, that now becomes obvious and questionable is---trust! My trust on you, I must admit, has been permanently broken, and I really don't know whether to maintain my trust in you again. But again, that all depends! Right now, if you can promise me never to repeat this behaviour again, I'll take everything into account, accept your apology and forget about everything. It will all be water-under-the-bridge, and, off course, everything will take a new course for sure. Is that okay with you…or have you got anything to say?"

Without a sound, Cathy tacitly gave a slow nod with her head to indicate her approval, on the terms and conditions, I put forward to her. But I was not satisfied with the gesture.

"Cathy, you have to say something, because I cannot hear you if you don't say anything", I demanded with ease, to make sure, that she spoke it out. Clearing her throat, "I won't, and don't think, I will ever repeat this behaviour again", Cathy finally muttered, with her head still bent low.

"It's good that you spoke it out, because I want to hear it coming out from your lips", I said, and added, "And because you spoke it out, I should accept your apology for now. And remember, it's a promise to keep" With that, I let out a grin and, looked across to Cathy with enthusiasm, and extended my hands. "Let's give each other a handshake, as a token of peace and reconciliation. And, off course, forget that this has ever happened, okay?" I suddenly, exclaimed to Cathy's surprise, with the grin replaced by a full warm smile.

Cathy's hands obediently reached out to take mine. Our eyes soon met. We smiled, then proceeded with our reconciliation handshake, and I believed, with affection and love.

We sat and talked for over two hours. The sun had already gone into oblivion. Nightfall gradually emerged. Higher up above us, there was a spread of clear sky across the empyrean, and a beautiful night was imminent. A little while later, in the cloudless sky, from behind the mountains in the north along the Bismark Range, the full moon, in the shape of a giant sphere, slowly appeared, its brilliance lighting up the entire valley. Countless stars began to fill up every cosmic space, and twinkled happily across the sky. Down on the valley floor, the temperature was gradually dropping. The cool alpine breeze from the towering Mt Wilhelm had precipitated to the lower grounds, gradually freezing the valley floor, sending everyone home, early to the fireplace. There was silence all around us, except for the crackling sounds of the courting insects.

When I looked across at Cathy, her head was still down for most of the time. She hardly broached on any topic for discussion, and responded very little, letting me do all the talking. She might have lost the faith, and the trust I had reposed on her, but she had not completely lost everything. Her physical charm was intact. In the dimly glow of the full moon, the perfect outline of her feminine beauty was visibly very clear against the stillness of the night---the smooth facial features, the gentle sloping shoulders and the perfect twin bulges across her teen chest were irresistible for my eyes to revert or ignore. Topping that she was prettier than before She was indeed a paragon of beauty and majesty. The more I looked at her, the more entranced I became of her, and soon I could feel my desires for her growing, and rising with increasing tempo inside me. The fire of desire, which had died out inside me, was slowly burning again. Hence, I was already at the mercy of Cathy Gior's beauty. A bushfire was imminent. And it did not take long for the burning flame to cause a bush fire to explode.

Drowned by lust, passion, envy and desperation, I slowly reached out to Cathy and gently pulled her arm towards me. Unaware, Cathy must have been prepared for this too, and instinctively moved without resistance, slowly and gently like the wind to my pull, and in no second fell into my arms. In the next second, we embraced each other, our lips touched and before long we fell onto the soft verdant lawn beneath us.

Cathy might have been timid, and kept herself almost silent during our entire afternoon. But, it was different during the coital session. She was a raging bull. She was active, and superb in everything she did. She knew exactly what to do, where to touch and reacted instantly to all my advances. She must have planned this moment to be a special one for me, and gave me everything she had. She was superb and excelled in all of them. Her superior performance so pleased me with unimaginable excitement that I soon became oblivious of her past erratic deeds. As the minutes clicked past, we forgetfully entangled in each other's grasps, enjoying every minute of our ecstasies, as the darkness of the night took us away into the many wonderlands we'd never seen before.

I walked Cathy back to Ende-naige-ingugl soon after our courtship was over. This time, she was all perked up after the pleasant night, and was in an elated mood during the walk. Her behaviour said it all. She had just mitigated my exasperation by compensating me with sex for her infidelity, and she appeared more pleased, satisfied and relaxed then she was, hours earlier. Her true persona was back, and during the long night's walk, Cathy did most of the talking. Like she always did in the past, she gabbed away happily with little concern at all for other ears that may be listening elsewhere, with her high note frequency. She uncovered more topics and agendas for discussion than I did. I didn't mind anything she came up with, and agreed to almost anything she said, proposed or enquired about. And before we reached Ende-naige-ingugl, our bond was re-established. We became one again, one more time.

I bade farewell to Cathy at the entrance into her village. I stood watch as she climbed over the style. And then, almost unexpectedly, "Goodnight and Sweet dreams", she teased, as she was on the other side. I smiled, but before I could respond, she faded into the dark and disappeared into the village. I headed back home alone under the dim moonlight. I thought back to what had happened, moments earlier, between me and Cathy and let out a complacent smile of satisfaction. I was pleased that Cathy Gior had come back to me again. Fortunately, I had not totally lost her after all, I thought. The power of love had clearly prevailed and bonded us together again. And I felt elated and superior, imagining what the Coca-cola salesman would do, when he finds out that Cathy had deserted him. But that was none of my business to know, and brushed aside the thought.

But then suddenly, as I continued up the road, an embarrassing spectre perturbed my composed mind, and caused a rather unpleasant disturbance. Cathy and her guy had caused a sensation over the Christmas period, and the taunts and stigma I feared that would be generated after our reunion panicked and scared me. It made me feel sick and I regretted my recent communion with Cathy Gior. Many had seen and witnessed Cathy's adventurous relationship with her new boyfriend only months earlier, and to see me associating with her again was not a good sight. It would raise eyebrows and gossip would spread like wildfire, and many would tauntingly condemn my action, stigmatising me as a blind-eyed fool for taking Cathy back. Paul had advised me to drop her, and he certainly won't be a happy man, if he learns of our reunion. He'll likely protest at some stage. "Why do you have to go back, and pick on 'someone's second-hand' when there are many 'fresh and decent' ones around to pick from", he'd most likely say. It would certainly be an embarrassment to me, and I don't like that.

The thought sent shivers through my nerves, and a restless feeling swept through my inside, as I pushed my way through the cold night. I realised, Cathy had played a pre-emptive game on me and easily won. Only months earlier, she inflicted, what I'd say, an unpardonable grief to my heart, and exhibited something immodest to the eyes of the many. And for those who knew me and Cathy personally, it was shockingly a disgusting behaviour. But now, she had propitiated my pardon skillfully and successfully with very little effort in a single afternoon, within a space of six hours, or less. For everything she did to me over the Christmas period, that had made me look like a fool, she only ingratiated herself by putting on a mask of sorrow over her face, sobbed profusely with a placatory exhibition, and simply performing extraordinarily on the cold lawn. And I fell into the trap! "I should have refused Tongia in the very first place. I shouldn't have come to Wai-mambuno", I bluntly complained to myself, as the thought boiled inside me.

"Should I keep my distance from her", I asked myself, as I walked. But, on the second thought, one thing was there to stay---love! Buried deep inside, and cemented firmly was my desire for Cathy. I loved her, and I did not want to lose her again. I had considered losing her, my childhood inamorata, forever to John Mitna after the Christmas incident, but the rapprochement was a miracle, a real miracle. And to throw her away again like that, this time around, was definitely not in my mind and favour. Moreover, I did not want any further disturbances to our association again.

But the embarrassment, I feared, that would cause after our reunion, panicked and scared me, more and more when I came to think of it. And, hence, I was a divided person in the chilling night. I tried to think of some practical ways, some plans to help avoid stigma and the frustration that was building up in my mind. "Should I avoid her, and quit the relationship?" I asked myself, thinking deeply all over again, but surely I loved Cathy, and had no intention of doing that. My lust for her, introspectively, still kindles and I did not want to lose her, nor do I want any further disturbances done to our association again. There must be a better option still, I kept reminding myself. When my family momentarily crossed my mind, a series of unanswered questions arose, too. Disregarding Paul, "Should I let my parents know of the reunion?", I asked, and uppermost in my mind, "Will they accept Cathy, despite her dark side?". I would never know the answer. But literally, there is, after all, nothing to fear about. "It's not their business", I thought, "I decide on who to choose as my partner, not them".

This sounded reasonable in my mind and I felt brave too but, for some reason, I still felt nervous to tell my family about it. They had seen more than enough of the dark side of Cathy over the holidays, and had told me about it many times before. And I again become restless about the negative approach to my decision. During the next hour, I tried to think up some practical ways that would keep Cathy within my grip, but my family, friends and public away from all criticisms, gossip and stigma over our association. Several options surfaced in my mind and I spent time weighing them out, but soon discovered that there was no other way, than to keep everything secret. Hence, I finally decided to keep my recent reunion with Cathy Gior confidential from everyone. It was a piquant bit of thought, and sounded simple in the mind. But in reality, it was practically a rather difficult scheme to plan and execute in a crowded valley of over 2000 inhabitants. It was certainly an impossible task, and I re-studied and gave thought for other options too, but there were no other possible and workable plans for substitution. I decided to stand by the confidentiality plan.

The mid-semester break holiday was a week long. I was soon to return to Lae after spending nearly five days at home. I furtively courted Cathy again twice, both during the video nights at Pokodame, and as per my plan, I tried to avoid her as much as possible during the day. I did not want to be seen with her by the village folks, or anyone else. As usual, we talked and shared our stories, but I remained silent over my new plan to keep the relationship confidential from everyone. I had a feeling, that I'll certainly frustrate Cathy if I divulge my plan to her, causing her to have doubts on our relationship, and I remained tightlipped over the plan during our two meets. "I'll write a letter to you when I get back to Lae", I assured her on the final night before my departure, which was to be the following morning. Cathy promised to do the same, but suggested writing first in order to recuperate, and instill back into me all the lost confidence, I had had in her earlier. I left on the following day with peace.

Cathy Gior did not lie. Almost a week later, I received her very first letter after our rapprochement. She apologised dearly again, and vowed to remain forever mine. A famous quote in her letter reads, *"I will remain yours from now on until death do us part"*. I clearly remembered the exact words being spoken out by Hollywood couples to each other at the weddings in the movies, and was glad she had adopted and quoted it for her own use. It sounded pleasant and touched me deep. Many other lines of apologies and repentance followed in the other paragraphs, and finally, Cathy ended her letter with the three-worded sensational postscript: *'I Love you'*.

I responded to Cathy's letter, the moment I finished reading it. *"Whatever happened yesterday is all gone"*, I wrote, and asked her to *"Forget the past and look forward into the future, but don't be so pliable as before"*. Other encouraging lines to settle her anxious mind followed in the later paragraphs with tons of endearments. And as usual, I mailed the letter away without any further delay. It did not take long to get Cathy's reply.

Cathy must have been pleased with my quick response, and acknowledged receipt of my letter at her earliest moment. I did not wait either. Soon our exchange of letters became obligatory, and our desires to have them in the shortest time possible intensified. She wrote four to six pages of letters. I responded the same, trying to outpace her by exceeding the number of pages she wrote. She was quick to match my earnestness and reciprocated by adding more pages in return. Without any objection, our relationship had resurrected again, resumed its track, and yes, was back on the road, though, only through the mail. And every letter said it all.

13

At Crossroads

The end of the academic year was approaching fast. In almost five weeks from then, my first year at Unitech was going to be over. In the next three weeks, everyone was expected to sit for the second semester exams. After the exams, of course, was the long anticipated Christmas vacation that everyone was looking forward to. As the days quietly rolled past, the excitement of the approaching holidays slowly gained momentum. I had longed to spend some moments with Cathy in seclusion and was already making plans to ask her out for a holiday somewhere, a destination away from home, where no one would see us together and avoid speculation. I planned for my cousin Kuglame's place in Goroka to be the ideal place for such a rendezvous. "I'll take Cathy to Faniufa, when I get home after the exams", I thought.

The study week finally arrived in November. All the students were granted two week's study leave to prepare for the forthcoming final semester exams, and to finish-off and hand in any uncompleted assignments. Formal classes ceased completely and there was silence all around, when all the students locked themselves up in their study rooms. The university campus soon appeared a ghost town within two weeks. Noise was also naturally kept to the lowest, except for the hustling, bustling and tooting of the busy traffic on the main Taraka drive, outside the campus' northern perimeter.

Like all other students, I sweated my guts during this period of time with endless nights of study, and ultimately passed the five exams I sat. Although the results will be posted to me in January, I knew I did absolutely well and was confident. As a non-school leaver, it was an achievement. I knew, I was not a bright student in the class, especially in the science classes, but I knew my success was a blessing from the creator above. Now, that it was all over, I had another two more years remaining before I'd be graduating with the planet's renowned paper, the 'Degree'. With my head lifted high, and soused with confidence and optimism I walked to the Red Lodge, and packed my bags for the long journey home for a much-deserved break, after the year long heading cracking.

Home, sweet home, was always the same, whenever I arrived. My loving and caring family would welcome me home ardently with wide opened arms. Unlike the pre-university holidays, they'd expect very little, or otherwise nothing at all from me, now that I was a student again. My presence was their joy, and theirs was my comfort. They would all make me feel kingly by doing his, or her bit of duty to please me, and make my stay enjoyable. My brother, Paul, would come home every afternoon with firewood for mother to light up the house, and cook food for us all. As usual, he would then retreat to the corner and remain quiet for most of the time, as if waiting for his next set of instructions. My mother would return from the garden with all the fine harvest: *Kaukaus* (sweet potatoes) of the Duma-ambu and Daka-ambu types, tasty green peas, prized giant cabbages and other attractive garden produce, she purposely left behind for me.

"I had left this behind for your handsome mouth", she'd say, smiling up at me, as she'd carefully prepare them to go into the pot.

My father would harvest the 12ft high sugar cane, he'd poled them up in the front yard of our house, and cut them up into required lengths for consumption during my stay. He'd make constant checks, and replace them with new cuts, once I finished everything up. And with all the royal treatment I was getting from my family, my stay in the village was never boring, or unpleasant, nor did I have any regret, whatsoever. Hence, every minute of my holidays was always enjoyable and splendid.

One evening, about three days after my arrival, we were all basking ourselves around the fireplace after taking dinner, prepared by my mother. We had no visitor in the house, and outside, daylight was slowly fading and darkness was gradually closing in. In the opposite corner, Paul was helping mother with the lantern lamp. He was filling it up with kerosene to light the house. And directly opposite them was father, sitting relaxed and gently puffing away his *brus*, enjoying every inhale, as his keen eyes were glued on Paul and Mother.

When the house was finally lit up, my father, who seemed to have waited for light in the house, broached on an agenda for discussion among us. The discussion initially had required my presence, in person, and that evening, when we were alone, my father perhaps resolved that it was an appropriate moment and mooted the topic. He began with the obsession of looking after our ten pigs: how my mother came home tired every afternoon, with *bilum* load of *kaukau* from the gardens to feed them. And himself struggling everyday to dig up, and fence in new plots to grow *kaukaus* for the pigs. "Son, it's all labor intensive, you know'" he said, "We currently have ten pigs. Two sows are pregnant, and another is expected to conceive soon. When they start weaning their piglets, we expect the number to rise dramatically. A second house will have to be considered to accommodate them all. And again, the construction of a new house will yet be another burden". He whined and highlighted further some common problems associated in rearing the animals: the payments involved, when the pigs wondered into somebody else's garden, the pains and aches they sustained in their everyday activity and the frequent aid post visits they made for medical attention.

"Really, we have to get rid of some of these pigs, somehow, to relieve me and your mother from all such hardship", my father said, with plaintive concern.

Seriously, this was a rare agenda, never touched before with such concern and emphasis in all our family discussions. And already, I sensed the importance of the subject matter, my father was broaching. It was sensitive too, and I remained attentively tight-lipped, as he rambled on. I briefly raised my eyes to check out mother if she was listening too, but she apparently was not. She had her back to the fire, her face to the lantern in the corner, and was busy working on her new *bilum*. But, with the theme of the discussion already in light, I knew that father was talking on their behalf, and she was obviously listening to him too.

"Your mother needs a helping hand, someone younger and energetic to assist her in the house with some of the workloads", father said, partly exposing the underlying message of his long spiel.

At twenty-five, matured and going towards my adulthood, father had finally decided that the time was ripe for me to choose a bride, a wife for me---a helping hand for mother. This was, after all, the ultimate objective, behind his long talk---to deliver this message. And even though, my father was circuitous, I was already beginning to feel and experience some kind of challenge and ultimatum never expected. I went mute, and a long moment of silence existed, as I ruminated over the subject.

But my father had no time to wait. "Maybe, you will feel strange about it", he voiced again, "…but don't you forget that you have already grown up into a fine young man", he said, gradually digging in to explicate his agenda. "And we are proud of you", my father moved on, "And like all parents of a fine young man like you, we have laboured tirelessly to rear these pigs; purposely in the event, that some kind-hearted young angel decides to leave her family behind and come across to live with us in the future. But when they multiply, they create problems for us. Your mother, and I are getting just too old, to bear with all the problems, and hardships associated with these pigs anymore. It's terrible, you know! You've seen our daily plights and the choking state we're always in. Perhaps, you won't find us here when you come around next time. We may be gone into the next world by then…so, all we want to ask you now is, have you got someone in mind---a girlfriend, or someone that we can engage to be your wife. I mean, it's all up to you, we're only too happy to wed any girl of your choice to be your spouse. And in that way, we can get rid of some of the pigs, and of course, remove this burden out of the way". Saying that, my father paused, presumably for a break, I guessed.

Reaching out to the fireplace, he picked up a burning ember to light his *brus*. My eyes followed his hand to the fire, and rested on the burning flames. I meditated on my father's words. He was succinct and correct. He had watched me grow from infant to become a man over the last two decades, and had finally decided he could not go on watching me grow forever. He had to draw a line somewhere, and send me packing out of his house to start a family of my own at some point. And he has decided to start the process that evening.

Sure enough, I was confronted spot-on without notice. But I cannot argue, because both my parents had their own calendar, and they go by that. They had prepared for this moment of my life. I have seen them both at work, and the hardships they've coped with. It was time for me to think seriously, and bail my parents out of these hardships, they had been enduring just for my sake. Surely, the pigs were a real burden to them, and the thought reverberated in my mind, as I tried to put something together, when father come on again. "You must consider your younger brother too", he said, after puffing out a cloud of smoke, that gradually reeked the house with raw tobacco smell, "He's catching up fast behind you. He's courting girls too, and one day he'll, most likely, walk home with a partner for himself too. First thing comes first, and you know that. As the primogeniture, we'll have to sort you out and settle you first, and then concentrate on Paul next. We cannot concentrate on both of you at the same time. This is important! Just think about it, and let your mother and I know of your opinion, before you go back to school. Otherwise, you can perhaps tell us now if you have something, or someone in mind".

There was air of finality in my father's voice, and correctly, nothing more came out of his lips. He was now concentrating on his *brus.* seemingly enjoying every inhale, as he waited and tuned in. It was my turn to talk now, to respond to my father about my views on the subject matter, and the house was in total silence. Everyone wanted to gauge my views. But, quite stubbornly, I found it almost difficult to open my lips. My father's agenda was something, more of a surprise, a bomb thrown at me without expectation and I found it almost difficult to open my lips. And on a more serious note, this was no ordinary discussion, where a compromise can be reached within the next minute. And I remained too dumbfounded to put forward my views.

As the silence prevailed, I revisited my father words again, as if to find some clues in them to start a discussion, or perhaps an argument to start a debate. But I found nothing. I realised without objection that my father was correct in everything he had said. I had witnessed all the travails in rearing the pigs. I had seen my parents going out in the mornings, and both returning home late in the evenings, weak, tired and exhausted, all in their relentless efforts to raise, and keep the pigs healthy. Everything they did was undeniably onerous, and labor intensive, and they certainly had had enough of the animals. And with me at the ripe age, it was an opportune moment to dispose of the pigs, in the manner they had envisaged---in payment for my bride. This was their ultimate goal for their tireless efforts. Even though my mother did not speak any word on the subject, father, as the patriarch, was speaking on their behalf. And I knew she was tuning in and waiting to hear from me too.

Sure enough, I accepted my father's decision to choose a bride wholeheartedly, and without any reservation. Both, him and mother had stoically endured the pains of excessive labor in these moments of their senescence age without any emoluments. I pitied them too. But, quite strangely, in my stubborn confused mind, I refused to entertain the subject. I grossly considered my studies at Unitech more important than women, despite their earnest concern. I preferred to complete my studies first, then talk about women later. I could be mean there, but this was the order of things I preferred to have them lined up for me. And without a second thought, "I have two more years before completing my studies, and right now I am not interested in women," I bluntly voiced, that I believed shocked my father outright.

Though, peremptory, in my tone, it was a pretty ordinary response, coherent and innocuous to the minds of a modern thinker, anyone who moved along with the change of time and technology. But in a rustic and primordial setting, where the primeval ways of life still took precedence over the time change, my response was flippant, harsh and invidious to the minds of my parents. It was intuitively, a total breach of customary obligation, I supposedly was to fulfill on my part. It was all part of the formalities and, likewise, it was my filial duty to obligingly co-operate and accept the decision. But I did not. Instead, I puzzled my parents who didn't expect me to respond negatively in such a manner. And neither spoke a word, nor wanted to continue on the subject again, especially my father, leaving the house in an eerie silence.

I speculated nothing at first, but, minutes later, the oddity of the silence alerted my nerves. Something had definitely gone wrong in the house, and I felt rather odd and more like a foreigner amongst my very own family members in the house. Something is wrong, I thought. I quickly took a furtive glance at my father, then at mother, and later at Paul to establish the likely cause. Paul appeared relaxed in his corner, taking in anything that went his way. But it was my parents that appeared most affected. Sadly, I noticed that my response was invidious, and not at all in their favor and expectations, especially my father who had been doing all the talking. He sulked, looking hopelessly defeated with his head, hanging down loose. He was not enjoying his *brus* anymore. I appeared to have psychologically put him off completely with his discussion, with my flippant response, and the pout on his face divulged the disappointment in him. He was now staring down at his laps in silence. Opposite him, across the fireplace, was mother engrossed in her *bilum*, like she was moments earlier. She did not talk, nor did she dare to contribute anything towards our discussion, but I intuitively sensed the disappointment in her too. It all showed on her face, as the *bilum* twine coiled rapidly around her spinning thumb and little finger in front of her.

The unhappy scene prompted me to re-assess my statement again, and even think deeper. I looked at Paul for the second time. He remained mute and forever silent in his usual posture in the corner, his back against the wall, and ears listening attentively to all the conversations taking place. I considered him neutral and singled him out as 'just a spectator', as the discussion was centered on me alone, and not on him. His turn would come later. But it was the parents, whom I hurt most, when I saw them and this began to worry me. It made me feel uncomfortable, somewhat uneasy and guilty. And I consequently felt more like a stranger, than being the primogeniture in the house. I should have responded nicely, I sadly thought. It certainly was going to be a very important decision, I was to make, a decision of a lifetime that would determine the next phase of my life. And I should have taken my time, thought over it, and, maybe, discussed it further before giving my family the unfilial response, I thought. But I did not. I rushed. I was ignorant and unrespectfully threw everything back at my loyal loving parents, who had been struggling to gratify me without any emolument. Perhaps, I was trying to act smart, like most arrogant university students do, as if they know everything when they go back home to their parents and village, I thought. Regretfully, I guiltily pulled back in deep thought, not wanting to blurt out anything again, thereby causing any further discontent.

It was after a long while later, presumably after regaining composure, that my father spoke again. Clearing his throat first, and drawing out attention to him, he let out his mind, putting us back into the discussion once again. "The pigs are all looking good now, nice and fat", he said, in a defeated tone, "...but anything can happen to them. In the gardens, there's not much *kaukau* left to feed them every day. And if they don't eat, they'll all starve, lose weight and reduce in size. Some may even die, and we don't want that to happen. Our prime goal is to get this 'thing' over, while the pigs are still in their peak form, nice and attractive". He paused momentarily, and then, "I mean, if you don't want a wife right now, we can pre-arrange with your prospective parents–in–law, and get some of the pigs away to them, as part payment of the bride price. We can then settle the balance later when you are ready to take a spouse. That's not as hard as what you may be thinking, son. All you need to do now is to name a girlfriend, or someone you intend to choose for a spouse. I'm sure you have some pretty girls following you right now. We can simply announce the engagement, with any one of them and do some advance payment by removing some of the pigs".

My father stopped, and picking up a burning ember, he lit his *brus* again. He quickly inhaled, as if he had not puffed anything in the last two hours, and exhaled a thick cloud of smoke, that spread right across the entire length of the house. I assumed him to be restless. I again mulled over his words, attempting to establish a decision. My father's latest suggestion on the advance payment was a convincing one, and I already had Cathy Gior's parents, and relatives lined up in mind to get the pigs across to them. But, otherwise, I still did not establish anything mature in my undecided skull yet. I was confused, obstinate and almost mindless to make a serious decision. Really, I was unprepared for this moment, and it was becoming more and more obvious that I needed help and consultations from friends, and even a counseling agency, like the *Life Line*, to get me through it, if there was enough time.

As my eyes ruminatively scanned the room, mother was still in her earlier fixture, her right hand vibrantly spinning above her crossed legs with the thumb and little finger fast gathering and re-coiling the twine around them with dexterity. How could she be so quiescent and remain like this the whole night, and not contribute one bit? I questioned myself in my mind. This family discussion was supposed to be an important one for her and why couldn't she open up, and say something on it. It's all about her future daughter-in-law, and why can't she open up and say contribute on it? Father remained unmoved with his head down, and I knew he was perhaps waiting for me to say something. And when my eyes rested on Paul, I felt a slight change inside me. Though I had considered him a spectator earlier, my mind started wondering to a new direction. I remembered father's earlier sentiments on him. Surely, he was already catching up with me, and father was not wrong in his judgement. He had gone past his teen, and was to turn twenty-one in three months. And he was courting girls too!

Premarital attitudes have changed, and differed from those of the primeval past, and what if Paul comes home with a girl for his spouse, if I continue to remain undecided? My mind started ringing the warning bell. We both cannot get married at the same time. Extraordinary cash and material wealth is required for a single bride price payment, and paying of two brides at the same time was unimaginable for any parent, and I began to realise that, as the primogeniture, it was imperative for me to think seriously. I couldn't be inconsiderate, and keep my parents waiting in suspense, and under immense pressure from the animals, during their current senescence age. They wanted to be free, totally free. In this period of their time, they wanted to sit back, and look forward to the arrival of their grandchildren, something elderly parents relish most. And for another thing, they wanted to focus on Paul alone next, after I'm cleared. I soon realised the significance of their decision, and embraced the fact that I had done my parents total injustice by giving them the negative response.

"Ok father… as you wish", I finally opened up, breaking the long silence, "I really don't know who to pick, but we'll work something out".

My father's head slowly rose. Immediately, there was sign of relief on his face, as what I thought brought smiles, spread across his face. Opposite him, mother smiled too. Both indicated a major breakthrough with their complacent smiles. And in no minute, "Thank you, thank you, my son", my father said happily. "I knew you would say something, and

I'm glad, you finally agreed", he ranted, and, "I mean, this is something you cannot avoid, and I am sure your mother is proud of you too", he added.

"I certainly am", mother voiced from her corner, her wrinkled face glowing radiantly from the lantern light.

I was glad, and proud of myself to have recanted my earlier statement, and for being positive towards my parents. I did, of course, cause some havoc in their minds initially, but, in the end, had not let them down totally. The discussion continued again, and this time, my father freely disclosed what he has in mind on the agenda. He shifted from topic to topic; first, the animals, then the potential bride, then all his creditors, as we all listened. But then, although I had agreed with my parents, some several minutes after assenting to the concession, an ambiguous situation of a debatable nature wafted through my mind. It was the problem of selecting the bride-to-be, when my father landed on the subject in his spiel. I had retrospectively focused my attention on Cathy Gior alone since childhood. And with Cathy already condemned for her infidelity, I was encountered with the problem on who to pick for the spouse-to-be in my mind. During the spiel, I momentarily tried to think of some local girls with whom I had flirted, or made irregular contact, or perhaps had a crush on me, but, strangely, none of them stood out tall and conspicuously in my mind, as Cathy herself. I tried to think harder, but soon realised that my assent towards my parent's decision was only one part of the problem solved.

"Maybe, I should admit Cathy Gior to my family", I thought, "…and tell them about the latest development regarding our relationship".

Certainly, this was the only crucial moment to disclose her to my family, observe their reactions, bag their views and, perhaps, together we could discuss the pros and cons of this choice amongst ourselves, I thought. There was obvious perception that my family would disagree, and dispute my disclosure at first, but apparently surrender to me eventually, if I stood by my decision. This was supposedly the likelihood, but, again, for some reason, I found it difficult and reluctant to speak out.

Then, suddenly and softly, as if she had noticed my problem, my mother spoke out for the first time from her corner. "There's a pretty girl who has been friendly to me every time I crossed her path", she said. "She is beautiful, kind, affable and, above all, generous in everything. She gives and shares with me whatever she has in her hands, no matter how little it is, and I like her. And I am for her too", she openly admitted.

"Who's that girl?" I asked with anticipation and curiosity, immediately wanting to know the girl.

"Anna, the Siako Councilor's daughter", my mother propounded, looking straight across to me for the first time, as if to seek my approval.

"Who is that Anna?"

"Anna Thortia", my mother, said.

Anna Thortia was no stranger to me. I had come across her many times before, and the disclosure of her name was a stunning surprise, and had me staring absent-mindedly at the dying flames. She certainly was another Siako beauty, and I liked her too. But, with my firm bondage to Cathy Gior, I was always respectful towards her, taking her as a kindred sister of Cathy from the same Siako clan. Her greetings, smiles and pleasantries were merely accepted as friendly gestures from someone related to Cathy, frivolous and trivial in every sense, and nothing more.

Then, my father, as if he had been waiting for mother to disclose Anna, "She does that to me too!", he said, in support of his darling, "And I particularly like her working attitude. She does everything for her mother, while she rests. She's sure to be a good wife, and you will never regret later on", father boastfully added, as If I had already given my nod for Anna.

On intuition, I already pictured my parent's reason for mooting the agenda for discussion. They had already got someone in their minds for my spouse, or more specifically, have already associated themselves with someone, and were waiting for this moment to get through to me. Again, it was all part of the formalities, but, disgustingly nothing tangible came into my stubborn head to offer my views on their candidate. I was literally confused, and undecided again, to make an immediate decision, and let out my views on Anna to my parents. Obviously, if I decided on Anna, I would have to lose Cathy Gior, my childhood inamorata forever, and deep inside, I didn't want this to happen. I was literally placed at a crossroads. I needed to take time, sit down properly somewhere and seriously decide first, before disclosing my opinion. And, I scrupled instead to respond immediately.

I was lost in deep thought, again. I glanced across to mother, and stared at her waving hand, as it was playing with the twines there, as if to gather some hope. But nothing helped. "Can we leave this talk pending for a while?" I said, looking straight across to my father, who was fiddling with his *brus*, and then at my mother for approval. Both did not respond. They heard me, but did not dare to look at me, or even made an attempt to speak a word. Most likely, they were not happy again with yet another inconsiderate response. But there was nothing else I could do. I had already run out of options and remained obstinate and maintained my insistence.

"I think, I need some time to think over it", I spoke, almost commandingly, "…just give me about a week to decide".

"Before you go back to Lae?" My father promptly asked, once again in a defeated tone.

"Yes, before I go back to Lae. Just give me this week to work out something, and I promise I will come back to you before I go back to school"

"Oh, okay…then, that sounds good enough. Please try not to drag this thing on", my father said, with a little bit of delight in his voice, "… remember, the sooner the better", he further added.

My mother, who had been listening to everything, praised me highly for my thoughtful words, and appreciatively hugged my knees. "I am going away sooner, or later. Many of my friends in my age group are long gone. You must be quick", she said, encouraging in a motherly tone. The clock was ticking towards midnight. "I will…I promise, I will", I repeatedly told my parents, as we ended our discussion.

I dilatorily temporised our discussion in order to wait for Cathy Gior when she would arrive from Hobe for the school holidays. She had, about a week, left before the schools nationwide closed for the end of year holidays. I was predetermined to discuss everything with her when she would come home. I wanted to let her to know of my parent's intentions, then discuss the subject further and bag her opinion. Maybe, she will have something for me too, I thought. A surprise, perhaps. Moreover, it was also the perfect opportunity to ask for her hand to tie the knot too. For sure, I had absolute confidence in Cathy to affiance me, if I asked for, and I was optimistic on that too.

The following week, I waited impatiently for Cathy to come home. Schools were scheduled for the Christmas holidays, and school children from the nearby Denglagu Community School and the Mt Whilhelm High School were walking home happily to enjoy the long Christmas vacation with their parents. Likewise, many of our local teachers, teaching elsewhere, in other parts of Simbu were coming home with their families. Cathy's uncle, Philip Koane, was the first to come home. He taught at Dirima Community School in Gumine, before the break. After him, many others followed. There was drinking sprees going on everywhere, sponsored by teachers who'd come home with their Christmas break lump sum payments. But Cathy did not show up at the expected time. At first, I suspected the rush hour delay at Negabo. Maybe, she was having trouble trying to get on the plane, I thought. It sounded reasonable too, especially when everyone was rushing to come out of that remote airstrip serviced only by a single Cessna. But after the second week, there was still no sign of Cathy Gior, and this time questions began to pound my mind. What's taking her so long to come home? Is the aging Cessna still servicing that part? Or, is she sick---malaria? Then, as the third week was coming to an end, something suddenly crept into my mind when there was no sight of Cathy altogether in Ende-naige-ingugl---the face of John Mitna. "Don't tell me, she's gone off with the salesman again", I anxiously mused, as I tried to brush aside the thought, and contain myself from ruminating further.

I quickly went around asking relevant people, Cathy's friends and others, whom I thought would know something about her whereabouts. I met my old friend, Thomas Goir, who was now a final year account student at UPNG and asked, but he shrugged his shoulders. "I want to see her too but don't know where she is. She hasn't come home yet. Maybe, she's still in Hobe", he said. Some close girlfriends of Cathy who were supposed to know something about her whereabouts, also indicated the same, when I inquired.

It was a few days before Christmas eve, that I finally received some information on the whereabouts of Cathy Gior. This time, from two tribesmen, who had come home from Mt Hagen for festive season, to celebrate Christmas with their families and friends in the village. "We saw Cathy cruising around in a plushy Toyota landcruiser in Mt Hagen, just days after the schools closed up. We could not identify the owner of the car, but it was sure to be owned by somebody 'up there", both men informed.

"Has it got any Coca-Cola stickers, or logo on the doors", I quickly cut in, after suspecting John Mitna.

"No! Nothing of that; the car was a station wagon, just plain gray in colour with radial wheels, and dark tinted glass all around".

"Oh, my gosh, what is she up to this time?" I mused, as my anxious mind flicked around the clock, to establish the vehicle owner. "Who would own such a flashy car, if it is not John Mitna, that she is going around with this time?" I thought.

I absent-mindedly tried to recall, any of her immediate family members, or kindred owning one such vehicle, but could hardly establish one---none that I knew of. After a futile cerebral search for her mysterious host, I conclusively deduced with reservation that she had reverted, and taken up with somebody else again, in retrospect of her earlier infidelity. But her new man remained a pestering question in my mind.

I was exasperated at the discovery. In the last five months after our reconciliation, Cathy had written six letters to me, with sensational endearments that clouded pessimism of any kind. And I never thought that the past would repeat itself again. But I was wrong in my judgement. These letters now seemed perfunctorily written with no authenticity in them. Cathy was seemingly demonstrating a Dr Jekyll and Mr Hyde character, and I was obviously 'dumped' again, for the second time. I briefly thought back to the earlier reconciliation night at Wai-mambuno after the first infidelity. Gentlemanly, I had accepted her apology, and repentance with open arms. I had delivered and filled her with some fatherly advice. And she had promised never to relapse again, but these all seemed to be a waste, and a total joke. She had reverted again, for the second time, off course. Why did she do this to me? Had she seen me fit for a dupe? I kept asking myself, and was irritated, the more I thought about it, but, ultimately, felt sorry for myself in the end. Clearly, a clever schoolteacher had fooled me again. Maybe, there was something in me that Cathy Gior detested, or something that was not quite appealing to her, but whatever it was, my lust for her was disenchanted, and dwindled for the last time. I was now determined to sit down, and reconsider my association with her.

Day and night, as the weeks passed, my anxious parents expected me to spit out something about the promise, I had made to them. Have I decided on someone, a potential bride yet? They would eagerly ask in their minds. I knew their anticipation for my opinion was burning inside them, but I carelessly ignored them totally. Seriously, the latest turn of events, regarding Cathy's disappearance and the subsequent reports had affected me tremendously, that I didn't want to talk about the subject again. In truth, I just did not feel like mentioning women, or any related subjects anymore.

Then, one afternoon, after the New Year, towards the end of January, as usual, I went out for a ramble to Mondiagl-kaugla to enjoy the evening with friends there, before ending the day. I met my old friend Thomas Goir and, as usual, we chatted and entered into a long conversation.

"Did you meet Cathy?" he suddenly asked. I was almost taken to my feet, and stared blankly into his eyes.

"Where is she?" I quickly asked.

"I heard, she came home yesterday afternoon", Tom said, "…and left this morning. And I am asking if you had possibly met her yesterday".

"No! Not at all. I didn't see her, Tom".

"Me too…I didn't see her. I spent the whole of yesterday at Kuaglke-nigle, and spend the night up there. I only learnt of her arrival when I came down here after midday today. But she already left for Kundiawa in the morning. That's what I heard".

"Was she in a hurry or something?"

"I wouldn't know anything about that either. Maybe, she was, otherwise, she'll still be here".

It was an astounding discovery. And after Thomas and I parted, I quickly waylaid Anasas, Cathy's young sister at Mondiagl-kaugla, later in the evening. She was also out on an afternoon stroll with a friend.

"I heard Cathy arrived yesterday afternoon, and left this morning. Is that true?", I asked.

"Yes, she came home last night, and left early this morning".

"What's the story here…is she coming back this afternoon?"

Anasas thought for a while, then. "No, I don't think so", she briskly responded with hints of hesitation.

I noticed the scruple, and quickly guessed that she was hesitant to admit something.

"What is it?" I demanded, with ease, as she tried to move on with her friend, "I can see, you are trying to hold back something form me. Is something wrong?", I asked.

Anasas paused for a while, as if trying to decide whether to tell me everything. And some seconds later, to my dismay, I received the most shocking news of my lifetime.

"Cathy's married", Anasas finally admitted.

"What? Married? It that true? You can't be kidding", I said, looking on with a frown.

"Yes…her husband is a prominent business elite from the Western Highlands, somebody from an area just outside Mt Hagen town. She arrived here yesterday to inform us all about her marriage to that man, and returned this morning to Kundiawa to arrange for her transfer to teach in the Western Highlands; at a school somewhere closer to her husband's home. The husband will be traveling down this morning to Kundiawa to pick her up. So, mother went along with Cathy to meet her new son-in-law in Kundiawa. She'll be back in the afternoon".

"So, Cathy is married", I finally reiterated, disbelievingly.

"Yes, she is married, Tom", Anasas said, in a muffled tone.

"Well, that is new", I said, looking away into the empty space, my mind already in a turmoil.

I never quite wanted to hear *'Cathy is married'*, from anyone on this planet, and found it almost difficult to digest every word that had come out of Anasas' lips. I felt quite lost, depressed, psychologically neglected and betrayed in my mind. And it did not take long for Anasas' percipient eyes to notice the peculiar state of my mind. To her disgust, she also instantly realised that I was not the right person either, to disclose any information on Cathy's romantic and matrimonial affairs. She seemed crushed inside and briskly excused herself to go, and eventually left with her friend. I stood alone, trying to put my disturbed mind together, but it was too much for me to end it from thereon. I was definitely lost and undecided. Finally, after some good sensible thinking, I conclusively agreed that Cathy Gior was only double-crossing me, and deriding my efforts with her many voluminous romantic letters. She has done it before and had reverted again. And there was no point in crying over spilled milk, either. With my head hanging down low in deep thought, I walked home to Bokan to end the miserable afternoon.

14

A Mad Scramble for Wealth

When the school year commenced in early February, I left for Lae to start my second year at Unitech. My brother, Paul boarded at Maina Vocational School to undergo his final year of carpentry training. However, my departure, this time, was not an appreciated one, as it was in the previous years. My shifty approach and intransigent behavior towards the affiancing proposition had incurred the odium of my parents, and both complimented me very little on this trip, even though my loving mother was always there beside me to hug me 'goodbye'.

"Safe trip, son, and look after yourself", was all they managed to deliver, as I bade farewell to them at Mondiagl-kaugla to begin my trip.

They were upset and uncomfortable. And I could see it. I had not disclosed my opinion on their proposition and, quite obviously, both were kept in suspense again, with Anna closely associating with them. I perceived the mental and physical stress they'd be subjected to during my absence. But things had not personally worked out well for me, and I was`not at all in a sane position to be decisive. Seriously, the latest turn of events was a disaster for me too. But I also disclosed nothing of this to my parents too. "Just stick close to Anna", I blankly advised, as I embarked on the PMV.

I wasn't too sure whether my line did sink in well into their minds, but that was the least I could do. I temporised the proposition to a later date, purposely to let my disturbed mind rest and resume normal function first.

But in Lae, I began the year with a terrible start at the campus. As weeks rolled past, I kept recalling Cathy's infidelity. I tried to compromise why she had to do this to me twice. Did she every really love me? Why did she write all those voluminous letters of romance and endearments to me, when she never really loved me? Has she been trifling with my affections all along then? The more I pondered on the subject, the more questions I began to ask. But, ultimately, nothing appealing or compromising settled into my head to put the matter to rest. I glanced at the mirrors to see for myself it I looked more like a stupid, or some kind of a lunatic released lately from the Laloki Psychiatric Camp. But the mirrors hid nothing of me. I looked all right, perfectly fine; perhaps handsome to some secret admirers. And I couldn't reason out why Cathy had to 'dump' me twice.

It was sometimes later, that a clear sense of understanding gradually settled into my head. "Why do I have to let a single, just one, woman out of the many thousands of others, dominate my entire life and cause me all these miseries, head aches and grief? Why do I have to really 'crawl' on my knees everyday, and night just for a single woman, when there were so many others out in pursuit of a gentlemen like myself? And why do I have to blow my mind everyday for a humbug, who considered me a dupe?"

And for the first time since I met Cathy Gior, I finally reached a compromise, that she was, maybe beautiful, but certainly not ideal for a life long spouse, let alone a faithful partner, and courageously decided to repudiate her. It was a tough decision, but I remained firm and stood by it. She no longer deserved my trust, and was not to be trusted anymore, and should never be trusted again, I finally decided.

With Cathy Gior dismissed from my life, Anna Thortia automatically became the potential 'spouse-to-be' candidate in my mind to settle the desires of my anxious parents. I did not have to retrospectively look far. The fact that she was closely associating herself with my parents, back home, already placed her as the next option after Cathy Gior. Further, Anna close association with my parents was an added bonus too, as obligations would work out accordingly, if I gave my consent.

But effectively, on the other hand, a certain face---the face of someone else, I had met in Lae, the previous year, was gradually sailing into my mind too: a lass, also from Gembogl from the neighboring Wandike clan. Her name was Druagle Peni.

A shop assistant at the Papindo Supermarket in Eriku, Druagle, completed her Grade 10 education at Bumayong High School, outside Lae, but missed securing a place at a tertiary institution. I got to knowing her some two months after settling in at Unitech, the previous year. Perhaps, it was easy knowing her too, because we had originated from the same area, Gembogl, in Simbu. Her Wandike parents migrated to Lae back in the early 1970s, when she was an infant and she lived at the Boundary Road Settlement ever since. She was into her late teens, pretty and gorgeous, and had all the looks of a highlands supermodel in her Papindo uniform, when I first saw her. Her beauty attracted me when I walked into the Papindo shop to cool off under the aircon with some schoolmates one Saturday. She was one of the cashier girls. After tracking her for some time, with a bit of research into her origin, we finally got to know each other. And after some brief meetings, I was invited to her home at Boundary Road. At first there were objections by some of the family members, but soon I was made part of the family, after getting to know me better.

Anna, on the other hand, lived all her life in the village with her parents, and little brother Gigmai. I wouldn't know anything much about her village background. But, according to my parents, under the strict guidance, discipline, care and mentoring from her respected father and mother, she developed into a hardworking and obedient young woman, loved, respected and envied by all. "She does everything, while her mother relaxes away in their home", my parents had said, of Anna. She was a kindred sister to Cathy Gior, and she fully aware of our relationship running errands between Cathy and myself when need arose. And she had always respected that relationship between me and Cathy initially. But it was on the day I was snubbed, and publicly humiliated by Kumo at Mondiagl-kaugla, on that fateful November afternoon, that things changed for her. She was deeply annoyed with Kumo for her invectives and condoled my predicament deep in her sympathetic heart. Her sympathy soon veered into affection. But she furtively remained silent over it. It was only after Cathy Gior's infamous affair with John Mitna, the Coca-cola saleman that she saw the door opening up for her, and started a relationship with my parents, which captured their attention.

There were several rare moments when Anna tried to confront me too, after Kumo's public outburst, but I was blind. The most notable, I remembered, was an afternoon where she bought me a handful of betelnuts at Mondiagl-kaugla market during one of the school holidays. I remember standing near a betelnut vendor, when she came along, produce a K1.00 coin and collected the nuts to the value of the money. Then, walking across to me, she said, "Your betelnuts here, take them", and passed me the nuts, suprising me.

"You bought them all for me?" I had asked. She had nodded

"All of them?"

"Yes"

"That's very kind of you", I had said, after collecting the betelnuts thankfully from her hands.

I had taken that generous act lightly, considering the betelenuts as a token gift coming from one of Cathy Gior's sisters. But she had not left immediately. Instead, she had posed some distance away from me, near enough where I could still be able to talk to her. Off course, we had talked and chewed the betel nuts together. I remember, she had maintained an affectionate smile, and eyed me with leers, as we conversed. But I truly had failed to decipher the true state of her mind. She definitely had had something in mind for me that moment, but I had failed to perceive the motive of her attitude.

I soon 'short listed' the two girls in my mind; Druagle in Lae and Anna back home. In Lae, I continued my normal relationship with Druagle, making sure that all was going well and smoothly, but in truth, deep inside, I was already standing in the middle of a cross road, lost and confused, which way to go. I was deciding between Anna and Druagle, juxtaposing both girls in everything, and making my comparisons, weighing out the pros and cons. With due respect, I could easily pick on Anna Thortia, who was already at home and undoubtedly, would elope to Bokan and live with my parents, if I give my consent. But I considered Druagle for other things too, the financial support I was getting from her. I'll surely be missing out on that in Lae, if I should let go of her, I thought. She had been my only financial source during my student life and I'll certainly miss out on that support if I put a stop to our relationship, and that would be a disaster in itself. With a year remaining to complete my studies, I didn't want to sacrifice that support.

Day and night, I put my mind into it, but still, there was no breakthrough. Easter was approaching fast, and I was still stubborn and indecisive. Then, one night, something good finally entered my mind.

"Maybe, I should let my parents decide for me between the two girls", I thought, "I'll brief them about the girls, and let them choose for me which one to take".

Bang! The puzzle was solved. I, for sure, knew that their obvious choice would be Anna, because they never knew who Druagle Peni was. But I needed their input to settle my undecided mind once and for all, and close the files on this matter. Moreover, this will satisfy, and please them enormously, and make them feel more responsible for Anna, should they decide on her, I mused. Yes, it was finally decided and settled at last. The parents would decide and choose for me between the two girls---Anna Thortia and Druagle Peni!

During the Easter break, in April, I took a bus ride from Eriku, the first bus that left for the highlands in the morning and traveled straight for home, arriving in Kundiawa at 4.00 pm. It was Easter Thursday or Maundy Thursday, as is commonly known and was a pay weekend. With the Easter long weekend coming up, the township was packed to its capacity. The street pavements were crowded and packed with people, all bumping and jostling into each other, as they struggled to move around the town. The main street, likewise, was jam-packed with cars and trucks of all makes, moving at a snail's pace to avoid knocking down the busy jaywalking pedestrians in the streets. The last day of business in town truly must have meant many things to the Simbus, and it seemed that the entire populace was in town, I thought, as I jumped off the bus.

I decided to take a quick walk around the town before taking another PMV home, just in case, I met up with someone I knew, or run into a regular PMV operator bound for Gembogl out in the car parks in front of the shops. I walked past the Police Station, and the John 47 Store. Across the street, on the far side, in front of the NBC studio, was a group of people crowding around a busker. The entertainer was Kundiawa's very own Kembri Kua. His distinct, uncompromised voice, could be heard from where I was, howling the ever-popular *Waikiki Tamure*, well above the uncoded strums of his plastic ukulele, while the crowd laughed and cheered him on.

Further down, next to the Post Office, was another mass of people, all crowding around another street entertainer. And, this time, it was Kura, another ever popular, but mentally retarded Simbu, famous all over the province for his unbelievable made-up adventure tales.

Walking bravely through the crowd, I continued down the street, wandered in and out of the shops, and eventually got to the front entrance into the Collings & Leahy Supermarket. It was packed to the fullest. After a quick look-around, I jostled past the crowd, and veered around the corner towards the airport. To my left was the graveyard of Simbu's only prominent politician to date, the late Sir Iambake Okuk, and on my right the busy street heading to the bank, the airport and all other shops located on the upper eastern section of the four-cornered township. As I was about to reach the top street, I noticed a plush Toyota Land Cruiser station wagon, driving lazily with hardly any sound up to the bend. It was a gray in color, had mag wheels and tinted glasses all round. I could hardly see anyone inside, but it certainly was a dream car for anyone eyeing the vehicle. The rear blinker to the right came on at the end of the street, and I thought it was pulling in at the PNGBC car park on the other side of the street, but the vehicle continued straight down the road, and headed towards the Dixion Oval.

I proceeded into the Sika Super Market. Like all other stores, it was packed with customers inside, and with no set purpose in there, I decided to turn back, instead of going all the way into the store. This shop also concluded my walk-about search. My next destination was the Gembogl PMV Stop, where I'd be catching a PMV home. Turning back, I jostled through the crowd made my way out towards the entrance, excusing a queue of customers who were busy at the serving counter with the cashier girls, as I passed. Then, as I stepped out onto the entrance door, after a brief body search by the security for any hidden stolen items from the shop, my eyes suddenly caught sight of the flashy station wagon again. This time, it was pulling into the car park in front of the shop. I was in such a hurry that I took little notice of it at first, but then, I saw a gorgeous looking young girl, stepping out of the car, when the front door to the left opened up. She momentarily lured my attention, and I paused for a while to take a quick look at her before proceeding to the PMV stop. She was cute, had dark sunglasses over her eyes, and was neatly dressed with the latest outfits of some kind. Her hair was nicely permed, and appeared professionally done at a hair salon.

However, despite the irregular appearance, the girl characteristically looked more like someone I knew. Mouth agape, I peered on with curiosity.

"She looked more like Cathy", I thought. "Could this be her?" I mused curiously.

Then, as if being instinctively aware of my curiosity, the girl somehow removed the glasses away from her eyes for some reason, and threw them back into the car.

Suddenly, everything broke loose, the moment the glasses came off. My heart in no time doubled its beat, and pounded vigorously against my chest. My breathing intensified. I was not mistaken. The girl was Cathy Gior. She was standing right there in from of me, only less then ten meters away. Although, there were some slight changes after the brief make-up and fresh clothes on her body, there was not much difference on her physical appearance. And the car? It was not a mistake, as everything began to piece together in my mind almost in an instant. The station wagon was the very vehicle Cathy was said to have been cruising around in Mt Hagen last Christmas.

The door to the right opened up and a hoary-haired gentleman, presumably in his late forties, stepped out of the car. He was thickly bearded, slightly paunchy and opulently dressed in King Gee khaki from the top to bottom. His face was well shaded by a Stetson, which fitted nicely over his head. Down on his feet, a new pair of tan polished Blunderston Stockman put the finishing touches to the striking ensemble. With his age, I admired the sartorial elegance in his dressing and envied him.

"That man must be Cathy's father-in-law", I said to myself, as I stood watching them both. "And the busband?" The question suddenly popped into my head, but no answer was yet evident.

There were some people sitting in the rear seats, but none of them dared to come out. It appeared Cathy and her man were out to collect a few things, then would return back soon.

Taking the lead, Cathy walked her way into the store with the gentleman following closely behind her. I had been eagerly watching her for the past moment with expectation, and suddenly our eyes met when she looked my way. On impulse, I let out a gorgeous smile with a fawning look. But quite strangely, and rather unbelievably, she masqueraded and ignorantly looked away. She pretentiously walked past, as if she had never known me before, and hurriedly led her man into the store, as if she portended danger looming behind her. My smile immediately disappeared. Her surprise and sudden change of attitude left me in wonderment, and I tried to comprehend why she did that. Maybe, she had not seen me properly, I thought. But there was broad daylight outside. And inside, the super market was brilliantly lit up by dozens of electricity light tubes, with the power source coming all the way from the giant, and most famous power plant in the country, the Yonki Power plant, and she could not be mistaken.

Then, I remembered the middle-aged gentleman. Something clicked in my mind. "That man is not her father-in-law", I said thoughtfully, "It must be her husband, the local businessman, everyone talked about at home. No wonder, she had to masquerade and looked away from me to please her man, for there was no other guy in Simbu apart from himself"

I cringed back with embarrassment, knowing how inane it was to force out that fatuous smile. Moreover, I had already repudiated Cathy in my life only weeks earlier: why do I have to try and get in her way again? I must be out of my mind. I am a damn fool, I thought. Sheepishly, without looking back, I walked out of the supermarket with guilt and embarrassment, and disappeared into the crowd outside.

It was getting very late in the evening. Across the sky, thick black clouds closed in, covering the entire township of Kundiawa and a rainstorm was imminent in the next hour or two. I scurried down to the

Piunde Gas Station, hoping all along that some car would be waiting to pull out when I arrive. But I was obviously late. All the familiar PMVs, operating along the Kundiawa-Gembogl route, had already left while the sun was still up, according to some passengers when I enquired. There was no other regular vehicle around, or still in town to lift our hopes either, and I felt slightly anxious, standing there. But seeing that there were still many unfortunate people around in dire need to catch a PMV home, I joined them with relief soon after learning that some of these passengers were to join me all the way to Gembogl station. At least there were some passengers around to numerically convince any PMV operator of the economical worthiness of the long-distance trip up the valley in this late hour, I thought.

We waited in anticipation for some PMV's to come along but, seemingly, nothing was forthcoming. And with the daylight slowly ebbing, I decided to pass the night in town, and travel up to Bokan the following day. It wasn't a bad idea, and as I was going to leave for the Gon hill to pass the night there at a friend's house, a two-wheel drive Mitsubishi L200, owned by a Goglme entrepreneur pulled to a stop in front of us. "Gembogl-Mondiagl-kaugla, Gembogl-Mondiagl-kaugla", pattered the driver, who was without an off-sider. Fortunately, the vehicle was making a Gembogl-Mondiagl-kaugla run, and the driver was announcing his travel route to lure the waiting passengers.

All of a sudden, the Mitsubishi L200 was probably one of the last vehicles to pull in at the PMV stop, and there was a mad-rush from the waiting passengers to get on the vehicle. There were passengers from all stops along the route who tried to board, but the driver was strict on Gembogl passengers alone. Regardless of the driver's direction almost everyone got on top of the L200. I was fortunate to secure a space and uncomfortably wedged in amongst the crowded passengers. But despite the overloading, many kept filing in on any available space they could find. And soon, there was no more space to take in anyone, even a child. Those sitting around the edges had their other leg hanging outside, with the other inside to keep them balanced on the vehicle. In the front three lucky passengers shared the cabin with driver, that was obviously meant for two people. Finally, at the end of the head count, there were twelve lucky people on board with their bags and everything, including trade store cargoe. The load was unbelievably more than what the Mitsubishi Company in Japan had recommended for that particular vehicle, but in PNG it was diffrent. I was wondering if the operator would unburden the load by removing some of us, and of coure, some of the cargo also, but satisfied with his load and his money that was forthcoming from the passengers, and from the cargo he loaded, he got into his car and started the engine. "Hold on tight", he bellowed, and pressing on the horn firmly to clear the crowd in his front, he gently released his clutch and stepped on the accelerator.

Packed like sardines in a fish can, we pulled out of Yuai and traveled at a snail's pace up the Upper Simbu gorge. But unfortunately the weather forecast for the Gembogl was not promising either. The thick black portentous clouds that had blanketed Kundiawa Township gathered further in the north, and a very heavy rainstorm was also imminent in the entire valley. Sadly, the first drops showered us at Mandime, almost 12 km outside of Kundiawa township. It was heavy and poured continuously without any respite, as if the gods had opened the floodgates of a mighty dam in the sky.

We passed Goglme under heavy rain. I was pleased, we made progress and arrived this far under such terrible weather condition, considering the dilapidated state of the Mitsubishi L200. And to my delight, almost half of the passengers got off along the route, and there was now adequate space for a comfortable ride home. In the next hour, I should be at home, nice and comfortable by the fireplace, I thought. Already, a mental glimpse of a high flame was burning spontaneously in my freezing mind. But sadly, we had not got far when my dream of home and the burning flame was shattered. We encountered yet another pluvial disaster.

At Oyame, just outside Goglme, this time, the heavy rain caused a major landslide on the upper ground, around the Boan escarpment, and the entire road was closed off to traffic. "It just came down only a while ago", a bystander informed us, when we neared the road block. From my assessment, it could be possible for a four-wheel drive to make its way through, but it was certainly impassable for two wheel-drive motor vehicle. Our driver pulled to the side and walked out to assess the situation and the condition of the road. Benumbed and torpid to do anything, we remained on the back of the car, waiting to get his report and decision. And after quick look around, the driver returned.

"I'm sorry fellows, the pile of debris is too much, and I don't think I'll make it to the other side", he reported.

He was evidently not wrong after all, and there was no point in arguing either. The mountain of debris in front of us was just too much for his two-ton Mitsubishi to drive across, and we all saw it. The only option available was to get off and continue the journey from the other side by any means available, perhaps in another vehicle, or resort to something else.

"It's alright, it's terrible out in the front and we cannot blame anyone here. We'll just get off and continue, maybe in another vehicle on the other side", we told the driver, accepting his decision, and got off the car. The PMV operator solicitously refunded a third of the total fare back to each passenger and wishing us good luck, turned back to Goglme.

Hopelessly, we crossed the landslide. The mountain of debris was too much and the mud was knee deep. Since I had traveled alone without any baggage, I helped the other passengers with their loads, as we floundered through the debris to the other side of the road. Everyone was thankful for my generosity and in return, some offered me betel nuts in exchange for my service. This was just what I needed at such a time---something that would defreeze my numb body---and I thankfully acknowledged their kind gesture, as the diaphoretic effect of chewing the betel nuts brought some temporary relief and comfort back into my benumbed body, as we waited in the rain.

There were five of us in total, including a woman, all soaked wet and bedraggled in the incessant rain. With nowhere else to hide, we slouched impatiently in the never-ending rain on the other side of the road, hoping that some PMVs would drive past and pick us up, but, with the murky and menacingly cold weather prevalent, not even one vehicle drove past. Most PMV operators sensed the menacing weather and had stopped for the day, long before. The longer we stayed under the rain, the more critical our situation became. I pitied one of the passengers, who had traveled with trade store goods for his canteen. The cartons of cardboard boxes got heavily saturated in the rain and tore open, spilling all their contents onto the wet ground. It was a real nightmare for him. We gathered what we could for him, but I don't know whether he'll ever line them on the self again for his customers. The rain continued and there was nothing else we could do to stop it.

It was about an hour later that we finally heard a fading sound of an engine in the distance, obviously coming from the south, where we had already covered. Our hearts jumped almost immediately with delight. Our hopes were resurrected. Over and over, we re-tuned our dumb ears for no mistake, as we rested all our hopes on the approaching vehicle.

"Yes! It's coming from the south", one said excitedly.

"Let's just pray that it is a four-wheel drive", another babbled between his shivering lips.

"I bet so," said another.

"And, there must be enough space for us all too", another muttered almost beggingly, as our eyes remained fixed at the final bend.

We briefly saw the illuminating rays of the headlights on the tree tops, grass and bushes on the adjacent bends and ridge tops in the front and above us, as the car meandered in and out of the elbows on the other face of the ridge-way. A little while later, the sound of the engine got louder, and louder, and soon the vehicle emerged at the final bend, and into visibile range. But sadly, our hearts sank to the bottom when a station wagon meandered around the carves towards the landslide. The vehicle was certainly not a PMV, or any other open back pick-up that could pick us all up, as we had hoped for. And we slouched hopelessly in dismay, as the station wagon pulled up to the landslide.

"This is an unusual car on this road", one of the passengers managed to open his shivering lips, as we looked on.

"You are not wrong…it is my first time to see it on this road too", said another.

The vehicle soon approached the pile of debris. All of a sudden, like an invisible lightning flashing up in my spine, I remembered the grey land cruiser outside the Sika store. Could this be it again? I wondered, as I eyed the station wagon with curiosity from the other side. But why would a rich man of very high reputation risk his life travelling up this way, especially at this time of the night under this weather condition?

When the vehicle finally got closer, in the ebbing light, I finally identified the station wagon. It was the same one, which I had seen in Kundiawa; the color, grey, mag wheels and tinted glass all around. Yes, it was Cathy Gior and her husband with their entourage, presumably up on their way to Ende-naige-ingugl to spend the Easter there.

It stopped some distance away from the pile of debris. Then under the shining lights of the headlight beams, a man stepped out to assess the situation. He was not the same man I saw in the Sika Store, but someone different, someone seemingly much younger, who was garbed in different clothing from that I saw in Kundiawa. He walked around the pile, surveyed its extent, and then went back and got into the car. For a while, the station wagon did not move. On perception, I knew a discussion was certainly taking place in the car---a discussion to either to turn back, or cross the landslide. And with the enormous pile of debris in front, I thought Cathy's man would simply turn the vehicle back to Kundiawa. Certainly, he'll not want to risk his plushy vehicle or, more importantly, his precious life, trying to get across the mass, and then end up many feet down in the Upper Simbu gorge along side the Simbu River. And far more important, he was just too important a person to travel on such a road in this weather condition, I thought.

But when the engine revved again, it was the opposite. The vehicle slowly moved forward, and with its engine responding very well to the engagement of four-wheel-drive gear transmission, the station wagon roared over the pile of earth, mud, rocks and debris with ease to the other side of the road. Amazingly, there was very little struggle in crossing the debris pile than we had anticipated. The station wagon slithered initially, then danced a little about halfway through, and finally reached the other side with ease and very little struggle. It was truly amazing, and full credit goes to the man from the land of the rising sun, or whoever brilliantly invented the four-wheel-drive transmission. Stopping briefly to release the four-wheel-drive transmission from L4 to H4, the vehicle accelerated past us, and disappeared at the next corner.

It was too dark to see who was in the car, but I knew Cathy Gior was in there somewhere, otherwise, this particular vehicle would not be coming up this way. She had got out from the front left seat in Kundiawa. So, she would obviously be in the same place. I knew, she saw me standing out there in the cold rain, wet, bedraggled and benumbed through the headlight beam. And she knew exactly why I was standing there at this time of the hour. Yes, I was on my way home, and she knew it, but it was a pity that she did not do anything about it, I felt. I stood watching as the car traversed in and out of the bends and finally disappeared in the final corner.

It was already past 6.30pm. The rain had finally subsided, but the possibility of getting on a PMV was slim because of the darnkness now creeping in. Losing patience, I decided to take a walk instead, and maybe, hitch hike on any vehicle that came on the way, rather than waiting all night. Maybe, I can walk into a *yagl-ingu* along the way, and spend the night, if I find I cannot continue any further, I thought. I was disclosing my plans to my four comrades when a fading sound of another vehicle echoed in the distance, again from the south. Our hopes were resurrected again for the second time. We remained slouching in anticipation, not daring to speak a word after our last experience with the station wagon. The sound of the engine got louder and louder, and finally the vehicle emerged in the fore bend. It was a white Toyota Land cruiser open-back and my eyes could never be mistaken for my uncle's *'Ambu Kindal,'* the name given to his jalopy, an old model HZ 74 Toyota land cruiser.

Already there was smile on the faces of everyone. We could see from the other side that he was traveling alone, without any passenger at the back. It crossed the debris pile, again with ease and pulled to stop beside us. He let out a smile, when he saw me and opened the front door to let me into the cabin.

"What are you doing here at this time and weather?", he asked, staring up and down, as I struggled to get into the front. "You must have been out here for some good hours", he said.

"Three good hours, I guess", I murmured through my benumbed lips, "Maybe more".

"Good grief, three hours? What happenered?"

"I'll explain later. Can you get us out of here fast? I'm freezing".

"Relax! Don't you worry any more, we are all going home. You'll soon be beside the fireplace. Let your other friends get on first".

"I can't wait, uncle".

My uncle laughed.

As the others were getting on, I briefly went through the tragedies we encountered in the last two hours, only to regret later that my uncle was still around in Kundiawa while I was struggling to get home on the two-wheel drive Mitsubishi.

"I pulled out late", he said, "There was a faulty engine, so, I put the car into the workshop at Wara Simbu. When I finally got it out, there was no one at the PMV stop. The heavy rain had dispersed everyone. So, I traveled up alone".

"I could have waitied for you, if someone had told me that you were still in town, and had not yet left".

There was silence during most of the trip. We passed Womatne, Womsike and Bendam, all under the cover of darkness. In the next three minutes, we would drive past Gembogl Station. Then, it would be a mere eight minutes drive to reach Mondiagl-kaugla. I was already dreaming of a burning fire, with high flames, to chase the cold away from my benumbed body. In the mean time, I had the door glass wound to the top to keep out the cold and forced my uncle to do the same on the door on his side.

But, despite the cold, Cathy Gior's rude and selfish bearing could not easily go away from my mind, and bothered me during the entire journey. I could not believe at all that Cathy deliberately ignored me out in the cold while traveling in style and comforts of a flashy station wagon. How could she do that after knowing me for almost twenty years? I kept asking myself in my mind. Maybe, she's married and does not have time for for me anymore, but being married does not mean that she doesn't know me. At least lending a hand in times of dire need and disaster would be much more valued than total ignorance, I thought. At least, I deserved from her a sense of compssion and humour at this difficult hour for someone who was so close to her only months earlier, but that was unfortunate and not forthcoming from her. Although Cathy had decided to drop me for someone new, I felt like a stab in my back over her recent selfishness. She could have said, "Stop! He's my brother, he must have been dropped off here due to the landslip. Let's give him a lift", and directed the driver, or her man to stop and pick me up. And, off course, as an intellectual and a victim of a dreadful catastrophe in dire need for a helping hand, I wouldn't have done anything stupid to upset her, or her new found love, but gratefully take the back seat or the rear compartment with the spare tire (if there was any in the car). But she was truly mean---mean and selfish, I thought. Pity it was and the thoughts reverberated in my mind, as my uncle navigated his way through the Upper Simbu gorge.

As the *Ambu Kindagl* jerked and joggled through the bumpy road of the gorge, I briefly thought back to the bygone years and sensed a twinge of jealousy against Cathy's new man. But, later, introspectively, accepted the fact that I was not the ideal man for her. Times had changed and she was becoming more and more unpredictable in recent times. More importantly, her change of attitude towards sybaritic pleasures was increasingly becoming evident and irresistible to her. I don't have a car, let alone a station wagon. I don't have a highly coveted house, and above all, I don't even have money or a single Toea in my bank account. I am only a lousy student forester, I thought, and not even on a paid job. And seriously it would become very difficult for people like myself of bourgeois status to keep up to Cathy's expectations. In this world of many things, where money seemed to become the pride and source of everything, many women are alike in their quest for men. They selective on their male partners unlike the past, and most women prefer the proletariat who are well educated, employed and highly paid, or a businessman who is living an opulent life with high reputation. Seriously, it is really the wealth of a person that attracts a woman nowadays, and not the physical appearance, I thought.

My mind started to open up to the everyday situation amongst girls in PNG. I soon deduced that the many classes of girls that hanker after wealth, riches and sybaritic luxuries are those that see, touch and value money as the only source of survival, joy and comfort in their life. It was as if someone had just imparted into my mind some sense of truth about the general behavior of the modern PNG girls. I started reviewing analytically some of the girls in my life, and soon, realised that the very few exceptional group of girls that remain submissive to the grandeur of western influence were those back in the village, those who know very little about money. But it was the total opposite with educated and town girls. And before we reached Mondiagl-kaugla, my attention was conclusively fixed on Anna Thortia as my future wife. She currently led a spartan's life working hard in the gardens, greeting people and looking after the old nicely and, above all, obedient and more diciplined in every sense. She was certainly going to be a good wife. Druagle was, maybe, beautiful but I empirically deduced that she might become 'another Cathy' in the future, because of her exposure to the many things of the city.

We passed Bomkane, my uncle's home village, and then Engre-mambuno, my clansmen's pig killing festival ground. After conquering the Tem-nigle ascent, we finally reached Mondiagl-kaugla. When my uncle drove past Endenaige-ingugl I saw the snazzy station wagon parked to the side at the entrance into the village, and well knew that Cathy Gior and her husband were now in the village. Briefly, the entire picture of Cathy introducing her millionaire husband to her family, and the queue of friends and relatives going in and out of the Giors' home to greet and welcome the couple flashed in my mind, with Kumo sitting by the fireplace, sweating all over, trying to prepare the best dish of her lifetime for this son-in-law. What a wonderful Easter weekend it would be for her, I thought, as my uncle pulled into Mondiagl-kaugla.

My uncle turned back to Bomkane after dropping me off. When I arrived home, my parents were shocked to see me in such a terrible condition in the shivering cold night.

"What happened?" they inquired, after greeting me.

"There was a landslide, so I couldn't get home on time". I said, and explained all the tragedies I had encountered.

I demanded my father, as a matter of urgency to make a very big fire for me. Seeing the condition I was in, he wasted no time, and quickly took a *dinbede* down from the firewood rack above the fire place. He got it split up and started a fire. It was a very big fire, just as what I had wanted all along. While defrosting my benumbed body, I did not waste any time too.

"About Anna…", I said, "how are you getting along with her? Are you both still maintaining your relationship with her?" I asked my parents, touching on the pending subject, I had temporised for a while too long, while my memory of the latest mishap was still fresh in my mind.

"My good son, she is very close to us now. What is it that you want to say about her?", my mother burbled excitedly, as if I had touched on something, that she had been waiting to hear for ages.

"Well, I think I've made up my mind now"

"Mind? What have you decided about her?"

"To take her as my bride"

"Oh, thank you, my son, thank you", my mother said, almost in jubilation.

But my father, who was still working on the fire, perhaps did not catch my words clearly from my trembling lips.

"Sorry, Joe. What did you just say to your mother? She sounds happy" he asked, tuning in.

"Yeah, about Anna…remember? I said, I have decided to take Anna as my bride now", I repeated.

My father stopped everything he was doing, as if something touched him. "Thank you very much, my son", he said, commending me with great delight. "We have waited too long, and that's absolutely good thinking. Anna is very close to us now, and that is very good of you to say that".

"Yeah, I was thinking hard and finally decided to choose her. And there's just one more thing to add here" I interjected disrupting their attention, "I've just made my decision, and you heard it, correct?"

"Yes, we did, son, and we liked it", both my parents chorused.

"It's final and you can take over from here with whatever needs to be done to formalise the engagement. But, do it after I go back to Lae--- that is after the long weekend! Is that clear?"

"Oh, that's not a problem, we will do it, the way you want it", my father said proudly, "We can arrange that, and let you know of the outcome through someone coming to Lae".

"Correct! That's a good idea, and that's how I want it done", I affirmed.

There was a complacent atmosphere of joy and satisfaction in the house. I had finally made my decision that my family had been waiting for a long time. My parents were both very pleased at my disclosure. I had kept them in suspense for a very long time, and now it was all over. Fortunately, I had precisely chosen the candidate of their choice and liking to be affianced. Both were jubilant, and had many things to rant about Anna Thortia, dragging the night along with heaps of encomiums about their candidate till late.

15

The Greener Pastures

The sun was already up when I woke up the following morning. It was a nice long sleep, but I was annoyingly disturbed from the sleep by some people talking outside my house. They were obviously baking themselves in the early morning sunlight, just next to the wall where I was sleeping. As I listened, I heard my father's muffled voice, and then that of some neighbours. They were talking of a big *mumu* taking place at Ende-naige-ingugl. I heard somebody mentioning the Giors, and Cathy, and later Cathy's husband. So, the Gior's are hosting a *mumu* for Cathy and her husband, I thought, as I woke up from my bed. When I came out of the house, I saw thick white clouds of smoke curling up lazily, and wafting away into the clear sky above Ende-naige-ingugl.

The peculiar smoke also attracted the attention of nearly everyone in the surrounding villages. Soon, Cathy's visit with her husband became the talk of the day. There was a rumour hawked around that Cathy's millionaire husband had come to make part payment of the bride price to Cathy's parents, but no one was really sure of that. I felt a bit sick to move around after that tiring journey, the previous evening, and went back to sleep again in the house. When I recovered fully later in the afternoon, I went for a leisure walk to Mondiaglkaugl. It was a beautiful Good Friday afternoon, and, as I crossed the bridge, I saw Cathy Gior and her husband together at the roadside near the market. They were in the company of some Siako clan brothers of Cathy. Across the road, in the far corner, I saw the other Western Highlanders, five in all, two middle-aged and the rest in their mid-twenties, excitedly going around, eyeing the various locally-grown fresh vegetables sold at the market. The fresh carrots, broccoli, cauliflower and the giant cabbages seemed to amaze them greatly, and they spent minutes talking and discussing them before loitering on to the next, as if it was their first time ever to see such things. Seemingly, there were marveled at the very low and cheap mark-up for the giant crop produce, something hardly seen at the Mt Hagen markets, and elsewhere.

Cathy faced towards the bridge, and my appearance was eye-catching from where she stood. Apparently, I caught her attention directly when she looked straight across the bridge. Our eyes met, but not surprising, like the previous day in the Sika store, she quickly looked away in denial. I smiled conciously at her childish reaction, as I ambled across the bridge. I was neither jealous, nor stirred up, as there was no real reason for that. But I was surely interested and curious to find out more about her husband and, if possible, how they managed to get together and, or course, the bride price payment that was rumoured to have been paid during the day. I plodded around the market, looking for a possible informer; someone I knew, or perhaps a Siako, who could divulge everything that had happened during the day to me. There was none. I scanned the market thoroughly again, and eventually sighted an old friend, Gumia, sitting at the roadside, all by himself. Though he was a Siako, he was from a different sub-clan and was not directly related to the Giors. He was curiously eyeing the Western Highlanders too, just like the many others, as they were going about excitedly, eyeing the agricultural products in the market.

I walked up to Gumia, cheered him up and, after some exchange of pleasantries, sat myself on a boulder next to him.

"Who are these men?" I knowingly, asked to put us into the conversation.

"Some Hagen blokes, they came along with Cathy and her husband Peter, last night: that's Cathy down there with her husband", he said pointing down the road.

"Oh, I see! I hear, he is here to make part payment of the bride price".

"That's correct. Peter paid K4,000.00 today, about three hours ago in a small ceremony at Ende-naige-ingaugl".

"Gee, that's a lot of money? There must have been a mumu too, because I saw the smoke above Ende-naige-ingugl from Bokan this morning".

"That's right; the mumu was prepared for that occasion. The Giors slaughtered a porker for the Hagen men, and presented their bride price demand with the food: K10, 000.00 cash, 20 pigs, a brand-new land cruiser, and some other small stuff like a radio. Peter promised to pay all that later during the coming Christmas period".

"My-Oh-My, that's an exorbitant price, a real fortune, don't you think? I said and looked astonishingly at Gumia.

"Well, it is---but that's nothing new to Peter. He's got the money, the car, the pigs and everything. He'll pay everything just like that", Gumia confidently said, snapping his fingers.

Gumia's revelation was surprisingly a great piece of news I collected from him. Looking back, I now know why Kumo was harsh on me for her daughter. Cathy was certainly reserved for someone special, the special one with money and material wealth, I felt convinced. And she has hit the jackpot now, I thought. A little while later, Gumina divulged something more of Peter Kupal's background.

"He's got two other wives in Mt Hagen" he said.

"Oh, yeah?

"Yep, Cathy is the third wife now. In fact, during his life time, he married well over ten girls, or maybe more. He simply divorced them all, those that he did not like or performed to his expectations. He is currently left with two and Cathy is the third now".

"How did you know all this?" I curiously asked, wanting to know more of Peter.

"I lived in Mt Hagen for two years, and know more about this guy than anyone else here. Peter is from the Jika Milakwub tribe, just outside Mt Hagen. His very high covenant house is only about 2 km in from the Okuk Highway, just across Kalakai bettlenut market. You wouldn't believe it, if I say that Peter's first daughter is about the same age as Cathy. She's currently a medical student at University of Papua New Guinea. In fact, Peter fathered many other children too from the many different wives. Usually, when he sends a wife away, he keeps the kids with him".

"Does Cathy know that?"

"Off course, she does. She is aware of that. I mean, she has to, because of a man of Peter's age and dignity, and who comes from an area where polygamy is rife and prevalent, and above all filthy rich, no one can expect him to be a bachelor", said Gumia.

"That's sad", I said, feeling sorry for Cathy to have blindly walked into a web of an extended polygamous family.

"You may say it's sad, but nowadays it's money that stands out tall, and speaks louder". Gumia unexpectedly cut in. "Girls don't care how handsome, ugly, old, young, or how many wives you have. Maybe, it was different in the past, but today it's the pecuniary wealth of a person that counts most, not the person himself".

"You are not wrong", I affirmed thoughtfully, "It's money that does all the talking nowadays. By the way, Gumia, I hear that Peter is a very rich man".

"Filthy rich, Joe! Peter is a very rich man, one of the respected and silent millionaires amongst the Western Highlanders", Gumia confirmed, "You see that vehicle over there? When that station wagon drives past in Hagen town, everyone knows who owns that vehicle. And quite often, you will see people pausing to take a glimpse of him. He hardly walks on the street. His name is one of the popular names amongst the list of other names of people like him in the streets of Mt Hagen."

Quite fortunately, I had come to the right person to elicit some good information I needed about the much talked about millionaire husband of my former girlfriend. I made a lot of important discoveries about Cathy's man. I learnt that he was not an ordinary person. He was somebody important and of high esteem, a very well-respected figure in the business arena. His business empire included a number of shopping malls in Mt Hagen, Lae and Port Moresby, some of which I'd shopped in, real estate, several coffee plantations in the Waghi valley and a huge fleet of trucks sub-contracted to Pangini Transport. He also served as Director and Chairman of various other organisations in the country. He was comparatively no person to collate against any other ordinary citizen and, in the end, I began to feel some respect for this great man. This was a rare submissive feeling for anyone who took his girl away. But, quite sanely, I was comparatively incommensurable against this great man's dignity, wealth and the plutocratic image he maintained at all levels in the country, the business community, his province and finally in his village. Cathy had decided for herself, I thought. She was no longer a small kid anymore. She knew what was good for her and what was not and respectfully there was no reason to interfere, I felt.

"Cathy had certainly landed herself in a garden of roses embedded with diamonds", I finally told Gumia.

"No doubt about that, Joe. It's just that she's lucky…that's all!".

The sun was gradually sinking in the west and, by now, the market was practically empty. There were a few people, about a handful, mostly betel nut vendors, still doing business with their demanding tax-free commodity. But the rest had gone home early to get prepared for the Easter Friday night service at Toromambuno. Gumia and I were still talking when further up the road at Pokodame, I saw a woman walking down the road, her head forced down by the double weight of a big *bilum* load, and a bundle of firewood over her head. It was a typical sight of hard working mothers returning home from the gardens with such loads and cargo, but it was terrifying to see the excessive weights overhead, and on the back, of the one up the road. And one could not possibly guess from a distance, who she was.

"Gumia, you see that woman up the road? That load is going to kill her", I said, as I stared in disbelief at the load over the girl's head and back, that was stooping her almost to the ground. Gumia turned.

"Oh, that's Anna, she is always like that", Gumia said, looking up at the woman, "That's nothing new to her, she carries almost half-a-ton everyday, and is used to it"

"Which Anna?"

"Anna Thortia, Councilor Bagle's daughter", Gumia said.

"The Siako Councillor?"

"That's right. That's his daughter".

My heart skipped a beat and pulsated faster at the establishment of the girl's identity. I realised that it was the very Anna, my parents had talked about most, the one to be affianced to me. They said her mother rests while she does everything for her, and here I was proving beyond reasonable doubt what my parents were really talking about and, of course, what Anna Thortia was really made off. She was really the work horse that my parents boasted about.

Shaking with great enthusiasm and expectation, I struggled to think up some banter, or anything that will lure her attention and maybe reveal my presence. I forcefully cleared my throat, and then extemporaneously managed to get my afternoon greetings across when she lined herself up directly with us. I couldn't be so certain, if she had seen us from up the road while on her way down. But she sure had her ears tuned, and after some struggle, looked up and responded back with a beautiful smile, a smile, I'd say, that completely changed my inside. I remember returning her smile. I remember what I'd said, but I couldn't clearly recall what happened therafter as it was something I could not describe with the appropriate words. Seriously, as if being touched by a magic welding rod, sparks of delight flew off in all directions inside my body, with traces of enthusiasm, desire and excitement exploding and glowing spontaneously like burning embers throughout my nerve system.

"Sorry to disturb you with that kind of load over you", I quickly mumbled out between my trembling lips. Anna paused in her track, turned with ease, despite the pressing weight over head, and briefly threw a glance at me. It was a provocative glance, a leer. She heard my distinctive voice, and already knew who I was. Then, "It's alright, I don't mind", she said, and timidly chuckled. And then with ease again, she turned and was ready to continue on her way down to Ende-naige-ingugl.

I remained still for some time but her sweet voice continuously replayed like music in my ears. Almost immediately my mind raced against time to think up some more banter to throw across to her. Furthermore, something suddenly clicked in my mind too. I felt that it was also an opportune moment to prove my parents right, if everything they had said about Anna was true. And by good chance, as if being reminded by someone, "Remember", I called out after her, as she was about to proceed down the road. "…you brought me some betel nuts last time. Well, it's my turn now. How about a chew before you go?" Anna stopped again, then turned and sheepishly smiled.

"Oh, thank you, that will be kind of you", she said moving to the roadside and resting her loads on a projecting stone, the *bilum of kaukau* dropping onto the stone in a heap behind her. Gumia helped her in bringing the bundle of firewood to the ground. It was a heavy bundle from the way Gumia handled it, and I can't figure out how the poor girl managed it together with the *bilum* of *kaukau*. But as Gumia had said, she was used to it. Unbelieveable! I thought.

After a shy handshake, I hurried to the nearest betel nut vendor, a couple of steps down the roadside, and pulled out the only K2.00 note I had in my pocket. For some reason, I had not released that money earlier, when I was with the Gumia all that afternoon, but, somehow, did when Anna came along. I collected all the betel nuts worth the amount and returned.

"You can chew one and take the rest home", I said, handing her all the betel nuts.

She was pleased and took everything that was offered. Gumia and myself stepped back with two nuts each. Gumia was, in fact, surprised at my rather quick and peculiar behavior during those few short moments, when Anna arrived, but he didn't ask. I could see the curiosity in his eyes, but it was clever of him not to ask, because if he had asked, I would have told him nothing.

While Anna was chewing from a *fri-kambang*, a quick thought came into my head and, just before she left, I quickly moved in closer to her and, in an inaudible tone, asked; "Can I see you later this evening?" I paused and panicked, shaking as well, to have asked that question, but with a guilty smile. Anna looked into my eyes and smiled back. Perhaps, she already knew why I wanted to see her, but she did not mention anything.

"Where?", she quietly asked.

"Here…right here", I quickly said, with excitement. Anna thought for a while, then said, "Alright, I'll come. You must have something big to tell me", she twitted with smile. Then picking up her load with Gumia's help, she continued down the road to Ende-naige-ingugl. This time Guima helped Anna with the bundle of firewood. "It's late and I must go home too. Thank you for the betel nut, Joe", Gumia said, as he placed Anna's bundle over his shoulders.

I remained with the betelnut vendor, and Gumia and Anna left, but I felt quite different from what I was only moments earlier. I could feel my blood pressure pulsating well above the normal pulse, and my heart pounding heavily against my chest. I was shaking, apparently with joy from the satisfaction of talking to Anna and it was likely that the excitement wouldn't subside for a while yet. When I looked down the road, Cathy and her sugar-daddy husband were no longer there. They had, most probably, retired back to Endenaigeingugl a few hours earlier. But who is Cathy Gior any way, I asked myself. And for the first time, my mind totally ignored and dismissed any links and traces of Cathy with someone else.

I could not hold back the excitement, derived from the satisfaction I had from the brief conversation with Anna. I was over the moon. Inside me, I felt like a prospector who had just discovered a very big gold field. My knees weakened, and my mind was inundated with joy and expectations. My thoughts were no longer with the betel nut vendor, or the other buyers anymore. New plans began to flood my mind, plans that will change the course of the original proposition, I had disclosed to my parents last night. Soon, I bade the others the end of day's greetings, and scurried home to Bokan to disclose the change of plans to my parents.

My parents were both at home when I arrived, dropping onto the wooden bed, flat and panting.

"What's the matter?" Is someone chasing you?", they asked, frowning.

"No, I am not being chased. But I've come to tell your something".

"What is it then?"

"I have just decided to change my previous plan". I ranted, almost excitedly.

"What plan?" my father asked, almost taken to his feet, thinking that I had changed my mind on Anna.

"Remember, what I told you yesterday?"

"About what", he came back slightly serious.

"I mentioned something about executing the *ambu yana* after I leave for Lae, remember that?"

"Yes, what is it then?"

"Well, I've changed my mind again. Can we do that anytime this weekend, say tomorrow or Sunday, after the church service?"

"Oh, okay! As you wish son", my father, said with a sigh of relief, "I'll arrange for that tomorrow".

"That would be good, go ahead and do it sometime this weekend", I urged, commandingly with excitement, and added, "I want to witness everything before I go back"

"That's good thinking. You'll bag Anna's opinion before you go. I'll inform the menfolk tomorrow to ready themselves, and go out for the *ambu yana* on Sunday".

The air of excitement derived from the brief moment with Anna Thortia at Mondiagl-kaugla, was so satisfying that I purposely permitted the formal *'ambu yana'* plan, and my subsequent engagement to Anna on the weekend. I wanted it all to happen while Cathy Gior was there, and right in front of her, so that she too could witness the engagement for herself. I'd like her to see that, I may be 'dumped', but I am not out yet. And above all, I'd like Cathy to see that I am not going anywhere to be affianced to someone else, but to one of her very own kindred sisters.

My mother, a dedicated Catholic, as is always usual for her, left early, not wanting to miss the start of any religious activity and rituals.

"Joe! Are you coming for the service?", she called back to me, as she made her way out.

"Yes, I am, mama, I'll be coming right after you with father".

"Your dinner is in the pot. Take it before you come".

"Oh sure, I will. I am starving". I called back to mother, as she disappeared behind the house.

My father followed mum some minutes later, after getting himself into his Sunday clothes. I waited a few more minutes to give him some distance first, then locked the house, ignoring my dinner, and dawdled behind. I knew Anna would be waiting for me and wanted to let my father go away first, before meeting her. But alas! Anna was already there waiting for me at Mondiagl-kaugla, when I arrived. I could see her from the other side of the bridge, as I was about to cross over. She was there with someone, a girl. I briefly waited for my father to disappear, then quickly crossed the bridge and walked over to Anna. Her girlfriend,

Molki, accompanied her and both smiled timidly, when I approached them.

"I'm sorry, I thought you won't be here yet. How long have you been waiting?

"We just arrived, about a minute ago. We never waited", Anna said, and smiled.

"So, we all arrived together at the same time then, our timing must be very good", I said, joking.

There was a moment of laughter, as we chatted. Both girls had spruced themselves up thoroughly, and were in their best Sunday dress. It was quite obvious that they were going to leave for the Easter Friday night service at Toromambuno after we'd finished. What was more amazing was, I'd seen Anna in rags only moments earlier, but she was quite different before my eyes that moment---she was truly beautiful and majestic. In fact, I had never seen Anna in that appearance before and marvelled at her style of dressing, and how she appeared when she really wanted to clean herself up.

Some few meters across the road, the flow of people going to the church service increased with the start of the service hour almost up. We already attacted a lot of curious eyes and would certainly attract a lot more, if we stay in the same place, and I disliked that. "Can we go over there?" I said, pointing to a nice secluded spot behind some boulders along the river side, "I don't like curious eyes", I added.

Anna smiled, then tacitly approved my proposition and followed closely behind with Molki, as I proudly led the way. But strangely all did not go well in me. Before we reached the spot, I began to feel a little bit nervous, and rather uneasy, for the reason that; firstly, I had not known Anna better personally and, secondly, I could not reason out why I had to call this rendevous. And coupling both, I did not know where to start. Certainly, I'll look stupid, if I beat around the bush, and I don't want to do that. I remembered the change of plans on the proposed *ambu yana* with my father only moments earlier, but should I disclose that to her now, I kept asking myself, as we finally reached our destination.

In our brief moment, Anna did most of the talking and responded nicely to all my puerile questions and banters, while her friend listened with chuckles. She was open and perky. That made me feel good. But she was not as talkative as Cathy, which I felt, was very good. This one part of her character was to prove a stimulus towards our healthy relationship in the later years, I felt.

After an effortless struggle to hold back everything, I kindly excused Anna, with a leer, if I could speak to her alone for a minute. Anna smiled for some reasons, looked at her friend, as if to seek her approval, and assent, then obediently followed me to a distance some few meters away from her friend. When she was near enough, I did not wait.

"My parents have been constantly telling me all about you", I began in an inaudible tone, "They've always boasted about your kindness, and the many good things you did to them every time I came home. And I was wondering if you were hiding something from me"

Anna smiled. She heard me but stood still. She did not make any attempt to respond. She was nibbling her fingernails instead, her eyes fixed firmly on the currents of the fast-flowing Simbu River. There was serenity all over her face and I deduced, on perception, that she had been expecting this moment for a very long time. And I also guessed that my parents were right about her, when they disclosed that she was very close to them, as she already and seemingly realised that I just about let lose the top secret. And, I sure did.

"My parents are so much convinced that you could possibly become my bride one day in the near future", I openly disclosed, "How about that? You know, old people are sometimes crazy and really don't know what they are talking about"

Anna stll did not voice anything, but, this time, the mention of the word 'bride' seemed to have some impact on her. I noticed a slight movement in Anna—something suggestively welcoming to the mind. She stealthily peered at me through the corner of her eyes, and smirked almost approvingly. That made me felt uncontrollable inside. I deemed it as a green light, that soon let open the floodgate.

"We are sending out a *ambu-yana* delegaton to your place this Sunday", I continued, as if I saw nothing, "I really don't know what your opinion will be, but this is all part of formalities, you know. It's all up to you to decide from there"

The *ambu-yana* is the very first step in the long customary procedure towards engaging, and marrying the young. And I surprised Anna almost instantly with my disclosure. There was a long moment of silence. Molki let out occasional smiles from her location as she waited for her friend. Then, looking up at me, "What time on Sunday?", Anna finally inquired for the first time, since I touched the subject with a relaxed and credulous countenance

"Sometimes in the afternoon, definitely after church service, of course". I replied, looking on with enthusiasm.

Anna said nothing more and continued with her nail paring, but again, on perception, she was certainly in deep thought too. I had in no doubt placed her in a position of a lifetime decision. and her eyes stared ruminatively at the fast flowing river, as if to grasp some answers flowing past. Though there were occasional smiles, when she lifted her face to peep at me, nothing positive was yet voiced from her lips. And with the prolonged eerie silence between us, I felt rather guilty, deep inside me. Had I erred somewhere? Maybe, I had made a mistake by blurting out everything, I thought. And between my trembling, "I'm sorry, I didn't mean to confuse you", I burbled, breaking the long silence. Anna's head turned slightly in my direction.

"No! It's alright. I think I'm lost for words…that's all", she muttered and smiled, a bit shy and looked into the river again.

Apparently, the shining face and the relaxed manner of her stand, coupling the frank responses she was giving, were suggestive of her approval, and this instantly ironed out my doubts. These were already positive signs for the near future, and importantly more than enough for me to draw my own conclusion on the final outcome of the proposed *ambu-yana*. She was clearly on my side of the table, and I could perceive that intelligence almost immediately in that brief moment, but I wanted to be really sure. I wanted to hear something from Anna's very own lips.

"What will be your decision on the proposition, if my delegation comes?" I asked, looking on with anticipation.

Anna smiled. It was a direct question, a question that needed time to think over, evaluate and make a decision. But, "Let them come", she snapped back confidently in a very plain tone, and timidly chuckled.

"We'll see to it when they come around", she added, amdst her chuckles.

I was taken aback inside, by Anna's prompt response. She responded as if she did not care at all. But she was plain and straightforward. It was going to be 'yes'. And it all came from the very own lips of the bride-to-be, and there was no need to pry further. Inside me, my excitement reached another peak, and I could not hold back anything behind.

"My father is leading the delegation of about four or five people down to your place", I opened up, "…but it all depends on you, and your parents. Everything will rest on, first your decision, and then that of your parents."

"I don't think, they'll have much to say when I make my decision, Anna cut in, interrupting my talk, as if being upset at the mention of her parents. I stopped.

She surprised me yet again, but it was well said, and I was pleased after all. We had certainly surprised each other with a few exchange of words. And I liked every moment of it.

"My delegation will approach your father and ask for your hand. You father will then turn to you for your decision", I concluded.

"I'll look forward to that", Anna said, as we ended our private conversation.

Anna's father, Councillor Bagle, was a great village leader, the chief. A conventionally eloquent orator and renowned village elder, his natural leadership qualities made him stand tall amongst his other Siako clansmen. He had been elected unopposed to the Mt Wilhelm Local Government Council Assembly for three consecutive terms. He was currently serving his fourth term in office as the Siako councillor. Apart from his little hamlets at Irugl, along the headwaters of the pristine Kualke to house his pigs, he had his permanent residence set up in the most central part of Ende-naige-ingugl and played his leadership role from there. My father eventually caught up with him after church service at Toromambuno, outside the church, on Easter Sunday. Facing a man of dignity and high esteem, my father went straight to the point after exchanging the day's greetings.

"*Yagl kande*, it gives me great pleasure to approach and talk to you" My father began, as they shook hands. "In fact, I feel relieved too, I must tell you that", he added. "Why? Me too," the Councillor responded, looking on with smiles. The councillor had been taken off-guarded perhaps, and traces of curiosity and doubt began to show signs all over his face, as he smiled and eyed my father. The frowning look alerted my father too.

"My Honourable Counillor', my father quickly said, "I don't want to take too much of your time, but if you don't mind, I just want to make an appointment to come around to your place this afternoon"

And with great anticipation, my father looked directly into the Councillor's eyes when he finished. With no former association, including family ties and connections to the Tamgos, the great Councillor, appeared apparently lost, but welcomed my father warmly. "No, not at all. You can come around at any time, as you wish." Bagle said, his face radiant and welcoming. Then he asked, "Have we got something to discuss there?"

"Yes!... Well, not exactly. It's something along that line, and I'll make it short", my father said, his lips slightly trembling. "I just want to come around with a delegation for a '*minge-yana*', my father finally said.

"*minge-yana*?" Bagle questioned. With no family ties, and family relations, Bagle was obviously becoming more curious this time.

"That's right, councillor. Maybe I'll elaborate", my father voiced, and as the Councillor Bagle listened, he said, "I am desperately in need of something, and I know you would have 'it' there. That's why, I want to come around and ask you for 'it' this afternoon. And it would only be a matter of asking, no big deal in it".

Indeed, my father was circuitous but Bagle was not a junior from the kindergarten school either. As if being touched by ice, he turned stiff and rigid at my father's disclosure. His lips quivered but nothing came out of it. It may have dawned on Bagle that my father was visiting him for nothing else, then to ask him for his daughter Anna's hand. It was all part of the customary protocols that my father had approached him, and Bagle was practically held spellbound to voice anything, or let out an immediate response too. The notional terms such as, *Appointment...Delegation'* and *'Minge-Yana'*, selectively used in my father's spiel conventionally meant business of some significant importance. And pursuant to customary rites, observances and obligations the terms literally hinted to nothing else but only one thing, and that was a possible *ambu-yana* mission. The councillor sensed it. He remained unmoved and consciously eyed my father thoughtfully with intent, perhaps contemplating on the question, 'And who is the groom to wed my daughter?' But the councilor did not ask. It was a long pause and my father felt a too little shaky in front of the great leader. A twinge of embarrassment sailed into him too but he brushed it away and remained rooted with expectations. He wanted to hear from Bagle, Anna's biological father, first before he would go away and mobilise a team. Then, all of a sudden, as if touched by something good in his mind, Bagle discharged a full smile. It was a friendly smile and according to my father's intuition, an affirmative smile. And, he was right. Moments thereafter, there were no further questions coming his way. "I see", was all councilor Bagle voiced for the moment.

Understandbly as a father of a young nubile daughter, approached by the father of a young forester son, with no pending business between them---and off course, perhaps after establishing who the potential groom would be---Councillor Bagle knew instinctively that my father's visit was certainly going to be an *ambu-yana* for his daughter, Anna, and nothing else. Maintaining the gorgeous smile and in a very gentle voice, "Alright, I'll be expecting you all, say around two or three o'clock in the afternoon. From here I will be somewhere else but surely after midday I should be home", he said.

"That is very kind of you. We'll see you there then. Thank you, very much", my father replied.

"No problem. We will catch up in the afternoon", the councilor said, and walked away.

Satisfied with the dialogue, my father thanked the Councillor again and immediately came out looking for me. He found me with a group of boys, next to the mission canteen, and called me out. As is always usual for him after a success in anything he does, he was smiling.

"It's alright for us to go to Ende-naige-ingugl. I've just talked to Anna's father, and he'll be expecting us this afternoon at his house", he proudly reported.

"So, what are you going to do now…and can you briefly tell me what will happen when you get there?"

"I'll call a few of our menfolk: Thomas, Kua, Gende and whoever is around to accompany me the in afternoon. They all should be attending church and must be here somewhere amongst the crowd. I'll find them. We will go to Ende-naige-ingugl and formally ask Bagle for Anna and, maybe, he'll leave it all to Anna to decide for herself. If Anna accepts our invitation, then she will be formally betrothed to you that moment. And if everything works out well for Bagle, he'll read out the price tag for us to take home, and prepare for payment. It all follows a sequence, you know, a primeval procedure".

"And what if they refuse?"

"Oh, come on son, cut this crap. Let's look at things positively". My father cried out almost with a shout.

I smiled, knowing very well that I was only joking.

"Alright papa, you have a nice day", I said, bidding him farewell on his mission, as I hurried off to join my friends for the Easter games at the Community School Sports Ground.

My father's face was all lit up and radiant when I arrived home later in the afternoon. He was already smiling, and I knew on perception that he had succeeded in his mission. I smiled back, as I made my way into the house.

"How did you go?" I asked.

He looked up at me, still smiling.

"Sit down first and make yourself comfortable, then I'll tell you everything".

I found a place near the doorway and sat on the earth floor with my back against the blind wall. My mother was sitting opposite father on the other side of the fireplace. Both seemed to have been discussing the subject when I arrived. I could see my mother's face all flushed and radiant.

"Where are the rest of the men?"

"We have all waited for you here to relay to you the outcome, but you didn't arrive early, so, they left".

"Oh, sorry about that. Anyway, how did you go? You can still tell me all about your mission, without them".

"Anna accepted the engagement", my father gabbled, and briefly went through the details of their mission, "There were no objections of any sort from anyone, when we put our proposal. Anna accepted the proposition instantly without a second thought, and so did the parents and everyone else there. 'Joseph is a good fellow', they were all saying of you. It all happened, as if we were predisposed in Bagle's favor. I mean, we were targeted for Anna long before we even got there. A meal of rice and tinned beef was provided with coffee after the discussion to close our session. The meal must have been the reason why he wanted us down there in the afternoon".

"I knew, Anna would accept the proposition", my mother boastfully interjected.

She was overjoyed and excited and couldn't sit still to anything else. Ignoring her, I asked father again.

"What else did you discuss…anything about the bride price?"

"Oh, yes, we discussed that too: K4000.00 in cash, seventeen pigs, seven birds of paradise plumes and two cassowaries; that shouldn't be a problem…the pigs, cash and plumes will be determined at the *ambu-di-kungugl*. Our pigs will all go. There is no doubt about that, but we'll have to look for the cassowaries. Generally, I don't think they'll refuse anything we put forward to them", my father said optimistically.

It all sounded nice to my ears. I was overwhelmed with the general outcome of *ambu yana* mission, particularly the bride price tag put on Anna Thortia. I knew, Anna was more an asset to Bagle than a daughter. Her performance in the gardens and home was way beyond comparison with the other local girls. And coupling that with her majestic beauty, I had expected the Siakos to tag her with an exorbitant price, some figure much more, higher than the K4000.00 revealed. But this turned out the opposite. I, therefore, felt happy. In reprospect, I was to learn later that the genuine price was all part of a 'consolation gift' package for the humiliation Cathy Gior's shrewish mother Angela Kumo, who had harangued me in front of the public. It was certainly the most terrible moment in my life and Anna had witnessed it. The predicament had also been the talk of the day. Like many observers who were around at that time, Anna and her parents had talked it over indignantly, and at great length, in their home, detesting and condemning Kumo for it. That evening, in their hearts, a seed of pity grew for me and eventually developed into an affection that remained furtive until the *ambu yana* delegation went. And the rest was to be history from now on.

The Giors and Bagles had their homes close to each other. I wished Cathy was there to see for herself, her nextdoor sister being affianced to her 'dumped' boyfriend, but, unfortunately, she was reported to be out on a leisure drive, with her husband, to the alpine grasslands of Kuraglba, when my delegation arrived. "Cathy and her man were out, but the parents were there", my father said, "Her father came to greet us, but the mother was nowhere to be seen, when we settled down to open the talks with Bagle". So, the mother and daughter were both not there, how unfortunate, I thought. But I very well knew that Kumo was probably guilty of her past and avoided my delegation, and, of course, disappeared. But she would have something interesting for her daughter's ears later in the evening when Cathy returns from her sight-seeing. Seriously, this was the entire reason, why I had orchestrated the *ambu-yana* to take place over the Easter weekend, so as to let Cathy know that her kindred sister Anna was engaged to Joseph Tamgo. And it worked out very well. She will surely collect the news, I predicted.

I was to travel back to Lae, the following day, Easter Monday. So, while there was still light, I suggested that we convene a small meeting within our family group to discuss the details and the tentative dates for the *ambu-di-kungul* and the matrimonial ceremony. A runner was sent up to Dinipene, our central communal village, where the majority of our clansmen lived. Late in the evening, some leading figures in the clan arrived at Bokan. A lengthy deliberative discussion took place. All unanimously agreed to June, during the four-week mid-semester break to be the tentative date for the wedding to take place with the exchange of bride price payment. I suggested December, during the Christmas period, but this was defeated by nearly everyone, who went to support my mother, who reasoned June as her preference. She desperately wanted Anna to be her daughter-in-law, and soon. After a long fruitful meeting, which included, among other agendas, the *ambu-di-kungul, di-minge-bugla* and other things related to the entire matrimonial ceremony, we finally dismissed late in the night.

I traveled to Lae, the following day, a very satisfied man. As the PMV turned to the Ende-naige-ingugl corner, I saw the grey station wagon parked along side the road. The familiar Western Highlanders were hectically moving about and circling the car, trying to load cargo, presumably some bags of cabbage, broccoli and cauliflower into the back compartment of the station wagon. I am sure they were loading some of the left-over *mumu* pork too. They were leaving. But I could not locate Cathy or her husband amongst them. They were probably still taking breakfast in the house, or maybe, still in bed---perhaps too cold for them to come out yet.

I reached Kundiawa just in time to catch a waiting 25-seater coaster that was heading to Lae. As the bus pulled out onto the road and roared down the Prenorkua declivity, I recalled the busy Easter weekend and let out a composed smile. But I did not last long to think further. The soporific effect of the jiggling and juggling along the crushed limestone coated carriageway of the Okuk Highway in the Sinasina-Yongomugl through to the Chuave country soon took its toll. My head dropped, my eyes closed and I was sent into a comatose sleep filled with snoring and snuffling until I reached Lae.

16

The Traditional Marriage Ceremony

The moves of the bride price payment and the subsequent handover of the bride to the groom in marriage follow an orthodox set of procedures, rules and protocols, primeval and inherited through many generations. It is a very special occasion and basically covers three major phases: the *ambu-yana*, the *ambu-dikugugl* and the *ambu-di*, with the last phase being the final and major event of the entire matrimonial ceremony. All phases involved a series of activities and the success depended on the participation of every member in the community.

Generally, the *ambu-yana* phase becomes insignificant, and is overlooked, if a bride eloped with the groom. The elopement, more often, would result from a stealthy pre-arrangement between the bride and the groom after a steady relationship. It would more often leave the parents and relatives of the bride with no alternative after the elopement, but to initiate further negotiations with the groom, and the people close to him to disclose the engagement. On the contrary, if the elopement is detested or rebuked, further negotiations remain stagnant until a compromise is reached between the two parties. However, for my case, the *ambu-yana* was accomplished over the Easter long weekend. And literally, this phase could have become non-obligatory had Anna eloped to Bokan, but this had not been slightly possible for Anna, as we never had established a lasting relationship that could intensify her inclination to elope to Bokan. Either way, the engagement of the bride to the groom had to be disclosed before implementing phases two and three of the matrimonial ceremony, and for my case, we had accomplished phase one with success.

During the remaining period, while I was away in Lae, preliminary preparation back home for the June event was well under way, as early as the first week of May, right after my departure. It was the same in the Siako camp at Ende-naige-ingugl. I dreamed almost every night about the proposed wedding date. And with the days and weeks going past swiftly like the wind, I could not easily settle down with my studies. I thought about Anna and the excitement of connubial life after the marriage, and how we would get along as a couple, though it would all be new experiences. In June, straight after the mid-semester exams, I took K3,500.00 out from the Westpac Bank, I had saved in an IBD, and traveled home. The monies were part of my going-finish entitlement with the Vanimo Forest Products Pty Ltd, and my refund from the National Provident Fund contributions collected from the Fund's Lae branch office.

Unlike my past home visits, this time I walked into the thick of things when I arrived. All the requisites for the matrimonial event were set and my parents and senior clansmen were all eagerly awaiting my presence before announcing the second phase. And as soon as I arrived, the *ambu-di-kungugl* was launched on the following day. It went on for a full week and *di-minge-bugla* came pouring in from all directions after the launch. Friends, relatives, menfolks and clansmen from all walks of life, far and near, walked into Bokan benevolently with cash and kind for the bride price. A literate clansman with the assistance of my father received and recorded the contributions, while my mother and some other relative women welcomed and applauded the contributions with *aglange*. At the end of the hectic week, my father reported K6,135.00 in cash, twenty-one pigs and eight bird of paradise plumes, a remarkable revelation of K2,135.00, four pigs and one paradise plume in excess of what was stipulated, leaving only the two cassowaries still outstanding. But we soon solved the problem later in the week. With the excessive contributions we bought the two birds at K500.00 each from two families in the neighboring clans, who were domesticating the birds.

My parents, as host members, brought forward five pigs for give-away and three porkers for the pork exchange.

The whole activity was much of a surprise for me. I had never thought or even dreamt that anything significant which could draw a lot of attention and people to happen to me. It was unbelievable, watching people coming, going, doing this and doing that, but, in the end, I embraced the fact that this was all happening for me. This happens only once to every male child in the Dengalgu Miuk clan, and now it was my turn. I felt proud and elated as I watched my clansmen and their wives going about handling the *ambu-di-kungugl*. Everyone was putting in every effort needed to get the ceremony going without any hiccup. I could now see that I was truly one of them and they were mine, when I needed them.

The *ambu-di-kungugl* was successfully accomplished by the end of the week. I thanked everyone in my heart when I noticed everything organized to perfection. The money, the pigs, the plumes and the two giant cassowary birds, were all ready for payment, but even still, late payments from distant friends and relatives made their way in. This, I owed all to my two energetic loving parents. They were terrific and punctilious. Despite their senescence age, they ceaselessly struggled to see that the beginning, and the end of this occasion for their primogeniture proved successful. The enormous flow of contributions would never have been so successful had they not actively participated in similar past *ambu-di-kungugls*, as most of the *di-minge-bugla* were return payments from their past gifts. Moreover, the three prized porkers, they produced, maintained pride and dignified the family name. This particular item was expected from them, as the immediate parents of the groom and they sweated all through these years to perfect that with great results. The porkers were so huge in size and weight that would certainly pose a challenge to the Siakos at the pork exchange when adiposity is compared, and many talked about it in their homes.

I perversely refused my parents and elders when they advocated to hold back the excessive *di-minge-bugla*, and pay only the exact price, which the Siakos had wanted from us, and disclosed to us during the *ambu-yana* mission. I wanted everything, which was contributed for the purpose to go and insisted that everything be paid out. "Don't hold anything back", I cautioned them, to which many were not happy. But I had one reason in my mind. And that was to prove to Angela Kumo that we could still afford to pay a hefty bride price, and pay even more than what was required from us in retaliation towards her obloquy and the blistering invectives of that fateful November afternoon. In truth, my hatred for Kumo, after the public humiliation, remained a lifetime nightmare that cold not easily be expunged from my memory. It was a total injustice done to me and I wanted to avenge this in any way I could think of---anything that will prove Kumo wrong and knock some sense into her. And this was one such opportunity, but I imparted nothing of the motive to the clansmen.

In the second week, a day was set for the Siakos, Anna's parents and relatives to visit Bokan to view and decide on the display of the *ambu-di-kungugl*. Then they have the opportunity, and option to decide whether to accept or refuse Anna's bride price. A huge crowd of beneficiaries was expected, and a *mumu* was prepared for the visitors with coffee, rice and stew boiled over the open fire in huge pots. The cash was segregated in hundreds and flaunted out on a linen in the main arena: K5,000.00 in all. The twenty-one pigs were tied to pickets planted in a straight row across the front yard of our house with tethers plaited from fig-bark fibers. In the eye-catching forefront were the three porkers, unavoidable for the public eyes to miss. The eight paradise plumes were nicely displayed alongside next to the money. Just behind the pigs, some metres out, were the two fierce looking cassowaries. They were confined to bamboo cages.

At about two o'clock in the afternoon, a typical war cry was heard over at Wai-mambuno. First, it was a single clamour, and then just when the solo voice died out, all erupted in unison. It was the harbinger of the Siakos approach to Bokan. "They are here now", my father announced, as we hectically rushed around in haste, getting the last-minute jobs done, and tidying up the place. Everyone made sure anything that was needed to done before the Siakos enter, was attended to within the short period. Finally, everything was set, the *di-minge-bugla* for their assessment and the food for their consumption. Moments later, Councillor Bagle entered, leading his group of beneficiaries. Being a councilor and village leader of very high dignity a huge crowd, numbering to well over thirty people accompanied him. They were greeted warmly by every one of us, present there. As their betrothed, I took a leading role in welcoming our visitors by upstaging bone-crushing hugs to every Siakos that came into Bokan with sincere warmth and friendliness, winning the hearts of everyone I came into contact with and the others too. Likewise, Anna, who had come along with her people, actively did the same, winning the hearts of everyone in Bokan. Coincidentally, we both stole the show even before everyone sat down to assess and decide on the *di-minge-bugla* and, of course, our fate after that assessment. "What a great couple they'll be", I proudly heard many commenting.

Soon after the exchange of greetings, handshakes and hugs, Councillor Bagle and some selected figures in the Siako camp settled down next to the cash and immediately went to work, counting out every note in the bundle. The Siako women wasted on time either. They were already moving around the three porkers and talked at great length amongst themselves, shaking their heads in amazement.

There was a lengthy discussion between the Siakos after the money was counted and a recount commenced soon after. It was no surprise. I knew instantly that the extra K1,000.00 had certainly caused some confusion and smiled, as the recount was underway. Immediately after the cash recount, Councillor Bagle and his team got to their feet and walked from picket to picket, counting and viewing the pigs as they walked along. Again, there was a moment of discussion at the last picket. A few moments later, Councillor Bagle let out his views.

Clearing his throat first, "I think you have many extras in your display, more than what we asked for", he said, in a pleasing note, "We really don't know whether these are all deliberately put there, but we have just decided to refuse the extra four pigs".

"No, it's not deliberate. You take everything", Thomas Kutne, our senior spokesman, rose to his feet and said. And then added, "It's the groom's wish, and he wants you to take everything".

My elder, Thomas was right. That was exactly what I had wanted, and was pleased when he spoke out.

An impressed Bagle said nothing more of the extras. "In that case, we'll take everything", he said, as he moved from picket to picket, set to give out the pigs to selected relatives of Anna who qualified for a pig from their share of bride price. We knew instantly that the Siakos were satisfied with our *ambu-di-kungugl*. Soon Councillor Bagle started apportioning the pigs to selected beneficiaries. There was no word of objection, protest or dissatisfaction against the *di-minge-bugla* which was more satisfying than ever. Had there been any dissatisfaction expressed the entire occasion would be in limbo. I later learnt that Kumo qualified for a pig too, but was reluctant to come along. But her mother-in-law, my friend Thomas Giors mother, came with the other Siakos and she was given a pig too, at the distribution. As a long-time family friend, she freely chatted with my parents all the while, as the counting, viewing and assessment of the *di-minge-bugla* were underway.

"Your brother hasn't written a letter once to us yet, and we are not quite sure where he is", she said of Thomas Gior, when I neared her to convey my greetings.

"He lost contact with me a long time ago, and I don't know his whereabouts either", I told her.

When the apportioning of the pigs was finally over, the Siakos settled down next to the dishes of food and ravenously helped themselves to the fullest. Most seemed to have starved themselves since morning for this occasion, and ate hungrily until satiated. The entire occasion was practically over after about one hour, thirty minutes. Many Siakos mothers were seen wrapping up the leftover foods, and tossing them into their *bilums* to take home, presumably for the little ones left behind. The coming Saturday of the following week was agreed upon for the final phase of the ceremony, the *ambu-di*, with Friday night set for the *endie-kaman* session. With that arrangement in place, the Siakos left Bokan, delighted and satisfied with the two cassowaries and the twenty-one pigs, leaving behind the monies and the paradise plumes to be delivered on the coming Saturday. The usual primeval clamour of appreciation sealed their exit, as they left. And with that, phase two of the matrimonial occasion was completed. I stood watching them go. Anna looked back and smiled. I winked my eyes in appreciation and 'thank you'. She smiled back, obviously satisfied too. "We did it at last", I told her in my mind.

It was a busy week in both the camps; the Denglagu Miuks in Bokan, and the Siakos at Ende-naige-ingugl. We prepared heavily for the last phase of the two-week event coming up at the end of the week. *Mumu* leafs, green vegetables and other prerequisites for the coming gigantic *mumu* were gathered from respective locations, and carted to Bokan. Food crops of varying types were harvested in great quantities to *mumu* along with the porkers and be enjoyed by everyone. As it was to be the final phase, my mother took out everything she had preserved in the garden, giant *kaukau* tubers, English potatoes, beans and anything that was ready for harvest. Every night, my house was packed to capacity with people. Apart from uncles, aunts, cousins and nieces, many of them were visitors and friends from distant locations, who had come to witness the occasion of my marriage ceremony. Others were close friends or neighbors, who popped in to watch and enjoy the women rehearsing the *gilanges* to be sung during the various stages of the occasion in the final phase.

On the early Friday morning, when the first cock crowed, the three porkers were clobbered with clubs. It was rather a sad moment to watch the hogs go down. My mother looked away and shed some tears at the sight of the pigs falling on the ground and struggling to rise up again in their final moments. She had reared them by name and they were certainly her very close 'friends' for a long time. And it was a truly pathetic sight and moment for her. I walked away to an obscured location and returned to the scene after the pigs were dead on the ground. Also clobbered was a fourth pig of average size for *ende-kambu* to be consumed during the *endie-kaman* session, later in the night. In total, there were four porkers on the ground.

The conventional cleaning of hog hair is by burning the hair, or singeing over the open flame, and it is a strenuous job. Paul and his young energetic comrades, numbering about six, and a host of other helping hands cleaned the pigs nicely, using firewood from the *dinbede*, and lined the porkers nicely in a row on banana and fig leaves for the local 'butchers'. Four proficient men immediately immediately went to work, disemboweling the pigs, while our women prepared vegetables and the garden produce to go along with the porkers into the *mumu* pit.

Four other women stepped up, and quickly walked away with the entrails to the nearby Mondia, and cleaned them up. They soon returned with the chitterlings, nicely cleaned and the entrails expertly plaited. After a perfect job, the porkers, the food and the vegetables were ready to go into the *mumu* pit. We quickly prepared the hot stones, and at around 10.00 am, the *mumu* was in progress. We placed everything; the porkers, the food and the vegetables, all into a large dug out pit, prepared the previous day. An expert was there to give directions and supervise the entire *mumu*, telling us what to do, which food to go first, what to go next and where the hot stones needed to be placed. When everything was nicely accommodated in the pit, water was the last ingredient to go in to produce stream, and then, the cover of the *mumu* to prevent the hot steam from escaping. There was a long rest from the hectic activities when the *mumu* pit was covered up with earth.

It was some two hours later that we opened up the *mumu* again, carefully picking out everything, one by one, out of the pit. Everything was cooked to perfection. The stones were red hot and we knew they would do a very good job, and they did.

"So far so good", many observes, said approvingly.

"Yes, it is. It's a good sign; there won't by any hiccups in our progress", some elderly clairvoyants murmured, as they viewed the *mumu*.

At about 6.00 pm, everyone gathered at Bokan to mobilise for the trip to Ende-naige-ingugl for the *endie-kaman* night. Our women arrayed themselves in meretricious *bilas* of face painting and flower circlets. Other were in gaudy feathers of red parrot and yellow bird of paradise plumes. We met in Ende-naige-ingugl for a very big reception. The Siakos welcomed each and every one of us fervently with open arms. Councillor Bagle was a well-respected chief and leader of high standing, and his status, prominance and reputation was displayed in the reception he provided that night. The food far too much to make any comparison. There was a bit of everything in the garnished mountain of food assembled in front of us; bananas, taro, *kaukau,* sugar cane, and nicely prepared consumable foods from the store in dishes and pots. Maybe, it was part of a retaliation exercise initiated by the Siakos for the previous week's meal, we provided for them at Bokan, but it certainly was unquantifiable to make any comparison against it. A pig was also slaughtered and prepared for *ende-kambu* to top off the list of consumables he made available for that night. We exchanged that meat with ours, we had brought along.

After a heavy meal out in the open under the brilliant lights of six Coleman pressure lamps, we were led into a large newly constructed house. Bagle had consciously erected the house in the previous month, purposely for use during his daughter's wedding. The building undoubtedly served its purpose splendidly by taking in everyone comfortably. Some moments later, the sitting arrangement was done and the Siako women entered. They took up their space opposite our women, facing them with the fireplace in between. Next Anna Thortia was directed into the house. She was directed to be seated in between the two groups of women, her back against the wall, and facing the fire that was burning with high flames. Within a short while, a *giglange* was sung with both groups of women taking turns, the rest of the vocals joined in the tune and, seconds later, the whole house rocked to the tune. It had started, the *endie-kaman* session, the second last ritual before the final phase, the *ambu-di.* During the intermissions between the *giglanges* the women would indoctrinate Anna with advice, rules and the 'do' and 'don't' she should live, perform and die with in the next phase of her life as a married woman.

We left Ende-naige-ingugl at first light in the morning. Later in the day we would execute the final phase, the *ambu-di* that would take place in a dramatic open-air ceremony to be filled with thrills and excitements. Off course, after the ceremony, Anna and I were to become husband and wife. We would have finally been married at last after the two-week event. I tried to imagine being a married man, as we walked, and whether this was all really happening to me but it sure was. Before the day ended, I would tie the knot with Anna Thortia, and we'd became one, as husband and wife. The true experiences of a married man should gradually move in, and so would begin the new chapter of my life. What an amazing chapter it would be, I thought, as we walked to Bokan.

Four tall bamboo poles were cut at Yandina and brought to Bokan. The cash money, all in bills, were divided equally amongst the poles, and carefully arranged and pasted in line against the poles, up the entire lengths, using twines and sticky tapes. Experts arranged K1,000.00 each onto the two shorter poles and K1,500.00 each on the other two taller poles. After midday, when the afternoon sun rested above Gunda-bugl, we regrouped for the very big open-air ceremony, the *ambu-di,* and the final ritual of the two-week event. Everyone, apart from the sick and the old, gathered for the dramatic cavalcade to Ende-naige-ingugl to pay the Siakos and walk Anna away in marriage to her new home, Bokan.

We departed Bokan when everything was set, on a high note in flying colours, with the four money poles hoisted high, and the *kaigale* pagent leading the way with their primordial dance in the front. Behind them followed men, women and children raising our voices to the tune of the *giglanges* and peans rehearsed in the past nights, captivating the attention of every onlooker along the way, in style, as we walked. We drew a large crowd at Mondiagl-kaugla. The news of the Siako chief's daughter Anna 'tying the knot' with Forestry Officer, Joseph Tamgo had fanned out to everyone long before, since the *ambu-di-kungugl* phase was in progess, and Mondiagl-kaugla was packed to capacity with observers when we arrived. Many came as early as 10.00 am, waiting the whole day to witness the occasion, especially the display by the *kaigale* pageant. They all joined us in the cavalcade, and together we proceeded towards Ende-naige-ingugl, consequently increasing our size to an unimaginable number.

Nearing the proximity of the Siako camp, we formalised our approach with harbingers of war cries, alerting the Siakos of our approach. They were equally prepared in anticipation of our arrival. The entrance gate into Ende-naige-ingugl was pulled to the ground to allow the influx of people, and allow trouble-free entry without any inconvenience caused to anyone. Like the crowd behind us, there were many people inside Ende-naige-ingugl, all looking out to the direction of our entry. As we stepped into the entrance gate, the Siakos *kaigale* pageant rushed out, and greeted us with a spectacular performance. Our *kaigale* group had been performing all along, and retaliated immediately. Soon, both dancing groups blended and executed a dramatic combined performance, which was applauded and cheered on by everyone with the Siako *agl-ange* women, fervently up on their toes during the entire moment.

The procession continued across the village to where the stage was prepared. There, we circled around their pork display, and retired to our corner in the direction of our entry. Councillor Bagle and his group took the opposite corner towards the village. While the women were still in singsing, we quickly displayed our pork opposite theirs, neatly stacked, one on top of another. They had slaughtered three porkers, equivalent to our number and, ironically, both displays matched each other perfectly well, comparatively, and there was no impression of defeat in terms of the pork exchange, at the very first glance. Many observers were marveled at this sight, and was later talked about it in many homes. The money poles, supported by pickets, were planted in the central arena along side our pork display. Considering that everything was set, our group circled around our display with a non-stop high note cry of *Puo…Puo…Puo*, and reaching our corner, we open up in unison with a shout of satisfaction, as we backed into our corner.

The entry observance of the *ambu-di* had been accomplished. We had officially arrived with our *di-minge-bugla* to Ende-naige-ingugl in the eyes of everyone to pay for Anna. We were officially accepted and welcomed. It was speech time next, and we had two orators each from both the camps that came out into the arena and spoke. Thomas Kutne and Anton Kama were the first and second speakers respectively in our camp. Both were renowned village elders from the Miuk Kwuiopa sub-clan of mine. The men walked into the arena with axes in their hands, the object conventionally symbolising a scepter or authority, and let out their speeches with oratorical gestures, as they perambulated the central arena, getting everyone up on their toes with tumultuous applause. In the Siako camp, Anna's uncle and father came out respectively and ended the speech session. All speeches were eloquently made with occasional banters from all orators, which sent the crowd into a frenzy. There was applauding from everyone, as the orator left the arena.

After the speech, the next protocol was the handover and takeover of the bride, but still, at this point, I could not see Anna in the Siako crowd, where she was supposed to be. Then, after a moment of hassle in the Siako corner, I saw a mount of black paradise plumes moving to the front behind the heads of the crowd. Gradually, a space was opened up and, for the first time, I caught a glimpse of Anna being led to the forefront. My heart trembled almost immediately with emotions.

"Good Golly, could this really be Anna" I thought, as I looked away into the opposite direction to avert my eyes.

I only knew Anna in a blouse, skirt or a *laplap* during the few times I saw her. And my eyes peeled wide open with the brows arched high when I saw her in full traditional attire. I never knew, she had such a beautiful body, seraphic and almost that of a goddess behind the regular nylon material. I was amazed, as she posed in the front to be led away. She was truly a beauty in disguise, back in the village. And as I peered, I recounted my father's words, "Son, you won't regret this day with the decision you've just made" on that miserable Easter Thursday night, after I announced my decision to him and mother to take Anna as my bride. He was truly a great man. He saw sunlight first, or otherwise, was born before me and knew what he was talking about. He knew what was right at the doorsteps and insisted, but I turned him down many times just to remain with, what I thought, was best for me. But he never gave up. I did. I was the one who finally gave in to him. And now I realised, I never erred in making that decision, as only a few steps away from where I was standing was my wife-to-be of angelic beauty, waiting to be led away to our corner.

Anna was the daughter of a village chief. And hence, her father bedecked her supremely with the most prized and sought-after *bilas* anyone would possibly want to lay his or her hands on. She was oiled with clean lard, which glistened in the afternoon sun, as it shone upon her marvelous body. Her headdress was buried with paradise plumes of all sorts, the tall black plumes being dominant, covering every little space of her head. Shielding her pectoral was a possum pelt that stretched from neck to her torso. The furs were snow white with scattered patches of gold and brown, and were one such, which I had never seen before. Down her groin strands of beautifully made *kaur,* dangled down her anterior and posterior from the waist to the ankles. The strands were intertwined with prized possum furs of grey, black, silver and white from the popular upper montane possum species of *mogl* and *towa,* most probably from the hands of her very own mother. Adding absolute beauty to her *bilas* were colourful ornamental leaves, crimped and tucked nicely away into her armbands and her posterior. Finally, the facial paintings of red, white and yellow, put the finishing touches to her adornment. I wished I had had a camera to take some pictures of her, but this had never crossed my mind earlier. It was a mistake, and truly a teribble mistake, as I was to regret that mistake in the later years of our life, after acknowledging that such occasions and appearances become possible only once in a lifetime.

Conforming to the established and conventional protocols, well before the entire matrimonial ceremony, a clansman's wife, who, obviously, must originally be from the Siako clan, has to be nominated as bridesmaid, or *ambu-kep* to take Anna's hand at the time of the handover. Her duty was to take Anna's hands and lead her to our corner. It was the protocol, formally officiating the marriage, the conferment, and the handover of Anna from her parents to the groom in marriage. Gambugl, a relative's wife, was nominated for the job and she crossed the arena, all dressed up for the occasion in full traditional attire. She took Anna's hands from the hands of Bagle, and gently led her out. Mid-way through, two strong men from our corner rushed out, meeting Gambugl and Anna midway. Standing right beside Anna on both of her sides, they reached out and gripped each other's hands from behind. Then, going down low, both formed a seat with their hands, and lifted Anna up into the air. In the next minute, they made two histrionic appreciation laps of honour around the main arena, as the crowd roared and applauded the ritual. When they finally rested Anna in our corner, it was all over. Anna was now a married Denglagu woman, wife of Joseph Tamgo, a student forester and no longer a Siako girl to go by her own inclinations.

It truly was not only sensational but also a moving moment in the Siako corner. Anna won't ever come back to Ende-naige-ingugl again. She had officially crossed the line to move out of Ende-naige-ingugl permanently and many friends of hers shed tears openly, as she was led away. Her mother keened openly. She was her strength and she knew it. Tears flooded Anna's eyes too, and dripped down in rivulets on her painted cheeks and awkwardly distorting her painted face. She knew, she would never come back again to the place where she began her existence. She was going out to start a new life on her own, away from them all, her loving parents, relatives, best friends and everyone in her Siako community. And, off course, when her hour comes, will be buried away from her fatherland. Indeed, it was a heart-felt and pathetic moment for Anna and her family members.

There was a recess after the handover. In the Siako corner, everyone was regrouping for the farewell presentations.

In our corner, everyone crowded around the new member of our clan, my bride. Some men were tidying up the *bilas* that had been disarranged during the appreciation lap. Then led by Councillor Bagle, the Siakos crossed over, individually, one at a time, and delivered their farewell presents to Anna. They presented cash, exchanged handshakes in farewell and retired back to their corner. The cash monies in notes were all tucked firmly into her armbands and the *kaur* loops around her haunch until no more space was available. Lastly, they presented three pigs to take along to start and build up her own wealth with her husband, who was myself. The cash later added up to K1200.00, an unexpected amount that was very much a surprise.

We were nearing the final stage of the ceremony and, obviously, the two-week event. All that was left was the snack bite of the *bugla-dane* that would be offered by the Siakos, the final ritual of the ceremony, before retreating out of Ende-naige-ingugl. Two sebaceous *bugla-dane* from the Siako porkers were heated over the flames, salted and held out by two men. Everyone took turns to take his snack bite. I joined the queue but stepped back, when my appetite dropped after the first bite, and watched others, as they went in for their second, third and fourth rounds. The entire ceremony was practically over when there was nothing more of the *bugla dane* left. Indeed, after all the singing and dancing during the long procession in the hot afternoon sun, I knew nothing would be left. We had punctiliously covered every step, and completed every ritual required under the customary observance in the marriage of the young couple. It was all over now.

We regrouped together, fervently chanting the famous "Thank you" war cry of *Sipu…Sipu…Sipu* and walked out of Ende-naige-ingugl, our *kaigale* pageant leading the way out with their spectacular dance. Again, there was singing, this time paeans, as we led Anna out of Ende-naige-ingugl, taking with us the exchanged pork, three live pigs and Anna's trousseau. The latter were all in a bag that was carried by my mother.

The wedding ceremony was a great success, and it drew praise from all those who had witnessed the occasion. Many summed it up as the best ever after a long period of time. Juxtaposing the event, the Siakos were comparatively terrific like us. The K1,200.00 and the three pigs they gave as farewell gifts to Anna were more or less a rebate of the total bride price we paid. Their porkers for the exchange, by comparison, matched ours perfectly in size, weight and adiposity. They were the talk of the day amongst the observers, and in the homes of many. Far more delightful was how Anna was arrayed in traditional attire and presented to us. As the daughter of a renowned village chief, she certainly was the attraction of the day with her magnificent *bilas*, and drew the attention of the crowd.

I felt proud, as we walked out of Ende-naige-ingugl. Briefly, I wished Cathy Gior could have been there to see how one of her clan sisters was wedded to her jilted boyfriend. But unfortunately, she was not around. However, her mother was there. She witnessed everything from the start to the finish. I had seen her standing with the other Siako women in the crowd, and even presented Anna with a farewell gift of a K20.00 bill. She closely watched how Anna was wedded to someone she had inveighed before, someone who was even more crazy about her very own daughter. She had seen the extremes of the exchanges of pork, the presentation of Anna, the crowd attraction and everything that had happened during the ceremonious event. On perception, I knew that Kumo had drawn up her own conclusions to the event and would have a lot of things to tell her beautiful daughter, when she comes around in her flashy tinted glass station wagon again. As I thought more about it, I wondered if Angela Kumo would ever bedeck Cathy Gior and send her out of Ende-naige-ingugl in a ceremonious event like Councilor Bagle and his wife did to their daughter Anna. Only time would tell!

17

Polygamy Has Its Incidence

The spirit and mood of the wedding ceremony was still fresh in my next two remaining weeks of the semester break. I was now a husband, not single anymore. The aftermath activities included the pork distribution to family units, the dismissal of friends and relatives who had come and stayed with us to assist on the occasion, and the introduction of Anna to her new home and environment. I was eager to spend sometime with Anna alone to discuss some very important things over these few remaining days, but, seemingly, there was not a moment of peace during the first week after the ceremony. Everyone was still busy. It was only towards the final three remaining days of the week when everyone left that I finally had some free moments to spend with Anna, now my wife. At first, I felt unusual and rather strange, at times, to call Anna 'wife' or heard people addressing her to me as 'your wife', or myself to her as 'your husband'. But I soon learned to accept the fact that I was now a married man, even though nothing of my pre-marital attitude changed. Furthermore, I began to realise that it would take sometime for me to adjust myself to the new role I would be playing as a husband.

Anna was different. She seemingly was well prepared for this next chapter of her life and the roles she would be playing from then on. She was more relaxed than myself. She had already taken over many routine duites from my mother; the feedings of the pigs, the cooking and many other domestic jobs with omniscience. And she seemingly excelled in anything she ventured into. But I personally foresaw the future differently from my perspective, that life would be no longer the same and as difficult from then on, for the reason that I was still a student and that Anna's welfare was my responsibility. Above that, I would certainly make it more difficult for Anna when I leave her alone, on her own, in the village with my parents and go back to school. Hence, I was placed in a situation to decide if I should could continue the next semester. The thoughts reverberated in my mind. Finally, I decided to defer my studies to the following year after settling Anna first. And when we were alone later in the evening, I let out my intentions to her.

But, alas, to my surprise, Anna asked, "Why do you want to defer your studies?"

"To settle you first, off course. I just can't leave you here like that to fend for yourself and go away". I openly told Anna.

Anna did not speak again. She looked out ruminatively into the empty space, as if to find some alternative solutions, but did not show any emotions of discontentment or even being fazed about anything. Then calmly, she said, "Why don't you go back to school and complete the second semester?"

"What?"

"I said…why don't you go back to Unitech and complete your studies. I can stay home with the parents".

With my eyebrows arched to the forehead, I stared stunningly into her eyes.

"Anna, are you really sure, you are telling me to go back to school, and continue my studies?"

She smiled.

"Yes! Yes---off course, I did", she affirmed aspiringly, "You need not worry about me; living in the village is not a problem to me. It's been part of my life. I've lived all my life here, and I know how to survive in the village. You should worry about your studies and not me?"

Anna's approach to the situation, and the response she gave me fascinated me and had me speechless for a long time. It was only twelve days since our wedding and already she was making some crucial and very vital decisions in her life that could have a daunting effect on her first eighteen months of married life. But deeply, there was substance, perspicacity and words of encouragement, in everything she said, and I felt proud. Not that I would be going back to school, but that Anna was somebody blessed with gumption and insight, whom I could certainly rely on in the future. She was sagacious, understanding and, of course, decisive too, attributes that I could fall back on in the future.

After a resilient return from Anna's response, I reconsidered deeply whether I should really go back to school and complete the semester. I thought of the unknown future that lay ahead of us, and whether I should really leave Anna alone. I also contemplated on the academic progress I made. In the end, after seriously considering the rising difficulty in securing scholarships and the one-chance Natschol award system, I finally decided to take the chance and heed to my young wife's call, i.e to retun to the campus and continue my studies. Maybe, it would be difficult for us from the start but, with an understanding wife around to support and make the ends meet, I knew, we would make it during the tough times and come out victors.

"Well! Anna, I really can't take that but, if that is what you want me to do, then I will and take the chance…thank you, for your understanding", I finally said, after a long thoughtful pause. Then, in a slightly relaxed, but uncomfortable tone, "I'm rather pleased with you for thinking wise", I said, "I really don't know how this will work out, but I know it would certainly be a bad start for us both, as a newly-wed couple. But let's not forget that we have a great future ahead. Whatever difficulty, or burden we encounter now, I assure you, will only be purgatorial", I told Anna.

Anna looked into my eyes, and smiled. It was a cool and devoted smile, rarely seen on the faces of many. There was understanding, trust and faith, all in her eyes, as she smiled at me. I smiled back in appreciation. And with tenderness, I reached out and gently pulled her into my arms for the very first time. "I promise that you won't regret this day", I said, as I held her in my arms, amply recalling my father's exact words when I finally got out, after getting stuck in decision-making.

Then, finally, on the painful morning of my departure to Lae, Anna walked with me to Mondiagl-kaugla to send me away on a PMV. She carried my bag that contained a few clothes, and some essential items. Before sending me away, Anna led me to a secluded section, away from the many eyes, and handed me an envelope, thick but folded squarely, that fitted perfectly in the palm of my hands.

"What's this?' I asked, looking at the envelope, as I took it.

"Money! The envelope contains money", she said, "…about K400.00; you take it with you and use it, whenever you need it".

"Where did you get them?"

"Father gave them to me on the night before the *ambu-di* in the house. He said, I would be leaving him forever to go on my own, and privately gave it to me as a consolation gift. But they're too much for me to use, so I thought it's best you take it along with you. I know you'll need it down there"

Anna yet again surprised me with another overture, her approach to pecuniary matters. But it was understandable. She was always a village girl her whole lifetime with little access to large sums of money and was, perhaps, scared to keep the large amount of cash in her possession, or otherwise, does not know what to do with it. I took the money, thanked her supremely and got on a PMV that pulled in. She waved me goodbye and stood watching as the PMV turned the Ende-naige-ingugl corner. I put the money in my pocket, and knew that one day, it would serve its purpose. The following day I opened an Interest-Bearing Deposit account at Westpac Bank in Lae.

The second semester went past quickly. Maybe, I was too occupied with my studies to realise the days and weeks going past, like the wind, but certainly in the next three weeks, after the final semester exams, the University would close for the long Christmas vacation. The excitement was gradually building up. As a young husband, I was glad of the approaching long vacation. I had certainly left my young wife behind, all on her own, and all I wanted to do was to go straight home and spend my holidays with her. I had missed her so much and soon after the last exam, I rushed to Eriku. I took a late bus to Goroka and continued to Simbu, the following morning. When I arrived in Bokan, I found my beautiful Anna smiling gorgeously at me. She was filthy, disheveled and grubby, a common sight of married women in the rural areas, but her distinguishing beauty could not be denied amidst the rags she was in. She had only returned from the garden and I could see her weary eyes sparkled with delight as soon as she saw me. I threw my arms around her and hoisted her up into the sky with happiness in greetings.

"Am I not glad to see you, *leva*", I exclaimed, as I held her aloft in the air.

She giggled and struggle to go free, which she did after I gently placed her back on the ground.

'Where did you come from?" I asked inquisitively when my eyes rested on the hugh *bilum* of *kaukau* and another *bilum* of vegetables and broad beans on the ground.

"Dunugl", Anna said shyly and smiled, her pretty cheeks hollowed with dimples.

Then, looking down at the *bilums*, she eyed me again with smirk, as if holding something back in her mind.

"What is it? Spit it out, I know you are holding back something", I asked inquisitively, smiling back.

"It's just coincidence; you just arrive in time to taste my first early harvest from Dunugl".

"Oh, really!"

Anna said nothing more, but continued to let the smile glow shyly on her face. I was speechless also. So, she'd been working in the gardens all the while I was away, I thought. I just could not think up anything better to compliment her, but after all, she was my wife, my very own wife, and that elevated my inner feelings to reach the acme of my life. She was truly someone I could rely on, I thought.

My mother, later, proudly boasted to me of Anna's performance.

"She's my number one daughter-in-law", she ranted, not wanting to let anyone interrupt her, "…she has taken over all the jobs; from gardening to everyday porcine duties, and I am almost free everyday. And she excelled in all of them".

I felt proud. I confirmed my mother's boastful reports of Anna when many people approached me in the later weeks to commend Anna's excellent performance as a young wife to me.

"She's a beauty in everything", many observers said with great satisfaction, "…she's someone you can rely on in the future", they complimented her.

Again, I owed all the credits to my parents. It was their initiative that made everything possible for Anna to become my bride and, quite frankly, their efforts had paid off richly in the end to rip the harvest. I was happy, just as they were, and so was everyone, who was part of the *ambu-di-kungugl.* Their contributions had not been wasted but instead went for a worthy cause.

Christmas was always a great moment for everyone in the villages. It was time for celebrations, partying and reunion of families, relatives and friends. It was also the time for relaxation after a year of hard work and to enjoy the reunion. But I had a lot to catch up and spent my entire time with Anna, upon arrival, helping her out in whatever problems she encountered during my absence. As a workaholic, she was inspirational, and soon I got myself involved in gardening and digging up new plots for her to plant. My hands had been accustomed to that small 'stick' called biro and, for the first time, I touched a bush knife, axe and spade. Before the first day ended, blisters riddled my hands, but I did not give up. I knew, it would take time to habituate and execute the full roles of a husband in the village, but the fact that I could prove to my wife that I could do 'this' or 'that' was far more satisfying than giving up, or doing nothing at all. And I worked tirelessly and relentlessly in whatever I did or touched.

In the villages around us, the number of visitors kept increasing. Every PMV that traveled up from Kundiawa dropped off at least four or five 'local tourists' daily, most of whom were relatives and friends, who had long gone to other parts of Papua New Guinea and returned to spend Christmas with their families. Some were public servants. Other were students like myself, who had come home for the Christmas vacation after sweating and blowing their heads in the classrooms all the year round.

I met a lot of old friends, with many of whom I had either lost contact, or had not seen them for quite a while. Thomas Gior, who was now employed with an accounting firm in Port Moresby, arrived in the last week of November. It had been some couple of years since I last saw him and I felt like meeting a long-lost brother when he came over to see me. Anna was out when he arrived, but he congratulated me personally on my marriage to one of his kindred sisters.

"I'm sorry, Joe, I contributed nothing towards the bride price", he said.

"It's all right, I think we handled that nicely. There was surplus *di-*

minge-bugla, so we overpaid them. And the ceremony went off without a hitch", I said, and briefly went through the June ceremony.

"At least you married one of my sisters. That's the most satisfying part", he came back.

"Thank you"

There was envy, and regret in his tone. I could sense the indirect condemnation of his niece, for all the infidelities that ruined our amorous relationship that he had helped to bridge. But he did not let out a word on his thoughts.

"Anna is nice", I frankly told Thomas, in the hope of bringing his mind back. "I don't have any regrets now. I wish, Cathy comes around to my place for a cup of coffee to see how Anna is doing", I added, laughing.

It was a joke.

"Forget about that swine", he bluntly said, as we burst into laughter.

Thomas Gior later mooted on his affair with a Papuan girl.

"She's pregnant", he said, "I'm not too sure whether I'll marry her". "Congratulations! That's good news", I commended, "You're certainly going to come up with a rare breed around here".

We laughed.

"Where's she from---Hunuabada?" I asked, as if I personally knew where Hanuabada was.

"No! Not there. She's someone from outside Port Moresby, Yule Island. That's miles outside Port Moresby, up the Bereina way, following the Hiritano highway. Can you remember a visiting Bishop from Central Province in Kondiu during our tenth grade and was said to be the first Papua New Guinea Catholic priest, ordained in Madagascar?"

"Yeah, Bishop Louis Vengeke. He spent a period with us during religion class".

"That's right. The girl is from around the same place where that Bishop comes from".

"Really?"

"Yeah"

"That place is filled with history, and historical sites. Have you been up there yet?"

"No, I just met the girl in Port Moresby, and the relationship started there. I have yet to see her place".

"I see. So, are you two living together, then?"

"No, she just comes around to visit me regularly, whenever she is in the capital".

"Then listen…why don't you just forget the girl. I think the pregnancy results from excessive fornication between you and her, and you just cant't succumb to marriage because someone is preganant". I cut in and foolishly advised. Thomas laughed without voicing any word. "Besides that, I don't think that girl of yours will habituate herself to the highland's climate. Just pick up the baby and send the mother away, simple".

Again, we laughed.

"I'll think about it", Thomas said, almost foolishly, taking in my ill advice.

In the same week, some two days later, Anna and I were both in the house, one afternoon. All of a sudden, she burst into tears when a gentleman stepped into the house. I panicked and sat wondering with a blank mind when Anna introduced him to me as Bonma Gumia, her elder brother, and now my brother-in-law. Bonma moved over to West New Britian, some ten years ago, and worked with New Britian Palm Oil Limited. He started as a young driver and eventually made his way to a supervisor's post in recent times. I have heard of him many times before, but never had a chance to meet him even once. I was surprised when he was introduced to me that evening.

We exchanged greetings with a hug. He took all the resemblance of his father Councillor Bagle, maintaining a robust and sturdy physique. He was open, and spoke nicely in an admirable tone that I began to like him almost immediately. We settled down and chatted, while Anna quickly started the fire and made us coffee.

"I'm sorry, I wasn't here to witness your wedding ceremony, but mother said that it was great", Bonma said.

We said nothing but looked at each other and offered our affirmative smiles. "It was really our wedding, so we cannot make any judgement on that", I told him, "You can make your own judgement from what you gather from observers, but truly it was something everyone talked about most in the weeks after the ceremony".

"Yes, many, who witnessed the occasion, told me that it was a great wedding".

"It sure was", I affirmed.

After Bonma finished his coffee, he slipped his hands into his side pocket and produced some money. He did not pause to count them out, or even look at them. "I really don't have plenty of money with me now, but this is for you two as my Christmas gift", he said, and then held out the bills to me.

He surprised us and it took some moments to stare at each other before I eventually took the money from his hand. It was K200.00 in all, neatly folded in halves. We thanked him for his kindness with hugs again, and I later gave the money to Anna for safekeeping. She carefully locked it away in her suitcase.

Bonma had planned other surprises too. Immediately, after Anna locked away the money, he excused her if he could take me out for a drink at the local pub. My understanding wife, without any objection, tacitly consented with an affirmative smile.

"Joe, I think your wife agrees…let's go! We'll be back in the night", Bonma appreciatively told his sister, and soon stepped out of the house.

"He has been tackling *pitpit* stumps lately, and blisters are all over his hands. I think Joseph appreciates your invitation. Make sure you look after him", Anna voiced from inside the house.

"Don't worry, we'll be alright", Bonma shouted back.

In a matter of minutes, we stepped into the nearest pub where he bought a lot of the favourite ale. It was a bottle after bottle situation--- that took us into the early hours of dawn. It truly was a memorable night, no drunkenness, no rough tactics, no shouting and no everything as commonly seen amongst many local drinkers. I have heard stories of him being a great man and superior in many things he does and legitimately proved this right that night. For instance, it is typical in any carousal to return some one's beer. And I was only a student with no money to return his beers, but he said, "Don't worry, brother…just drink up", and I did exactly that obligingly, and truly enjoyed his companionship during the night. And before the we ended the night, we omitted our given names, and called each other 'brother' instead.

One afternoon, during the third week of December, just before Christmas eve, I stood watch over Bonma, as he gambled with a group of men at Mondiagl-kaugla, a nice secluded spot, some few metres outside the market perimeter. The spot was a popular hotbed for card gamblers and there were three other gambling groups in the adjacent areas near us. To the left, in the east, was the mighty pristine Simbu River, purling noisily over huge boulders, rocks and stones, heading south. And to the west, a couple of metres out, was the main Kundiawa-Gembogl road, obscured from the shrubs and thickets growing in between. No one could see the gamblers from the road, but anyone gambling could clearly see through the bushes who was on the road or what was happening out on the road.

It was a beautiful afternoon and the market was packed with people. There were many new faces, that had come home to spend their Christmas holiday. They could be seen wandering around in the market, admiring the fresh garden produce sold by the local farmers. Others just stood, or were seen loitering around and enjoying the afternoon sun with friends. Equal in number were villagers, who had retired home from work in the gardens, but stopped to pass time in the market before retiring home. Out on the main road, PMVs roared past, leaving billows of dust behind them. Many stopped to let out their passengers before continuing to Niglguma and Kegesuglo. And after the PMVs left people could be seen crowding around a new arrival, if a friend, or a relative was off-loaded.

Our attention was suddenly drawn to the engine of any approaching vehicle in the south. The sound got bigger and bigger and within seconds, a red Mitsubishi L200 showed up on the road. It zoomed to a stop at the roadside next to the market. It was the same PMV I had traveled on some months earlier, that could not cross the landslide debris at Oyame. About three people got out, but my attention rested on a young woman who appeared modern in her outlook, but seemed sick in her movements. I tried to establish her identity but couldn't, as it was rather impossible from where I was. She had a Queensland maroons cap over her head, wore a blue jacket that was zipped to the neck, possibly to keep out the dust, and a pair of blue Jean plus-fours, cut at knee length. Her feet were well hidden without socks in a pair of KT26 Dunlop runners.

Held firmly in place by the maroon cap was a white face towel that hug down in her front, shielded most of her face to avoid the dust, perhaps. A school kid's lunch backpack, that seemed to have contained almost nothing, drooped loosely behind her back.

With the impossibility of establishing her identity, my attention was drawn back to the gambling again after the Mitsubishi pulled out, but things did not look good for Bonma in the games that he played. In the next twenty minutes, it was all over for him.

"We lost", he said with a grin, as he stood up.

"You have to be careful. These people here sometimes play dirty. They'll cheat and win all your money", I cautioned, him.

"It could be that. There were only four wins in my favour, out of the thirteen bets. But I held back a K2.00 note for our betel nut. Let's go to the market and chew", he said.

I said nothing more and followed closely behind, as he led us out onto the road to proceed to the market.

As we stepped out onto the road, we noticed, far down on the roadside, just a few meters away from the entrance into the nearby Christian Life Center church, a group of people convening there. They were nearly all Siakos, crowding around, almost in a full circle, discussing or just observing something amidst them, with the unfortunates peering over the shoulders of others.

"Something is happening down there. I don't know, they are probably discussing, or viewing something. What could it be?"

"These are Siakos; let's go and find out", Bonma said, and wasted no time.

I followed closely behind, as Bonma led the way. The Siakos were in the middle of a fierce discussion; more of a debate than an ordinary talk, perhaps an argument too. I was less curious about what they were actually doing, or talking about, as it was practically non of my business. Bonma appeared more concern as it was his clanmen and women grouping there, and he wanted to find out. Thus, I towed along slowly behind him. Then, as we neared the group, through a gap that was partly opened up between the crowd, I noticed the young woman who had got off the Mitsubishi sitting in the middle of them all. She still had the face towel over her face, and quite seriously seemed to be the center of the attraction there. Sitting right beside her was Angela Kumo, Cathy Gior's mother. She appeared to be doing all the talking while the others listened, and as I neared, I could already pick up her voice too.

At first, I suspect nothing but, as I stepped up to the group, I noticed a rather suspicious reaction from the girl. She quickly turned away to hide her face from me, when her eyes somehow caught mine, alerting my instincts almost immediately. But I still had trouble recognising her, with the face towel still over her face. My curious mind instantly started to ask questions. Who could that be? Why did she have to do that? Do I know her? But it did not take long for the answer to come forward. With Kumo alongside her, and garrulously doing all the talking, my mind started resurrecting the past almost immediately.

"Could this be Cathy Gior?", I mused, as we approached. "If she is Cathy, then she must be in some kind of trouble", I wondered.

I was not wrong. Seconds later, her name could be heard in the discussions taking place within the group. The girl, in fact was Cathy Gior.

The circumstances surrounding the nature of the discussion was not known yet to me, but as suspected, Cathy was certainly in some kind of trouble. I overheard Kumo detesting and complaining bitterly over something tragically serious. But I did not stay long to take in everything. It was truly none of my business and, after all, I did not want to be seen in the group, especially by my wife Anna or anyone from Bokan, to avoid gossip.

Leaving Bonma behind, I quietly stepped back onto the road and surreptitiously walked my way up to the market, to wait for him to join me there. I sat on a boulder, but curiosity took the better of me as I waited. It was some good minutes later that Bonma caught up with me again.

"I decided not to stay there and came back up here. What happened to Cathy?", I asked.

"She got bashed up", Bonma said.

"My gosh! By whom?"

"Her husband's two rival wives…and an elder daughter too, that's what she said, but whoever did the harm, sure did it thoroughly", Bonma said, referring to Peter's two other wives and his elder daughter who was out on school holidays.

"Three women against one? Unbelievable!" I said looking astounded.

"It was a combined effort from her three rival women, and Cathy's face is in such a terrible state. Cuts and bruises are all over; that's why you saw the face towel over her face, most of the time. She is trying to hide the wounds and bruises from everyone".

It was shocking but also a surprise. And almost immediately, a smile of approval swept through my entire system. I retrospectively absorbed her beating as a retributive justice for jilting me, a penal consequence for trying to be too smart. And though I have nothing in store for her this time, I became overwhelmingly excited and, as curious as ever to know what exactly had happened in the mishap.

"Was her husband around? He should have intervened and stopped this", I voiced, as though showing my genuine concern.

"He is out of the country", Bonma revealed, "…that's what Cathy said. But who knows? He may be gallivanting off in Port Moresby, hugging another woman at Travelodge, or Islander at the moment. Never trust local tycoons nowadays", he grinned.

"I know that"

Cathy did not elaborate on the cause of the commotion between herself and her three women rivals, or the reason why she was beaten up. "I don't know why, they are jealous", was all, she was telling everyone, who asked.

Perhaps, she was frustrated to divulge or disclose the cause, but the truth came to light a day later, when I came around to Bonma again. "It was her fancy and possessive attitude over her husband, coupled with the favoritism she's been receiving from him that incurred jealousy and anger, in the two other wives, resulting in the fight. The daughter stepped in, in support of her elderly mother", he elaborated.

"That's sad", I said, without voicing any further concern.

But Cathy's marriage to the millionaire had certainly hit the headlines in the Maugl-wak tribe, only months earlier, and her tragedy was the most talked-about stories in the next few days. Many discussed, at great length, the fairy tale life of the Siako beauty and her down turns in the aftermath of her marriage. And in turn, I soon learnt many things.

Obviously, Cathy's teaching career took a different turn after she was transferred to Mt Hagen. She was so absorbed in her husband's wealth and fortunes that her interest in teaching declined. Maybe, Peter's business empire proved too much for her to go out and waste time in the classroom with little kids in the bush. Perhaps, there were other reasons too, but she eventually left teaching at the beginning of the year, obviously declining a posting to West Kambia. Her reasons were straightforward---too remote and high security risk area. Her wealthy husband was not at all bothered with her decision. Eventually, money is the bottomline, and he has it all. Why, allowing his latest 'find' into the bush, or to stay away from him, just for a lousy pay packet every two weeks. He welcomed Cathy's decision and allowed her to be with him in his fabulous Mt Hagen mansion, away from his two other wives, who had their own homes in the village.

In the course of her stay with her husband in Mt Hagen, Cathy was privileged to almost anything in life compared to the other two wives. She traveled extensively with her husband, accompanying him on his many business and leisure trips, to the parties, enjoyed all the perks, and recived all the glamour and attention of a businessman's wife. This flared up frustration and jealousy between the two other wives, especially the second wife, Kossip, who was in her mid-thirties. She felt neglected and missed out on the many things, that she believed she was supposed to get, share or equally enjoy. Tension gradually built up and a physical confrontation was imminent almost every day, but there was no better time than that Christmas when her husband, Peter Kupal, was out of the country.

Kumo and the Siakos viewed Cathy's misdemeanors with disgust. They discussed her tragedy at great length again at Ende-naige-ingugl, but nothing conclusive and constructive was yet reached on the possible actions to take against Cathy's rival women for the infliction caused to their daughter.

"Peter will look into it and sort that out when he comes back from overseas", many said, referring the matter back to her husband.

Others lamented that the encounter was something common, inevitable and unavoidable in any polygamy.

"That's quite correct; she cannot circumvent infighting, especially when she has two other rival wives", Kumo was heard blindly telling everyone.

Maybe, she was conventionally right in a logical sense. But, in oblivion to the fact of polygamy, it was the start, the beginning of a painful road for herself and that of her daughter's much dreamed about endeavor to a sybaritic lifestyle.

Those who saw them, described the facial injuries sustained by Cathy from her encounter with her women rivals, as severe and terrible for any eye to see. But I never saw her wounds myself to make my own judgement. She avoided my eyes, as much as possible, everytime I was in her path. She either looked away, or dropped her head with the face towel still over her face. I could see slight indelible stains of dry-blood on the face towel from far, but could not see the actual wounds behind the towel. It was not until some days after Christmas that I finally had a chance to view her bruised face. She was receiving treatment at the aid post. I went in for my usual weekly chloroquinine dose and accidentally stumbled into her. She was sitting at the end of the bench with the Aid Post Orderly attending to her wounds.

It was an unexpected meet. And I must have certainly surprised her with my presence and she was shocked to the nerve, just as I was to see her wounds. She was obviously trying all she could to avoid my curious eyes. But I was appalled and horrified at the sight of her squeamish wounds and bruises, some of which were gradually drying up, while the most severe cuts were festering. Her right eye was still blackened by blood clotting from a good blow that must have landed there. There were swellings all over too, but it was gradually abating. But they certainly distorted the true complexion of her face, with some part still turgid. Cat-scratch bruises were everywhere on her face and extended down to her neck. It was indeed a terrible sight. The elegance of the once beautiful face I had admired was no longer there. It was gone, and now replaced by scars, bruises, hollows and patches of lumps. What a real pity it was, when I saw her sitting there helpless and cringed without a word, trying desperately to avoid my gaze. I noticed the awkward situation I created for her, and quickly walked out to the lawn outside to wait for my turn to be called in by the Aid Post Orderly.

Sitting out on the lawn, I reviewed Cathy's face again and her encounter with her enemies in my mind. With the ratio at three is to one, I recreated the possible situation that might have possibly happened; three giant Western Highlands amazons swooping in on her, pinioning, hitting and dragging her around helplessly on the ground. She was a foe, an intruder in their domain, scooping up all the perks and privileges and they gave her all they got. I imagined Cathy Gior, most probably stripped to the pants, wriggling on the ground, all smeared in her own pool of blood, desperately calling out for help with no one coming to her aid in that distant place. It was truly a nightmare for her. She escaped now, lucky to be breathing. But that was not the end. To her women rivals, she was their life enemy, their obstacle to wealth and fame. She has to rival against them in order to make her presence felt. And she must plan and strategize too in order to win her spot amongst them. I wondered if she would ever do that, and succeed.

18

Nemesis Brings in Poignant Feelings

The Christmas season and the New Year period were finally over. It was now time for the working-class elites around the country to return to their respective work places. In the neighboring villages, the number of visitors slowly declined, as more and more people left. My brother-in-law, Bonma, left for Kimbe after the Boxing Day and exchanging best wishes with Anna and I. He left behind his contact number and address, urging me to write to him, as often as possible, to remain in close contact with him. He was quite nice to me during the holidays and I was sad to see him go when he boarded the PMV. He left his wife and kids behind in Kimbe so he traveled alone. I promised to write him letters as soon as I go back to school. I wished him a pleasant trip when he left. My friend, Thomas Gior, also left for Port Moresby just after the dawn of the New Year.

For the many school children and students, the beginning of another school year was just around the corner. It was time for the 'back to school' preparations. Amongst the many prerequisites, school fees turned out to be a major setback in many family units. And a number of anxious parents were seen desperately looking around for ways to secure schools fees by whatever means available to them. Many of them resorted to marketing pigs. It was a golden opportunity to buy a pig after using up and exhausting almost everything in the *ambu-di-kungugl* six months ealier. And with the money Bonma gave us, Anna and I quickly bought a piglet at K30.00.

"We will celebrate at the end of the year with this pig if you successfully graduate", Anna twitted, as we walked home with the piglet, as if the animal would balloon within the next ten months.

I smiled at Anna with an askance look over her remark.

"It's only a piglet, I don't think it will be ready to go into the *mumu* pit by Novermber".

"You think so?"

"Come on, Anna. You can't make me believe that".

"Then wait till you come back and find out".

"Well, lets hope so", I chuckled as we headed towards home.

Apparently, time was running out for me too with the approach of the new moon. There was not much time left for me to accomplish everything as a married man, and I did whatever I could to please Anna in the limited space of time available. I concentrated heavily on digging up new plots for gardening in the few remaining weeks. I knew, Anna would ultimately takeover after my departure, with the assistance of my father, to finish off whatever unfinished jobs I would leave behind and work tirelessly to get something done. When the holidays were finally over, it was time to once again separate for the time being. I will have to return to Unitech to complete my final year of studies, and Anna will have to stay on her own in the village again, I mused. It was painstaking, but we consoled each other to endure the pains of missing each other. Anna had always understood, and remained natural and relaxed when the time came. It was also going to be my final year in Unitech, and she was just as eager as I was to let me complete my studies. I hugged her in appreciation and in the first week of February left for Unitech. This time, Paul joined Anna and my parents at home. He was no longer a student at the Maina Vocational School. His three-year carpentry training ended last November and he was presented with his trade certificate and a set of complimentary carpentry tools at the graduation ceremony. He would be with the family and was sure to take care of them with father during my absence.

In the campus, I started the year in an elated mood. The year was going to be my final year of studies at the University and I felt high after registering for the academic year. Looking ahead, it would be some ten months later that I would graduate and I hallucinated with joy how it would be like to possess a degree in my suitcase, and where I'll fit myself in the society and Papua New Guinea as a whole. I was optimistic in all my hallucinations only to discover soon after settling in the classroom that I was never to get my dream paper on a 'golden plate'. Like in any other challenging task, the higher one climbs the Everest, the tougher it gets. And I soon noticed that I had to work hard all the year round to earn the degree. I had to study hard, commit extra time and put in extra efforts on anything I had to do in that final year to achieve my goal, as strictly as I realised soon after, nothing was free in this world after all.

Apart from the many courses offered in the final year was a project. Every final year student had to choose from a series of forestry-oriented project titles to conduct research, write up a thesis and present it to the faculty at the end of the year. It was part of the course, compulsory and a prerequisite for every student in order to graduate. Friday of every week was allocated to the students to work on their respective projects.

From the potential list of titles that went up on the notice board, I noticed a project title that would require extensive travel up to the highlands for research purposes. Immediately I went for it, putting my name besides the title. The Project title was, *Diameter and Volume Increment of Coppice Saplings of Eucalyptus grandis in the Waghi Swamps*. The project title was put up by Mr Richards Towsand, the Forest Management and Mensuration lecturer. I noted later that it was part of a major research project Richards was undertaking himself on the coppice of *Eucalyptus grandis*. He was to be my supervisor all along during the year. Since the entire data was to come from the *Eucalyptus grandis* plantations in the Waghi swamps, it appeared that I was to travel to Mt Hagen more frequently. This was confirmed later when I was briefed by my supervisor of the quarterly trips to the Waghi swamp plantations during the year.

"You'll have to officially write and work closely with the provincial forestry officers in Mt Hagen", Richards said, and added, "in most of the times you'll need their assistance to get along up there". He was not wrong, as I found out later.

With Richards at the helm, I quickly drew up a work plan for the whole year on how to go about executing the research. Dividing the activities equally within the given time frame, I proposed to make my first travel to Mt Hagen in the second week of February, obviously to hold discussion with the forestry officers there, have a look around in the plantations in search of potential research sites and, if possible, set up my research plots. I also planned to trace up on any previous data kept in the Kagamuga provincial forest office, from past research. Richards agreed and my intention was later made known to the Provincial Forest Officer through the fax. After a further telephone call, I made my first trip to Kagamuga Forestry Station in mid-February. Fortunately, the Provincial Forest Officer was a Simbu man, Peter Kopin, a former college mate. He was surprised to see me when I arrived, and offered to accommodate me in his Kagamuga home. "I got your fax and was expecting you", he said. After a quick visit to the potential research sites in the plantations at Mugmamp, later in the evening, we traveled back to Kagamuga for the night. The following day, with the assistance from some of his laborers, I pegged out and established my plots, as directed by my supervisor, tagging and measuring every coppice in the plots. It was a laborious work and took me almost three days, the whole weekend to get everything done before returning to Lae.

In my second trip in May, I preplanned my stay for a few extra days, and contacted Peter in Kagamuga.

"Come around, we'll be expecting you", Peter assured me over telephone. And to my delight he also promised to make available some helpers to assist me. I thanked him sincerely before hanging up. And, on a Thursday, in the last week of May, I traveled up the Okuk Highway for Mt Hagen with the intention of spending Friday, and the weekend at the Mugmamp plantation to work on my research project.

Peter had prearranged two of his most senior field assistants on standby to wait for my arrival. On Friday morning, he assigned them to me at the office front and directed his driver to take us to Mugmamp. Both men were very experienced field assistants, who were experts in reading the compass, clinometer and tapes, and I was amazed at their work rate in the plots. They were fast, accurate and, above all, obedient. We soon finished measuring the plots after lunch. Coincidentally, the driver got back in time to check on us. "We are finished here, and are ready to go back", we told him, and soon we were on our way back to Kagamuga. I was pleased that we completed everything in a day and decided to spend the following day in the township of Mt Hagen on a sight seeing tour. Peter agreed to take me around when I revealed my plan to him.

At about 10.00am, the following day, I drove into town with Peter. It had been a quite a while since I last walked through the streets of Mt Hagen .and was amazed at the ever-expanding township. It was Saturday and there was not one street or town corner free of people. The erection of a six-storey Komkui building in the heart of Mt Hagen Township was the central attraction. But it was still under construction. After doing a few rounds in the nicely-gardened streets, I directed Peter to drop me off at the market.

"Market is always a place to find some one you know. Maybe I'll walk into some *wantoks* here", I said, as I stepped out.

"Simbus are everywhere here, I think you will find plenty in there", Peter said, "I'll pull in at the far end corner of the car park; just keep an eye out and join me there when you finish in there".

"Great! I'll catch up with you there".

The busy market was jam-packed with people, buyers and sellers, all alike. There was strict ban on littering. A spot fine of K20.00 was charged for the offence, and I was careful not to throw anything on the ground. Peter also warned me of the same when I got out of the pick-up. With my eyes out for some familiar faces, I was jostling, weaving and pushing my way towards the market. As I neared the entrance gate, all of a sudden, a high-pitched female voice called out my name from behind.

I had a cousin sister living somewhere in Mt Hagen with her husband. I had last visited them at the Kiminiga Police barracks, where the husband was a Police Officer. At first, I suspected the female to be that of my cousin, and quickly turned around with great anticipation. But, to my surprise, a couple of metres away with a gleeful smile, stood Cathy Gior. I turned virtually frozen inside, the second I caught a glimpse of her. The smile opened up to a certain extent when my eyes rested on her. I smiled too, but already panic-stricken and with traces of fear down my spine, my eyes briefly scanned the market, as I do not want to be seen as a former boy by Cathy's new family members. Further, it was the very first time for Cathy to come forward and talk to me after eloping to Peter, and I found myself almost dumbfounded to open my lips. For some reasons, I was scared too.

"What are you doing here?" I finally blurted, but then withdrew with a pardon when I realized how foolish the question was. "How did you see me?" I changed the question. Cathy smiled.

"I was standing only a few metres away from where you got out of the pickup", she said, "I beckoned, but you did not see me, so followed you here. Who was that guy who dropped you off?"

"A friend; I'm sorry, I missed you back there".

Cathy's face wounds had healed up. There was no more face towel over her face and I could see the scars clearly from where I was. I felt sorry for her, eyeing the damage there. The once beautiful complexion had partially gone and she was now in a sorry state.

"I thought, you were in Lae", Cathy said, as she tried to maintain a smile on her distorted face.

"I arrived yesterday. I'm just on a sojourn for a day or two here before returning back to Lae".

"And Anna?"

"She's back home, at Bokan"

"All by herself?"

"No, of course, not: she's with my parents. She prefers to stay in the village while I complete my studies. She's doing fine and has not yet let me down once. She is my nugget", I proudly boasted with the implicit intention to push her mind back into the glorious past.

Cathy smiled almost guiltily without lamenting any further on Anna. She paused for a moment, thinking hard, as if trying to think up something to impart to me. I wanted to asked her about the injuries she sustained during the Christmas period, and how, and when she got back to Mt Hagen, but I did not want to drag the conversation on. In truth, I did not want to be seen as a stranger talking to a rich man's wife in the market center by Peter Kupal's acolytes.

"Well, I better go now", I said, when nothing further was forthcoming.

"What? That's quite soon", Cathy voiced with astonishment. I seemed to have surprised Cathy with my sudden excuse to leave. And she quickly looked up at me, as if to check if I was truly serious. I was. The answers were all on my face. I was serious. I was no longer the same Joseph Tamgo she once knew. This time, I was somebody different, somebody struggling to make ends meet with a young intelligent and workaholic village girl. My love for Cathy was long gone. The room that she had occupied in my heart was no longer there. And she could see them all in my eyes.

"Alright, you have a nice day", she finally said, in a sad tone, after a long silence.

"Same to you", I replied back, as I left.

But I had not walked far when Cathy called out from behind again.

"Can I meet you here tomorrow?" she asked.

"Oh, what for?" I asked, turning around, stunned and pervaded with curiosity. Obviously, something had definitely crept into her mind, and I was eager to find out.

"Not a big deal; I just want us to go to Rebiamul and watch the rugby games; that all…and, maybe, we could talk."

"Talk? Talk about what?" I suddenly asked, surprised at her latest proposition.

She did not respond. Perhaps, she was trying to comprehend a more convincing reason to get me to meet her. But, anything to do with her was absolutely beyond my interest, and I did not give the chance to voice again.

"Just forget it", I said, "I'm sorry about that too, but I don't think I'll be around here tomorrow. I'm a bit busy and, besides I think, the good old days are over. We are both happily married now, and I don't think we have anything to discuss, or talk about this time. Or, even hang around together".

My firm response stunned Cathy, and I could see her standing back there in disbelief, but I did not bother to look back, and walked away into the populous crowd and disappeared.

For the first time, I was truly brave to have spurned the advances of the girl who was once my inamorata and idol. But, in retrospect, she deserved it more than anyone else. I had persevered long enough to keep her in my grip despite her many dark sides, but was ignorantly let down on many occasions. I had trusted her many times despite her infidelties, and gave her many opportunities to change her mind and attitudes, but she turned them down. And now that we both were happily married to our respective spouses, the bridge between us had been washed away. All that we had to do now is to stand on the riverbanks and 'wave' pleasantries across to each other without coming any closer. The encounter at the Mt Hagen market should be the start of all future similar encounters, I thought.

But that night, before retiring to bed in Peter Kopin's house at Kagamuga, I recalled Cathy again in my mind. I recalled her every word, her every attempt and the doleful state of her scar-riddled face. I never asked where she lived or what she was doing in town. She was certainly trying to tell me something, but I refused. The more I thought about it, the further my mind traveled down the memory lane, reminiscing the past good old days. Gradually, I felt a sudden change of heart in my body. I was rude and truly ignorant, I thought. I should have stayed back and listened to what she was trying to tell me, and, better still, accepting her invitation to the games. Maybe, she 'dumped' me but that does not mean that I didn't know her. I was truly inhumane and ignorant in my attitude.

I didn't see Cathy again after the Mt Hagen trip until June, some five weeks later, when I went home for the mid-semester break. This time, I was told that she had separated from her husband, an amazing disclosure. I never anticipated that this would ever happen to Cathy. I was again, as curious as ever and, in the house, during the absence of Anna, I consulted Paul. Paul wasn't interested in the subject, but forced himself.

"She was here since May", he said, "But she's not teaching anymore".

"Why?"

Well, some say, she left teaching when she was transferred to Mt Hagen, and others say, she had been waiting for her personal files to be sent to Kundiawa from Mt Hagen before she could go back to teaching again. So, everyone is unsure of the truth. All we know is Cathy is no longer teaching.

"So, what's she practically doing now?"

"Nothing! In many instances, I've seen her in the gambling arenas. But one thing is clear".

"And what's that?"

"Money! She needs money, Joe", Paul said, "She is finding the everyday life here in the village quite difficult to adapt to without money. All her make-up is gone, her hair is dry without pomades, and I think she is wearing the same clothes for some time now. You saw her; the raddled and unkempt appearance should tell a story".

"But that's impossible. She lived the life of a fairy tale queen only months ago".

"Well, that's true, but it's different now. Her attitude has changed completely. She has become a pervert, and is taking alcohol, and dominating all the dance floors. Her tomboy attitude is attracting the attention of many men, both single and married alike. She was a real goer in her brief stay, and has already engaged in some physical confrontations with several wives of public servants in the district"

"Did she?"

"Ask others and they'll tell you more. Really, her immodestly lewd and unorthodox attitude and promiscuous life style has disenchanted many of her former friends and admirers".

"You mean she's losing face?"

"Exactly".

Paul was not wrong. During the week, I saw her nearly everyday at the gambling places, either playing or just sitting around, watching others play. Incidentally, she smiled at me occasionally for some reason, but I ignored her, knowing very well that her reputation has disintegrated. It was not until about a week later that I accidentally walked into her. I was in Kundiawa to shop for some kitchenware for our house. Before I began my search in the stores, I went over to Yuai market for betel nut after I jumped off the PMV. As always, Yuai was packed with people even though it was still morning. As I loitered through the narrow, crowded walkway eyeing the betel nut display, someone suddenly poked my back hard from behind. Annoyingly, when I turned around, I found Cathy Gior with a provocative smile. Almost immediately, my anger was gone.

"Cathy", I said, smiling back, "When did you come down?"

"This morning"

"This morning? I never saw you on the PMVs we overtook. Are you on your way back to Mt Hagen?"

"No, I am not going back there", she said, pouting her lips.

"Oh really! What are you up to now? Why aren't you going back there then?" I inquired, as a matter of personal interest.

"I don't like him anymore. He's a womaniser, even though he is too old for that and I am already separated from him".

"Have you?"

"Yes".

Shaking my head in disapproval, as if to show my genuine concern, I asked, "So, what are your plans after this?"

Cathy did not say anything further and, instead, tittered with a leer, as if the answer was right there on her face for me to see. "Listen, I think you made a mistake", I quickly cut in, "Why did you leave him? He's got plenty of money to look after you. He is rich, and I think you are safe and better off with him than running around on you own like this. I mean, look at yourself now. I'd say you're in rags. I suggest you go back to him again, and settle down, perhaps start a family and enjoy the connubial life like myself".

I was bold, frank and almost didactic, like a father advising his daughter, and she said nothing in response. But, deep inside, I was implicitly trying to convey a message across to her that 'life' is not always pleasant where there is plenty of money, and it is a fallacy to suppose that wealth and riches deliver goodness. I wondered if she ever perceived the message I was sending. Above all, it was none of my business to pry deeper. "Look, I've got to go now. What are you doing here anywhere?" I asked.

"I came into town to go up to the Education Office. I am trying to go back to teaching again, but my files have not been sent down from Mt Hagen yet. I'm going there to check on that", Cathy explained.

I was already aware of her struggle to get back into the classroom again, and did not bother to inquire further. Instead, I offered my suggestion.

"Why don't you go up to Mt Hagen, and arrange it from there?" I said.

"I can't do that", Cathy said, "I don't want to walk into that old man again. And if word reaches him that I'm there in town, he is certainly going to come after me. He'll send his acolytes to hunt me down".

"I see…so, you both have not really separated. It's you who decided to run away. Correct?" Cathy did not respond, and I did not want to hang around with her any longer, either. "Well, I am in town to look for some kitchenware for Anna in the hardware shops. I haven't started looking in the shops yet, and will do that right now. You have a nice day", I said and disappeared.

Cathy was truly as adventurous as Paul had said. After our Yuai encounter, I noticed a tremendous change of her attitude towards me back home. She was slinky and slobbery in all her demeanors to attract my attention every time I crossed her path. She openly behaved in such a way---despite my marriage to her kindred sister, Anna---to revamp our old relationship again, and went completely out of proportion. In a sense, I pitied her, as the once elegant looking and much sought after girl was now already a spoilt soul. Her future was already tattered and shattered. She was now in ruins with no set goals and purpose. She was lost and psychologically affected by the depressions in her life. Quite clearly, she did anything to please herself, and fit into the society. But adversely, I personally sensed that Cathy was a threat to my young marriage. She had been a threat to all other wives of the working-class elite with her tomboy and immodest attitude towards their husbands. I feared that the same will happen to me if I stayed any longer in the village. Her slobbery approaches towards me were conspicuous and detestably not appealing to me personally. They were sure to raise suspicion in the minds of many, and I feared my wife, Anna, most, if Cathy continued to try and bug with me. With a week remaining before classes began, I reluctantly excused Anna and returned early to the campus for an overdue assignment. I had lied, but seriously, that was the only option opened to me to avoid Cathy Gior's further undue attentions.

With the year gradually coming towards an end, I found very little time for leisure. There were so many things to do; assignments to tackle, tests to prepare for and the voluminous research project report to write and key into the computer, all within the short space of time. Hence, I kept myself busy almost every day. There was very little time for anything else, apart from the Sunday rugby league matches at the Lae rugby league grounds in support of my Lae Biscuit Spiders team, captained by a rampaging countryman from South Simbu, Mathias Kin, coached by Victor Kaugla and pivoted by another tribesman, Andrew Goime, in the number seven jumper. I cancelled my entire trip home and kept Anna momentarily out of my mind.

But, in mid-October, the excitement of the Morobe Agriculture Show fever in Lae took its toll, and there was never a moment to spare in the campus over the Show weekend. There were so many exciting activities and events happening at the Show Ground, that I had little time to think about studies or anything else. On the second day of the show, I was standing with some schoolmates near the northern entrance into the Show Ground, when the familiar grey station wagon turned into the Show Ground from Salamanda Street and pulled into the spot where we stood. It parked some few steps away from us among the many other cars that were already parked there. Instinctively, my mind clicked. Had I seen that car before? I was trying to recall the car, when the front door to the right opened up, and a tall familiar man, elegantly dressed in sumptuous clothes, stepped out. My eyes made no mistake. The heavily bearded man was Peter Kupal, Cathy's husband. The rest of the other doors opened up, and several other people got out. Amongst them were two young girls, college type in their general outlook.

They grouped beside the car for some minutes, and then were slowly making their way to the paying entrance. I had my eyes fixed on the two girls and noticed that one of them was a familiar face.

"It has to be Cathy", I thought, as I fixed my gaze on her, and I was not wrong. "But she had separated with her husband, and was at home when I saw her last time. It can't be her".

But, as they neared, the girl was obviously Cathy Gior herself.

"They must have got together again", I mused, looking on. Looking around Cathy's eyes suddenly caught my gaze, and the familiar smile of surprise spread all over her face. Leaving her group behind, she hastily walked towards me without bothering to look back. I returned her smile as she approached, but my smile suddenly faded when she stood in front of me. She was bruised all over. The sight of her face was terrible and in a horrendous state. I was shocked to the nerve at the sight of the cuts and wounds all over her face; some of them still purulent as others dried up.

The dark blood clots around both the eyes were severe, and could easily be mistaken for sunglasses at a distance.

"Good grief! What happened? Who did all that to you?" I blurted, as we exchanged hands.

"The old bastard did it again", she said, looking away to the other side of the road to avoid my eyes.

"When did he do that?"

"Three days ago".

"But why? Why did he have to do such a terrible thing to you?"

Cathy was just going to impart something, perhaps was going to answer my question when her husband joined us. She hastily introduced me to him instead, and for the very first time, I formally met his wealthy husband, the spouse of my former inamorata. We shook hands.

"This is Joseph Tamgo", she introduced, "He is one of my sisters' husband. You remember Anna? Councillor Bagle's daughter?"

"The Councillor's daughter…yes".

"This is her husband", Cathy explained.

Quite surprisingly, I found Peter Kupal to be a charming man with amicable gentility. He spoke nicely and softly in a businessman accent, and I began to admire him in the brief moment. There was no doubt, why Cathy gullibly fell into his net of charms, perhaps in their first meet. Peter was briefly speaking about their tiring journey to the Show by road from Mt Hagen, when a member of his group returned with their entry tickets. They bid me good luck, and left for the showground.

I stood watching them go, as they disappeared into the crowd. Cathy walked closely beside her husband without ever looking back again. She had not told me anything about the recent cuts and bruises on her face and, as I watched her go, I wondered how she managed to go back to her husband and ended up with the cuts and bruises again. I remembered advising her to return to her husband at Yuai market, in Kundiawa. Has she suffered all these after following my advice? On the contrary, a partial bride price was already in lieu to her immediate ones, and she strictly belonged to Peter Kupal. She was his wife and, no matter what happened she would still be his wife all along, perhaps till death. And the cuts and bruises? Only God knows what happened.

Fate has its own destiny. After knowing Cathy Gior for almost two decades, the Lae Show Ground encounter was to be my last glimpse of her. And I was to realise that two years later.

19

The Interlude

I finally completed my forestry studies at Unitech by the end of November. After the exams were over, I packed my bags and bade farewell to my classmates for the last time. Maybe, I won't return for the graduation if I had failed in the exams. But I knew I did well, and went home in high spirit. Anna was well aware of the finality of my studies, and was just as enthusiastic as I was, about the results of my final exams. She was eager to know everything, whether I had succeeded in attaining my degree when I got home.

"How was the graduation?" she asked with enthusiasm, when I settled down with her, later in the evening.

"I have not graduated yet", I conceded.

"Then what happened?" Anna asked with a frown, deducing failure.

"I will have to be informed by the University if I am eligible to graduate", I said, "We sat for the examinations, and the academic staff will let me know of the result in the near future".

Anna listened attentively with wonder, taking in everything I said. "You should have explained that to me earlier", she chuckled later. "I thought, you graduated already, the same time like the high school students".

"It's different at the university", I explained. "Graduands will be notified through the mail, and the ceremony takes place in March of the following year".

Anna smiled. "Then, when and how will they inform you?", she asked.

"I don't know when, but it will be through the mission address".

"I see...so, we'll keep our ears open on Sundays after the service, when the mail is read out".

"Precisely"

The graduation date was set for March 23 of the following year. In the months that followed, we waited patiently for a letter from the University. We kept alert and had our ears opened for the incoming mail read out on Sundays, by the mission workers. Finally, in mid-January, I received the long-awaited letter from the Student's Registrar at Unitech. It was good news. I was eligible to graduate with my Bachelor of Science degree in Forestry. I felt proud and happy of the achievement, and could not help the excitement steaming inside me. Deep inside, I owed it all to my wife's support and patience during my long years of studies, and could not wait to rush home and impart the news to Anna.

Anna was getting herself out of her Sunday dress when I arrived, but before I talked, she spoke first.

"What's all the excitement on your face about?" she asked.

I smiled but can't wait to disclose the news.

"We are graduating", I whispered into her ear, and leered at her provocatively.

She looked up into my eyes in surprise, and a complacent smile followed next. It was a smile never once seen on her face before. There was no secret. She was part of the success. Her patience, loyalty and sacrifice had paid off, and she knew it. And the smile said it all. She was pleased and was truly satisfied to take the news.

"Did you get the letter from Unitech?" she asked.

"I did…today, after the church service".

"I didn't stay back for the mail call. So, when is the graduation?"

'In March, and we are traveling to Lae together for the occasion".

What? Me to Lae? Are you crazy?"

"Yes, I am taking you and Paul; both of you will travel with me to Lae and witness my graduation".

Anna stopped short for any more words. She had never been to the coast before and was overjoyed when I surprised her. Paul had been the support and strength in the family during my absence and Anna was pleased when I mentioned him to accompany us. It was a perfect reward for him, and Anna quickly hawked the news to him. Like Anna, Paul had not set foot on the coast yet also, and jumped up in jubilation when he took the news from Anna.

We had all prepared ourselves in advance for the trip. Two days before the graduation, we departed for Lae. Paul and Anna were in their best outfits. I had not seen both in such splendid appearance before, particularly Anna, who was normally in rags everytime I went home. And for that trip she was totally transformed. She was extraordinary and I was careful not to mistake her for someone else this time, or be jealous in any way.

We passed Goroka, Henganofi and Kainantu. Both were wide-awake during the entire trip, enjoying the scenery outside, as we meandered down the Okuk Highway.

"What's that?", Anna suddenly asked with surprise, when the Yonki Dam came into view in the Arona valley.

"That's the sea", I tricked Paul, and Anna at first.

Both gaped at the huge man-made sea of water, without removing their eyes.

"I can't see a ship", Anna said, her eyes all over the water, possibly checking for one. I chuckled, and later uttered the truth.

"It's the famous Yonki Dam", I told them, "…where the power source to Kundiawa and the rest of the highlands provinces get their electricity".

Both were amazed at the huge extent of the water.

"So, this is the Yonki Dam! We've only heard of it, and now for the first time we are actually seeing it", they sighed, and murmured in amazement.

Some moments later, we descended the famous Kassam Pass and onto the Markham valley below. Paul and Anna saw the coconut trees for the first time, and hardly removed their eyes away from them, trying desperately in vain to count every nut hanging on the trees, as we zoomed past them. I tirelessly answered the many puerile questions about the wonders of the coast and the lowlands, as we traveled. The stretch of the vast flat plains of the Markham valley, with the rigid road network, was another surprise to the two mountain people, as we scudded along the endless bitumen-coated highway. They remained disbelieving until we finally reached Nadzab, and eventually Lae.

The following day was tour time for Anna and Paul around the city of Lae. I was their guide. Before commencing the tour, we went to the

Westpac Bank in town and took out the K400.00 I had left in the IBD, while Anna and Paul waited outside.

"This is your money", I said, and gave it all plus interest to Anna.

Surprised with astonishment she looked at me, then at the money in her hands.

"Where did you get it?", she asked.

"From the Bank, this was yours, ok. Remember, you gave it to me last year in June before I came to Lae?"

"I remember, but I thought you used everything up already".

"I didn't. I put them all in the Bank. I left it there purposely for this moment. You can use it to shop now, as you wish".

She thanked me softly, and kindly shared the money, K100.00 each to Paul and me. She used K100.00 and kept the rest for betel nuts along the Markham, when we would return to the highlands after graduation.

We moved in and out of the shops, and later stood at the oceanfront towards the far end of the old abandoned Lae airport. Paul and Anna saw the seascape for the first time in their lives and marvelled at the spread of this great body of water. The sight of the huge ocean liners, moving in and out of the busy port of Lae, thrilled them both.

"They looked no different from a huge house moving on top of the water", Paul said.

"In a way, it is. Whatever you find in a home is all in there, people are living in there", I explained, as they gazed in wonderment, as a cargo ship from the Lutheran Shipping sailed into dock at Voco Point.

They stood by the edge of the sea front and dipped their fingers into the sea to taste the salinity of the seawater.

"People used to say, the sea water is briny, and it is. It tastes just the same as the cooking salt", Anna called up, after placing a wet finger on her lips.

"That's right, because that's where all your cooking salt comes from, and be careful with the sharks", I jested, scaring Anna back to the beach.

"Do sharks wonder to shallow waters", Anna inquired, looking out into the sea, as if checking the water to find one.

"Yes, they do. They come onto the land for food, especially in the night, but when they are really hungry they can come out anytime. And they don't like strangers".

Anna stood in silence with her eyes on the sea, as if believing everything I had said.

"But in school we learnt that a shark lives in the deep ocean. Our teacher said, it is a fish", she said, still looking into the sea.

"Who was your teacher?"

"I forgot her name now. She was from Wabag"

"Well, if you sever see her again, tell her that she was wrong, remind her that she taught you the wrong thing".

We were still at it when Paul joined us.

"Do you believe him?" Paul asked.

Anna stood still in confusion.

"Well, if you do, then you are believing a lie".

Anna looked at me and tried to hit me, but I jumped clear from her arm's distance. We all laughed.

"It was a lie; sharks don't come out of the water", I conceded later.

The following day was the graduation day, the moment every graduating student was looking forward to. Friends, relatives and parents of the graduants filled the front yard of the Student Services Building and at 10.00 am, the ceremony began. Attired in gowns, four hundred and thirty-three students graduated in the ceremony. Anna and Paul stood watching me in the crowd, as I went up to collect my degree, the dream paper I had struggled to secure for three years. And when I returned it was all over.

We did not remain any longer in Lae after the graduation. Paul and Anna both complained about the sultry tropical climate of the coast that made them feel uncomfortable. On the following day, we traveled back home, the way we went. This time, we made several stops along the Markham valley and bought some betel nuts for Anna, who was eager to market them when we got home. It was betel nut fruiting season too, and we bought two bags at K40.00 each. When we finally arrived home, she went into business at Mondiagl-kaugla market, the following day.

I had written several letters out to the public and private sector organizations in the forest industry for possible employement, while I was still in school, and also during the months of January and February while in the village. Soon after the graduation, I arranged with the

Faculty's Secretary to hold onto all my incoming mail in the Faculty office and expect a call from me in the future. Some three weeks later, after arriving in the village, I rang the Forestry Faculty from Kundiawa to check if I had something in the mail tray. Clara, the Faculty Secretary, was on the phone.

"You have a couple of letters here", Clara asked, over the phone, "Should I mail them up to you now?", she asked.

"Don't send them yet, I'll come down and pick them up personally. Just hold onto them, till I get there".

"Alright, if that is how you want it, then they'll all be here".

"Good! I'll show up anytime when I am ready", I said, thanking her.

I traveled to Lae, the following day and spent the night at Nine Mile settlement with friends. Next day, I went over to Taraka Campus and collected all my mail from the Forestry Faculty office. There were about four letters in all. The first three came from timber companies around the country, where I had expressed employment interest with them, but the fourth one came all the way from Kerema in the Gulf province. It came from the Department of Gulf Province, and had the signature of Assistant Secretary of the Human Resource Division. In the content, I was offered a substantive position of Harvesting & Marketing Officer to work along side the Provincial Harvesting & Marketing Officer in the Forestry Division, to be based in Kerema. Fortunately, I was lucky to have written my letter at a time when the Department of Gulf Province was undergoing a major restructure program, and according to the Provincial Forest Officer, weeks later, I was fortunate to have applied and hence secured the position.

I immediately discarded the three other letters, as they were of no use for my personal files. Using the Faculty's telephone, and with the help of Clara, I quickly rang the Provincial Forest Officer for Gulf province, Ronold Apelis in Kerema. He sounded a nice man on the phone, and I was to learn later that he truly was a very good man from Namatani area in the New Ireland province. I quickly briefed him on the letter I had received, and gave my assurance to accept the offer. He was equally aware of the letter and immediately responded by demanding my personal details.

"Are you married?", he asked.

"Yes".

"And your wife's name?"

"Anna Tamgo".

"Any children?"

I paused momentarily to think of the response. Anna and I had earlier planned sometime ago to adopt her younger brother, Gigmai, but we had not sought the parent's approval yet. And I was unsure whether to mention this to Ronold.

"Are you still there?", the PFO came on again, after I became silent on the phone.

"Yes, just one", I gabbled absent-mindedly, and later provided Gigmai's name and age to complete the dependant list.

I heard papers flicking on the other side over the phone. After a moment of silence, the PFO directed me to check the forestry office in Kundiawa for any fax messages, or letters that would be coming my way from him or the Personnel Division.

"Should I ring the Division of Personnel management in Kerema, as directed in the letter?" I asked.

"No, no need. We need someone here urgently. So, I'll take care of things for you here. You just do as I told you. Just keep checking our Simbu office", Ronold urged.

I thanked the PFO appreciatively and hung up. It was the most satisfying conversation I had ever made by telephone. I had been a student, then a husband, then both---all without a formal employment to sustain my family. And after the telephone talk with Ronold, I was over the moon. Without wasting any more time, I left for home the following day.

Anna was pleased when I told her everything when I arrived home.

"Are we both going?"

"Yes, both of us...and little Gigmai too".

"What? Gigmai too?" she asked, surprised.

"Well, there is no one else to accompany us. All we have to do now is to ask Councillor Bagle and his wife to let their boy go with us, or we take someone else in his place. Remember, I already gave away his name, as my son, and three tickets would be purchased for us all".

"I don't think, mother and father will disagree to let Gigmai come with us", Anna said, and she was right.

I made weekly trips to the Provincial Forestry office in Kundiawa and checked for any letter or fax message coming up from Gulf. It was in mid-May that I finally received a fax letter from the Gulf PFO, informing me of my travel to Kerema with Anna and little Gigmai. Airline tickets were arranged through the Air Niugini office in Kundiawa for the three of us. We were booked to fly out from Kundiawa to Kerema, via Port Moresby, after lodging in at the Granville motel. I was excited about going to live and work in Kerema. I wanted to see what it was like at the place of *Yu yet kam na lukim*. Equally, I wanted to take Anna out and let her see the world, to see it for herself what it was like out there, and enjoy the many different environments after being in the village for far too long. She had sacrificed her freedom just to marry me, and then later allowed me to continue schooling while she stayed in the village. And there was no better moment to reward her for all her sacrifices, than today. She was equally pleased and excited when I brought the news back home, and produced the airline tickets to her.

We quickly set off to Ende-naige-ingugl and arranged with her parents to take Gigmai with us.

"He's my only boy", Gigmai's pathetic mother said, amidst tears, as she reluctantly gave her assent. "Make sure, you look after him well", she advised us.

"We sure will, mother. Don't you worry too much about him. We'll take good care of him", Anna reassured her mother, and we soon returned with Gigmai, who was eager and very excited about seeing the outside world.

We finally left home in May after a huge farewell, amidst wailings at Mondiagl-kaugla. Paul accompanied us to Kundiawa and returned after we boarded the Px Dash 7 aircraft. It was Anna's first experience in an aeroplane along with Gigmai. And for us all, it was our first trip to Port Moresby. We were all looking forward to seeing the nation's capital with delight, as we cruised in the air. A seat away from me was Anna. She sat motionless with her eyes closed, avoiding all the simpers and snacks offered by the air hostesses. The light air turbulences almost had her screaming, and the same with Gigmai too, who was right beside her. I knew, both were scared to the nerve, hoping that we return to the ground soon. I showed them the paper bag, in the pocket of the seat before them, should they feel uncomfortable in their tummy. But both were brave and shook their heads negetively. I remained calm, but anxiously wondered how we would find our way to the Granville Motel.

We finally touched down at Jackson's airport at around 3.00pm in the afternoon. We collected our baggage at the arrival lounge and exited to the car park. It was 3.15pm on the wall clock in the terminal, and I quickly rang the PFO in Kerema from the pay phone, outside the terminal.

"You are in Port Moresby now, are you?", Ronold enquired.

"That's right. We are standing at Jackson's airport terminal".

"Good, you are safe and sound on this leg of the journey. Now the Motel is only two-minutes drive from where you are standing. Just get into a cab outside the taxi rank and mention Granville Motel to the cab driver. He knows where to drop you off"

Taxicabs were everywhere at the car park, which made our search easier. In fact, some cab drivers waved to us with welcoming smiles, as if we had known them personally for ages. But we finally got into the nearest one, a sedan that was parked just in front of us.

"Granville Motel", I said to the cab operator, as I got in beside him.

Without asking any question the cab pulled out, and in less than three minutes we checked in at the Motel. The Provincial Forest Officer was not wrong. "It's still possible to walk from the airport to the motel", I told Anna later.

In the morning, we got dropped off at the airport again by the Motel's Bus, and we boarded the first Talair, Kerema-Ihu-Baimuru-Kikori flight to Kerema. Flying time was one hour, or perhaps slightly more. The boss himself was at the airport to meet us. He introduced himself as Ronold Apelis, the name I had seen in his many letters. He was from New Ireland Province. I shook hands with him, and later introduced Anna and Gigmai to him. He appeared a nice man, spoke the usual New Guinea Islands tone and presented a sociable character. I intuited that he was sure to be a good boss to work along with, and he sure was later on. After a brief stop at the Provincial Forest Office, Ronold drove us to a residential area, and gave us a set of keys to one of the three-bedroom, NHC houses, which was recently renovated. It was furnished about a week earlier in preparation for our tenancy. We removed our baggage from the pickup onto the verandah. This was to be our new home during our entire stay in the Gulf Province.

<h1 style="text-align:center">20</h1>

The Denouement

Kerema was a small town. Our first year was quiet, peaceful and enjoyable. We made many new friends. They were kind and generous. The Gulf Province being the confluence and tributary of many rivers from the hinterlands, and off course, the highlands and home to many aquatic creatures, there was constant supply of fish and other seafood in our house from our local friends. I traveled extensively to project sites in Ihu, Baimuru, Kikori and up the Turama river to Kuri more often on duty trips and, on return, brought back home prized catches of Barramundi, prawns and crabs. Anna and Gigmai relished all of them. Both were also introduced to sago. And soon, Anna came up with some of the best sago dishes I had ever come across or tasted elsewhere in my life. *Kaukau* was a rare consumable item in the Gulf and was temporarily out of our minds. Back home, Paul kept us posted with all the happenings there in his frequent letters. We responded the same, highlighting our everyday Gulf experiences, and the year past without any hiccup.

In the second year, when Gigmai turned seven, we enrolled him at Hikaraita Community School in Kerema, where he began his Grade 1. He enjoyed his schooling and soon made many friends on his own. In May of the same year, I finally completed my two years of service required under the Public Service Regulation, and was eligible for my 6-week rec-leave. We had all missed Simbu badly and were eager to go home. Little Gigmai was eager to see his mother, whom he had missed dearly, and so were Anna and myself. I applied for my rec-leave and when that was approved and processed, we were all set to go. Taking out a leave of absence from the headmaster of Hikaraita Community School for Gigmai, and leaving behind a caretaker in our house, we flew out of Kerema to Port Moresby for our connection to Kundiawa.

Fortunately, the flight to Kundiawa was on the following day. After checking in at Granville Motel, we spent a pleasant afternoon touring the city of Port Moresby. It was also a golden opportunity to shop for our dear parents at home. While Anna fastidiously shopped for our two mothers, I carefully selected two Stetsons for our two fathers at the Garden City in Boroko. The bus service provided along the major routes in the city was efficient and soon we visited almost all the major centers in the city---Badili, Koki, Ela Beach, Down Town, Konedobu and finally Waigani, before retiring to the Motel. We departed Jackson's airport on a Px Dash 7 flight, the following morning. I had written to Paul sometime earlier, when I was in Kerema about our vacation, and the flight schedule. He was already waiting for us at the airport in Kundiawa when we disembarked from the plane. He helped us with our baggage, and before the day ended, we were in Bokan.

Our homecoming was a great moment for everyone in our village, especially our parents, friends, relatives and ourselves too. Gigmai's mother took him, her little long-lost son into her arms and sobbed uncontrollably, as if he was returned dead. My poor mother held Anna, her long gone daughter-in-law into her arms and cried too. She keened as if one of her missing parts was returned. In the evening neighbors and friends came to visit us with dishes of food, which resurrected almost immediately all our long-lost appetite of home dishes. Some even brought uncooked *kaukau* tubers and vegetables to be enjoyed during our stay.

It was a great holiday and we enjoyed every minute of our stay at home. Little Gigmai spent his entire time with his parents at Ende-naige-ingugl. Anna spent most of her time with mother in the gardens, and instantly took over the kitchen duties. Ironically, it was holiday time for mother too. In the days that followed, we were not left alone to fend for ourselves. Friends and relatives visited us almost everyday with fresh home-grown vegetables, firewood and many other requisites to make our stay in the village as comfortable as possible during our vacation. I had great moments with old friends and clansmen, gambling or taking a few drinks at the local pubs to enjoy our reunion. After the hot humid tropical climate of the Gulf Province, it was truly pleasant and refreshing with a bottle of SP under the cool temperature of the towering Mt Whilhelm.

However, despite all the diurnal comforts of home the nocturnal discomfiture caused by the highland climate was unedurable. After a long absence on the coast, we found the freezing cold air outside miserable and unbearable to cope with. We would either swathe in warm clothes to remain outside, or close our door as early as six o'clock to keep ourselves warm inside. During these detestable times, I found a cup of hot coffee the only remedial 'medicine' to battle the cold and keep me warm and comfortable all night long when the alpine temperatures started freezing the valley floor. Thus, I made it compulsory to have the teapot next to the fireplace at all times in the evenings.

One evening, on the second Thursday of our vacation, I saw some people gathering across the other side at Kama-mambuno. It was a cold afternoon. The sun had already sunk behind the mountains above Pugl-angil. It had cossed over our Yandina Range hours earlier. I went about outside gathering firewood onto my arm. Inside the house, Anna was preparing dinner. She had returned with mother from our garden at Kundu-kowai, one of our plots located upstream along the headwaters of the nearby Mondia River, and was preparing some *kaukaus* to go into the pot. I had gone outside to gather some firewood I had prepared earlier in the day to start a fire, obviously to heat the water for hot coffee. The crowd attraction raised my curiosity and on careful observation I noticed that many people were crowding around and listening to a man, Kolkia Andambo, who seemed to be doing all the talking. Kolkia was our neighbor whose house was located some hundred meters behind our home. The crowd around him swelled as many more moved in to listen to him.

"The guy must be telling these people a very good story", I said to myself. I quickly brought in the first lot of firewood and started a fire for Anna. Then, later, when I came out to bring in the remaining firewood, I saw Kolkia crossing the suspension bridge to walk past our house and head home. Like his many listeners I was curious too.

"You drew alot of attention across there, Kolikia. I guess, you must be telling them with a very interesting story", I called out to him after exchanging the afternoon greetings.

"Oh, yes! I was, but I'd say it's not an interesting story after all", he said.

"What was it all about?"

"It's Cathy…Cathy Gior. She's dead".

"What? Did you say Cathy Gior?"

"Yes! Cathy Gior…the daughter of James and Kumo".

I stopped in my tracks and curiously stared at Kolkia in disbelief with the firewood in my arms dropping back to the ground, one by one, as I rose up to my feet.

"Where did you hear that?" I slowly asked.

"From the Siakos at Mondiagl-kaugla. This is late news. All her immediate ones are gathering out there, discussing her death. No one is yet quite certain how she died and her uncle Philip took a late PMV this afternoon to Kundiawa to find out more. He's traveling all the way to Mt Hagen".

We were still talking when Anna came out of the house after she overheard me talking to someone. She found me conversing with Kolkia with a pale inquisitive face.

"What's the matter, something wrong?" she asked curiously, wanting to know everything, "…I overheard you two mentioning a dead person or someone dying. Who is that?"

"Yes! It's Cathy Gior…she's dead", Kolkia said, and recounted everything again while I stood back and listened.

Anna expressed shock on her face, but did not ask any further question for a while. Cathy was her sister and she was startled to take the news, just as I was.

"How did she die?" Anna finally asked.

"I don't know. We'll find that out tomorrow".

"Thers was constant infighting between her rival wives, someone must have finally put an end to it this time", Anna said.

"It could be that, or somethings else. Her uncle Teacher, Phillip over at Wai-mambuno is gone to find out and will return tomorrow", Kolkia said, and with that he walked away.

After Kolkia left, for some reasons, nothing came out of me, or Anna's lips. Neither of us wanted to talk about Cathy or her death, although we might be sharing the same feeling about the reported death. The water eventually boiled and I made coffee for us in silence while Anna kept herself busy with the preparation of dinner. She was working on the vegetables this time.

It was a long while later that I suddenly broke the silence.

"Something terrible must have happened to Cathy", I said in a plain tone after taking a sip from the cup of burning coffee. Almost immediately Anna questioned the circumstances surrounding her death in a pathetic tone. I cleared my throat but couldn't remember what to say. The news was abominable and shocking to the mind and I had not fully recomposed myself to open my lips or even talk.

"We don't know anything yet, we'll have to find that out tomorrow", was all I managed to say, as I stared at the burning fire over the rim of my cup.

The news of Cathy's death was a spine-chiller and soon became the talk of the day, the following morning. We soon learnt that Cathy's uncle, Philip, returned from Kundiawa in the night with all the news.

"I rang Cathy's husband from Kundiawa and confirmed the death", he appraised everyone. "She was knifed by his second wife. And her body is lying in the morgue now".

It was tragic news for the Siakos, the Wandike-Auke-nigl-endes, Cathy's immediate family members, uncles. And at Kama-mambuno and Wai-mambuno, little crowds were seen discussing the death, as they basked in the early morning sunshine. At Ende-naige-ingugl, a huge crowd had already gathered when Anna and myself arrived there to find out about the death from my in-laws. Present amongst the crowd were some Wandike Auke-nigl-endes, some of Cathy's immediate uncles and relatives.

Among them was Anna's father, Councillor Bagle, who appeared to be the central figure and kinpin, doing all the talking. They were all discussing a trip to Mt Hagen. We soon learnt that the Siakos and the Wandike-Auke-nigl-endes, Cathy's uncles, had jointly hired a Mazda T3500 truck from the neighboring clan for their travel to Mt Hagen to view, grieve and mourn the death of Cathy. Many were seen going around, preparing themselves for the trip, in a hectic way.

On the far end corner, just in front of the Gior's family home, several women were grieving and consoling a woman, who appeared too tired and languid to sit up by herself. She appeared to be Cathy's mother, Angela Kumo, with Anansas next to her in a similar state. Both were daubed in mud, their faces bloated to a stage beyond recognition from the grieving and mourning taking place all night. Several women gathered around them and hugged them in mourning. Anna wept too and joined the other women to extend her condolence to the two women. I later hugged Kumo when she was free, as a gesture of respect, to pass my condolence.

The discussion among the men stopped when the hired truck finally arrived and parked at the main road opposite the entrance gate into Ende-naige-ingugl. Kumo was helped onto the truck. Other mourners followed. Soon, there was no more space left on the truck. Many reluctantly stayed back. My father-in-law spruced himself up in his gentleman's attire. With his Councillor's badge pinned onto the chest pocket of his shirt and his new Stretson from Garden City over his head, he got into the truck and took the middle seat in the cabin. Cathy's father, James, was teaching at Kangir Primary School, further down, opposite Goglme, and it was pre-arranged for him to join them at Goglme, when they arrived there. The hired Mazda T3500 finally pulled out at around 10 o'clock in the morning, leaving behind those who could not find a space on the truck, the old and the disabled.

Anna and I walked back to Bokan.

21

The Great Trauma

Cathy Gior's death was said to have been caused by knife wounds inflicted by one of her husband's other wives, but nothing concrete could yet be established from an eyewitness account. It was two days later, after the mourners left that every detail of the tragedy reached home. Two women, who had gone to Mt Hagen, along with the mourners, returned. One of them was Anna's aunt, Katrina Miane. Katrina told us everything and reported on the new developments taking place at Mt Hagen.

"A 'tug of war' of words is going on at the moment", Katrina revealed. "The Siakos want to take Cathy's body up to Ende-naige-ingugl for the interment to take place here, while her husband is disputing that with his tribesmen".

"Why did the Siakos want to do that?" I asked.

"Well, Cathy's death was a murder and coupling that with the non-payment of the full bride price, the Siakos want to take the body home for burial here. I really don't know what they have come up with, but they were still at it when we left", Katrina said.

The Siakos proposition sounded genuine, but again still cast some doubts in our minds on the latest turn of events in Mt Hagen. It was two days later, when my father-in-law finally returned home from Mt Hagen with some of the mourners, that he brought back the entire news we had wanted to know, disclosing everything to the last detail.

"Cathy's husband has finally agreed to allow the body for interment to take place here", Councillor Bagle told everyone, "And the casket is leaving Mt Hagen morgue with the Western Highlands contingent tomorrow morning. They are likely to arrive here after midday. This place will be packed with people in the coming week. Peter also disclosed to pay some *wari pei*. So, he'll be coming along with his clansmen to do that".

Then, later in the afternoon, when we were all alone in the councillor's house with a few Siako clan members, my father-in-law mooted and divulged everything he had learnt of Cathy as part of our family discussion about the death. He spoke of her marriage, her breakdowns and the suffering she endured, culminating in her death. The others in the house also put out what they knew about the tragedy and also about Cathy's marital life. Soon, Anna and I learned and pieced together every little detail of Cathy's ill-fated marital life. It was really a sad tale, indeed.

Cathy Gior's marriage, retrospectively, collapsed, after she ran away to Ende-naige-ingugl when she was involved in a commotion with her husband's other two wives and his elder daughter, while her husband Peter was away overseas. It was in December, almost three years ago, that she took the beating. And I clearly recalled the white face towel over her face, hiding the wounds, when she had disembarked from a PMV at Mondiagl-kaugla in the afternoon. For some reason, she stayed on for too long at Ende-naige-ingugl and eventually got herself together with John Mitna, the Coca-Cola salesman again. John was out on holiday at his Sitnigle village at that time. Her prolonged stay upset the anxious husband and he soon followed her to Ende-naige-ingugl, only to discover Cathy in the middle of an affair with John Mitna. Angry, hurt and disappointed, Peter took Cathy back to Mt Hagen and unforgivingly castigated her on many occasions to bring her conscious back from apparent comatose. As punitive measure, she was strictly banished from making any further trips to Ende-naige-ingugl or even to Kundiawa unaccompanied.

In Mt Hagen, all did not go well for John Mitna too. His life was threatened and he fled his place of work without notice to Lae, where his employer arranged his transfer to a new location, in the New Guinea Islands. Retributively, Cathy was doubly punished, shouldering all the penalties intended for John Mitna instead.

With the personal trust in Cathy diminishing, Peter Kupal was not the usual sugar daddy Cathy had come to know and love. His attention was diverted to the two other wives, overlooking Cathy as 'just-another-wife' and attending to her needs, as and when was required. Coupling that, some of the perks and privileges previously enjoyed were gone too. Seeing the love and the usual care fading from her husband, Cathy fled to Simbu again, in May of the following year. This time, she stayed three months at Ende-naige-ingugl with her parents. She disclosed to all, to the surprise of everyone, that she had separated from her husband forever, and did whatever she could to make ends meet for her in the village. Her attitude changed from that of a wealthy man's wife to that of a humbug. She lived a very immodest and promiscuous life in the village. I briefly recalled the Yuai encounter and her deception. She had lied to me about her separation from her husband, but it was actually Cathy who ran away from Peter, according to the truth revealed by Councillor Bagle. She approached the education officials in Kundiawa to get back to teaching there and asked around if there was any vacant space was available in Simbu schools. She was unsuccessful in every attempt she made. One contributing factor was that she was an unregistered teacher at the time she was moving around with her files between Kundiawa and Mt Hagen.

When worst followed worst for her in the village, and no formal employment, Cathy finally decided on the option of 'give and take', to barter sex to go back into the classroom. She had tried every orthodox means to get the job and failed, but nothing was impossible, she thought. If our biblical ancestor Eve could convince Adam to change his mind finally, and take the apple from her hands, nothing after all was impossible on this planet for a woman to change a man's mind. And she knew it too well. In this world of opportunity, where greed and corruption are rife, there is always a 'back door', left open for people with the right kind of entry 'pass'. With money and women being the key players in any unorthodox deals, she decided to use herself to go through that "back door". She knew that the mirrors hid nothing from her. She was young, pretty and beautiful, something most men would never reject or refuse, and her ravishing beauty and charms were more than enough to do the job for her. They were the perfect bait needed in such endeavor.

As anticipated, it was very easy going through the 'back door' and shortly thereafter, an adulterous affair followed next with a senior government official in the Provincial Education wing. Within less than a fortnight later, she finally got what she wanted. In August, she was given a teaching post at Womatne Community School along the Kundiawa-Gembogl road, less 10 km before reaching Gembogl station, and 30 km out of Kundiawa. The school was situated at a convenient location. Firstly, it was close to home and secondly, it was safe and away from the many troubles that were sure to haunt her.

Nevertheless, Cathy Gior finally solved one of her problems, i.e. formal employment. She finally got back into teaching again and her pay packets were on their way. But that was not the end of all her troubles. In the process of getting the job, Cathy brought in other predicaments for herself, the problems that were to haunt her for almost her entire lifetime. First, the wife of the senior education official stormed into the education office, demanding Cathy's instant removal from the teaching job, after she learnt of the adulterous concubine affair with her husband. Worse still, she kept a watch for Cathy in Kundiawa with a knife to slit her throat if she ever came into town. Secondly, there was Peter Kupal, her wealthy husband. Although Cathy claimed to have broken up with him, Peter still kept Cathy in focus as his third wife, perhaps for the reason that K4000.00 cash payment was paid in lieu as brideprice. In early October, after he was told of her affairs with a government officer in the Provincial Education office, Peter traveled to Kundiawa and demanded Cathy's immediate release and transfer back to the Western Highlands. He exerted pressure and breathed down the necks of the education authorities to effect the demand without delay. With a man of Peter Kupal's stature, there was very little the educational officials could do, but to obey. They sent a memo to Cathy in Womatne, informing her of her husband's decision, but she frightfully ignored the memo. She knew what was in store for her if she ever went back to Mt Hagen. Pitifully, Cathy was in double trouble.

The intelligent Peter did not give up. Surely, for a woman of Cathy's beauty, height and build, one would not easily give up. He knew that nothing would be done to Cathy from Kundiawa, as she was already absorbed into the Teaching Service Commission in Port Moresby. And it would take time to make arrangements for her dismissal or transfer,

Peter felt convinced. He decided to physically remove his wife from Womatne. One Friday afternoon, some five weeks after Cathy went back into the classroom, the familiar grey landcruiser station wagon zoomed down the Okuk Highway, and in Kundiawa had its left blinkers turned on. The crowd at Yuai market made way and the station wagon picked up speed again, hitting the Gembogl road. In about an hour and a half later, it pulled into Womatne and was parked in front of the Catholic Church, next to the entrance into the school. The front door opened and Peter Kupal stepped out of the car and walked straight into the school. Behind him were his acolytes, numbering several persons. Cathy had already dismissed her class for the long weekend and was chatting with the other teachers on the lawn at the assembly ground when the entourage arrived. It was a surprise, a totally an unexpected visit. Cathy was shocked to see them all at first sight. She knew instantly that something terrible was going to happen to her in just a few moments. And she was not wrong.

"Pack your bags up", was all Peter ordered.

His face was pale, and stone cold. Cathy could see the anger in the giant's eyes. Her other teaching colleagues stood in confusion, as the headmaster tried to intervene, but Peter asked him to stay away.

"I'm sorry but she has gone loose for a long time, and I am taking her back", he told the headmaster.

Cathy was also confused too, but she knew outright what was going on. She refused to go, but Peter asked for the way to her residential apartment. With no options, she led the way to her residence. She doesn't want to feel embarrassed in front of her other teaching colleagues. And after being with him for some time, Cathy knew what kind of a person, Peter was. He can do anything. He carrys licensed guns too, like all other wealthy businessmen, for security reasons. When he wants something, he gets it. And for him to personally travel to Womatne to pick up his wife, was something that he will never go back without her. And Cathy Gior knew it.

Peter Kupal and his gang followed closely behind Cathy. Once inside the house, Cathy stood speechless in a corner, as if in readiness for her next set of instructions. "I had just told you to pack up your bag", her husband commandingly repeated. Tears welled, and soon rolled out of her eyes and then slowly dripped down her cheeks. She knew, she was going to lose her job again, maybe forever. Quietly, she collected the few things she had had with her into her bag and walked out to the road. She got into the car, without even a word of farewell to her other teacher friends and colleagues. She never talked, or explained to the headmaster, either. She was lost in thought, and remained silent in the car, as the station wagon pulled out of Womatne, all along wondering what the future held for her this time. The more she thought about it, the more mind-boggling it became for her. Only God knows what was in store for her.

When Cathy and her husband reached Mt Hagen, Peter imprisoned her in his room and summoned her to explain her affairs with the education officer in Kundiawa, as a matter of urgency. "Is that why you ran away from me? To get screwed by someone else?", he roared. It was all too much for Cathy to answer. And when nothing came out of her lips, it was as if more and more fuel was added to Peter's temper and a severe flogging followed with censure. The chastisement continued until Cathy went into a coma. Whether Cathy feigned a comatose to avoid further beating, like many guilty females do when faced with such situation, or was it a real coma that she went through remained to be answered only by herself. And for a man of Peter Kupal's age, dignity and status to fatally inflict such beating and damage, done on purpose, or out of sheer jealousy and frustration, or to teach Cathy a lifetime lesson remained only to himself. But Cathy was rushed to Mt Hagen hospital. By western standards Peter was legally wrong and could be charged for inflicting such bodily harm, or charged for crimes under 'Violence Against Women' laws, but by custom Cathy was clearly wrong and rightly deserved some form of punishment which she did. Peter paid a partial bride price and she belonged solely to him, and him alone, and no other man. And many, if not, all, supported Peter's action. Apparently, Cathy was discharged at the insistence of Peter after spending only a night at emergency wing because the annual Morobe Show fever was taking its toll in the highlands, and Peter had planned a trip to Lae for the show. He did not want to leave Cathy behind. "She can be treated at home", he told the nurses and doctors. And three days later, after she was discharged from the hospital, the couple traveled to Lae for the Morobe Show.

Cathy Gior's last two years were the most difficult and torturing moments of her life, even though her marriage was gradually picking up in the end. She could no longer go back to teaching again, the career for which she had been trained, and had endeavored to take up in her lifetime. In the Western Highlands, the education authorities, despite the plutocratic influence of her husband, turned her down when she enquired for a placing to teach in a school in Mt Hagen.

"Sorry, you refused a previous appointment to West Kambia. There are now more new graduates coming in, and we don't have any vacancies available now", was all that the appointment officer told her.

She walked out of the education office without daring to ask any further question. She knew, it would be useless begging for a posting after turning down the first offer.

Hence, Cathy spent most of her time at home, Peter Kupal's house doing menial inhouse duties, the flower gardens, the dishes, the laundary and any odd jobs that presented itself. Her husband was tough on her. Any trip to Simbu was disallowed. She wasn't allowed to even travel past Minj. Perhaps, the most painful burden she had ever lived up with was the infighting with her women rivals, the two other wives of her husband, something inevitable in any polygamy. And regretfully, it was the infighting that was to eventually take her life away.

Cathy wrote many letters home, demanding her parents talk to the relatives and repay back the K4,000.00 to Peter Kupal, but the money was just too much a sum to pay back. Worse still, Cathy's father did not receive any favorable response from those relatives that shared the partial bride price payment.

Kumo and James Gior tried relentlessly, in their capacity as the biological parents, to bail their daughter out of her problems, but as inveterate gamblers, and the father, an addicted alcoholic, there was almost nothing they could do with practically a nil balance in their savings account. Alternatively, every avenue seemed impossible and Kumo's heart broke, when she saw scars on Cathy's face, or heard terrible stories of the life she was going through. She repeatedly urged her husband to do something about it. But, as an average breadwinner, the part bride price of K4,000.00 payment was just too much to secure within a short span of time. With very little hope, Kumo and James pathetically lived with Cathy's predicaments, praying all the time that everything will eventually work out right for their daughter in the end.

Their prayers were finally answered. Almost miraculously Cathy Gior's shattered marriage picked up again when her husband decided to create a job for her. He placed Cathy behind one of the cash registers in one of his shops in Mt Hagen. Cathy was momentarily happy to keep herself busy and occupied, just as Peter was, but on the contrary, her appointment to the cash register irritated the jealous Kossip, Peter's second wife. She would walk into the store, harass and attack her continuously, causing inconvenience to the customers and damage to goods and property in the store when Peter was away.

Peter Kupal, unhappy about the continuous harassment from Kossip, removed Cathy from the store to allow peace and harmony to reign amongst his wives. But that did not deter Peter from using Cathy elsewhere. A little while later, after noticing Cathy's intelligence in communication and probably paper work, he temporarily tried her out as his private secretary. She might have pleased him and, at times, allowed her to accompany him wherever he went, to which Cathy quickly acquired the skills of a competent private secretary. With her intelligent brain, she mastered the skills, outwitted several other employees and was outstanding in her performance. From a businessman's perspective, Cathy was the best private secretary anyone can afford. She, therefore, won Peter's heart almost immediately. To top it all, it was a 'wife' and 'husband' combination at the end of the day. And that pleased Peter Kupal most. But most of all, peace, love, joy and harmony was restored in their marital life again, as never experienced before.

From the outset, Peter, as a polygamist, was not selfish to his wives. He treated each and every wife equally, and with fairness in everything he did for them. But as a businessesman, he favored and patronised Cathy most, primarily for her intelligence and secretarial competency. Peter considered her more resourceful then the other two. He regarded Cathy as a pivot and, more importantly, an asset in his business than a wife and treated her supremely compared to the other two wives. The favours she received were double, even though she was on the company payroll with all the other employees. And this did not go down well with Kossip, Cathy's prime enemy. Her jealous mind did not accept the treatment Cathy was receiving. She was frequently heard raising baseless, and menacing complaints against Cathy, and even instigated commotions when opportunity presented itself.

On the day of the murder, Kossip traveled to Mt Hagen in the morning from Avi. She walked into her husband's store, greeted the workers as usual with banter and enquired about the husband, who was away in Port Moresby with Cathy. She knew it well that Cathy accompanied Peter on that trip, and did not enquire about her, nor did she make a mention of her. She had a much more frightening, and more tragic surprise in store for her. "He's coming back this afternoon on the 1.00pm flight", the shop workers advised Kossip, only to regret later that it was to become a fatal mistake in their lives.

"Oh, alright, I'll wait around for him", she said, and went out of the shop.

She did not return, and was never seen again for the rest of the morning. It was normal to see her in town. She only walked in to enquire about her husband and was gone. Thus, nobody suspected anything.

At one o'clock in the afternoon, the Px flight from Port Moresby touched down at Kagamuga airport. Cathy Gior and her husband were on that flight. A flashy Nissan Patrol, the replacement of the Toyota Station Wagon, pulled into the car park some few metres down the road to pick them up. In the car were the driver and an acolyte.

The exit of the national flag carrier opened up, and the passengers disembarked. Out at the terminal, a huge crowd gathered at the arrival entrance to meet the friends and relatives coming home from the nation's capital. The Kupals decended from the carriage stairs and stepped onto the tarmac. Without stopping they proceeded towards the arrival lounge. Cathy followed closely behind her husband across the tarmac and stepped into the arrival lounge. After collecting their baggage, and their baggage tags checked, they walked out to the car park, where the waiting driver received them. He helped them with some of their luggage and led them to the car, the driver taking the lead, Peter in the middle and Cathy following closely behind. Like the inside, the outside was crowded with people too. As they walked towards the Nissan Patrol, a hand suddenly reached out from behind and grabbed Cathy around the neck. In split of a second, before Cathy Gior knew what was happening to her, a cold steel blade made its way into her abdomen. It was quickly pulled out, and thrusted into the same spot again. By the time Cathy realised what was happening to her, the blade penetrated her for the third time, and this time in the chest.

"Oh, I am knifed, please help me…he-e-e-", she whined in agony, broke free and ran forward, but did not gain any distance before collapsing onto the car park.

The terrified crowd screamed and fled the scene in fear. When Peter turned to check out the stampede, he found his second wife, Kossip, standing with a devilish face, smiling at him. In her hand was a long kitchen knife, all covered in fresh human blood. In between them, on the murky bitumen surface, lay Cathy Gior in a pool of her own blood that was oozing out profusely from the wounds she sustained from the knife.

"That should do good for your young wife", Kossip shouted to her shocked husband, who was trembling with fear, and walked to the airport police, where she surrendered herself. She was eventually led away to the police station, charged for willful murder and locked in a cell.

Peter Kupal and his driver, with the help of the escort, tried to get Cathy up, but her consciousness had long gone. It was only her heart that was still struggling to function. They rushed her to Mt Hagen General hospital, where she was pronounced dead upon arrival. She had already died along the way. The knife wounds were severe and fatal. There was excessive loss of blood. This was later confirmed in the doctor's autopsy report.

Peter, like many other respected Western Highlands leaders, was a man of intelligence, reasoning and clear understanding. He knew that he was at fault in the death of Cathy. It was his other wife that murdered her, and indirectly held him responsible for Cathy's death too. When the Siakos demanded the body to be taken to Ende-naige-ingugl for burial, Peter consented without any hassle, even though he objected to the idea initially. He agreed to personally deliver Cathy Gior's body to Ende-naige-ingugl, and meet all the funeral expenses, and other associated costs that were to be borne therewith. He assured the Siakos to pay them a *wari pe* when he would deliver the body, the amount undisclosed.

In the week leading up to the departure for Ende-naige-ingugl, Peter arranged and paid for the most expensive funeral items at the funeral pallor in Mt Hagen. He purchased a red casket, which alone was worth over K1,000.00, flowers and wreaths, store food items, to be taken along to Ende-naige-ingugl and used during the mourning period. About K3,000.00 worth of assorted food items were taken out of his bulk storeroom. Two long-wheel-base Toyota Dynas, one Mazda T3500 and an open back Toyota land cruiser were arranged to take them all, and deliver the casket to Ende-naige-ingugl.

After witnessing these arrangements in place Councillor Bagle left Mt Hagen for Ende-naige-ingugl, to be with his people when the body would arrive.

22

The Curtain is Drawn

The news reached everyone that Cathy Gior's venerable millionaire husband, Peter Kupal woud be personally delivering the body of his late wife to Ende-naige-ingugl for the interment. He would accompany his contingent, comprising of friends, business associates and clansmen. And a huge crowd of mourners waited the following day to receive them. Many had their faces all smeared with mud to show their grief and commiseration. Anna and myself had heard everything that had happened to Cathy from my father-in-law and others, the previous evening and, quite obviously, it was not necessary for us to attend the mourning, especially me. But, since Cathy was Anna's clan sister, she insisted that we attend as a sign of respect to the Gior family in this moment of their grief. At first sunlight in the morning, we left Bokan for Ende-naige-ingugl. Like everyone else, Anna rubbed her face with mud along the way. But it was still too early when we reached Mondiagl-kaugla. I decided to try my luck at the gambling place at the market place, or just hang around there to pass time and allowed Anna to move on. "The Western Highlands contingent should be here around midday, I'll join later", I called out to her, as Anna continued down the road alone to join the other mourners at Ende-naige-ingugl.

After mid-day, at around 1.30pm, everyone was taken to his feet by the resonance of tooting and sounds of alarm, reverberating from an approaching convoy of vehicles, advancing up the road from the south. It was the harbinger of Peter Kupal and his contingent's approach with the casket containing the body of late Cathy Gior. "They're here", everyone said, as mourners and curious folks starting heading towards the direction of Ende-naige-ingugl. Women started wailing, as the sounds of tooting and alarms got louder. Everyone knew that the casket had finally arrived. The gambling groups stopped their games too and soon just about everyone hurried down to Ende-naige-ingugl. I scurried along with the many others, and was just in time to see the convoy of trucks pulling to the roadside at Ende-naige-ingugl. There were about six trucks in all, conventionally bedecked in red ribbons of nylon all around every truck to disclose the purpose of the convoy and the cargo it was transporting.

The Nissan Patrol led the convoy. In it were Cathy's father James Gior, some Western Highlands elders and some other gentlemen, who appeared more like Peter's business associates. Peter Kupal himself was at the steering wheel. Directly behind the Nissan Patrol was an ambulance from the Mt Hagen General Hospital. It was obvious that Peter Kupal had arranged with the hospital management for the release of one of their ambulances to transport the casket. There were a couple of heads in there, but due to the non-transparent glass surrounding the ambulance, I could not work out who, or how many were in there. But later when the door was opened to bring out the coffin, I noticed only a few people, probably less then five in it. The casket was of an expensive kind and was red in colour. Among the few people that traveled in the ambulance, were Kumo and Anasas---late Cathy Gior's mother and sister. Both women were leaning against the coffin for support, and were beyond recognition in their swollen and disheveled faces from the non-stop mourning. Pitifully, I guessed that there were no more tears left in both women.

Right behind the ambulance was a blue Toyota Dyna and three other long wheel base Mazda trucks. Peter Kupal's plutocratic image and status had attracted and filled these three trucks to capacity with people and mourners from all walks of life, and I believe different vernaculars too. They had boarded these trucks at Mt Hagen, Kudjip, Minj and even Kundiawa. Many smeared themselves with clay and had red ribbons of nylon tied around their head, arms and necks to address the nature of the situation to the oncoming traffic, by-standers and on-lookers during the journey. In the fifth truck, a Mazda T3500, that had been parked some distance further down the road, were garden harvest of varying food crops from the rich fertile plains of the Waghi valley which had been provided by Peter's tribesmen. The fine harvests filled the entire length of the vehicle, from the front to the tail end. The final vehicle, a Toyota land cruiser, that had followed some distance behind, had all the comestibles, that I believed, Peter had removed from one of his bulk storerooms in Mt Hagen. There were bags of rice, sugar, cartons of tinned food items and many, many more which could feed the hungry during the entire mourning period. The trucks lined up one after the other in the order they had traveled.

A lot of mourners howled and keened around the ambulance, as the casket was carefully lifted off and carried into the village center. Peter Kupal had pre-arranged his men to be the pallbearers. In this instance, the Siakos were refused any hand in the handling of the casket. After a slow and mournful procession into Ende-naige-ingugl, the casket was carefully laid down on a floor mat that was spread out in the village center. Mourners in mud-drenched faces wailed and keened incessantly around the coffin. Many of Cathy's close friends either collapsed, or threw themselves to the ground, keened and wriggled in mourning, as the casket was put down on the prepared mat. It was truly a very, very sad and moving moment. Out on the road, the flow of people did not abate, as both mourners and curious individuals convened, and soon Ende-naige-ingugl was slowly filling up. Despite the plentiful, many kept coming, bawling and howling elegiacally, as they entered. From the road everyone entered the village and soon the village center was packed with people, mourners and observers alike. The crowd was reminiscent of my ceremonious wedding held there, some three years ago, on that same ground. But this time, it was for a different occasion---to mourn the death of a jilted lover.

After settling in at Ende-naige-ingugl, the Western Highlands contingent retreated to the corner reserved for them in the direction of the road, leaving Peter Kupal alone in the center. He stood adjacent to the Siakos with the casket in between them. It was quite obvious that Peter had pre-planned a speech before handing over the casket to the Giors and the Siakos. He looked around, possibly for silence, but the deafening sounds of the keening and wailing was so extreme that Peter remained standing for some time in silence for calmness until Councillor Bagle stepped in. The councilor directed the mourners for silence. In his deep powerful voice, "Okay, your attention, please", he announced, and when there was a slight pause "…our daughter has finally been brought home", Bagle said, "And I think the husband is waiting to say something before handing over the body. They have come a long way and need to rest too. So, I ask you all to remain silent for a while, so that we can listen to what they have to say. We will continue after they finish. And for those who cannot keep quiet, please keep it low" As soon as Bagle delivered the announcement, both men briefly discussed something, and then the councillor retreated back to his corner, leaving Peter alone in the center.

The Western Highlanders are powerful public speakers and entertaining orators. The knew what speech to deliver and on which occasion to keep their listeners happy, sad, bring joy or sorrow, or put smiles and laughter on their faces. They can even deliver speeches to lift or drop morale. And Peter Kupal was no exception. Clearing his throat, Peter began:

"My good people of Gembogl; firstly, I feel enormously guilty to stand out here before you and talk to you all on this occassion. But I hope you all understand the situation I am placed in now. This tragedy is something I least anticipated, and never thought it would ever occur. I know, you never expected it either. In my life, I have married so many women, divorced them, married another one, and so on. But never had I come across this kind of incident, the kind that I am faced with now, before in my life. This is the first such incident of its kind. Though infighting is common among my many wives, death is something I never expected from them, because I treated my wives fairly and equally in everything I do for them. But today, I have not yet recovered from the shock I got at the airport, or from the fact that Cathy is dead. Cathy was no ordinary woman, and for those who don't know, many will say that she was one of my other wives, but she was not. She was more than that. She was my business partner, apart from being my wife. She assisted me greatly in my everyday running of my business as my private secretary. I will greatly miss her from today onwards. I am truly sad that I have lost one of my vital parts. Her murder is inhuman and diabolically barbaric. I personally condemn my second wife for this detestable act. She is currently locked up in the Police cells in Mt Hagen, but I promise you all that I will personally see to it that she gets the maximum penalty for her crime"

Peter Kupal went on to briefly explain the last hours leading up to Cathy's death, as the grieving crowd listened and looked on. He described the Port Moresby trip and the landing of the Px aircraft that fateful afternoon, and how the tragedy happened at the Kagamuga airport. It was a sad and moving tale. Then, in a heartfelt tone and deep remorse, Peter Kupal formally apologised to the Siakos for everything that had happened to Cathy Gior. As Peter apologised, he slowly turned around to his corner and motioned one of the Western Highlanders, a young man in his thirties with a small handbag to come forward. Peter Kupal took the handbag from him and with everyone looking on, opened it and took out a bag containing, what appeared to be money of a substantial amount. Turning back to the Siakos, he continued again:

"I know, you all are deeply hurt and in pain, just as I am. The pain will not be something ephemeral but everlasting. It will continue to live in us for a very, very long time, and I regretfully blame myself for causing this everlasting pain for the fact that the one who inflicted that pain happened to be one of my other wives".

Then, after a brief pause, putting his left hand on this chin, as it to think up some more words, he said:

"Cathy was my wife, and I insisted that she be laid to rest in Mt Hagen, my place of birth. So that when I see her resting place she will remind me of the wonderful times we had shared together as husband and wife and in business. But you adamantly refused and wanted the internment to take place here. As the guilty one, I had no choice and co-operated with your decision. And as you can all see, we finally brought Cathy home, to the place where you wanted her to be laid to rest. I am now formally handing over the casket to you for burial with K10,000.00 cash as wari pei together with the pile of foodstuff here for use to feed the hungry during this period of mourning. This wari pei is to lull any anguishes and animosities that may be borne in our minds during this period of grief. I will return to make a full payment in compensation for the murder later after putting Cathy to rest".

Saying that, and with an air of finality, Peter Kupal held out the bag of money, and called on James Gior, Cathy's father to come forward and take the money bag from him. All eyes rested on James, but he did not move an inch. Instead, he looked across to Councillor Bagle and beckoned him as the village chief to go forward and take the *wari-pei* from Peter Kupal.

Stepping out from the crowd, Councillor Bagle walked slowly forward. Standing opposite Cathy's husband he took the bag of money from Peter's hand. For what ever reason there was no handshake between the two men to signal peace or a 'thank you'. Then, standing back a few metres away from him, Councillor Bagle responded to Peter's speech.

"We are all saddened and deeply hurt by the tragedy. Cathy is dead and when someone is dead we cannot get him or her back to life. And now we cannot wake Cathy up again. She is gone for good and we are deeply hurt. In situations like this, where broad daylight murder is the primary cause of the death, there is nothing we can do about it but to let the law take its course and decide the fate of the killer. We hear that the murderer is in the Police cell. We understand that she will be dealt with accordingly, which means the law will take care of her. We welcome the arrest, as she deserves to be punished and pay for what she has done. One thing you will be assured of is that, we, the Gembogl people, are an exceptional group in the entire Simbu province. We are peace loving and understandable people. We will not retaliate or do anything absurd to avenge the death. I really don't know why we are such a peace-loving group. Perhaps it is because the Word of God came across from over those mountains over there and landed here first before spreading out to the other parts of the highlands. That could be the reason. But we have the mother laws of this country, the Police and the courts, to deal with our daughter's death and we hope that the murderer answer for her crime in the court. Before I go, my final word, on behalf of everyone here, is our many 'thanks' for delivering the body of our beloved daughter home in such a fine and an extraordinary way, thank you! And as you said, we hope to see you here again when you return".

Councillor Bagle looked across to Cathy's father, James Gior when he finished his speech and motioned, if he had something say. But James was too emotional to open his lips, and shook his head. And so was Teacher Phillip Koane, Cathy's uncle, when he was asked if he might want to add something. Noticing that there was no one coming out, Councillor Bagle looked across to Peter Kupal, extended his right hand and both men shook hands, in what appeared to be, a sign of peace, or thank you, or whatever! Then both men walked in their opposite directions to their respective corners to join their group.

I stood in the background with the other onlookers. The mourning and keening was slowly picking up again. Anna had joined the other mourners and wept profusely over the death of her clan 'sister'. She sat next to the coffin alongside Kumo and Anasas. Her eyes were flooded and wet all over with tears, as she watched the *wari pei* changing hands between Councillor Bagle and Peter Kupal. In the Siako corner, I saw Councillor Bagle retreating back to the Siakos with the bag of money in his hands. A handful of Siakos, including James and Cathy's blood relatives, closed in around him. They were all hectically discussing something, presumably of some importance. In the Western Highlands corner, I saw Peter Kupal standing amongst his men with a face of contentment. He was conspicuously satisfied with everything that was happening at Ende-naige-ingugl, and what he had done so far. The Western Highalnds contingent remained quiet in their corner, perhaps contemplating on what the Siakos might do next, as the village center was gradually packed and expanded with people. All around, mourners began to wail and keen plangently again that soon erupted with resonance, as if picking up from where they had left off. As my eyes wandered around, I suddenly caught sight of the eye-catching red coffin in the crowd center amongst the mourners. Sumptuous in its design with brass handles and embroideries, the decor was magnificent unlike other caskets I had seen. Spreads of fine linen covered the total length with wreaths. Bouquets from flower shops and the funeral parlour, splendidly piled high on the coffin lid, covering the entire length from top end to the bottom.

As I admiringly viewed the expensive coffin, I suddenly remembered the one lying supine in it. It was the body of someone I knew--- someone, a beautiful girl, I had known better than anyone else. As my eyes remained glued to the coffin, I could see her beautiful face smiling at me in my mind, and her soft sweet voice calling out my name. I could smell her refined body aroma and feel the curves of her soft marvelous body pressed against mine in the silent night under the stars, and her warm breath amidst the silent romantic whispers of endearments in my ears. Suddenly, as my eyes blinked for a second glance, I felt my vision blurred and a lump in my throat. For the first time, I could feel a well of tears damming in my eyes. It certainly was a painful journey traveling down the memory lane, and as I looked on helplessly, the floodgates suddenly burst open. I couldn't hold on any longer. As if gushing out from a dam, I felt a flood of tears rolling out of the lower lids of my eyes, dripped slowly over my cheeks in rivulets onto my shirt.

"You are a free bird now", I said in my mind, recalling all the miscarriages in her ill-fated marital life. "You can fly as high as you may want to fly, and as far away as you may want to go, to that far away place of no return, and everlasting peace. Rest in Eternal Peace"

I did not feel like remaining there any longer. Without arousing anyone's attention, I quietly stepped back, turned around and walked out of Ende-naige-ingugl to the entrance gate. I stood on the main road, lost for a while. Eventually, I decided to travel back to Mondiagl-kaugla and, perhaps continue with my gambling, or occupy myself with something else, while waiting for Anna there. I walked past a lot more mourners on the road, all heading towards Ende-naige-ingugl. They were either keening and wet all over on their faces, or were ready to explode when they would reach the entrance into Ende-naige-ingugl. As I walked, the plangent, keening and bawling taking place inside Ende-naige-ingugl resounded in my ears, immediately prompting me to recall the various scenes that took place there. I evoked Peter Kupal's speech, the apologies, the *wari pei* and the mountain of comestibles piled high next to the coffin. I also evoked how Cathy's casket was bedecked, delivered and handed over to the Giors. Certainly, it was amazingly terrific. Peter Kupal was a man of dignity and every little detail was carefully assessed, ticked off and done to perfection, something well expected of a millionaire husband. But, sadly and unforgivingly, I disapprovingly shook my head in disgrace. Seriously, these posthumous activities and material items pragmatically have no value, compared to the loss of human life. The Gior family, including James and Angela Kumo have certainly lost a beautiful daughter, who would never be replaced again.

Cathy's tragedy was not the first incident. I have heard tales, seen and read many stories of similar incidents happening at home and elsewhere around the country in the past, through friends, the mass media and other sources, where many teenage girls and spinsters, including school girls and highly educated women, one way or the other, ended up in the same fate. Many because they lacked the acumen to think and use their heads correctly and the gumption to avoid such tragedies. Cathy Gior was no exception. She was 26 years old at the time of her death. She could have lived for another 26 years, had she been wiser and decisive at the very first opportunity. But, it's all over now. There is no more Cathy---Cathy Gior, the name and the girl that once dominated my entire life. She had gone, and gone forever.

23

Nostalgic Memories of Inamorata

Cathy Gior's body was finally laid to rest outside Ende-naige-ingugl on an eye-catching hilltop, a few hundred metres away from her parent's house. It was her mother, Angela Kumo's wish that she be buried there, where her daughter's resting-place could be visible from her house front. Many people attended her funeral to see the wife of Peter Kupal, the venerable businessman, finally laid to rest. Fr. Tobias, the parish priest at the Catholic Mission station at Denglagu, held a special requiem of her later in the week, followed by a huge *kugl-gaugl*, putting the long weeks of mourning, grieving and keening to rest.

Peter and his group of mourners and contingent returned to Mt Hagen after the burial, promising to return at a later date to pay the outstanding compensation payment. When and how much they were going to pay was never disclosed. "I'll be back", was all Peter Kupal confidently announced to everyone after the funeral, before he got into his car to leave. Sadly, that afternoon was the last of him and his party to be seen at Ende-naige-ingugl. His promise was a load of claptrap and he never returned to make the payment he had promised.

The distribution of the *wari-moni* paid to the Giors during the mourning at Ende-naige-ingugl by Peter Kupal was unfairly distributed amongst the relatives, uncles and family members. Kumo's frigid and domineering attitude again had a devastating impact. This time, it severely ruined the family unity by failing to close the ranks. There was disharmony and rift between the family members, and relatives over the money. Many disengaged themselves from the Giors, and vowed never to associate with them again, especially the mother, for being occasionally too greedy.

"She never fails to become rapacious and selfish when it comes to pecuniary matters", many relatives were heard complaining, and hence refused to take part in any future pending pursuits against the Western Highlanders in relation to Cathy's death.

The family rift was a total blow to the Giors, when solidarity, family unity and team effort was the utmost requirement in any pursuit, when the compensation claim, the court sessions and many other issues were still outstanding.

The Kossip murder case was heard at a National Court sitting in Mt Hagen, presided over by a National Court Judge. Ruefully, not one of the Giors nor the Siakos, or anyone closely related to the Giors, attended the court sessions after the first and second adjournments. Many blamed the PMV fare between Gembogl and Mt Hagen as the setback and hindrance.

"Too costly to travel to and from Mt Hagen these days", many relatives were heard complaining about the K4.00 fare between Kundiawa and Mt Hagen.

And no one followed closely on the murder case. Hence, nothing was heard of the verdict, nor the fate of Kossip. It was about a year later that Kossip was seen walking around freely in Mt Hagen by Phillip, Cathy's uncle, who had gone there on a private trip. She seemingly appeared to have been exonerated. He knew Kossip and was not mistaken when he saw her. According to sources from Mt Hagen based relatives, who attended the final court hearing, the witnesses collusively perjured themselves in order to protect Kossip. And she was subsequently acquitted of the murder charge by the trial judge with lack of witnesses in the prosecution box.

As a son-in-law of a prominent Siako Councillor, I made frequent--- in fact, many visits, to Ende-naige-ingugl in the later period after Cathy Gior's demise to see my parents-in-law, sometimes with my wife Anna accompanying me. Unlike in the past, I noticed a tremendous change of attitude in Kumo, particularly towards me. She was no longer the hellcat I once knew. This time, she started coming into my in-law's house to greet me whenever she learnt of my presence there. Sometimes, she invited Anna and me over to her house for tea or a meal. At other times, she brought us food to take home. We soon became very good friends. There was intuition that she had realised her mistake finally and was trying to atone for her past errant behaviour against me, but I pitied her eventually. In retrospect, it was clearly too late to look back now, as she had already lost a loved one through her feeble-mindedness. Perhaps, had she respected my intentions on her daughter earlier the situation would have been different. But its over now, definitely too late!

When I looked up at the cemetery from the Gior's house front, I could see the shiny white paint on the headstone cross over Cathy's grave, projecting above the colourful garden of flowers. To everyone else, the cross marked the permanent resting place of a young and gorgeous Siako lass of seraphic beauty, the wife of a venerable millionaire. But for me alone, beneath that cross laid the remains of someone special, someone that once dominated my entire life---a beautiful indecisive woman who was gone too early!

The End

Glossary

aibika Vegetables from *Abelmoschus manihot,* especially the fresh leaves and shoots.

ambai Girl

ambu-yana Mission undertaken by delegates from the bridegroom's camp to seek formal consent from bride for engagement to the groom

ambu-di-kungugl Contribution of cash and kind from the parents, friends, relatives and neighbors towards the bride price.

ambu-di Open-air ceremony involving the formal payment of the bride price and exchange of bride in marriage.

ambu-kindagl Old woman

aglange Traditional shout of applause and appreciation echoed by women.

APO Aid Post Orderly

bilas Dressing, especially in traditional attire

bro Abbreviation for 'brother'

bilum Net bag or string bag

brus Raw or unprocessed tobacco

bugla-dane Pork belly, especially with lard.

dinbend Firewood, usually oven dried over the firewood rack above the fireplace and reserved for use, as tinder and/or during occasions of urgency.

di-minge-bugla Axe-money-pig; items collectively for the bride price.

endie-kaman   Night session held prior to *ambu-di,* where the bride is advised of the 'dos' and 'don'ts' for betterment and success in married life, interluded by *gilanges.*

ende-kambu   'Meat-of-the-Fire'; porker prepared for consumption during *endie-kaman* night.

fri-kambang   Free lime provided by the betel nut vendor for chewing by the customer after purchasing his/her nuts.

gigl-ange   Folk songs.

kaukau   Tubers from *Ipomea batatas* or sweet potato

kai-gagle   Ceremonial dance peformed during giving or taking of bride.

kaur or purpur   Traditional nether garment for the anterior and posterior made from entwined strings worn by women.

kugl-gaugl   Feast held in honor of the dead after the burial to end the moment of mourning, grieving and keening.

kumo-kwimbo   Sorceror

laplap   Loincloth, commonly worn by women around the waist, extending to the knee or ankle.

leva   Sweet Heart

mumu   Food and vegetables cooked in the pit oven over hot stones

PMV   Public Motor Vehicle

PFO   Provincial Forest Officer

sipu   Appreciation shouts or tune of appreciation echoed in unison by men after accepting or taking something from someone.

SSRDP   South Simbu Rural Development Project

tulip   Vegetable from *Gnetum gnemon,* especially the young shoots, leaves and buds.

wantoks   One-Talks; friends, relatives or anyone whom you know personally sharing the same common dialect.

wari-pei/ moni   Blood money paid in expiation to the parents and relatives of the decease prior to the formal compensation payment.

yagl-ingu   Men's house

yagl-kande   Big man.

Acknowledgement

This book would not have been completed without the cooperation and support I got from many good people. My log export inspector colleagues at SGS (PNG) Ltd deserve my utmost gratitude for being very supportive during the penning period when we were locked away in some of the loneliest and most remote logging camps in PNG.

J Menge and H Turadawai deserved my recognition for lending me their Oxford Dictionaries, the writer's 'handyman tool' when I needed them most in Open Bay and Alotau forest camps respectively. George Reu and Macky Kupa, kindly allowed me to use their desktops in Open Bay and at Aiambak camps to convert my manuscript into soft copy. I thank them sincerely.

L Peni, A Allai, A Patma, U Dixion and F Hurhura briefly read through the manuscript and offered helpful comments, suggestions and corrections. I thank each and every one of them.

I also thank my wife Betty and children; Getrude, Elice, Thomas, Natasha, Tony, Shane, Ryot, Libocedrus for their loyalty and patience when I was away for most of the time on SGS inspection duties.

Lastly, but not the least, the publication of this book under this imprint would not have been possible but through the generous efforts of a remarkably kind-hearted and hardworking person who submitted it to the FNWF2024 Book Award Judges, where it eventually won a Book Award. Thank you, Anna Borzi, all the FNWF2024 Judges for selecting my book for an Award and the wonderful team at First Nations Writers Festival Internation Ltd.

No other private enterprise is publishing these
magnificent stories of the
First Nations peoples of the Greater Pacific.
In the unfiltered voices of the writers.
On a global distribution platform.

We are a registered, regulated, audited Charity, with
Australian Charity and Non-Profit Commission [ACNC]
And DGR tax exempt with the Australian Taxation Office.
All expenses are paid with private bequests and donations.

We have no government support.

All the team workers are unpaid volunteers.
All net funds received through sales are reinvested
in the publications of future stories.

PLEASE DONATE
In Australia by phone PAYID 79655932979
OR Global on our website
https://firstnationswritersfestival.org

IN OTHER BOOKS WITH SPARE PAGES WE HAVE
INCLUDED THE COVERS OF OTHER FNWF BOOKS.

Other books by FNWF

www.ingramcontent.com/pod-product-compliance
Lightning Source LLC
Chambersburg PA
CBHW020334120726
47904CB00002B/413